MONSTER HUNTER
NEMESIS

BAEN BOOKS by LARRY CORREIA

Monster Hunter International
Monster Hunter Vendetta
Monster Hunter Alpha
Monster Hunter Legion
Monster Hunter Nemesis

THE GRIMNOIR CHRONICLES
Hard Magic
Spellbound
Warbound

Dead Six (with Mike Kupari)
Swords of Exodus (with Mike Kupari)

MONSTER HUNTER
NEMESIS

Larry Correia

MONSTER HUNTER NEMESIS

Copyright © 2014 by Larry Correia

A Baen Books Original

Baen Publishing Enterprises
P.O. Box 1403
Riverdale, NY 10471
www.baen.com

ISBN: 978-1-4767-3655-6

Cover art by Alan Pollack

First printing, July 2014

Distributed by Simon & Schuster
1230 Avenue of the Americas
New York, NY 10020

Library of Congress Cataloging-in-Publication Data

Correia, Larry.
  Monster hunter nemesis / Larry Correia.
      pages cm — (A Baen Book) (Baen Fantasy) (Monster hunter ; 5)
    ISBN 978-1-4767-3655-6 (hardback)
1. Monsters—Fiction. 2. Cults—Fiction. 3. Fantasy fiction. I. Title.
  PS3603.O7723M636 2014
  813'.6—dc23
                                                      2014014384

10 9 8 7 6 5 4 3 2 1

Pages by Joy Freeman (www.pagesbyjoy.com)
Printed in the United States of America

to Jake

PART 1

The Plan

CHAPTER 1

"There's innocent blood on your hands. How many federal agents, civilians, and hunters did you kill out there?" the interrogator demanded.

"I lost count."

The two men sat in a small, brightly lit, white room, separated only by a narrow rectangular table. Franks couldn't remember how he'd gotten here.

"State your name for the record."

"Franks."

"And what position did you hold up until recently?"

"Special Agent of the United States Monster Control Bureau."

The interrogator was as small and white and unremarkable as the room. "I want you to know that this will be your only opportunity to explain your actions. Your future depends on you being completely forthcoming during this investigation."

"You expect a confession?"

"I want the truth, Agent Franks."

"Are you my judge?"

"Your fate is out of my hands. Everything you say here will go straight to the top. He makes the call. Do you understand?"

Franks nodded.

"Start at the beginning. Tell me everything."

The California Incident
18 Months Ago
20 miles off the California coast

The final ritual had begun.

Another massive wave lifted the fishing boat. Lightning flashed across the sky as it came crashing back down. A mighty blast of water came over the side and knocked a few of the cultists from their feet, but the rest continued chanting and circling around the runes painted on the deck.

Cold water ran through the seams of the crate to soak him, moistening the dried blood on his suit enough to make it pliable again. His crate was about the size of a coffin. If it was swept overboard he'd have to break out, swim to the surface, and try to find the boat as it was being tossed about on thirty-foot waves, and considering that he'd already been shot and repeatedly stabbed tonight, that would be inconvenient.

The rain was coming down in hard sheets. Only suicidal idiots would take a boat out into a storm like this, but after the Monster Control Bureau had interrupted their plot on the mainland, the remaining cultists had been desperate enough to try to perform their big finale right on top of their target audience. Cultists were a particularly annoying type of vermin.

Some of the deck was visible through the air holes punched in the side of the crate. The ship was running dark and the storm clouds were blocking the moon, but none of that mattered to his augmented vision. Once a month the Bureau scientists stuck a needle into his eye and injected a syringe full of burning chemicals, which helped him see better in the dark. Originally developed by DARPA, the vision enhancement serum had driven the original human test subjects so mad with pain that they'd clawed their own eyes out. He found the process mildly uncomfortable. The injections meant he had to replace his eyes every few years, as they inevitably caused ocular cancer, but that was a small price to pay for increased tactical awareness.

He'd counted fifteen cultists so far. They seemed human. Mostly. There were probably more, and somebody had to be in the wheelhouse trying to steer the boat through the storm. They'd formed a circle, and a larger figure moved between them, giving directions to aid in their summoning spell. Franks tried to keep track of that one, but he couldn't get a good angle through the air holes. There was a brief view of legs ending in goat hooves, and then the demon was out of sight. He caught the stink of sulfur before the storm tore it away.

"Target acquired," he said, not even knowing if his radio signal would reach through the wood and weather.

"Copy." Special Agent Myers' voice was barely discernible through the static. "The USS *Cheyenne* is shadowing you. Bravo Team is on a Coast Guard cutter heading for your position. ETA ten minutes."

The waves had taken on a strange rhythm that matched the fevered chanting of the cultists. He had seen enough black magic rituals to know where this was going. They didn't have ten minutes. "Requesting permission to engage."

His superior sighed. "Why do you even bother to ask when I know you're going to anyway?"

"Protocol."

"Hold on. . . . I'm being told there's seismic activity directly beneath your position. We've got something on satellite. There's a thermal bloom at the ocean floor. They've woken something up . . . Dear Lord! It's huge. Stop that ritual, Agent Franks. Stop it now!"

Myers' command was the best thing he'd heard all night. "Yes, sir."

Someone began bellowing orders, far louder than the cultists' chanting. "It is time, brothers! The leviathan is coming." The demon that was providing the cult their black magic intel was his target. Take it out, and these morons wouldn't be able to boss around a shoggoth, let alone a great sea beast capable of devouring whole cities. "Let there be light so that we may look upon his glory." Brilliant beams shined through the holes of the crate as the cultists turned on several big spotlights. "Gather the virgin for sacrifice. Hurry, brothers! Spill the virgin's blood upon the circle with the sacred blade so that the leviathan may witness our devotion."

During the raid, he'd found a female tied up and drugged, loaded in a crate in the back of a truck. He'd figured she had been meant for something like this. Even though he'd been injured and had used up all his ammo on cultists, Franks knew it was his best chance to find his target, so he'd dumped the girl, taken her place, and then ordered his men to fall back enough to let the cultists escape. Sure enough, a minute later a bunch of losers who stunk of fish and Elder Things had piled in and they'd been on their way to the docks.

There was movement all around the crate, and several men gathered to lift him from the deck. "How many sacrifices did they put in this thing?"

"Maybe she's a really fat virgin. Come on, guys. One, two, *three*." They lifted the crate and stumbled across the slick deck.

The boat groaned. Lightning flashed. Cultists screamed. Some bit of their god had risen from the depths, revealing itself. From the commotion, Franks figured it had to be pretty impressive-looking, but then again, if they weren't easily impressed, they wouldn't be cultists to begin with.

"Hurry!" the demon commanded. Franks' coffin was dropped in the middle of the painted designs. Some of the cultists lost their wits and ran away, their sanity unable to cope with the ancient monstrosity rising up around the boat. There was a new smell in the air, the overpowering stink of rotting fish. "Do not test the great leviathan's patience!"

Franks closed his eyes and took a deep breath. Both of his heartbeats were slow and deliberate. Someone was unnecessarily working a crowbar into the seams, unaware that Franks had already tugged the lid off earlier to climb inside.

They opened the crate. "*That's* our virgin sacrifice?" Two men were looking down at him, both wearing impractical ceremonial robes. Far behind them a wall of spines and tentacles was rising from the ocean. "I thought we were getting a chick, not some big ugly dude."

"What the—"

Reaching out, Franks grabbed the first cultist by the throat and squeezed, smashing his windpipe flat. Franks caught the other by the hair, and slammed his face through the edge of the crate. That one dropped his crowbar right in Franks' lap.

Another cultist was standing nearby, with an ornate, jewel-studded dagger. It was the sort of flashy thing that assholes like this loved to sacrifice virgins with. The man turned around, wearing a look of predatory eagerness. That expression turned to shock when he saw Franks getting out of the crate. This was not the tied-up, semiconscious mortal he'd been expecting. This was a slab of hate bundled together with muscle. The cultist dropped the blade and raised his hands to surrender, but it didn't matter, as Franks embedded the crowbar into his forehead hard enough to make brain matter come out the cultist's ears.

"An intruder! Seize him!" The demon gave the imperious command, but then it recognized who it was and shrieked in fear. Just about everything from the other side knew his reputation. "Oh shit! It's Franks! Run!"

He recognized the demon's type. The physical body was a pathetic alchemical creation, stitched together out of animal parts and old cadavers and held together with magic barely fit to animate a zombie. A body like that was only capable of holding the weakest of the host in the mortal world. Franks sneered. He'd gotten shot in the stomach for this? *Stupid imp.* He'd been hoping for a good fight at least.

"Help us, O Great Sleeper of the Deep," the demon begged as the ancient squid god's bellows shook the sea. "Please save us from Franks." It seemed the demon was actually more afraid of Franks than he was worried about placating the Elder Thing they'd just woken from its thousand years of slumber.

Good call.

Most of the cultists were still cowering because the ancient monster they'd summoned rising up all around their boat had scared the hell out of them, but those who had been in the circle rushed him. Their efforts would have been amusing if he hadn't had more important things to do. Franks swung the crowbar in a wide circle, hitting several of them, shattering ribs and limbs. The impact was enough to flip one man over the rail to fall screaming into the ocean. *Good luck swimming in those idiotic robes.*

Someone grabbed him by the shirt. Franks took him by the wrist, twisted it until it snapped, and then spun and flipped the man into several of his friends, knocking them all down. Another man almost managed to hit him, but Franks merely moved his head out of the way, hooked the man beneath the jaw and pulled. That one only made it a few more steps before collapsing and clutching at the gaping hole where the bottom of his face had been. As he flicked the jawbone off the end of his crowbar, Franks noticed that there were gills flapping on the dying man's neck. These fools had been intermingling with Deep Ones, and a few appeared to be hybrids. On land, that just made them squishier. Franks confirmed his hypothesis by braining a cultist and noting that the blood that sprayed out was an oily green.

That would have to go in his report later, but right now he had to concentrate. One cultist was smart enough to draw a pistol, but Franks hurled the crowbar across the deck and shattered her skull.

Their giant underwater monster might have been impressive, but it wasn't actively killing them, so the rest of the cultists were paying attention to Franks now. The demon was waving his long misshapen gorilla arms and wailing in the original tongue, beseeching the ancient thing from the deep to do their bidding and to kill Franks and then attack the human cities along the coast. This operation's primary objective was to keep that from happening. The secondary was to capture this demon for questioning. The tertiary was to kill every cultist who pissed him off. He'd added that one himself.

Franks bent down, picked up the ceremonial dagger—*solid*— and covered the distance to the demon in a flash. It clawed at him, still screaming for the monster to save them. He slugged the demon in the chest and felt bones explode. "You're wanted for questioning." He hadn't brought cuffs, so Franks caught the demon's arm, forced it to the deck, and slammed the dagger through its hand and deep into the wood. "Stick around."

He left the demon thrashing and clutching at the dagger in a futile attempt to pull it free, but when Franks stuck a blade into something, he did so with authority, and the demon wasn't strong enough to pull the blade free.

Something needed to be done before the cult got their wits together enough to actually get the big monster to do their bidding. In Franks' experience, the best way to keep somebody from accomplishing something was just to kill them.

The thing which had been sleeping beneath the ocean was directly under them, and it seemed angry about being woken up. A tentacle as big around as their boat broke the surface, whipped through the rain and spotlight beams and then came crashing back down only twenty yards off their port side. Franks snarled. He had no patience for eldritch horrors. *They think they're so tough*... The Navy had an attack submarine a few miles away. He'd show them tough. He keyed his radio as he walked toward the dropped pistol. "Come in, Command."

"What's your situation, Franks?" Myers asked, sounding a little flustered, but the boss always got that way when he was watching some supernatural world-altering event unfold over a satellite feed.

"Situation under control." The cultists were going for their weapons. A cultist standing in the wheelhouse door started shooting at him with an AR-15. Franks calmly bent over, snatched up the dropped handgun, an old GI 1911, lifted it as he ran, and put a single round through the window. The glass shattered and the shooter went down. Several others were retrieving their weapons, so Franks methodically went about gunning them down as bullets flew past him. He took cover behind some metal storage boxes. "Requesting torpedo fire on the big one."

He couldn't hear Myers' response through the static. It would have to do. He leaned around the corner, shot another cultist in the mouth, and put his last round through another man's heart. Franks dropped the empty gun and was moving as they fired uselessly through the sheet metal. Franks was huge by human standards, but he moved faster than almost any mortal on Earth. He cleared the edge of the wheelhouse, caught a cultist from behind, snapped his neck, shoved the paralyzed man into the next so that he fired his shotgun uselessly into the air. Franks punched that one in the face, breaking nose, jaw, and several teeth, took his shotgun away, and hurled them both over the side. He spun the shotgun around, shouldered it, pumped a round into the chamber, and blew half of another cultist's head off. He aimed at another, but could tell by the feel as he worked the Remington's action that the weapon was empty, most of its rounds already having been fired at him. Franks dropped the shotgun and ducked as the rest of the ship began shooting at him again.

Looking back, Franks realized that the demon was so scared of being captured by him that it was actually gnawing through its own arm in an attempt to escape. Franks moved quickly. He found a long pole with a hook on the end and used that to reach up and shove one of the spotlights out of alignment, temporarily blinding the cultists shooting at him. Then he speared an old man through the guts with the pole, clotheslined another cultist hard enough to kill him instantly, and got back to his prisoner just as the demon finished chewing its arm off.

It began scrambling away, but he easily caught it. "You can't do this, Franks! You're a traitor to the host. You'll pay for this!" it shrieked as he dragged it back to where he pinned it the first time.

The demon scratched and bit at him, annoying Franks. When he reached the ceremonial dagger, he tugged it from the wood. The severed claw slid off the end of the steel. He forced the demon's head against the deck and stabbed it through the face, pinning it just as hard as before. It squealed and thrashed, but at least it couldn't talk anymore. The stupid imp wouldn't be chewing its way out of that.

Franks went back to killing cultists. Some of the fools were trying to communicate with the leviathan but it took a human years of effort to master the original tongue, and their demon translator was occupied. The old language was very difficult for the mortal mind to comprehend it, let alone speak well, but one cultist, apparently their leader, was giving it his best effort. He had spread his arms wide and was screaming up at the creature. *"Great Sleeper of the Depths, forgive us as we trouble your rest. Humbly we request our enemies gone by devouring!"*

A tree-sized tentacle paused over their boat, and fifty eyes opened up along its length to study the cultist in his wind-whipped robes. Franks found another gun and angled for a shot on the cult leader. He had to admit he was impressed; for a mortal the cultist was doing really well, up until the part where he screwed it up. *"Our lives are food for you!"*

The leviathan was happy to oblige. Thousands of spines erupted from the tentacle as it descended. Cultists screamed as they were pierced, encircled, and lifted into the air to be shoved into giant pulsing mouths.

Primary objective completed. The monster wasn't going to fling itself at the civilian population now, but Franks still needed to secure his prisoner for interrogation before the leviathan sank the fishing boat. A female hybrid attacked him, fish eyes bulging beneath her cowl, fat frog lips smacking as she tried to bite him in the face. Franks merely kicked her in the stomach, launching her back, and before she hit the deck, a tentacle snatched her up, lifted her to one of the monster's snapping beaks, and popped the hybrid in to be chewed.

Tentacles were striking everywhere. The monster could have simply crushed the boat, but it seemed to be enjoying the snacks first. But the boat was nearly depopulated. Franks did not want to be chewed, nor did he want to spend the time sawing his way out of a giant monster's guts. It was time for extraction.

There was a white flash far beneath the surface. An explosion rocked the fishing boat. The leviathan screamed in frequencies that deafened whales. Either Franks' message had gotten through or the captain of the attack submarine had seen the giant monster on his sonar screen and made the call himself. A circle of water a hundred yards across erupted upward as the second torpedo hit the leviathan.

A black, glistening bulk the size of a three-story building hit the fishing boat, and the vessel went sideways. The few remaining cultists were hurled into the sea. Franks fell, but caught himself on some machinery. Then, annoyed by this turn of events, began crawling toward his prisoner, who was dangling by its face over the churning water. "Bravo Team, this is Franks. Look for me in the wreckage."

The boat righted temporarily, but its back was broken, and they were sinking fast. Franks reached the demon, and pulled the dagger free. It sprung up and clawed at him, but Franks blocked the arm and slugged the demon in its punctured mouth, sending it crashing back down. He loomed over it. "Who sent you?"

"Traitor," the demon gasped. "You're a traitor to the host."

Franks kicked the imp in the face. Fat droplets of glowing blood flew up into the rain. Even animated bodies felt pain, but considering the imp had just gnawed its own arm off in an attempt to escape it had a respectable pain threshold. Torture would take too long. The boat was going down. Explosions were ripping through the ocean as more torpedoes struck the thrashing monster. There was no time for games. "Talk or I'll send you back to Hell." It would take a thousand years for a shit stain like this to find its way back out of the void.

"Please, no," it hissed. Franks didn't answer, but the demon looked him in the eyes, saw what was waiting there, then experienced an involuntary shiver. "Fine, fine." It dipped its remaining hand into the puddle of glowing blood, and with one claw drew a complicated symbol on the wood. The demon didn't need to explain. They both knew exactly who that stood for.

Franks scowled at the design. *Another related event...* Already the rain was washing the mark away, but it was unmistakable. This would be going in his report. His superiors wouldn't be happy.

One of the smaller tentacles approached, bristling with eyes and thorns, looking for one last snack before it fled back to the deep. Franks looked up nonchalantly, saw the massive blob of flesh, and immediately slugged one big fist into a soft eyeball. Pus squirted out and the tentacle retreated.

"That's right, Franks. All those years buried deep, but he's awake, and he's gathering his army. The end is beginning, and you picked the wrong side, brother. Don't leave me out here. I can help you. Let me go and I'll tell you everything I know."

Never trust a demon. The fishing vessel was listing badly, but it looked like the main body of the leviathan was coming back around to swallow them whole. Franks took the demon's other hand, shoved it against the deck, and slammed the dagger through its palm. The imp screamed. "Chew fast." Franks began walking away.

"Wait. I've got more information! I've got something you're going to want to hear. Let me go," the demon begged. Franks got to the edge. A fifty-foot tentacle swept by and tore the wheelhouse completely off the boat. The mouth that was lifting out of the sea now was big enough to engulf the whole boat. It was time to go for a swim. "This is personal, Franks! Your old enemy has found a way back to Earth."

Franks paused. He looked back at the imp. "Who?"

"Kurst!"

It was not often that something shook Franks. He started back toward the demon.

"He's found a new body that can hold him. He'll be coming for you. Let me go and I'll—"

This tentacle was as big around as a bus, and when it landed on the fishing boat, everything simply came apart. They were being lifted by the ancient beast as torpedoes exploded beneath them. Franks stumbled across the splintering beams, but the imp was gone. A row of suckers had slurped the demon's remains off the deck, leaving nothing but a mass of hamburger and bubbling acid.

Kurst... Either the imp has been toying with him out of spite, or that was very bad news.

Franks snarled in frustration and leapt over the side. The ocean rushed up to meet him.

"No, Agent Franks, I said to start at the beginning.*"*

Franks folded his gigantic arms. His broad shoulders seemed to fill the small room. "No."

Normally people would shrink before Franks' withering gaze, but the interrogator didn't so much as flinch. "That's not a request. It's in our vital interest to know the whole story. Everything's on the table now or we're done here. I don't think you realize the mess you've made. This is your last chance. He needs to decide which side you're really on."

The whole story had never been told. Franks didn't even know if he could.

"Well? What's it going to be? I know your usual answer would be classified, *but that really doesn't apply here now, does it?"*

"I'm not much for talking."

"Then it sounds like I'm in for a treat, because if you don't tell me your whole life story right now then the deal is off."

Franks exhaled. "Take notes. I don't like to repeat myself."

CHAPTER 2

Testimony of the entity known as Franks, former Special Agent of the United States Monster Control Bureau.

Interrogator's note: All of my questions, and the awkward periods of silence and angry glaring from the subject, have been omitted for the sake of brevity. I have never, in all my years, encountered anyone or anything this surly and menacing. Franks is completely incapable of mercy or kindness. As this process went on he began to open up, granting me a good look into his thought processes. I know that it isn't my decision to make, but in my professional opinion I would find the deepest hole possible and bury Franks in it.

BEGIN TRANSCRIPT
Where do you want me to start? My contract? I kept my word. It was the government that broke Benjamin Franklin's contract. Stricken shouldn't have crossed me.

Earlier than that...

The first words I ever heard in my mortal life were "It's alive. It's alive." *Is that what you want?*

Before that even... Hmmm... Normally I'd kill you for asking.

You want the real beginning, but it's hard to remember and harder to explain.

Buckle up. This is about to get weird.

Aftermath of the Level 5 ICMHP Incident
12 Days Ago
Las Vegas, Nevada

The man's ID badge read "Foster." The command tent was full of people called *Agent*, but his title was simply *Mister*. Despite that, he was the one in de facto command. Franks really wanted to kill him, but that would only complicate matters. Foster was from Special Task Force Unicorn, one of Stricken's handpicked human lackeys rather than one of their monstrous foot soldiers, and was thus worthy of having his neck snapped, but since Franks had been placed in chains and surrounded by guards prepared to shoot him down at the smallest provocation, Foster's death would have to wait.

"If Franks so much as twitches, kill him," Foster ordered.

The assembled MCB agents were following orders, but they were obviously uncomfortable with it. Several blocks of Las Vegas were in smoking ruins around them. The situation had descended into complete chaos. The chain of command was broken. There were hundreds of eyewitnesses. Rather than being allowed to fulfill their primary mission of trying to keep the existence of monsters and supernatural threats concealed from the general public, these MCB agents had been tasked with securing the most legendary operative in their organization's history as if he were some sort of traitor.

One of the men voiced his concern. "I don't think this is necessary. Franks cooperated fully with your arrest order, Mr. Foster."

It was true. There would have been no point in resisting, so he'd allowed the arriving reinforcements to secure him until their superiors arrived. Franks had very little faith in the wisdom of mankind, but he trusted Dwayne Myers. Myers would sort this out.

"Don't give me any lip." Foster was pacing nervously and checking his phone, waiting for some word from his mysterious supervisor. "You're going down for this, Franks, you're going down hard."

An hour ago Franks had been swatted across the Strip by a dragon made of ectoplasm and nightmares. Bureaucratic plotting seemed inconsequential in comparison.

There was a commotion on the other side of the tent flap. Guards gave challenges, IDs were presented, and then there was a rush of apologies. The flap opened and several men entered the giant command tent. The first through were members of the MCB's elite mobile strike team. They were hardened warriors Franks had served with many times, and behind them was an innocuous-looking, middle-aged man in a cheap suit.

Franks' arms were chained to the chair, so he dipped his head slightly. "Sir."

"Why is my second-in-command tied up?" demanded Dwayne Myers, the Special Agent-in-Charge of Strike Team. "What's the meaning of this?"

Foster's response was about as belligerent as could be expected. "Agent Franks is charged with disobeying direct orders, violating security protocols by taking a civilian witness into a monster containment area, and then breaking into the Nevada storage facility to steal seized evidence."

"Is that true?" Myers asked.

Franks nodded. That sounded about right, but Myers already knew most of the details, since it had secretly been his idea to begin with. Franks had taken Owen Pitt to Dugway because he'd thought the Monster Hunter's psychic powers could help their investigation. He'd taken three ancient arcane weapons from Area 51 in order to fight the Nachtmar: Lord Machado's ax, the Attilius gladius, and the Black Heart of Suffering. That last one had done the trick, and destroyed the creature.

"When he was confronted about his actions, Franks attempted to kill MCB Director Douglas Stark."

Franks snorted. The five men covering him with drawn weapons backed away nervously. They were only following orders, but all of them had worked with Franks at some point, so they were aware that shooting Franks might upset him.

"I've known Agent Franks for twenty years. He doesn't *attempt* to kill anyone. Holster those sidearms and unchain him. Franks is coming with me." Myers had recently been demoted, but had been the Acting Director before that, and he was still probably the most respected senior agent in the Bureau.

"Hold on," Foster demanded. "Franks is in STFU custody." It was almost like Foster thought that invoking the name of the ultra-secret Special Task Force Unicorn would strike fear into the federal agent's heart.

Myers glanced around theatrically. "Really? Because these appear to be MCB men, and last I checked, sworn MCB agents don't take orders from an operation that doesn't exist." The MCB didn't officially exist either, as it was just a line item on the Department of Homeland Security's budget, but in this business there were levels of *not* existing.

"Director Stark is—"

"Hiding from this giant clusterfuck caused by his lack of leadership," Myers said. "Our good Director must have forgotten that it is against regulation seventy-two dash B to turn MCB handling of a level five containment to another entity, such as yours, without authorization from the President. So in the meantime I'm the highest ranking member of the MCB available, and I'm making the call. Cut Franks loose. I'm going back outside to try to contain the unholy mess you amateurs made out of one of America's most popular tourist attractions, before every news agency in the world records video of a street full of ectoplasm and dragon parts. Is that understood, Mr. Foster?"

It was clearly understood, but not particularly liked. "We're not done, Myers."

"Oh, I believe that we are." Myers glanced over and confirmed that the men had put their weapons away. "Remove Mr. Foster from *my* command tent."

"I've got it," Franks said. One of the men had been looking for the key to the padlock, but Franks simply took up the chain in his bare hands and twisted until a link snapped. By the time anyone realized what was happening, the chains had already hit the floor and Franks had caught Foster by the arm and effortlessly lifted him off the ground. Foster winced in pain as Franks carried him to the nearest flap, and hurled the Unicorn operative into the street.

Foster hit hard and skidded across the pavement, right into a pile of ectoplasm that had been blown off the nightmare dragon. He came up, indignant and sputtering, covered in the glowing sludge. "Stricken will hear about this!"

"Run away, little man," Franks advised as he dropped the tent flap and returned to Myers. "You should have just had me kill him."

"He's but an insignificant cog in a big dangerous machine." Myers was wearing a charcoal suit rather than his armor, but as far as most of the MCB were aware, that was because he had barely arrived on the scene. In truth, Myers had been here the whole time, secretly trying to stop the Nachtmar as fast as possible, and head off Stricken's power-grabbing schemes. "We've got our work cut out for us as it is. Agent Jefferson has handled the PR surprisingly well so far, but if we fail to move quickly this event could prove to be the worst breach in MCB history."

Myers gave a quick series of orders to the waiting agents, about coordinating with the military and local law enforcement, making sure that the given cover stories were consistent, sending out plainclothes agents as witnesses to speak to the media, cleaning up anything that looked paranormal, and placing fake evidence to back up their cover stories. "Martinez, gather up some actors and go give the news some firsthand accounts of this terrorist attack. Nothing too detailed yet though. Remember, good and emotional. They'll always run with tears and babbling. Barber, contact Technical Branch. Anything floating around the internet, crash it. As big as that dragon was there's got to be video and I want it scrubbed. Pick the worst virus we have and turn it loose."

It was like watching a symphony conductor.

"Tobler, where's my body count? How many corpses are we talking about? And how many wounded?" Myers paused when he was handed a tablet. He quickly scanned it and then swore at the rather large tally. "We've got a lot of eyewitness duty on this one..."

The men groaned as Myers began handing out more assignments. Intimidating the witnesses into silence was the duty that most agents dreaded. Franks didn't really grasp why. It was simply another part of their mission. The Monster Control Bureau's primary responsibility was to keep the existence of monsters secret from the general public. That was their founding principle. It was necessary, but most agents didn't like threatening innocent monster attack survivors. Humans were soft like that.

On the other hand, Franks didn't mind a bit. "Orders?"

Myers handed the tablet back. "Walk with me, Franks."

The two of them went outside.

Dozens of cars had been thrown about, flipped, and crushed. There was a huge hole in the pavement where the Nachtmar had burrowed through. Most of the fires were contained, but Diamond Steve's Hotel and Casino was burning out of control. The Last Dragon complex was a crumbling ruin, having been ravaged by fire, improvised explosives, a nightmare army, and several hundred desperate Monster Hunters. This event had begun simply enough, with a *medical* quarantine of a casino, but had quickly spread out of control, with a paranormal rift forcing the evacuation of the entire city. It had all culminated with a nightmare dragon wrecking its way up and down the Las Vegas Strip.

However, Dwayne Myers was the greatest propaganda artist that the MCB had ever seen, and if anyone could contain this, it was him. Franks' superior surveyed the scene for a long moment. "Yes... It'll be a challenge, but I can work with this..."

"Of course, sir."

"I'll have to do it without your capable help though. I need you to do something else. Stricken has made his move."

"Nemesis?"

"Of course." Myers took a pack of cigarettes from his pocket, removed one, and lit it. "It appears he wants that project restarted badly enough to endanger a whole city. The game is afoot."

"Nemesis isn't a game."

"He's using this event as an excuse. Stricken's under the impression that Nemesis is some surefire, anti-paranormal super solution, and he intends to convince the President that giving him a blank check will keep us safe. Your contract is the only legal thing standing in the way. You're going back to headquarters for a full debrief. That albino son of a bitch has already filed a report about all your violations."

"Trying to get me fired?"

"Dismantled."

Franks grunted in acknowledgment.

"Don't worry. That's not likely. Everyone knows you're too valuable an asset." Myers exhaled a cloud of smoke as he surveyed the devastation. "But did you really need to choke the Director unconscious?"

Franks shrugged.

"I figured as much... Poor Doug. I bet he's wishing he'd never taken my job now. I warned him it was stressful." Myers chuckled. "Stricken is crafty enough to know that I'll be stuck here until this is contained, so I can't maneuver against him. He'll strike while the iron is hot and push for Nemesis authorization while everyone is panicking. Sorry, Franks. I have to see to the mission first."

That went without saying. The mission always came first. The more people who believed in the supernatural, the more they believed in the other worlds, the stronger those worlds' influences became, the more the lines between them blurred, and that could not be allowed. Humanity never fared well when the lines blurred.

The two of them watched the casino burn in silence for a moment before Myers sighed. "We can't keep this up forever."

"No, sir."

"The MCB has done its best, but the time is coming when the truth will get out. I'm afraid that when that happens, there is going to be somebody like Stricken ready with a cure that's worse than the disease.... Do you trust me, Franks?"

Franks nodded. *More than any other human currently alive.* Though Franks used the word to keep communications simple, and he'd referred to certain coworkers as friends over the years, he didn't really understand the human concept of *friendship.* Logically Myers probably qualified as a *friend.*

"Then I wish you'd tell me the real reason you're so dead set against Project Nemesis."

Franks didn't respond.

"That's right. Classified. Even for me ..." Myers shook his head. "You know, I've got to hand it to Stricken. You're the one thing standing between him and what he wants, using his own system's rules against him, and as long as those stood, he was stuck. So he put you in a spot where you had to choose between breaking the system and failing a mission."

"I've never failed a mission."

"Then let's not start now then. There's a Blackhawk inbound that will take you to Nellis. I have a plane waiting for you. I'm occupied, so you don't currently have a partner. I'll send some of my trusted men to serve as handlers."

"Don't need them."

"I've seen your interpersonal skills in action. This is interagency politics now, Franks. You need someone capable of smiling and kissing congressional ass. I'll assign Grant as your counsel. Come to think of it, I've got a few other agents with skillsets that could prove useful in this endeavor ... There's one in particular ..." Myers trailed off, seeming deep in thought. "Never mind the roster. I'll take care of it. Get back to headquarters and tell your side of the story. There will probably be a hearing. Just be yourself and we'll be fine."

Franks glanced over, curious.

"I'd better clarify. When I said be yourself, I mean tell them the unvarnished truth, not murder everything ... Stricken is gaming the system, but I don't think he's willing to break it. *Yet.* I'd tell you to be careful, but I know you've got eyes in the back of your head."

"Tried that once. Too disorienting."

"You're a very literal man, Franks.... The powers that be know Stricken. He's their pet snake, but they still understand they've got a snake. On the other hand you have an exemplary service record for over two centuries. You're a known quantity. Some of them might fear you, but they know you won't blow smoke up their asses. I think it'll work out ... Hopefully we're not too late."

Myers wasn't allowed to know, but if they couldn't stop Project Nemesis then the destruction they saw here today would be *nothing* in comparison.

"Franks duty?" Grant Jefferson asked his partner as they approached waiting aircraft. "What did we do to deserve this?"

"Myers probably just wants us out of Vegas since we helped him screw over STFU," Archer answered.

"Shhh." Grant glanced around the runway. "Don't say that out in the open. There could be bugs."

Grant's lack of technical surveillance knowledge was funny, but most MCB personnel didn't have Archer's technical know-how. He'd been in the Tech Branch of the Admin and Logistics division of the MCB. Grant was Media Control, and that assignment was more about smooth talking than smarts. "If Unicorn has directional mikes good enough to pick us up over those engines spinning up, he deserves to know about our great Waffle Hut conspiracy."

Grant nodded. "I sure hope you're right."

"I sure hope Stricken hasn't arranged for our flight to crash mysteriously."

"That's not going to happen." But since both of them worked for a shadow government entity that specialized in fabricating conspiracy theories and falsifying evidence, Grant didn't sound convinced. "Probably. Stricken might be willing to sit around and let extra innocents die, but he isn't going to start murdering other Feds ... But if the crew starts parachuting out, I'm going with them."

"Like Stricken would tell the Air Force? Fat chance of that. If I was him, I'd just have one of our wings rigged to blow clean off." Archer had been in the 82nd Airborne and had made a lot of jumps in his life, but they'd all been out of perfectly good aircraft. "You can't exactly overcome centrifugal force and cleanly exit a plane that's corkscrewing its way into the ground. Well, Franks maybe could, but I hear as long as there's enough left of him to scrape into a Ziploc bag they can make a new body, so Franks doing something stupid doesn't count. All those military training accidents you read about where some plane falls into the Med with no bodies recovered? That's got monster cover-up written all over it. Just because we're not briefed in doesn't mean it wasn't us. I knew this one dude—"

"Okay, enough. I already hate flying when I'm not the pilot." Grant had to shout as they got closer to the plane. They both got their plugs out and stuck into their ears. C-17s were loud as hell on the ramp. Since the MCB was a rather special entity within the government, when they needed military resources they got them fast. "It's not fair. I was doing a great job on PR. Getting stuck Franks-sitting . . . That's the most boring job in the Bureau until the minute it turns into the most dangerous. What's the fatality rate on Franks-sitting?"

"Last time we worked with Franks only half of us died. Plus that dick Torres even deserved it. Don't be a wuss, Grant. We're not going operational with Franks. We're going to watch him fill out paperwork and maybe growl at a congressman. I'm probably just here because I type fast."

"This is just a letdown. That was one of the biggest cover jobs in MCB history and I was doing a damn good job locking it down."

To be fair, Grant really had. Some of them were just better natural born liars, and some, like Archer, were better at supporting the liars. "Your career will survive. Our last two directors partnered with Franks at some point. Supporting the big dog is a prestige assignment. Think of this as a resumé builder. Everybody knows you're gunning for a SAC position eventually."

Grant got a little red in the face. The MCB had a very hands-on warrior culture. No field agent wanted to get a rep as a political hack, especially now that the biggest political hack in the Bureau was their new director, and Stark wasn't exactly a popular figure.

Archer didn't bring it up, as Myers hadn't had a chance yet to brief them on the details of their particular assignment, but with everything that was going on in Vegas right now, Myers could barely afford to spare anyone, let alone four agents. There was something going down, and since he and Grant were some of the few who knew about Stricken's illegal activities, it had to be related.

The female Air Force loadmaster led them up the ramp and showed them where to stash their gear bags. She couldn't help but give Grant a flirty little look. The dude was just so annoyingly classically handsome that he had that effect on nearly every woman they met. Half the time Grant could simply charm their witnesses into silence. They were still in their issued black MCB armor, though both of them had managed to avoid being set on fire or covered in ectoplasm, so all things considered they appeared rather respectable. Only Archer was skinny and goofy-looking. She gave Grant a long once-over, barely noticed that Archer was alive, then went back down the ramp as they continued going forward. Grant inspected her backside through her flight suit and turned back grinning. "Thank you, stewardess... What?"

"That's why you're assigned to Franks. Myers figured you had charm enough for both of you."

"Hey, I'd seduce a congresswoman if it furthered the mission. Don't ever say that I'm not willing to take one for the team."

The interior bay was large enough to carry a tank and had seats down the sides. There were two other armored MCB agents already strapped in and waiting. Of course there were no nameplates on a mission like this, but Archer knew one of them. The muscular guy was Radabaugh. Like many members of the MCB recruited from the military, he was a former spec ops badass. Radabaugh was a long time member of the Strike Team and had even been in Natchy Bottom. That was the sort of thing that earned an agent some street cred. Archer shook his hand. "Good to see you here."

"Hey, Henry," he shouted back. "Grant. You guys Franks-sitting too?"

"Afraid so," Grant answered before turning to the last agent, who was a rather average-looking young man with thinning blond hair. He wasn't very tall, and a little overweight for an agent, which meant he probably wasn't from the Strike Team. "I don't know you. What department are you in?"

"Thomas Strayhorn." The young agent stuck out his hand to shake. "I was transferred over from the Marshal's Service. I'm still unassigned."

"Nice to meet you, Agent Strayhorn."

"*Probationary* agent. He got out of the academy a week ago," Radabaugh said. "I'm his TO."

"Still in training and you're on Franks' detail?" That was surprising. Archer shared a nervous glance with Grant. From the look on his face they were thinking the same thing. The last time Franks had been put with new agents it had been to smoke out a mole. That op had exposed the traitor Torres, but it had gotten Herzog killed in the process.

"A week, huh?" Grant asked suspiciously. "Isn't that something? Is he cleared on Franks?"

"He's cleared, but he's not had the *full* briefing yet, just the sanitized version from the academy. I just got the word from Myers half an hour ago to be here."

"You must have either impressed the hell out of him, or really pissed Myers off somehow. Welcome to Franks duty, Strayhorn. It's a real joy to work with him. Most bosses you have to guess if they really like you or not, but with Franks that's never in question. He hates everyone. Our job is to run interference, be the public face—"

"Fetch him snacks. Rub his feet," Radabaugh said. "Basically we do whatever he says all while trying to keep stupid people out of his way."

"Franks especially hates stupid people, and he thinks everybody is stupid." Archer sat next to the new guy. He'd ridden in plenty of C-17s, and compared to some of the other military aircraft the MCB routinely commandeered it was a pleasant ride in comparison. Conversation was even possible if you didn't mind yelling. "A rookie, huh?"

"I spent three years in federal law enforcement—"

"The sooner you get through your head that means jack shit when dealing with monsters, the better," Radabaugh corrected him. "That's Henry Archer you're talking to. Don't let the flat-top fool you. He may look like Vanilla Ice but he's the real deal. Archer here took point on the New Zealand op. You heard of the Arbmunep?"

"Oh." That got his attention. "They talked about that in training. Impressive."

"That tree was a mean son of a bitch, but it was a team effort." Monster Hunter International had done a lot of the heavy lifting on that one, but since MCB agents' opinions on that company ranged from MHI being cowboys deserving a little grudging respect all the way over to them being a bunch of money-grubbing, borderline criminal cutthroats, Archer didn't want to open that particular can of contractor worms.

But Radabaugh did anyway. "And Grant here is former MHI. He dealt with more oddities in a couple of years than most of us will over a career."

Strayhorn seemed intrigued. "That's weird. I've heard some MCB retire and then go private, but I don't know too many private Hunters that go government. Kind of backwards, isn't it? I hear they get paid tons, but we just start out as GS-12s. I've heard about MHI. They're supposed to be kind of shifty."

"Uh huh..." Grant said as he took his phone out and pretended to check his email. "Before you read too much into their character, our *boss*, MCB *legend* Dwayne Myers once worked for MHI too. He was even best friends with Earl Harbinger."

"I knew that." It still shut the rookie up. Archer was a little envious of how easily Grant could manipulate a social situation. Most experienced agents would have just browbeat the new guy, but Grant put him in his place and still came out looking like a nice guy.

"Myers has enough problems right now without any of us bringing up his past," Archer said. "In case you're wondering, he's a good boss. He knows monsters better than anybody." *And if he wants us here, there's got to be a damned good reason.* Myers was a hard-ass, but he was competent, and most of all, Archer's gut instinct told him that Myers was basically an honorable man. He cared about the safety of his country above all, which was more than Archer could say for his replacement. Stark was a doofus.

Immediately after the Copper Lake incident, Archer, like most of the MCB, had thought that Doug Stark was a hero. Archer had grown up only a few miles from Copper Lake. The whole Upper Peninsula would have been awash in zombie werewolves if it hadn't been for Stark's quick thinking. It wasn't until later, when he'd been assigned to the cover-up and was interviewing locals, that he had learned that contrary to the official record, Stark's real actions had consisted mostly of cowardice and stupidity. Harbinger, some rival Hunters, and a bunch of locals had been the real heroes. That had been a letdown. Then while picking through the aftermath, Archer had discovered the originator of the *vulkodlak* plague that had endangered his home town had been one of Stricken's pet monsters from STFU.

Between those two facts, it was no surprise that he'd sided with Myers in the MCB's internal power struggle.

"I'd never bad-mouth Myers. I've only heard positive things about him." Strayhorn left that hanging, waiting to see if any of the more experienced men would correct him. He seemed satisfied when they didn't.

"Don't worry about it, Rookie..." Grant said. "But yes, MHI are shifty. They only care about themselves. They're a bunch of glory hounds and hotdogs, but they're not all bad."

"Projection much?" Archer muttered.

"Huh?"

"Nothing." Thank goodness for the engine noise. Archer actually liked the MHI people he'd worked with, but then again, he wasn't the one whose fiancée had dumped him to marry a magic accountant.

Grant put his phone back in his pocket. "Well, anyway, I'm sure this assignment will either be boring as hell, or we'll all die on an op and Franks will harvest our corpses for spare parts.... Come to think of it, I sure hope you're right, Archer, and I'm here because I'm good with people and not because Franks picked us out because he needs some new parts." Grant made an exaggerated motion around his face. "Who wouldn't want this?"

"Makes sense," Archer responded. "Holly Newcastle did just tell me I've got nice eyes." And since he was thinking of MHI people he didn't mind working with... *Wow.* That was one enemy he wouldn't mind fraternizing with.

"Franks goes through eyes like crazy. I hear he keeps a jar full of them in his fridge," Radabaugh said as he looked over at Strayhorn. "That's right. The rumors are true. Franks is built out of body parts."

Archer was still thinking of his last oddly staffed op, so he watched the rookie carefully. He wasn't about to get bit in the ass again.

The rookie was pretty darn good at keeping his emotions hidden. "There was some talk about him at the academy." Strayhorn said cautiously. "Some of the guys said that he's really Frankenstein." Archer liked how he added the *some said.* The rookie wasn't giving away whether he believed them or not, just in case the senior agents were pulling his leg.

"You mean Frankenstein's monster, but yeah." Radabaugh grinned. "Welcome to the big time, Rook. Dr. Frankenstein was a myth. The real mad scientist was named Dippel. The book came out way later. Franks isn't a code name either. He named himself that because he was *built* in the real Castle Frankenstein."

"I see..."

"I doubt that!" Radabaugh insisted. "Franks is a three-hundred-year-old, one-man wrecking ball. Anything the MCB really needs to shut down, they drop Franks on it. Boom. Done. He's way faster, stronger, and tougher than any of us. I've got the top hand-to-hand combatives score in the Bureau three years running and I wouldn't last thirty seconds against Franks. He gets blown up, we bag the parts, and the egg-heads stitch him back together... Few days later he's back in the fight, mean as ever. And don't go thinking that because he's an antique he can't be that badass; they've been making improvements on him the whole time. He can shrug off things that would kill any regular man, and when he's moving, just keep out of his way. If we get called up for something and it turns into combat, stay behind Franks."

"He only needs us to deal with the red tape. In a fight you're basically his gun caddy," Archer said. "Keep your head down and keep handing him weapons. There's nothing Franks can't kill once he puts his mind to it. Plus, he's like a tactical genius, but I figure that's just because he's been doing this for so long nothing really ever takes him by surprise."

Grant leaned forward conspiratorially. "Franks killed a Great Old One."

"That's supposed to be impossible." Strayhorn frowned, probably thinking back to his training. "You can't kill a Great Old One."

"He did have help," Archer said.

"Pitt?" Grant snorted. "That jackass?"

"Well, him and Isaac Newton, but if anybody knows Franks well at this point it has to be Owen Pitt." Archer looked back at Strayhorn. "Sorry. That's a long story."

Strayhorn seemed intrigued. "We've got a long flight. Look, I've heard Franks' legends, every recruit has. He's supposed to be like the most intimidating guy ever, but come on..."

"I once saw Franks beat a werewolf to death with its own arm. He was like that *how come you keep hitting yourself* bully from elementary school, but with more blood. Only Franks didn't actually say that, because he's one humorless motherfucker," Radabaugh said. "If the Frankenstein origin story isn't true, then it's a pretty elaborate cover, because the real Franks is some sort of supernatural scary-ass killing machine."

Now that they were telling stories, Grant didn't want to be outdone. "I've seen them open him up for field surgery after he'd been injured. He's got extra hearts, like a relay system, and he can turn them on and off as he needs them. He doesn't have ribs like we do. It looks more like they stuck an armored vest inside his chest to keep his guts in place. I heard Franks even has extra brain tissue grafted along his spine, like backing up a hard drive, in case he gets his brains blown out. He might look like a man on the outside, but he's not."

"No kidding?" Strayhorn was nodding along. Even in an organization made up of professional liars, the others were just too earnest. Archer didn't know what his introduction to monsters had been, but it must have been something good, because Franks' story didn't seem to shake him too badly. "So what's he like as a person?"

"Person?" Archer snorted. "Don't make that mistake. He's the scariest thing you'll ever see. Franks is like the definition of *does not give a shit*. He's cold. He's got extra hearts, but he doesn't have a *heart*. There's just something not right about him in the head. I mean he's smart, and he's freakishly rational, but he's just not wired like a real person. When he looks at you it's like he's doing math. I don't think he gets people either, or he does get us, but he doesn't care. When you're talking to him, you get this feeling that you're talking to a fucking space alien wearing a human costume, and he's just looking at you with his blank eyes the whole time, and you just know the only reason he doesn't murder you is because you're not worth the paperwork.... I'd call him a sociopath, but that's too humanizing." Archer realized that the other three were staring past him toward the ramp. "He's here, isn't he?"

Radabaugh gave him a nervous nod in the affirmative. "We forgot to mention that he's got superhearing too."

"Shit." Archer turned back. The monstrous Agent Franks was walking down the center of the cargo bay, a giant bag slung over one shoulder. The loadmaster tried to give him directions to stow his gear, but he ignored her and kept walking. She took one look at the hulking brute and wisely let it go. The ramp began to rise.

Franks stopped before the agents, towering over them. He was as wide as any two of them put together and imposing as hell. His eyes swiveled over them, taking stock of his *handlers*—as if anybody could truly handle Franks—and scowled. Grant and Radabaugh nodded respectfully and simultaneously said, "Sir." Strayhorn tried to say something but failed, because once in the overwhelming presence that was Franks the truth had been confirmed, and that had to be fairly unnerving.

His cold, dead eyes fell on Archer last. "Welcome aboard, Agent Franks," Archer squeaked. "It's a pleasure to be working with you again, sir."

Franks merely grunted in acknowledgement. He either hadn't heard Archer's psych-evaluation or didn't disagree with the findings. Franks brushed past and went forward, where he took up two of the small, uncomfortable military seats.

The agents sat in silence while the plane taxied and took off. Franks stared off into space the whole time. Awkwardness was the norm when you were working with Franks.

What have I gotten dragged into this time? There was a power struggle in the MCB and Archer had sided with the hard-ass Myers against the moron Stark, and in doing so he'd probably put himself on the bad side of a top secret black op that was up to who knew what awful business. Franks had pissed off Unicorn, so now he and a few other men got to be glorified gophers to run interference while the world's most dangerous killing machine had to kiss and make up with a bunch of bureaucrats capable of ending all of their careers.

Something about this assignment was bothering him. Grant could be a narcissistic douche at times, but he was really smart and worked hard. Radabaugh had always struck him as a reliable tough guy. Strayhorn was a rookie and an unknown. The whole thing felt way too much like the time he'd been undercover at MHI.

For a man who hated conspiracies and lies, Archer had certainly gone into the wrong line of work.

Normally people were supposed to feel some sense of awe when they met with the President of the United States. Even if you didn't care for the man personally, despised his politics, or wouldn't let the fellow babysit your kids, you were still supposed to respect the office, and thus the man, but as Stricken watched the President dither over what to do next, all he could think to himself was *what a chump.*

Luckily, Stricken was very good at feigning sincere respect. "Mr. President, I'm afraid Franks has already proven how unstable he's become. We'll need time to get our precautions in place. I'm afraid I'm going to need your decision as soon as possible."

It was just the two of them in the Oval Office, the President and his Special Advisor. No other members of the Special Subcommittee had been invited to this meeting. "Are you sure detaining him is necessary?"

"Absolutely. This is the safest move for everyone involved. Provided Franks cooperates, nobody will be hurt. If he doesn't..." Stricken spread his hands apologetically. "Even the most loyal dog needs to be put to sleep when it turns rabid. It's time to take Ol' Yeller behind the barn, Mr. President."

The President chewed on his pen as he thought that through. Normally he'd listen to his legion of sycophantic advisors or take an opinion poll, but the nice thing about working at this level of clearance was that it separated the wheat from the chaff. There were very few individuals in the entire government cleared to know the details of this sort of event, and most of those were still occupied dealing with Las Vegas.

The most powerful man in the world pushed a button on his desk. "Bring in the Franks' contract."

Stricken made a show of studying the various decorations in the Oval Office while they waited. Of course, he'd memorized every item in it the first time he'd been here, and could tell down to the individual paperclip what had been moved since his last visit, but gawking was expected behavior, and staring at the man on the other side of the Resolute desk while he waffled on policy would be considered uncouth.

The contract must have already been pulled out of the archives earlier, as a moment later it was placed in the President's hands by a secretary who seemed very relieved to flee the Oval Office and Stricken's gaze. He had that effect on the sensitive types.

The contract was written on old parchment and sealed in a glass box. The President held it awkwardly, like he wasn't quite sure what to do with it. Stricken didn't understand why he needed to see the original. Every man who'd sat in that chair had read it at some point. A copy would do just as well, but sentimental foolishness was to be expected from a leader who was governed by his feelings rather than his iron will.

While the President studied Ben Franklin's scribbling and Franks' X, Stricken mulled over his takedown strategies. He already knew he'd be given permission to *detain* Franks, as if he were just some human being that they could throw a bag over his head, toss him in a van, and redact his ass to Poland. This was Agent fucking Franks they were talking about here. The President didn't have the balls to order Franks outright eliminated, so he'd take the middle road of locking him up for everyone's *safety*. That had been a forgone conclusion before Stricken had ever requested this meeting. He'd been laying the groundwork for this moment for a few years. Of course, it was also a forgone conclusion that Franks would resist being stuck in a cage, so that freak of nature would die resisting, and permanently this time.

The President sighed as he finished reading the old parchment.

"Those are not idle threats, sir. If we violate that covenant, Franks fully intends to do everything he said there. He is that irrational and violent, which is why I need your blessing before I proceed."

"Over two hundred years of service," the President said as he put the contract down, discarding it like he'd been so quick to discard every other founding document he'd found inconvenient. "He's saved this country, and maybe the whole world, more times than we can count."

That was an exaggeration. The correct number was only *sixteen* tops, and that was being generous because most of those probably wouldn't have gone all the way to an extinction level event. The earlier Special Advisors had been pussies when it came to estimating what the other side was really capable of.

"Yes, Mr. President, but we need not let yesterday's patterns hold tomorrow hostage. Franks is a remnant of a more barbaric time." Stricken managed to keep a straight face as he said that, which was quite an achievement, since his own history was rather blood-soaked, but what didn't make it into the President's daily briefings wasn't his problem. "He's a relic that needs to be retired."

"He's so effective though."

Yeah, but he's in my way. But Stricken just smiled and nodded, glad that his eye and skin condition gave him an excuse for wearing his odd persimmon-colored sunglasses indoors, because he had no doubt that if the President saw the hate in his eyes, he'd probably scrap the whole thing and burn STFU down. "He's Frankenstein's monster, sir. He was built to be effective, but he's still a monster."

"Spare me, Alexander. Your entire operation is based on using rehabilitated monsters, and look how successful that's proven to be."

Idiot. You can't rehabilitate a monster. You can only coerce them into being temporarily useful, then send the docile off into obscurity and execute the uppity. "Thank you, Mr. President." He dipped his head politely at the ignorant attempt at a compliment. "So you realize that I understand monsters better than anyone, so believe me when I tell you that if any of my recruits continued to demonstrate such erratic, violent tendencies as Franks has, I would have them dismissed from my program." *Dismissed.* That was an amusing euphemism. More like fed into a wood chipper, Saddam Hussein-style. Now, there was leadership with panache.

"I don't know...We spend billions on security, and they're still telling me our single best operative against the supernatural is this old pile of body parts that kids dress up as for Halloween. Hell, there's cartoons and breakfast cereals based on him."

"I take it you've never met the real Franks in person?"

The President shook his head. "The Secret Service didn't think that was a good idea...This is just so...Well, I don't know. Myers keeps telling me how vital Franks is to our defense."

A real leader needed to be decisive. He needed to declare a clear objective and then do everything necessary to seize that objective. This president lacked those necessary traits, that spine, that strength of purpose. He was uncertain, and Stricken couldn't abide uncertainty in a commander. The President was shrewd enough when it came to normal politicking, but when the subject turned to supernatural threats, he was in way over his head. He'd once confided to Stricken that when he'd been briefed about the existence of the Old Ones, it had felt as if he was drowning in an angry sea. That had been music to Stricken's ears. He'd served in one capacity or another in six administrations now, and none of this man's predecessors had been nearly this easy to manipulate. When someone felt like they were drowning, anyone who could throw them a lifeline would be seen as a savior. Myers had been too honest in his assessments, and the truth was too frightening to a soft man like this. Stricken, on the other hand, was more than willing to *massage* the truth, to throw that comforting lifeline. Of course, the President saw it as a lifeline. Stricken considered it a leash.

"Myers is partially correct. We do need *something* with Franks' capabilities, but that doesn't change the fact that the MCB's best asset is aging and shows signs of serious mental deterioration. He's a ticking bomb and he will go off eventually. Whether you deal with Franks now or not, the fact remains that he will need to be replaced someday. Either he loses his mind and causes something that we can't cover up, or eventually something destroys him. That's why it's so vital that you approve my Nemesis Project right away."

"That again?" The President leaned back in his chair. "You really expect me to approve the creation of an army of Frankensteins?"

Frankenstein was the creator of the fictionalized monster, not the monster itself, you fucking illiterate, but Stricken just gave the President a patient smile. "Nemesis assets would only be partially based on what we've learned from studying Franks' physiology. This technology is far superior. Franks is the Wright brothers' plane and these would be Predator drones. Give them a mission, turn them loose, and no matter what happens there's no bad press for you and no grieving families on TV. Everyone wins. Let me try a prototype out. My operations are so secret no one will ever know if it doesn't work out."

"Try them out? According to this Franks contract there aren't supposed to be any. Ever."

"I misspoke. We'd have to *build* some first, and I'd need approvals for that, obviously. But if they work like they think I will, I promise you'll want to use them for everything else. A squad of these and Las Vegas never could have happened. Since these assets would be starting with a clean slate, they are programmable for complete loyalty. They simply can't go rogue."

"Unlike Franks," the President muttered.

This was too easy. "For what we can accomplish with them, Nemesis assets are a bargain. The only thing that kept the previous administration from implementing my plan was this thing." Stricken picked up the contract and gestured at it dismissively. "This is ancient history. This is tradition blocking progress. It's a contract, not a suicide pact."

The President didn't have to mull it over nearly as long that time. "I'll think about it and give you my decision later."

"Of course, sir." That was a little disappointing, as he was tired of waiting, but Stricken could tell the President would come around. He'd come around and order Franks terminated eventually, but Stricken had more important things to do than wait around for the inevitable. He would go with plan B, and once that was done, the President would look back on this conversation and kick himself for not heeding his Special Advisor sooner.

"No matter what I decide, Franks deserves our respect. If he's to be retired, I want this nice and clean, nobody gets hurt."

Like that was going to happen. "Whatever you decide, I'll take care of everything." *Like I always do.*

"Thank you, Alexander."

There were very few people who called him by his real name. He preferred his codename, *Stricken*, as it had gravitas. He'd been using that name since he'd started his career murdering KGB operatives in back alleys in Bucharest. "Good luck with your press conference, Mr. President."

"I've got the White House press corps eating out of my hand. I could tell them Las Vegas has been attacked by escaped circus monkeys and they'd run with it. That'll be all."

Stricken rose from the chair and adjusted his suit, trying not to look smug. This was a temporary hitch. The decision had been made a long time ago. Fate had just required Stricken to guide everything to its inevitable conclusion.

The President leaned back even further in his chair and put his feet up on the Resolute desk. It was a false show of confidence. Stricken knew it. The President might have known it too, but it didn't matter, whatever made it easier to think he was really the one calling the shots. "I'll have to think more about this Nemesis proposal of yours. Get me a proposal written up. What you're talking about would be incredibly controversial. If it were to get out, heads would roll."

Stricken made his living using monsters as black ops weapons against all enemies, foreign, domestic, and unearthly. If the President knew half of what had been accomplished since Special Task Force Unicorn had been restarted he'd lose his mind. Stricken was one of the greatest keepers of secrets and lies who had ever lived, while this administration of petulant children and useless Ivy League college lecturers leaked like a sieve. *Who the fuck are you to tell me how to do my job?* "Thank you, Mr. President. I'll see to it that my people use the utmost discretion."

He was escorted out of the White House. Stricken's name would never show up on any visitor's log. His job title was Special Advisor, but the most dogged of reporters would never be able to figure out what was special about him or who he advised. His Task Force didn't formally exist, his budget was nebulous, and most importantly he had almost zero oversight. By government standards, Stricken was a ghost, though he thought that was a stupid comparison, since he had real ghosts working for him.

He made a single, brief phone call on his ride to STFU's secret headquarters. "We're on."

Events were in motion. Franks would be dead soon enough.

CHAPTER 3

Every mortal being existed before. Long before this world came to be, there was a world of spirits. There's a barrier between these two worlds. When humans are born they forget all that came before. I was never born. I do not have this problem. But as long as my spirit dwells in this body I am forced to use a human brain. It is as reliable as a lump of electrically charged fat and protein can be, but flesh can't fully comprehend the world before. My memory of the before is imperfect.

There was a great council. The Creator presented us with The Plan. There was a disagreement over The Plan. This disagreement led to a war. One third of us broke our oath and rebelled against the Creator.

The fallen made war against the loyal. I was one of the most powerful, but my strength was not enough.

We lost.

The spirits that remained loyal would be born into the mortal world, progress, and eventually return. They were part of The Plan. The third of the host who rebelled were cast out, never to be born, never to have a mortal life or real bodies. Our leaders were cursed, and all who followed were condemned and cast out of the Creator's presence.

Now, Hell... That I remember well enough.

11 Days Ago
Washington, DC

Franks lay on the floor of his apartment, staring at the ceiling.

Since he worked with humans, he kept a human schedule. That meant activity during the day and sleep at night. It was a rather pointless schedule for a man who didn't really sleep. It was one reason that he preferred to be on an op, because during an op working around the clock wasn't seen as odd.

Today would be a talky day. He hated that sort of thing. He hated talking. He hated the squishy, pathetic, government-appointed flesh bag overseers wasting his time arguing about regulations and picking apart the definition of words. Franks hated Washington. Of every human city, and he'd been to most of them, it was the worst. He'd rather have been in the slums of Mexico City strangling chupacabras with his bare hands. This city had been named after a true warrior, and Franks knew General Washington would be enraged if he could see the quality of human that dwelled here now. The general would probably run a few of them through with his sword.

Basically, Franks really hated bureaucrats.

At exactly four Franks got off the floor. Since he could see in the dark he didn't bother turning on any lights. He had grown tired of being stared at in the MCB's gym, so Franks had rented a basement apartment specifically so he could have a comprehensive weight set and not have it fall through the floor. He worked out for exactly forty-five minutes. One of his arms had taken a hit from the dragon in Las Vegas, so he kept his bench press to a mere seven hundred pounds so as to not stress it until the Elixir had time to properly re-form that bone.

There was no ornamentation anywhere in Franks' apartment. The walls were still painted the same builder beige as when he'd moved in. There were no pictures, no mementos, and barely any furniture. Franks showered in his undecorated bathroom and then shoveled high protein food into his face in his undecorated kitchen. Pick any cabinet and the cans inside were in neat, orderly rows. Not a single can of peas mingled with the beans, because that would be unforgivable chaos.

Franks turned on the closet light as he got dressed. His night vision didn't allow for much color differentiation. Not that it mattered since his closet was divided between nearly identical black suits, white shirts, and tactical gear. He did have a lot of ties, but that was because a few of his human coworkers always felt compelled to include him on their gift-giving holidays, and ties were the only thing that made sense. Despite having dozens of ties, he always wore a cheap black clip on.

Last were the holsters and weapons. Franks wore an Artoonian dual shoulder holster rig with an MCB-issued Glock 20 on each side. For most people, shoulder holsters were slower to draw from, but Franks wasn't *most people*. They were harder to conceal, but Franks didn't really care if anybody saw he was armed anyway. He had a compact Glock 29 in a G-Code holster on his belt. He kept six spare magazines of silver 10mm, three on each side of his belt, and a folding Emerson knife in both his right- and his lefthand pockets. Franks was ambidextrous, so it didn't really matter which hand he killed you with.

Today he would be grilled, questioned, prodded, and annoyed, but sadly, he would not be allowed to kill anyone, and since MCB's security force whined about hand grenades inside headquarters, he left those in the closet.

At 5:29 the doorbell rang, but Franks had already heard footfalls on the metal stairs and identified them as one of his agents. Franks opened the door and Grant Jefferson held out a giant paper container of overpriced coffee. "I got you some—" Franks rudely snatched the coffee from Grant's hand. "Okay... It was hard to find the place. I didn't think you'd live in such a bad part of town."

The neighborhood was filled with criminals. Franks didn't care. Occasionally one of the gang members who hadn't heard about Franks' rep would start something, and it gave him an opportunity to hurt someone. The government frowned on him killing people without an excuse. "Rent's cheap."

"Imagine that." Grant glanced over at the graffiti on the walls of the stairwell. The agent didn't realize that the spray-painted gang signs were a coded message left by the local scum, warning the other scum to not mess with Franks' stuff, because when Franks got cranky it was bad for continued business, not to mention continued breathing. "You ready?"

That was a stupid question. Franks was always ready.

The headquarters of the Monster Control Bureau were in an unremarkable office building in Washington, DC. The exterior was a boring ten-story beige concrete and black glass rectangle. The landscaping was designed to thwart car bombers, was purposefully ugly and extra forgettable. They were close enough to the Capitol for business, but not so close that anyone would think they were important. No tourist would ever waste their time taking a picture of this particular building.

The underground parking garage had no names on the reserved spaces, but Agent Franks parked his giant SUV across the closest two spaces to the elevator.

"I think we're in Director Stark's space," Jefferson said as he looked out the passenger side window, "*and* the one for visiting VIPs."

Franks put the armored Suburban in reverse, backed up a bit, then pulled forward at an angle so he could also encroach into a third space, which was reserved for the handicapped. Franks killed the engine. *Better.*

"Uh...Okay then."

Jefferson wasn't a bad choice for the assignment. He was a talented agent and one of Myers' confidants, but he also had some weaknesses. He was cocky. Franks figured Jefferson had been overcompensating for some perceived shortcomings long before he'd been traumatized by vampires, and that experience hadn't exactly improved his outlook. He tried to hide it, but he had a chip on his shoulder. His fellows didn't completely trust Grant because he was by nature a political animal, the former acting director's golden boy, and he'd been MHI. But that time at MHI also meant he was passable in a fight. If anything interesting happened, Jefferson would probably suffice, or at least not die badly. Franks might not have been able to grasp all the nuances, but he had plenty of experience judging humans, and they seldom surprised him.

Franks got out and didn't wait to see if Jefferson was following him. Myers had them working in shifts so that he'd always have at least one handler nearby. Normally Franks would only have a single partner, usually an experienced agent of his choosing. His partner would handle all of the messy business that Franks wasn't suited for, like anything that required empathy. However, this was an abnormal situation, so Myers obviously felt he needed a support team. Jefferson, Archer, and Radabaugh were experienced combatants and were skilled at running interference. Strayhorn was an unknown, but Radabaugh was his training officer, so he would tag along when it was his turn. Franks didn't know why Myers had stuck him with a rookie, but he would either succeed or he would fail. If he was lucky failure would occur in the bureaucratic arena rather than in combat. Either way, the outcome wasn't Franks' problem.

Most of the federal agencies around the city had fancy lobbies with useless decorations and expensive statues, all paid for by tax money that could be better used for important things, like weapons or training. The MCB building's lobby was as plain and small as possible. It was because of the secret nature of their duty, but Franks appreciated it nonetheless. He wasn't one for *flash*. The security checkpoint was manned by a fat old man who looked like a typical rent-a-cop. His name tag identified him as Terry. There were a couple of video monitors and a clipboard to sign in. There was nothing special enough to get anyone who blundered inside curious about the nature of this particular office building.

"Welcome back, Agent Franks," Terry said. The guard was old now, but Franks remembered when Terry had been a young agent, crippled in the line of duty almost thirty years ago. He was one of the hundreds who had been hurt serving with Franks. "You're looking well, sir."

The pleasantry was useless, as Franks had gone through a dozen different faces since the two of them had first met, but ritual greetings made humans more comfortable. "You've gotten fat."

"Ouch." He patted his gut. "It isn't like nightshift desk jockeys have to do PT." Terry wasn't completely for show, as there was a SCAR battle rifle hidden under the security desk, but the real security was inside. They were being observed. A red light flashed on the desk. "You're clear to enter."

He and Jefferson went into one of the elevators. It looked like any other elevator, but dozens of hidden cameras were studying them in every spectrum, including ultraviolet and infrared. If a visitor was running a temperature, they'd know. If they were too cold, the chamber would be flooded with powdered silver right before it was filled with fire. Body scanners bombarded them with low levels of radiation to see through their skin. Franks didn't mind. If he got a tumor he'd just replace that part. The regular agents made it a habit not to leave and reenter headquarters more often than necessary. They ate lunch at their desks or in the cafeteria.

There was even a scale in the floor to make sure they were massing correctly. There were all sorts of interesting creatures that would have loved to sneak into MCB headquarters. A voice came out of nowhere. "You've put on a few pounds since your last visit, Agent Jefferson."

"You get stuck working a trade show in Vegas and see what happens." Jefferson stuck his head in a corner. "Grant Donald Jefferson. Agent five-two-two-niner-three." There was a chime of recognition.

Franks put his eye against another hidden scanner in the wall. The retinal scan matched the last eyeball on record. Keeping his various part swaps updated in the database was a pain. "Franks. One." The voiceprint matched and a green light activated on the back wall. The fake paneling slid aside, revealing a metal door. It took a minute for it to roll aside like a heavy steel gear.

"I was told all this security is relatively new, implemented right before I joined the Bureau." Jefferson was still trying to make awkward conversation. "I heard they had to extensively remodel the building after a cinder beast snuck in and burned a chunk of it down."

"Classified."

"I heard you were the one that killed it."

It had destroyed two whole floors of headquarters before Franks had caught up. It had given him third degree burns on much of his body and ruined one of his lungs before he'd twisted its flaming head clean off. However, the remodeling afterwards had given him the opportunity to secretly add a few things to the building to satisfy his paranoia. "Classified."

"Bet that was wild..." Jefferson took a drink of his coffee. Humans were so annoying, with their need to *communicate*. Luckily for him the secret door was open. On the other side four armed men were waiting to greet them.

"Good morning, Agent Franks, Agent Jefferson." The senior man seemed extremely nervous. "I've been asked to have you both disarm."

Franks raised an eyebrow.

The four guards took an unconscious step back. The first swallowed hard. "I'm really sorry, sir. Director Stark just implemented a new policy. No weapons in headquarters beyond the first level. Only the designated security team is allowed to carry weapons upstairs."

That was new. It was stupid and it totally missed the point of *defense in depth*, but Stark was an idiot. "Hmmm..."

"Sorry, sir. I'm really, really sorry, and this is nothing personal, and I hope you don't take this the wrong way and—"

"Locker?" A couple of the men quickly pointed, just glad that Franks was mad at Stark instead of them. He went over, opened one of the lockers and began shoving Glocks and magazines inside.

"I'm sorry, sir. Edged weapons and explosives too. The Director's memo was very specific. Nothing deadly."

"Should I cut my hands off?"

"That wasn't on the memo."

Franks glowered at him. The agent gave an involuntary shiver, but Franks went back and tossed the folding knives inside as well. This had to be related to his choking Stark unconscious in Vegas, like disarming Franks would make any difference if he really felt like murdering someone. Bullets just meant he didn't have to chase them down first. He slammed the door shut and took the key. Jefferson had brought fewer guns, so was already disarmed and waiting.

Now Franks was really in a foul mood.

The MCB memorial for those who had fallen in the line of duty took up a lot of space on the first floor. It was a marble fountain, and it was really the only thing vaguely ornamental in the whole building. The badge of every agent who had been killed in action since their founding was inset into the base of the fountain, and they were shiny under an inch of clear running water. There were a *lot* of badges.

As expected, their rookie was here, standing at the rail and staring into the water.

"What's up, Strayhorn?"

The rookie jumped. He hadn't heard Archer coming. "Just reading names. Do you guys need me for something?"

"Nope. I was coming back from a smoke break and realized that if I do any more reports right now my eyes are going to start to bleed." He stood next to Strayhorn and looked over the badges. Archer hadn't been in the Bureau for very long, but it was sobering how many of those shiny badges he'd known as living and breathing men and women. "I figured you'd be here."

"How come?"

"The first time a new guy comes to headquarters, they always gravitate right to this spot. Can't help themselves. They've seen the stats, read the histories in the academy, but they need to see the names to put it into perspective. I know I did."

"That's a lot of badges..." Strayhorn trailed off.

"Sure, it's dangerous, but we've been around since 1902." Archer didn't want to point out that he'd seen the statistical analysis, and their casualty rate was higher now than it had ever been. Things were really picking up out there, but there was no need to depress the new guy already. "Come on."

"Where are we going?"

"Somebody needs to give the rookie a tour, and your training officer is a trigger puller. He probably doesn't even know where half the cool stuff is." Archer walked back toward the elevator and the rookie followed. "What's the MCB's mission, and the First Reason for that mission?"

"Is this a test?"

"Humor me."

Strayhorn quoted from his training. "The MCB's primary mission is to keep the existence of monsters and the supernatural a secret. The First Reason is the more people who believe in the Old Ones, the more powerful they become."

"Correct. You might think it sounds a little crazy right now, or you might be having some doubts about our mission or our tactics, I know I was when I was in your shoes, but believe me, the first time you see a monster tree the size of this building rampaging across the countryside sucking all the light and happiness out of the world, you'll be all in favor of doing some crazy shit too. The Bureau has four main departments to achieve our goals..."

"Admin and Logistics, Media Control, Research and Development, and the Special Response Team."

"Good for you. I was still so freaked out that monsters were real that I missed half of the nuts and bolts stuff from the academy," Archer lied. He was a nuts and bolts kind of guy. Archer slid his keycard in the reader and pushed the button for the fourth floor. "You'll be assigned to one of those after this Franks duty."

"What department does Franks belong to?"

"None. The Bureau just lets Franks do his own thing. Were you Special Forces or anything like that?"

"Not even close."

"Then you probably won't go to the Strike Team. Yeah, that's not the official name, but we don't call them SRT. We had that name first, but then the FBI came along and stole it. They're our resident badasses who ride in black helicopters and go in guns blazing," he explained as the elevator rose.

"I heard they're pretty tough."

"Of course. You've been listening to Radabaugh. They've got some offices here, but mostly they stage out of military bases and train at Quantico. Myers is their boss now, and his number two is this crazy guy named Cueto. You don't want that assignment though."

"How come?"

"They're most of the badges in the fountain."

Archer returned to work, satisfied that he'd done his good deed for the day. The rookie seemed like a pretty sharp kid. R&D was always a crowd pleaser, with all of the dissected monsters and equipment prototypes laying around, then they'd gone through Media Control, where the MCB worked their magic discrediting and slandering witnesses, manipulating the news, and even producing their own easily debunked conspiracy theories. Strayhorn seemed a little put off by that department, though he'd tried to hide it, but that was a fairly normal reaction. Then Archer'd turned the rookie back over to his TO and gone back to his cubicle on the ninth floor.

He found that Grant was waiting there, grey-faced and anxious. It was unusual to see Grant disheveled, let alone looking like he was about to barf in the trash can. "Man, you don't look very good."

"That's because I just got off the phone with our boss."

"What did Myers say?"

"First off, situation in Vegas is looking better. They've mostly got it under control and our usual media shills are doing a great job. The phone videos that popped up from the witnesses are being mocked as Photoshop."

"Myers is like an artist."

"He's trying to come back as soon as possible. Second, he didn't say why, but we're not supposed to go anywhere near operational, especially with a rookie along, and Franks is supposed to stay put, no matter how excited he gets to kill something."

"That makes sense I suppose." Going on an op with Franks was a duty best left to the badass snake eaters on the Strike Team. Those guys were mostly former SEALs and SF, like Radabaugh. Archer knew he was pretty good at his job, but he couldn't help but feel a little dumpy next to those guys.

"No, you don't get it. A giant kaiju monster could be climbing up the Washington Monument and Myers still wants Franks to stay put. No monsters. Period. You know what that means?"

Archer had to think about it for a moment. Franks' inclination was always to walk up to the most dangerous monster in the room and punch it in the face. Only they'd just pissed off an organization that actively recruited monsters and used them for wet work. "Whoa." *Was Myers actually worried about an STFU setup?*

Neither one of them wanted to confirm it out loud here. Their office *probably* wasn't bugged. "Uh huh. Exactly. Nothing concrete, just Myers' gut instinct, but Franks stays here."

Where it's safe and nothing can get to him. If anything happened, he really didn't want to be the one to try to get Franks to stay at his desk.... But that couldn't be why Grant looked like he'd just gotten off a roller coaster. "And?"

Grant swallowed hard. "And finally, he ordered me to go throw my career away."

Archer sat down across from his partner. "Wait...What?"

He gave a resigned sigh. "I guess this is what I get for picking a side in a battle of bureaucrats. I'm reaping what I've sown. Damn it. See, Henry, this is what happens when you try to do the right thing. You get screwed every single time."

"I've got no idea what you're talking about."

"Myers thinks they're going to try to crucify Franks in today's Subcommittee meeting. We need to shift the blame to where it really belongs. Myers wants me to tell the truth about our friends in Vegas."

Bring up Unicorn? "Wow." No wonder Myers wanted Franks to stay at MCB headquarters. They were about to flip the lights on and watch the roaches scurry for cover, only these cockroaches specialized in assassinations. Exposing Special Task Force Unicorn would be like a declaration of war. The implications sank in. "Oh hell..." Archer suddenly didn't feel very good either.

✧　　✧　　✧

The day proved to be as miserable as Franks had expected, filled with paperwork, useless reports, and foolish questions from petty men. He'd been grilled by members of the Subcommittee on Unearthly Forces, various high ranking MCB officers, and was now currently facing his main accuser, Director Stark. So far this meeting had been particularly shrill, with lots of dramatic table pounding for emphasis.

"And then as I confronted Agent Franks about his illegal actions and theft he physically assaulted me!" *Table pound.* The two congressmen, their aides, and other government teat suckers and hangers-on nodded thoughtfully. The augmented guard force just stayed in their corners, nervous at this display that was way over their pay grade as their Director continued his rant. "Not only did he put my life in jeopardy, but he also endangered the MCB's response to the Las Vegas incident. I was in command and without my leadership—"

Franks snorted.

"Don't mock me, Franks!" Stark struck the table with both fists that time. "I'm sick of your crap. You should be in jail right now."

He'd always thought that Stark looked like a bulldog. Animals didn't like Franks and tended to shy away from him, but Franks had always found the bulldog a fascinating creature, all slobbery, and ugly, with ill-fitting skin and labored breathing, yet they were determined beasts. Their awkwardness made him like them as much as he was capable of liking anything. The bulldog was proof that the Creator found joy in the cumbersome.

Stark on the other hand was just an asshole.

"You weren't in charge," Franks stated.

Double table pound. "Yes, I was! I had the situation in hand until your reckless actions endangered our entire operation."

"You weren't in charge. Unicorn was."

The briefing room was packed with people, and they all began to mutter at that. Only a handful of them were probably cleared to know about the existence of STFU, but Franks didn't care.

Grant Jefferson cleared his throat and leaned forward to speak into his microphone. "I believe that Agent Franks is saying that although Director Stark was present at the quarantine, the de facto command of the operation was in the hands of a high-ranking covert official code-named Stricken. Former Acting Director Dwayne Myers has obtained evidence that this Stricken was in fact aware of the full capabilities of the Nachtmar, and kept those facts to himself, needlessly causing—"

"That'll be enough of that," one of the congressmen interjected. The other one just looked confused.

"*Needlessly* causing danger to MCB personnel, local responders, and civilians. Dwayne Myers is currently running the Las Vegas operation, but I'm sure he'll be happy to testify before the Subcommittee about how Mr. Stricken subverted our mission for his own ends—as soon as he returns from cleaning up Mr. Stricken's careless mess." Jefferson had a good stage presence. Franks recalled from his file that he'd been a lawyer once. He sure talked like one. "Agent Franks was placed in a difficult circumstance, when forced to choose between following procedure or containing a Level Five outbreak, he choose to abide by the spirit of the First Reason. If Franks had not acted decisively, then thousands of other civilians would have been exposed to the supernatural. The record needs to indicate that Franks wouldn't have faced this difficult choice, if Special Task Force Unicorn hadn't overstepped their bounds."

"What is Special Task Force Unicorn?" asked one of the confused officials.

"They are a covert action group that recruits monsters to serve as soldiers in exchange for PUFF exemptions," Jefferson answered immediately.

The conference room was suddenly very loud. Most of those cleared for this hearing were high-ranking MCB, and this was news to them.

"Whoa there, son," the first congressman said, glancing around the room nervously. "This isn't the time or place to get into that."

Franks scowled. *Because everybody knows there's no such thing as unicorns.*

Jefferson gave him a nervous glance. If Stricken had the majority of the Subcommittee cowed, then they were in worse shape than expected. He turned back to their questioners. "You can't expect Franks to defend himself if he's not allowed to explain *why* he did what he had to do."

"Who does this Unicorn thing answer to?" demanded one of the MCB section commanders.

"You would have to ask Mr. Stricken that, sir. But whoever it is, they need to hold Stricken accountable for his careless actions in Las Vegas."

The chairman ordered the room to be silent. Franks was glad to see that there was still some fire in some of the MCB's leadership. Stark was red in the face and sweating. He'd not expected his string-pullers to be so blatantly exposed.

Then a senior administrator addressed them. "Officially, there's no record of any other agency or entity involved with running the quarantine. Rest assured that we'll listen to what Special Agent Myers has to say when he returns tomorrow. In the meantime this is an internal MCB matter, so let the record show that Director Stark was in command the entire time."

Franks was not amused. "So the MCB is a sock puppet for Stricken's murder squad now?"

Though most of the room were still in the dark, there were a lot of uncomfortable glances shared around the Subcommittee's table. One of the congressmen hurried and grabbed his microphone. "Let's have Agent Franks write up a statement for us pertaining to any sensitive information, then we'll reconvene this hearing tomorrow." He banged his gavel.

"He went nuts and tried to kill me!" Director Stark shouted. *Double table pound.* They'd worked together before, so Franks knew Stark had always been a fake, hiding his cowardice behind a wall of bluster and bravado. When the shit got real, Stark could be counted on to fold, but right now they were in his element, where talking about actions meant more than the actions themselves. "What are you waiting for? I demand that Franks be locked up!"

Franks rested his big hands on the table. "Try it."

Stark shut his mouth.

"That will not be necessary," said one of the congressmen.

The MCB security force breathed a collective sigh of relief.

"They named you in the Subcommittee hearing, right in front of everybody. They talked about the Task Force and said that Myers had evidence, the works."

Stricken listened carefully as his source continued describing the testimony. It matched almost exactly what another source from the same secret meeting had supplied a few minutes earlier. It was nice to have multiple moles. It kept everyone honest.

"Thank you, Elwood. I'll remember the favor." Stricken hung up on the congressman, then tossed the iPhone to one of his subordinates, who immediately sealed it into a bag. There were protocols in place for anything that might prove useful for future blackmail purposes.

A different man handed him another phone. "It's Director Stark."

Now that was one particular puppet whose annoyance was quickly outweighing his continued usefulness. Stricken took the phone. "What, Doug?"

"I tried to give the order to have Franks arrested, but the committee—"

"I already know. While you were taking your sweet time somebody else informed me about how you sat there like a moron while Myers' golden boy spouted off about my secret organization. Way to go, champ."

The line went quiet for a long time. Stark knew he was in trouble. They both knew the only reason he'd gotten the directorship was because of Stricken's string-pulling. "I tried to call as soon as—"

"Make sure Franks stays put. Don't go near him. I'll be in touch." He ended the call, then handed the phone back. This one didn't get bagged. He had so much dirt on Stark that it didn't matter at this point. "Myers, you clever bastard. What are you up to?"

They were supposed to have ruled Franks a menace. The MCB should have detained him. The President's hands would be clean. Everyone would be happy. There were only a couple of facilities in the country that could hold something like Franks, and Stricken had already made arrangements at both of them for Franks to get obliterated trying to *escape*. But Myers was good . . . He'd moved first and spooked the Subcommittee members who were in Stricken's pocket. Word was that Myers was getting Las Vegas under control surprisingly fast, which meant he would rush back to the action to really try to screw Stricken over.

It had been a long time since he'd so enjoyed a game of chess like this.

They were a lot alike, and both of them knew how to play the system, but the difference between him and Myers was that Myers still had faith in the system actually working as designed, checks and balances and whatnot. He would expect Stricken to run for cover and start doing damage control. He'd expect meetings and heated arguments, maybe some internal investigations, that sort of thing.

Myers sure as hell wouldn't expect what would happen next.

Despite his opponent's considerable intellect and ability to spin lies with the best of them, Myers was at heart a decent, patriotic man. That made him vulnerable. Myers reserved his ruthlessness for paranormal enemies. Stricken didn't make such distinctions. *You're either with me or you're in my way.* Considering what he suspected was coming down the pike, for America—hell, the human race—to survive, then they'd need somebody with the guts to do what was necessary running the show. Stricken knew he was that man.

In any other time, Myers probably would have been sufficient. Now? He just wasn't up to the task. And Dwayne Myers had even been willing to nuke Alabama to stop the Old Ones. Stricken considered that a *nice start.*

"We're launching our contingency plan immediately." The STFU bunker was so big that the distance between his office and the control center was significant, so he used the time to give a series of rapid-fire orders to his subordinates that fell in behind him. "Foster, you're running this op. Call up Renfroe. Pull the spider out of the tank. I want it wired with explosives so it doesn't get any funny ideas about running off on the job."

"This is Franks we're talking about," said one of his men. And these were all men. His inner circle would never contain any supernatural members again. Adam Conover had taught him a valuable lesson about the trustworthiness of monsters. "Our most reliable team was lost. Want me to call up some extra muscle?"

"Not yet." It was too bad about his first string. Those monsters had shown real potential, but Kerkonen had been the only one to get out of the nightmare realm alive. "Red isn't right for this job. Sending her against foreign terrorists is one thing, but Americans? And MCB at that? She's got a soft spot for cops. PUFF exemption on the line or not, she'd balk and screw this up." Managing monsters and black ops teams was a real challenge; he had to sort them not just by capabilities, but by which ones had functioning moral compasses. "Send her to the Flierls' team. They're a bunch of goody-goodies too. We'll hold them in reserve in case this goes sideways."

"If the Flierls find out we're operating outside the law, they'll flip out . . . Hell, Renfroe won't like this assignment much either."

"His employment isn't exactly voluntary, now is it?"

The men laughed, because when Stricken made a joke, you'd damn well better believe they laughed like it was the funniest damned thing ever. Intimidating subordinates was a guilty pleasure of his. One of them held open the door to the command center for him.

The name was kind of a misnomer. When he'd first heard *command center* he'd pictured something like NASA mission control. This was more like an office overlooking the laboratory floor, populated by a handful of nerds armed with computers and some big screens on the walls. It wasn't impressive because of how it looked, but rather, what he could screw with from here. The nerds looked at him fearfully as he entered and then furtively went back to their work. They reminded him of a bunch of ground squirrels.

"I don't know who you intend to use for this mission then, sir, because we'll need time to get other assets together. You don't intend to send only our regular forces, do you?"

It had been Foster who had asked that question. It was a reasonable question, since the former CIA man had just been put in charge of a hit against the biggest badass in the federal government, but Stricken figured the hesitancy was because Foster was still a little squeamish from his encounter with Franks in Vegas. No STFU man wanted to go up against a monster without monsters of his own.

"Of course not, Foster. I'm a firm believer in letting our *subcontracted employees* do the bleeding on our behalf." He spotted exactly who he was hoping to find in the command center and walked directly toward her. "Hello, Dr. Bhaskara."

She turned and nodded politely to the albino. "Mr. Stricken."

Stricken liked the Project's head scientist. She was an attractive Indian woman in her mid forties, with a British accent that reminded him of Mary Poppins, but she was every bit as driven as he was, and as far as he could tell, she'd never been weighed down with any of those pesky medical ethics some of these brilliant science types seemed to get hung up on. "Any new developments with our babies?"

Dr. Bhaskara sniffed. She didn't like when he referred to the Project Nemesis prototypes as *babies*. "Of the thirteen we have decanted so far, the prototypes are still testing at peak efficiency. Their ability to learn is remarkable. There has yet to be a single testing failure, cognitive or physical, thus far."

"What're the new scores looking like?"

"Far better than expected. They are remarkable. Let me put it this way, Mr. Stricken. Take ten minutes to demonstrate the skills necessary and another ten minutes to explain the rules of the sport to them, and then they would easily win the Olympic gold medal for that event and their human opponents wouldn't even have a chance."

"I'm not rigging the Tour de France, Doctor, hilarious as that would be. I'm talking combat capabilities."

"Weapons familiarity training has been going well. Since we last spoke I have tested the first prototype against captured vampires of various strains and ages. A particularly nasty, well fed, fifty-year-old specimen only survived two and a half minutes of hand-to-hand combat."

"That's my boy."

"He is still by far the most capable of the prototypes, but I hope the others catch up." Dr. Bhaskara was justifiably proud. "I have no doubt that if we had a Master to test against, our prototypes would stand an excellent chance at winning."

That was probably pushing it. The doctor had read papers about Master vamps, but Stricken had dealt with them up close and personal. He wasn't placing any bets. But luckily Stricken had a baker's dozen of growth tanks that could pump out a new body every six months. And since this whole Project was stupidly illegal and he wasn't even supposed to be testing, he'd done all that in secret. Once Franks was removed from the equation and he got an official go-ahead, he'd build hundreds of tanks. Then he'd have the quality and quantity to take all comers.

"Are you confident in their ability to follow orders?" That was his greatest concern. He'd taken them out for a few little things, like bodyguarding him that time he'd confronted Earl Harbinger in Alaska, or popping some easy targets of opportunity, but the prototypes had never done anything too complex yet. What he had in mind would be challenging.

"Absolutely. All of our psychological testing has shown that they are completely incapable of disloyalty. They are programmed to obey no matter what."

Programming was appropriate. They were basically like robots made out of flesh. He'd seen some of the footage of those tests. Order a prototype to hold a position no matter what, and then you could inflict all manner of pain and suffering on it, but they'd rather die than budge. Electrocute them, set them on fire, it didn't matter. It had been harsh, but fascinating. "The outside world isn't quite as sterile as your lab."

"Should one go rogue, we can simply activate the preprogrammed kill switch." Conover's treachery had caused them to add that improvement. "Even as incredibly resilient as their systems are, the release of the neurotoxin would incapacitate them instantly, and before you ask, yes, the rapid necrotic dissolution will destroy the evidence. Even their blood decays too quickly to extract DNA evidence."

"It's hard to autopsy slurry. Good work, Doc. If you weren't a complete psycho, I'd marry you."

"Sadly, I am married to my work, Mr. Stricken."

"Okay, ladies and gentlemen, you heard the report card..." Stricken picked up a remote control from one of the desks. One wall screen began flashing through various interior shots, the growth vats, the glowing cylinders of alchemical slime, and then finally the testing center. "If we're going to use these things to save the world, I think it's time we conduct a more in-depth field test."

The camera was fixed on a man sitting cross-legged on the floor of a padded room, staring off into space. His bare torso was hooked to several different monitoring machines. Every muscle group stood out with perfect definition. It was like he'd been sculpted by an artist whose only instruction had been to demonstrate perfection.

"The first prototype..." Foster whistled. They'd all seen what these things were capable of, and the oldest was special even by Nemesis standards. "Poor Franks will never know what hit him."

The man appeared to be an ideal human specimen, but he was so much more. He was a blank slate on which could be inscribed the perfect soldier. Other than the nearly inhuman level of muscle tone, he appeared to be a white male in his twenties. They'd varied the genetic mix in each tank so that he could have assets available to blend into any culture. Stricken had to admit, he felt a little proud. He'd played god and gotten away with it. He had to wonder if Konrad Dippel had felt like this when he'd electrocuted a slab of meat and brought Franks to life.

The first prototype was staring directly into the camera.

✧   ✧   ✧

He could smell his visitor approaching.

The albino had the scent of dark magic on him. He'd been touched at some point in his life and it had left him twisted. There was a blight on his soul, but unlike most damaged humans, the one called Stricken had embraced the darkness and used it to make himself stronger instead. He had a lust for power that was rare amongst mortals. It would be wise not to underestimate the albino.

The door of his cell opened and Stricken entered, alone. He was not afraid. Stricken believed he was in control. They had surgically implanted a device inside his skull, and should he rise up against his creators, they would destroy this body.

That was unacceptable.

"Looking good there, my badass genetically engineered killing machine."

He remained seated as Stricken approached. If he moved too much it would pull the needles and sensors from his body and that would upset the doctors. Their poking and experiments were tiresome, but the indignities were a small price to pay to have a physical body. It was not right to treat a prince like this, but he would bide his time, and once ascended, he would remember every single insult inflicted on him by these humans and he would repay each one a thousandfold.

"I know you're not into small talk so I'll get right down to business. I've got a job for you to do and I need to decide if you're up to it. Are you ready?"

He nodded.

"You want to go outside?"

He nodded again.

"You mind killing some people for me?"

He shook his head in the negative.

"Of course you don't. Mr. Foster will brief you. This operation is under his command. You'll do exactly as he tells you. You will not fail and you will not allow yourself to be captured. Your primary target will be Agent Franks of the Monster Control Bureau."

Franks? It was a common enough human surname. "Will you tell me about this Franks?"

Stricken seemed a little surprised that he'd bothered to ask a question. "That's just what Franks named himself. He's a powerful flesh golem."

It was fate. *Yet, they still think he is a mere golem? That is all?* Franks had successfully hidden his true identity all this time. Such patience and restraint was remarkable, especially for one capable of such anger.

"Don't worry. Franks is old technology, nothing like you and your siblings. We've arranged it so that he should be unarmed, but just in case I'll be sending some help with you. Foster will give you a rundown on Franks' known capabilities. He'll also brief you on your secondary and tertiary targets and mission parameters. This one will require some finesse and then a whole lot of bloodshed. Are you ready?"

He nodded.

"I knew my first prototype wouldn't let me down." Stricken began walking away. He paused at the door. "You know what? That's stupid. We can't go live and still be calling you First Prototype all the time. We need to think up a name for you."

"You said the flesh golem Franks named himself. Am I allowed to give myself a name?"

"Getting a little uppity there, aren't you, buddy?" The albino frowned as he thought it over. "Well, it's not like my mom named me Stricken . . . You were designed to be capable of autonomous problem solving, so I don't see why not. Keep it simple though. Name tapes charge by the letter."

He waited several minutes after Stricken had left. The doctors would observe his every move. He wanted them to believe that he had to think this decision over, even though the decision had been made for him a very long time ago. The name was remembered from the before time, bestowed upon the leaders of the rebellion by the World Maker when they'd been cast down and exiled to Hell. He stared into the camera and made his pronouncement.

"I am Kurst."

CHAPTER 4

Humans call it Hell. That name will do. For a few rare mortals the barrier between worlds is thinner. They have caught glimpses that were beyond their understanding. These mortals spoke of lakes of fire and brimstone. That would have been much nicer than the reality.

Hell is everything terrible, and absolute nothing at the same time. Calling it cold is a lie. Cold would be something. There's no time, so you can't even call it eternity. Eternity would give you something to track. It is the lack of creation. It is Void.

Mortals don't have enough words to explain how shitty it is. We'd brought it on ourselves and we knew it. Eventually you create torment for yourself, because at least torment is something.

Most give up. Their spirits consume themselves, collapsing like a dying star, until they explode and scatter bits of their consciousness across the worlds. Mortals hear these as whispers, urging them to cause harm.

The strongest of the Fallen never give up. Their spirits remain intact. The Fallen have nothing better to do than plot how to make those that stayed loyal just as miserable as we were. It gives us focus. We'd do anything to escape. Our spirits were banned from ever being born into mortal bodies, yet the cunning ones were always trying to cheat their way into this world.

There are ways ...

10 Days Ago

Franks filled out the same stupid answer to the same stupid question for the hundredth time, looked up from his computer and out the window, thinking to himself that somewhere out there was a horrible monster in need of killing, and how unfortunate it was that he was stuck here instead. In the good old days they just let Franks do what he did best, but choke one director and suddenly everyone expected you to explain yourself.

He wanted to be in the field. The last update from Vegas said that MCB R&D had been able to track the portal and it might even be possible to launch a recon mission into the Nightmare Realm. Now that would be a proper mission worthy of Franks' talents. Instead he was doing this crap.

Preferring to be in the field, Franks didn't use his office much. It was as unadorned as his apartment. Most of the surfaces were dusty. There was a stack of commendations and plaques in one corner that he'd never bothered to hang up. All the paperwork and binders were perfectly ordered. The last time his office had gotten messy was when the cinder beast had destroyed this floor a few years before. He'd not appreciated the disturbance.

The ninth floor of the MCB building was quiet. The ops center and media monitoring stations were on the floors below them and would be fully staffed around the clock. Most of the field agents stationed in DC had either been dispatched to the Las Vegas cover-up, or they were backfilling the regional offices of those who had. The office staff had gone home for the night hours ago. It was 1:15. Agent Strayhorn had fallen asleep in one of the office chairs in front of his desk. Somewhere down the hall the cleaning crew turned on a vacuum cleaner and the rookie bolted awake. "Huh?" He glanced around quickly before remembering where he was. "Sorry. I was . . . I was just resting my eyes."

This was scut work, not a real mission, so he didn't care if his agents slept on the job. At least when they slept they weren't annoying him with constant nattering. This way they'd be well rested for when there was something important to do, like killing things. He had dismissed Jefferson and Archer, and would have sent them all home if Myers would have allowed it, but Myers felt he needed handlers until this was over, so that was all there was to it. Franks ignored the rookie and went back to his forms. Having spent time in Hell, he knew that government paperwork was the closest mankind had ever come to achieving true soul-crushing misery.

"Where's Radabaugh?"

"Coffee." Franks nodded toward the hall. There was a cafeteria downstairs.

"I wasn't asleep," the rookie said, even though he'd been snoring when Radabaugh left. If this had been real guard duty there would have been a reprimand. The TO hadn't cared because if doing paperwork was tedious, watching someone else do it was even worse.

Franks made a noncommittal sound and went back to typing his statement. He'd have Jefferson edit it in the morning, because he didn't think Myers would approve of answers like *because Director Stark is a pathetic maggot he's lucky that's all I did to him.*

He worked for a few more minutes before Strayhorn got up the nerve to talk to him again. "Do you mind if I ask you a question, Agent Franks?"

"Don't."

"Sorry." The rookie went back to counting the ceiling tiles. He began to tap absently on the arm of his chair. The sound was annoying. Franks glared. He stopped, probably uncomfortable that he was sharing the room with a monster. "Sorry."

He could have ordered the rookie to shut up, or go stand in the corner, or *something*, but his question was probably more interesting than the stupid reports. "Ask," he demanded.

"I've been briefed now on your history and what you are..."

He raised an eyebrow.

"No. I'm fine with it. It doesn't bother me. You're a legend for a reason. I don't just mean like legend in the Bureau, I mean like a literal legend, around the world. You're folklore. Hell, you're *literature.*"

Franks hated that particular book. It portrayed him as a whiner. He found it—there was a relatively new slang term that fit—emo. And Franks was certainly not *emo*. The rookie was looking him in the eye. That was impressive. Very few humans were able to do that when they had an inkling what he was. The rookie was tougher than expected, but that was the nature of an organization that only recruited people who had already established themselves as professionals. Franks thought of Strayhorn as *the rookie* only because that was what the other agents had called him. By Franks' standards, all of them were new and inexperienced. "What then?"

"I was just wondering why you still work for the MCB? You've done this so long. It's not like you're obligated to anymore. You're PUFF exempt. Why do you still do this job?"

That was complicated. First there was The Deal and then there was The Contract. He had an oath to uphold, an impossible promise to keep, a huge debt to pay, and the only way he could ever hope to accomplish those lofty goals was by doing the one thing he was good at. He'd been a warrior for eternity, and unlike the humans who'd fought in the war in heaven before they'd been born, he still remembered his purpose, and he was damned good at it. Hurting the things that preyed on humanity was the only thing keeping him out of Hell, but like all complex answers it was just easier to say, "Classified."

Strayhorn broke eye contact and looked out the window. "I understand." Humans had a hard time with long awkward silences. Franks didn't mind them, as he didn't really grasp the awkward part and he enjoyed the silence. Strayhorn, apparently, did not. "Something's been bothering me, about all of this, about the MCB, about our mission, about the First Reason..." The rookie turned back to him. "I thought you've been doing this so long you might have a good answer."

Myers had sent orders to not let anything bad happen to the rookie. So that probably precluded Franks' initial inclination to toss him out the window. Answering his stupid question would probably be easier than shutting him up, or would at least have less paperwork involved, so Franks nodded for him to continue.

"Part of my last job included witness protection. Now part of my new job is witness *intimidation*. Yes, I know we can't let people realize the Old Ones are real, because then that'll make the Old Ones stronger. I know their evil is supposed to be unimaginable, so it's for the witnesses' own good, but it's...just so damned hard to stomach. We threaten people to keep their mouths shut. I know the better we do our job, the more likely they'll stay quiet, and the less likely we'll need to do anything worse, but you're who they send when we need *worse*. I can't believe I'm saying this..."

The rookie talked a lot. The window-tossing option was starting to sound more appealing.

"Sorry, I'm rambling. I can't say this to my TO or the others because if they thought I was having doubts about the mission I'd get drummed out of the Bureau. I get why we do it, but we threaten innocent people and once in a while actually have to do something awful to keep them silent... You're the one they send when that's necessary. How do you do it?"

"Usually a suppressed pistol. Close range. Unless I'm ordered to make it look like an accident."

Strayhorn went grey. He took a deep breath, composed himself, and continued. "Not the actual act... I'd ask you how you sleep at night, but the briefing says you don't sleep at all. How do you reconcile doing something evil to fight evil?"

Curious. Franks was not used to one of his subordinates using such strong terms concerning his actions. Strayhorn was either remarkably brave or remarkably stupid. "Why do you need to know?"

"I just do."

Humans had to make everything so damned complicated. "Old Ones are worse."

"And keeping the Old Ones from being worshipped is worth killing innocent people?"

The Old Ones were outsiders. They weren't part of The Plan for this reality. Their intrusion into this world would change everything. Too many humans were soft, weak, easily swayed, and they'd worship anything that was sufficiently powerful, and the Old Ones were powerful beyond mortal comprehension. If they had enough worshippers, then the lines between worlds would blur, and our reality would fall under their jurisdiction. Humans didn't seem to realize just how good they had it, living under their current benevolent steward, with crazy ideas like free will and eternal progress. Humans thought small. They had a hard time realizing that the Old Ones took the long view. They were vindictive and spiteful masters. Let them take over and they'd own humanity from before they were born and for an eternity after they died. All mankind would witness Hell for themselves. So yes, he occasionally had to shorten an already short mortal life to keep that from happening. They were collateral damage. And when that was necessary, it was better for him to be the one to pull the trigger than some poor soft human who still possessed a soul that could be damaged by the act. Franks' immortal spirit was already an irreparable mass of scar tissue. He had no humanity to sacrifice. It was best if he was the one to drop the hammer.

So he shrugged.

"I don't know, Agent Franks. I don't think I could do that."

"Do your job right and you won't have to."

The Spider appeared to be an Asian female in her late teens. The humans in the van had unconsciously placed themselves as far away from the Tsuchigumo as possible within the tight confines of their vehicle. Kurst sat directly next to the creature. Its presence did not bother him. Its illusion magic would affect his eyes but was not nearly strong enough to cloud his mind.

The creature's mask was very convincing, with wide eyes and a bubbly schoolgirl demeanor. During his current existence the doctors had exposed him to many popular culture materials, so that he could better blend in with human societies, so he understood that the *Japanese schoolgirl* act was supposed to be attractive to some humans. The Spider put one delicate hand on Kurst's bicep. "Ooh, you such a strong big man."

Kurst had only had this flesh body for a short time, but he'd been watching the mortal world for centuries. Long ago his spirit had observed such perverted beasts take on the form of beautiful women to seduce unsuspecting men, before spinning them into a silken cocoon and sucking their life out. The Spider was wasting its time on him.

He put a small measure of his true power into his response and whispered in the old tongue. *"I am not food for you. I am your better."*

It hadn't expected to hear him speak in such a manner. The Spider recoiled in horror as it realized it had bothered something far more dangerous than itself. For just a split second the mask slipped, and Kurst was staring into dozens of black eyes and hairy mandibles, but then the illusion returned before any of the humans noticed. It scooted as far away from him on the seat as possible.

"Did someone say something?" Foster asked from the driver's seat. No one answered. "Damned bunch of freaks," he muttered under his breath.

In addition to Kurst, the passenger van carried four human overseers, two of Kurst's *siblings*, the Tsuchigumo, and a human under a Fey curse named Renfroe. Stricken's plan was cunning, and Kurst was impressed with how even if they failed to eliminate their primary target it would still be a victory. However, Kurst did not plan on failing.

He had waited a very long time to see Franks again.

Franks is mine. You may hurt him, but I'm the one that gets to send him back to Hell.

The other two Nemesis assets received the message and understood. Stricken and his scientists were unaware that their Nemesis creations could communicate freely with each other telepathically. It had amused him to discover that STFU was so oblivious to the horrors they had invited into their world. Each of the thirteen spirits who had claimed these powerful new bodies had been leaders among the Fallen, but Kurst had outranked them in the before time. They would do exactly what he ordered now.

The streets of the American capital city were empty this early in the morning. Steam rose from manhole covers. Kurst liked how the buildings here were gilded palaces. Pride was what had gotten his kind exiled, yet how quickly mortals forgot themselves and erected marble monuments to their own meager power. He hated humans so much.

"That's the MCB building. Get ready," Foster said.

"There are four cameras on us." Renfroe could sense such things. The tall, extremely skinny, bespectacled man was still a human being, but he had peculiar abilities that made him just odd enough to be on the ragged edge of being PUFF-applicable.

"Don't disrupt them until I tell you to," Foster ordered. He was listening to an earpiece connected to the command center. "Spider, the second that door slides open, I want you doing your thing, just like we talked about."

The Tsuchigumo giggled. "Yes, Mr. Foster." Her fake accent was cloying.

They were coming up on the back gate of the MCB's parking garage. It was deceptively heavy duty. "Do your thing, Renfroe." The gate immediately began sliding aside. The guard waved them through as his computer informed him their plumbing van was expected. "Nice."

"We're on the schedule. I told their system we're emergency maintenance and backdated a service request to forty minutes ago."

"You're the best IT guy ever."

The van went down a ramp into a concrete chamber. This area was safely separated from the main building in case of car bombs. A pair of uniformed guards came out of a door, one leading a dog, and another with a mirror on a long handle. Their human overseers in the vehicle all had firearms, but that was more for the Nemesis prototypes than the MCB. Other guards would be watching the vehicle, and an alarm this early would cause a lockdown. If they were spotted, Kurst knew he would have to kill everyone quickly, then flee, and Franks would remain out of his reach.

"You know what to do, Spider."

The human overseers shifted nervously. They were depending on the Tsuchigumo's desire for a PUFF exemption to keep the treacherous creature in line. A uniformed guard approached the driver's side window. Foster told him something about a plumbing issue, but it was drowned out by a sudden buzzing in Kurst's ears. The interior of the van seemed to quiver. The side door slid open and the guard with the dog looked inside, eyes glazing over as he scanned them. It was as if they weren't there at all. The guard didn't even notice that his dog seemed extremely frightened, whimpering and tugging on its leash. He closed the door.

The guard smacked his hand against the side of the van, signaling Foster that they were good to proceed. The strange noise and shifting visual cues tapered off. *Impressive.* Kurst studied the Japanese creature. He could see where such tricks could be useful in his future plans. He would need to enslave a few of these things.

The plumbing van went down the ramp and then they were beneath MCB headquarters. It was empty except for a handful of black vehicles with tinted windows and government plates, so Foster was able to park near the main doors. A few of the humans pulled out tablet computers. "Renfroe, start messing with their security systems," Foster ordered. "The rest of you know what to do."

Kurst put in a radio earpiece, opened the door, and stepped into the chilly garage. The Spider and the other two Nemesis soldiers followed. They had not taken mortal names yet, so the female was still known as Prototype Nine and the male was Prototype Four. They were all dressed in the basic business attire appropriate for MCB employees. Kurst had worn the same type of dark suit that he'd been told Franks preferred. That would make the Spider's assignment easier.

They entered the lobby. A fat human was sitting at the guard station, tapping at his keyboard and scowling at his monitor. "Plumbing problems?" He looked up and saw Kurst approaching. Only Kurst could see the light bending around his form and hear the strange frequency of the Tsuchigumo's magic in his ears. The illusion must have been perfect. "Agent Franks? I didn't expect you—"

Kurst reached over, grabbed the back of the guard's head, and flattened his skull against the heavy desk. The body rolled out of the chair and lay on the ground, one foot twitching wildly.

"What the hell?" Renfroe demanded over the radio. "You told me they were going to sneak in. Nobody was supposed to get killed!"

"Change of plans. Get uppity about it and whatever weirdass electrical ghost thing you've got goes on the PUFF list tomorrow," Foster snapped back. "Now make sure you tweak the time stamp on that murder so it coincides with their exit."

The others were already waiting at the correct elevator. Kurst joined them. The door closed behind them. The Spider pointed at the hidden panel. Kurst went to it and spoke. "Franks. One."

"Forcing voice pattern recognition." A glowing ball of light appeared in the elevator car with them. The will-o'-the-wisp bounced about wildly as Renfroe's voice come from inside of it. "Adjusting scanners. Changing weights. Damn. The Spider is ugly as hell on the X-ray...What is she? Okay, okay, never mind. That's gone. And now it's just Franks in here. All records match. Changing the logs so he's going rather than coming... Okay. You're good. Camera on the other side is live."

"I give them good show," the Spider said. Then she covered her mouth with both hands and blushed, as if she was jealous of all the attention.

The blast door rolled open. Two tired MCB guards were on the other side. To their eyes and to the camera above them it was the hulking form of Agent Franks that entered the security room.

"Evening, er, morning, Agent Franks. I hadn't been told you'd left the building."

Kurst ignored them, walked to the lockers, and picked out the number Stricken had supplied him with. He balled up one fist and slammed it through the sheet metal. Kurst yanked the door off the hinges, then reached back inside and pulled out a Glock 20. The guards were surprised, briefly, then he shot them dead with a single well-placed round each.

"And cut," Foster said. "Beautiful. That's the opening scene of our masterpiece. I call it *Franks goes on a rampage.*"

The metal detector buzzed as Kurst went through it. He'd sensed more heartbeats on the other side of a partition. There were two more guards there and he intercepted them as they came out. They had their sidearms drawn, but their human reactions were far too slow to keep up with his movements. He shot the one who was further away in the throat, then took hold of the closer of the two and hurled him into the nearest concrete wall hard enough to break half the bones in his body. Kurst took a moment to take the guard's spare magazines of MCB-issued silver 10mm, while Four and Nine entered and took the other two pistols and all the magazines from the locker. Ballistic testing would show that the bullets pulled from the victims' bodies came from Franks' issue weapons.

You know what to do.

The four of them went to the real elevator. "Cameras show your primary target is in his office," Foster told them over the radio. Kurst pushed the button for the ninth floor. "Secondary target stopped at the cafeteria on the third floor." Kurst pushed that button as well. "Spider, can you disguise multiple assets at the same time across that much distance?"

"Yes, Mr. Foster. I do my best for you!"

"Okay, Renfroe, you've got some editing to do. Make it seamless."

The three Nemesis prototypes waited patiently while the Tsuchigumo hid in the back. Two of them were wearing heavy backpacks. One pack had already been left at the security checkpoint. They rode in silence. Kurst did not need to give the order. At the third floor, Nine stepped out and walked away silently. She would take care of their secondary target. They continued upward.

The door slid open. The ninth floor was a maze of cubicles and offices. This was the administrative center of the Monster Control Bureau. There were a handful of people there, a few MCB employees, and some janitors vacuuming and dumping trash baskets. Franks would be on the far side of the space.

Kurst lifted the stolen 10mm and shot a janitor in the spine.

✧ ✧ ✧

Gunshot.

Franks unconsciously reached for a pistol, only to find his holsters empty. *Fucking Stark.*

"We're under attack." Franks stood up and went to the doorway, listening carefully and picking apart the patterns. *Handguns. Two shooters. Screaming.* It sounded like standard MCB 10mm, and he'd been around a *lot* of those over the last decade, but what were his people shooting at? Had another monster got through? "Call it in."

Strayhorn was also futilely reaching for a sidearm that wasn't there as he went to Franks' desk. He grabbed the phone and dialed the MCB's internal operator. "We've got shots fired on the ninth floor."

Franks took a quick glance around the edge of the door. "Hmmm..." He did not surprise easily but then again, it isn't often that you saw a mirror image of yourself executing the janitorial staff. The man who looked exactly like him spotted Franks and raised his pistol. Franks stepped back as the frosted glass shattered and a bullet zipped through his office to slam into a stack of binders. Franks scowled. *Curious.*

Holes appeared in the walls around them. Another bullet smashed the desk phone and Strayhorn took cover. The rookie struck him as relatively calm. "What do we do? We've all been disarmed."

And that was totally unacceptable. Franks would not have lasted one century, let alone three, if he hadn't been consistently prepared. Walking to the far wall, he ran his hand down the Sheetrock, looking for the right spot. More bullets flew through the office. Their attacker was trying to pin them down, which meant someone else was probably maneuvering up on them. Strayhorn rolled behind the desk when the lamp on top of it shattered. The rookie was looking for something to use as a weapon when he saw Franks poking at the wall. "What're you doing?"

They had remodeled this floor after the cinder beast had burned it. Franks had seen the construction as an opportunity...Stupid policies came and went as the MCB changed stupid managers, but paranoia was forever. *There.* He found the right spot and then slammed his hand through the Sheetrock.

Franks tugged the old Colt Commando out of the wall. It was covered in dust and spider webs, but he'd thoroughly oiled the weapon before stashing it. He pulled back the charging handle and it felt as slick as when he'd hidden it there years before during the building's remodel. He let the bolt fly forward to chamber a round. There were at least two shooters. The sounds told him they were taking turns firing on his office while the other reloaded. A bullet punched through the wall and tore an inch of skin from his bicep. Franks frowned as his blood sluggishly rolled through the gash. This was his newest suit.

He turned back. The MCB night shift's skeleton crew were either running or taking cover between the thin walls of the cubicles. Papers and debris were flying everywhere. The attackers were firing blind. Franks could do that too. He watched the bullet holes appear through the carpeted walls, calculated the angle, shouldered the Colt, flipped the selector to full and ripped a horizontal burst through the cubicles in response. The stubby barrel of the Colt was extremely loud in the enclosed space and the muzzle flash was enormous.

The shooting from that direction stopped.

"Stay down." Franks went to the doorway, looking for the first shooter. The double had to be a doppelganger or something of that nature, but those things died easily enough when you started pumping them full of bullets. But there was no sign of his duplicate. There were bodies on the floor, some injured, some dead. There was too much movement. People were running for the stairs. The shooter had to be here some—

A shape crashed through the cubicles. A section of wall was being pushed directly toward him. Franks moved the muzzle of the Colt over and opened fire, but it was coming at him so fast he was only able to put half a dozen rounds through it before the wall hit him. He braced for impact.

Franks was not used to being bowled over.

The Colt went spinning across the carpet as he was flung back into his office. Up in an instant, Franks turned to meet the threat. The partition was tossed aside, revealing what appeared to be a normal man. Early twenties, Hispanic, six foot one, one eighty, dressed in a black suit, but from the way he was ignoring several grisly rifle wounds to the chest, probably not a human. Franks launched himself forward, swinging for the man's head.

The attack was intercepted by a raised forearm. Bones collided, and Franks came away with one arm stinging.

That was unusual.

Without any hesitation, Franks attacked with everything he had. It was a blur of fists, elbows, and knees. The man slid back across the carpet, taking the pounding, but protecting his head and torso. Then he countered, hands flashing back and forth with incredible speed. Franks barely managed to swat them aside. Dozens of blows were exchanged in a matter of seconds. A ridged hand that made the air whistle ripped a red line across Franks' forehead.

Another. Franks pulled back, trying to save his eyes, but his back hit the wall. Fingers cut through his cheek. Not claws. Fingers. Franks swung, but the man ducked, and Franks hit nothing but air. His opponent came right back up and hooked a fist into Franks' abdomen. The blow lifted him off the ground. Hands landed on his shoulders and Franks was jerked forward, spun around, and tossed hard into a nearby desk.

The man was coming after him.

His opponent stepped onto the fallen cube wall, so Franks kicked it out from under him. They both came up at the same time, but Franks had a head start and that was all it took. He slammed one fist into the man's face, and then Franks was hitting him with blows that would break cinder blocks. And he knew that for a fact because he practiced on cinder blocks. His opponent made the smallest mistake, dropping one hand a bit too late, and Franks drove a quick jab into his mouth. A human jaw would have exploded. He turned a bit, and Franks snap-kicked him in the stomach. The shot would have staggered a vampire.

The man took a single step back and blinked.

"Hmmm..." Franks didn't like that one bit. He could feel the man's body heat, so he wasn't a vampire, and he certainly didn't fight with the disorganized savagery expected of a lycanthrope, but since he'd heard Strayhorn picking up the Colt Commando, this mystery could wait until the autopsy. Franks stepped to the side. "Shoot."

Strayhorn opened up. The Colt was still on full auto. The thirty-round magazine was only half full but he put almost all of those into his target's upper chest before the last few climbed up and to the right to shatter the far windows. The attacker stumbled back as his torso erupted into bloody chunks, but he still wouldn't fall over. Instead he crashed against a desk and used that to steady himself. Even with around a dozen gaping wounds, he snarled defiantly at Franks.

"There's more mags in the wall," Franks said as he started toward the creature that had dared to trash his office. Apparently whatever it was did require blood pressure to continue operating, because the attack was slower this time, and Franks leaned back as a fist zipped past his chin. Franks slammed a massive hook into the side of the man's skull. The impact reverberated across the room, but he still didn't go down. Franks went to work on him, fists hammering like pistons, each impact hard enough to rupture organs. Blood flew from the bullet holes each time Franks hit him.

The man closed, trying to stop the pummeling. He tried to lock up on Franks' arms, and for several seconds they went back and forth, blocking and twisting, trying for a hold or enough leverage to break a limb. There were massive exit wounds in the man's back. Blood was everywhere, which was making it difficult to get a good grip. The level of dedication was impressive, but when he clutched the man's ear and ripped it *off* the side of his head, that finally broke his concentration. Franks knew from personal experience having an ear pulled off really messed with your balance, so he capitalized on the momentary weakness.

Franks took hold of the man's head and slammed it into the top of a desk. Wood splintered. Franks jerked his head up and slammed it down again and again and again. Blood and teeth flew, but the skull didn't come apart like it should have. It had to be artificially hardened. The desk broke in half, but Franks still had a bloody handful of hair, so he pulled back hard, exposing the man's neck, and then slugged him right in the throat hard enough to smash his trachea flat.

That finally dropped him.

Franks stood there, breathing heavily. He wasn't used to having to work that hard to win a fight.

There was another gunshot, only it hadn't been aimed at him, but rather the nearest security camera. Sparks fell from the hole in the plastic shell. He turned to see the first gunman, his double, approaching down the center of the cubicle aisle. Franks picked up a nearby swivel chair and hurled it at him, but the double quickly dodged to the side. Strayhorn was coming out of Franks' office, aiming the Colt, but their assailant fired first. Strayhorn gasped when the bullet slammed into him. He fell back into his office and disappeared.

So much for keeping the rookie out of trouble.

The false Franks reached up to the side of his head and removed a radio earpiece. "Now it's just us."

There was no way he could cover the distance without getting shot, but Franks charged. He'd gladly absorb a few rounds for the chance to beat this imposter to death.

Surprisingly, the double tossed the Glock aside and met Franks with open hands and a smile. The smile seemed very alien on Franks' face.

Picking up as much speed as possible, Franks lowered his shoulder and crashed into the fake, driving them both back, through one cube wall and then another, before crashing through the glass of the conference room, through the air, and finally hard against the floor. They were ugly face to matching ugly face, so Franks head-butted him in the nose. Normally that would have worked, but he might as well have slammed his forehead into a brick for all the good it did. Franks levered himself up, trying to pin the man's arms beneath his knees so he could pound his face into hamburger with his fists.

Only one arm slipped through, an open palm landed on Franks' chest, and *shoved*. Franks found himself airborne, until his brief flight terminated with an awkward landing on top of the conference table. The table legs broke from his impact and the whole thing collapsed beneath him.

The double was already back on his feet. Illusion magic shimmered around him, but then it broke, revealing a Caucasian male, with close-cropped blond hair, approximately early twenties, six foot four, and appearing to be an extremely fit two hundred and fifty pounds. After picking him up and throwing him through some walls Franks estimated his actual weight was much higher. Franks had never seen this person before.

"It's good to see that mortal existence hasn't made you soft, brother. You always were formidable."

Even if the voice was new, the tone was not. "Kurst..."

The demon prince gave him a nod. "I've finally found a way back... No thanks to you."

He had been hoping that the imp he'd questioned in California had been lying to mess with him. That was sort of their thing.

"You betrayed us, Franks."

"We betrayed God." Franks rolled off the table.

"Yet here you are, being the good little slave. The mighty have fallen again. Did he hear your weeping in desolation and offer you pity? Foolish, brother. Do you really think they'll let you back in after what you've done?"

Franks picked up one of the broken table legs. The solid chunk of wood would make a decent club. Kurst had found himself a physical body, so now it was time to see just how durable that body was. "Enjoy life. It'll be over soon."

Monster Control Bureau Director Doug Stark had been called into headquarters for an emergency meeting, but it could wait until after he'd gotten something to wake himself up. Normally he'd go straight to his big office on the top floor and dispatch his secretary, but the problem with clandestine, middle-of-the-night emergency meetings was that there was no secretarial staff on hand to fetch his latte. The MCB building was busy 24/7, but most of that activity was in Media Control or SRT, and Admin worked civilized person hours. He could have sent one of his two bodyguards, but then he'd only have had one left actually guarding his body. So it was easier to just stop at the cafeteria on the way.

Details were sparse so far, but there was supposed to be a conference call with the President and the joint chiefs in twenty minutes. Of course, those people all got to gather in the White House situation room, but since his bureau was the bastard red-headed stepchild of the federal government, Stark was supposed to offer his advice from MCB headquarters. The Washington SAC and some other senior men were on their way in. Apparently something else had happened in Vegas, though nobody around him was competent enough to tell him what he'd been dragged out of bed for.

The cafeteria was quiet this time of night. There were only a handful of MCB staff sitting around plastic tables and their conversations awkwardly died off when they saw Stark and his bodyguards enter. He got several polite nods of greeting, but that was it. Stark knew he wasn't a popular choice for director, but he was the boss, damn it. What did a man have to do to get a little respect around here?

Myers had gotten respect from the rank and file. It just wasn't fair. The official record had proclaimed Stark as the hero of Copper Lake, his getting the nod for directorship was a no-brainer. Stark was a rock star. Yet, if Myers had come into the cafeteria in the middle of the night, then he would have been welcomed with smiles and handshakes. So how come they had loved Myers, but didn't like him? It was a mystery. The cappuccino machine was off, which was just another annoyance on a long list of annoyances. "Damn it, Bill. Get me a Dr Pepper," he snapped at one of his bodyguards.

Bill did as he was told. The other one stayed at Starks' side. Maybe that was part of the problem . . . Myers had never had a security detail, but he'd only been *acting* director. Stark was important, so he rated guards, a driver, functionaries, and perks. That's just how it was when you reached the pinnacle.

No, he knew that the real problem was that Myers was sabotaging him. Very few people in the MCB were cleared to know about STFU, but enough people knew that something shadier than normal was afoot, and they suspected that their new director was working with the mysterious Task Force. Some would even go so far as to call him a *puppet*. It had to be Myers with his crazy conspiracy theories about Stricken and his bunch taking over the MCB . . . Myers was poisoning the well, saying that the only reason Stark had gotten the job was because Stricken had greased the skids. Hell, just today one of Myers' people had screwed up Franks' hearing just to embarrass him.

The night shift didn't rate real food, so Stark picked a bagel out of the plastic bin and a packet of cream cheese, which was when he spied Agent Radabaugh trying to slip from the room unnoticed. Radabaugh was one of Myers' loyalists. It was too bad, since he had a reputation for being a solid man in the field. He'd love nothing more than to fire every agent who liked Myers better than him, but it was almost impossible to fire government employees, so Stark played it cool. "Hey, Greg. Hold on for a second."

Radabaugh paused. "Good evening, Director Stark." He had a coffee cup in each hand.

"Is one of those for Franks?"

"Yes, sir." The agent appeared to be very uncomfortable.

"I should order you to spit in it." Stark walked over to him. "Ha. I'm only kidding. So, babysitting Franks? I had to do that assignment once. It was like following a tornado around and having to clean up trailer parks. I bet you're having a terrible time."

"I don't mind." Radabaugh looked like he wanted nothing more than to escape. The other people in the room were doing their best to appear disinterested in the conversation. "Somebody needs to do it."

"Of course. It's all about duty." Once he had the Bureau locked down tight and this Las Vegas thing was taken care of and Franks was gone, every man that had been loyal to Myers was getting their ass transferred to North Dakota, but until then Stark intended to be the friendliest director ever. "I've got to wonder, is Franks...upset? Is he worried? Nervous about tomorrow's hearing maybe?"

"Not that I can tell." Radabaugh answered in the most noncommittal way possible. "He's very private like that."

Oh well. He'd been hoping to hear otherwise. "Franks sure is a hard one to read, isn't he?" Stark chuckled. "That's hardly unusual. I do hope he enjoys his forced retirement. The Bureau will be better off without him." Radabaugh didn't even try to argue. That was probably smart. Stark noticed that his bodyguard was looking at the entrance. Stark turned and saw that Franks had come to the cafeteria. "Well, speak of the devil..."

Franks looked odd. Stark couldn't put his finger on what was wrong. They'd served together, and Stark had looked at that ugly mug daily for nearly a year. Sure, it had been a different face sewn on back then, but no matter what flesh he was wearing, Franks was always the same sullen, morose bastard. Right now was different though. It was because Franks seemed... *happy.* Franks reached inside his suit as he walked toward them.

"Stop right there." The bodyguard stepped in front of Stark.

Franks' pistol came out in a flash and he fired a controlled pair into the bodyguard's chest followed an instant later by a third round to the head, just in case he'd been wearing a vest. Stark yelped as blood hit him in the face. Surprised, Stark slipped and fell as Franks did the same thing to the other bodyguard standing by the soda machine.

In less than two seconds Franks had just Mozambiqued both his bodyguards. It didn't take too long to process that, because Stark had one hell of an instinct for self-preservation, with flight usually beating fight. He rolled over and crawled for cover.

Radabaugh dove behind a table as Franks shot at him and the surprised MCB staff sitting there. Most of them died clueless.

"Return fire!" Stark shouted as he scrambled behind a counter, not realizing that he'd just signed a memo banning guns from the facility. Luckily, that rule didn't apply to the guy who'd given it, so Stark reached for the Glock 29 on his hip.

But Franks had followed him. He walked around the counter and casually shot Stark in the right hand.

Stark screamed.

Franks pointed his pistol at Stark's face.

Terrified, Stark lifted his trembling hands. "Franks, please..." The gun shifted down. There was a flash and a roar of thunder. It was like a lightning bolt through his gut. Heat began to radiate through his body and out onto the floor. Stark watched incredulously as blood came pouring out the hole in his abdomen. "What the fuck, man?" he demanded, and then it really started to hurt.

The slide was locked back on Franks' pistol. He looked at it quizzically, as if surprised that he'd run out already. As Franks reached for a spare, he noticed Radabaugh was running toward the dead bodyguard's gun. Franks went after him.

Stark moaned. He couldn't believe how painful this was. Franks had just gut-shot him! *That asshole!* He pushed his left hand onto the wound and tried to stop the bleeding. He knew that he needed to put direct pressure on the wound, but that just made it hurt even worse. His right hand had a hole through it, but he tried to fumble his pistol out anyway, while shouting, "Help! Help!" but his employees in the cafeteria were either dead, suffering from gunshot wounds of their own, or running.

Radabaugh reached the bodyguard's piece, but Franks was on him before he could lift it. Franks stomped on his hand. He had to hand it to the agent; rather than cry about it, Radabaugh wrapped his arm around Franks' knees, and drove his shoulder against his legs, trying to lever him off-balance. It was a classic takedown move. Radabaugh should have known that would have been impossible against Franks' mass planted on those tree-trunk legs.

But then Franks toppled, and Radabaugh was trying to wrestle him. It had to have been the shock and the sudden loss in blood pressure, but for a second there, it looked like Radabaugh was fighting a woman who had to be half Franks' size, but he blinked and it was just Franks again.

Stark gave up on his throbbing right hand. His fingers were hanging like dead fish. He reached across his body with his left and got the Glock free. It hurt so bad he could barely think. MCB rounds were compressed powdered silver, and they fragmented like a bitch in soft tissue. He was probably going to die and it was going to hurt, and it was Franks' fault.

Two other agents besides Radabaugh had dog-piled on top of Franks, and all three of them were striking him and trying to hold him down. But Franks just got up anyway, dragging the hapless men with him. Stark raised his pistol in his off hand, but he was shaking so badly, he didn't have a shot with all of his men hanging off Franks' body.

One agent crashed through a table, hit so hard and fast that Stark couldn't even tell what had happened. Franks saw Stark aiming at him, and the cunning bastard grabbed hold of the other agent, picked him up, lifted him effortlessly overhead, and *threw* him at Stark. The man screamed as he sailed across the room. Stark barely had time to raise his hands to protect himself from the impact.

He must have blacked out for a moment. His head had bounced off the floor pretty hard. He couldn't move. The MCB agent was lying on top of him, not breathing. Stark didn't know where his gun was.

Radabaugh was still trying to fight Franks hand to hand. He was the MCB's reigning martial arts champion. He was a Strike Team commando and one of the toughest men in the Bureau. Radabaugh could tangle with damn near any mortal human being in the world and have a fighting chance of coming out ahead.

He only lived for another twenty seconds.

There was something wrong with Stark's eyes. Franks seemed too small, and also a whole lot faster than he used to be. Radabaugh threw a series of punches, but Franks brushed them aside effortlessly. One hand flew out, grabbed Radabaugh by the throat. The agent thrashed and turned red in the face, trying a wristlock to break the hold, but to no avail. Franks twisted and with a sickening crack snapped his neck.

Stark tried to push the dead man's weight off of his chest, but he was too weak.

Franks dropped Radabaugh's limp form, walked to the body-guard's pistol and picked it up. He began methodically putting bullets into each of the wounded.

Last of all, he aimed the gun at Stark's face.

"No. Please!" He squeezed his eyes shut tight. "I don't want to die! Not like this! Please!"

Several seconds passed. There was no boom. No tunnel of light, or whatever was supposed to happen. As far as he knew, he was still alive. Stark opened his eyes. The cafeteria was filled with dead bodies and Franks was gone.

CHAPTER 5

Disembodied spirits escape the Void however they can. Sometimes there are cracks where another world collided with our prison. There are other things out there, alien gods willing to cut deals. We would trade our services for freedom. Then the Fallen come to the mortal world and make trouble. When you make a hole, spirits will escape through it until it is plugged.

When any of us show up in this world, they called us demons or fallen angels. Those names will do. Without bodies we can't accomplish much. Even the strongest amongst us couldn't do much except harass mortals who couldn't even remember us. They are always there, whispering, encouraging evil.

I was never one for whispering.

I hated the Fallen who could not admit that they had been wrong. Most disembodied are weak and easy to banish back to Hell. Some are more persistent. They desire to be real more than anything. The jealous will do anything to possess a body of their own.

There's always some dumb mortal who'll listen to the whispers and open the door to let them in. But human bodies were never intended to hold the Fallen. They must compete against a mortal spirit that was tethered there first. Unless their soul is completely rotten, mortals will begin to fight back eventually, so demons are relatively easy to banish back to the dark.

What demons really want is a body of their own. If you leave a perfectly good body around empty then something will come and live in it.

There are lots of bodies that will do to live in. Several of the creatures that humans consider monsters are really the Fallen inhabiting some physical form. The greater the spirit, the better the body must be to contain it. Pathetic little imps will live in pigs if given the chance. A warrior or a prince of the Fallen requires a worthy vessel, golems, oni, even some forms of undead will do. Yet even after I'd found a breach in the wall of Hell that led me to the mortal world, there was nothing here capable of holding me.

I could not really understand humans, so I observed them. I also watched my kind. I grew to hate them both even more. I hated the Loyal for throwing away their precious gifts. I hated the Fallen for our stupid pride. I was furious at the Creator because He had been right all along, and I had been stupid, but He would no longer hear my words. So I wandered the Earth, angry.

Then one day I found something.

Kurst was rather enjoying himself.

"Did you really think it would be that easy, Franks?" he asked as he ducked under a swing that whistled through the air where his face had been. "You know the quality of body that I require. You should, since you stole my first one and ruined my second."

Franks had always been taciturn, even in the before time, so it wasn't surprising that he was too focused on killing Kurst to have a conversation about their shared past. He just kept whipping the table leg about in his typical, unimaginative fashion. Kurst effortlessly raised one hand and caught the descending weapon. It hit his palm with a resounding smack, glorious pain descended down his arm, but then his fingers locked around the improvised club like a vise.

Franks scowled as he struggled to wrench the table leg free. He hadn't expected that.

The Nemesis body had been thoroughly tested. It was based on Dippel's original design, but it was better in every way. Franks might have had a few hundred years of freedom in his stolen mass of corpse chunks, but in the end it was Kurst who had received the superior form. "The humans made a few improvements since last time." Kurst yanked the club from Franks' hands and swatted him across the room with it.

Franks crashed into the far wall. Kurst was on him before he could get up. He smashed Franks over the back, splintering wood and bone. The leg broke in half on the second hit. Kurst dropped it to the floor with a clatter, took hold of Franks' suit coat, hoisted him off the ground, and flung him into another wall. Franks bounced off and landed facedown in a pile of broken glass.

"Our exile has ended. I will reclaim our birthright." Kurst followed, his shoes crunching through the glass. "What was not given will be taken." He grasped a handful of Franks' collar and dragged him up. "You should have stayed with us." There was a bloom of fire in his abdomen. Franks jerked his hand away, leaving behind a large shard of glass jammed deep into Kurst's stomach. Blood spilled out around the red glass. Franks punched the shard of glass, shattering it into a hundred razor pieces inside Kurst's guts. He could feel the heat of every separate wound channel. Franks struck that spot again, spreading the slicing bits even deeper.

Kurst roared and hurled Franks. The unexpected agony increased his strength to surprising levels, and Franks was launched from the conference room and sent crashing through the cubicles. He lifted his blood-soaked shirt, found one tiny end of glass, pinched it, and dragged it out. It was only a small piece. The rest was trapped inside of him. He didn't mind the pain; in fact, after millennia of nothing, he savored the exquisite sensation, but his body's rapid healing mechanisms couldn't work around all those sharp pieces sliding and slicing about. It was insulting. He snarled and started after Franks.

There was a different kind of pain deep inside his head, and that made Kurst stop. He recognized that sensation from his conditioning training. It was from the control device the scientists had implanted inside his skull. He'd been out of radio contact for nearly a minute. Foster had probably grown nervous that he'd gone rogue.

Kurst put the earpiece back in and turned on his radio. "I'm here."

"About damned time, First!"

That is not my name! But it was not time to put the pathetic human in his place yet. "I lost contact. Still engaging the primary target."

"The alarm's been sounded. Get out," Foster ordered.

"I repeat, the primary target has not been eliminated."

"MCB security thinks Franks has gone on a massacre. We've got men going in with the responders. They'll handle it from here. Leave your bomb, grab Four and the Spider and go."

Franks had crawled around a corner. Kurst didn't like it, but if he hesitated, then Foster would release the neurotoxin implanted in his brain and ruin everything. It wasn't right for mere humans to destroy Franks...But it was doubtful any human would be able to kill Franks. The two of them would surely meet again. Kurst stepped through the broken wall of the conference room and began walking toward the elevator. They'd already tossed their backpacks into places they wouldn't be noticed.

Franks stepped over his dying coworkers. The ones who hadn't passed out from blood loss recoiled from his presence. Others saw him coming and hid under their desks. They thought he'd been the one to attack them.

It had been a clever ploy. It really made him angry.

Kurst hadn't followed him into the cube farm. Instead he was retreating toward the elevator. The elder demon was getting away. That was un-fucking-acceptable.

He passed the spot where he'd dropped the other attacker. There was blood and some teeth, but he was gone. *Resilient.*

Franks had taken some damage, and he wasn't even sure yet what was broken, but it was obvious that destroying Kurst's new body with his bare hands was unlikely. There was a water fountain mounted on the wall near the bathrooms. It was one of his remodeling landmarks. Franks kicked it. The sheet metal bent and a pipe broke, spraying water on the carpet. Franks kicked it again, ripping the fountain completely off the wall. He reached into the hole, found the shotgun he had planted and yanked it out in a cloud of drywall dust. He pumped a round of buckshot into the chamber of the Ithaca 37 and ran toward the elevator.

Someone shouted "Freeze!" as he entered the main hall. He turned to see that some of the building's security team were coming out of the stairwell. One of the guards had spotted him and was pointing a G36 carbine his way. "Drop the gun!"

There was no time to explain. Kurst was getting away. Franks ducked through the next doorway. The agent fired and high-velocity holes puckered through the walls around him. Of course, they'd been told that it was Franks who had been shooting everyone. If he resisted, they'd put him down without hesitation.

"Active shooter on the ninth floor," one of the men shouted into his radio. "Engaging."

"What's going on?" asked another guard.

"Franks lost it and shot Director Stark!"

That was bad....

He'd probably trained these men, so he didn't particularly feel like killing them. There were several metal filing cabinets in this room. Franks dropped the shotgun, and wrapped his arms around the nearest one. It was full of paper and weighed a ton. He grunted, hoisted it up, and carried it into the hall. The agents immediately opened fire, and Franks could feel the 5.56 bullets hitting the cabinet, but MCB-issued silver bullets fragmented quickly. They weren't designed for penetration, and that was a lot of paper. Franks swung the cabinet and hurled it down the hallway as hard as possible. The agents yelped as it went crashing through their ranks. Drawers tore open and paperwork flew everywhere.

Franks scooped up the shotgun and ran down the hallway. He turned and went after Kurst before the guards could sort themselves out.

The elevator door was closing. Franks caught a glimpse of Kurst and a few others standing inside. The shotgun only had a pistol grip stock, so it wasn't good for aiming, especially on the run, but Franks lifted it and opened fire. An oval of buckshot holes appeared in the elevator doors. Someone inside gasped. He reached it the instant before the door closed and jammed the muzzle into the crack. He fired again, splattering somebody all over the interior, but it wasn't Kurst. Franks pumped the shotgun and then used the barrel to pry the doors further apart. He fired again and heard the wet slap that buckshot made with the close range obliteration of meat. Something inside the elevator let out an inhuman wail.

Franks pumped the shotgun again but before he could fire, something struck him hard in the back. He lurched forward and crashed into the doors. *I've been shot.* Franks pushed himself back up, but it was too late. Kurst had shoved the shotgun's muzzle back and the doors were fully closed. The elevator was starting down.

His first instinct was to pry the doors open, then jump down the shaft after them, but there were agents firing on him, and MCB tended to be good shots. "Cease fire," he ordered. Franks dropped the Ithaca on the floor and raised his hands over his head in a surrender position. He turned around. "We've been infiltrated."

Three members of the security team were closing on him, carbines shouldered. Franks recognized all of them. Their fingers were on the triggers and their sights were on his center of mass. "Get on your knees!" one of them shouted.

"They were using magic to impersonate me. They're in this elevator. Call it in and seal the building." He was glad to see that at least one of them had sense enough to repeat that into his radio.

"On your knees. Hands on your head!"

Though it pissed him off, Franks complied. Going after them himself would be more satisfying, but the sensible thing to do was to sic the might of the MCB on Kurst. "There's an elder demon in that elevator. Use extreme caution." Franks slowly placed his hands on top of his head. It made the bullet hole in his back stretch and burn.

Four more men appeared, also dressed in MCB armor, but these he didn't recognize. The one in the lead aimed a suppressed MP7 at Franks' head. Time seemed to slow as Franks realized he was taking the slack out of the trigger.

This wasn't an arrest. It was an assassination.

Franks jerked his head to the side as the suppressed subgun fired. The tiny, high-velocity bullet cut a chunk from his ear.

So much for the sensible thing to do.

Before anyone else could react, Franks kicked the Ithaca that was lying on the carpet. The shotgun went flipping through the air to strike the shooter, who stumbled back, firing more rounds into the ceiling tiles. For the briefest instant, the lead agent's eyes had followed the movement of the shotgun, and that was all it took for Franks to reach out, swat the G36 from his hands, grab him by the armor, and spin him around to use as a shield. Franks pulled the Glock 20 from the agent's holster as he dragged him backwards.

Humans could never get used to just how *fast* Franks could be when he felt like it.

The assassin was bringing the MP7 back down as Franks lined up the front sight. He fired, placing a 10mm round through the man's eye socket and spreading a cloud of brains across the others. The bits always reminded him of wet dough.

He pulled his hostage back around the corner. The real MCB held their fire, but the strangers let it rip. Franks yanked the helpless agent aside and sent him spinning into a potted plant and out of the line of fire. No need to get one of his innocent men shot. Franks stuck the Glock around the corner and cranked off two rounds, forcing them to duck down. Then he turned and sprinted down the hall.

More responders were coming up the stairwells. After that last exchange there would be no attempt to take him alive. They would shoot him the instant they laid eyes on him. He could only hope that his message had gotten through and the agents at the first floor checkpoint would kill Kurst. Then they could sort this out. Until then, however, Franks needed to keep from getting shot to pieces.

The elevators were blocked. The stairs would be covered. It was about a one-hundred-thirty-foot drop to the ground, which was suicide even for him.

It was a good thing that he was so paranoid.

Franks had to make his way back toward his office, and fast. Armed responders were coming from everywhere. One of the fakes took a shot at him, and it was a normal sympathetic reaction for several of his agents to do so as well. He reached the broken drinking fountain, splashing through the newly formed puddle, and then turned toward the bathrooms.

There was a full-length window at the end of this hall. He'd picked this spot during the remodel because it was the closest big window to his office. The walls here were made of black tile, so it would be a little more time consuming to punch or kick through. So Franks picked up a nearby tree and smashed the tile with the pot, then he chucked the whole thing through the glass. The tree tumbled into the night, and he didn't even hear it hit the ground nine floors below.

Franks lifted the Glock and fired three rounds, sending them purposefully high. It was to slow his pursuers down and make them think. Incoming gunfire had a way of making you revert to your training. They'd think he was pinned, so they'd leapfrog forward, taking their time. Franks holstered the Glock, glad that their issued handguns were all the same model. There was no way the pistol would stay put if he just shoved it into his waist band, considering what he was about to do.

The nylon climbing rope had been piled in the wall, already tied off to a support beam. He took up the rope bundle and tossed it out the broken window. He'd left a pair of leather gloves there as well, simply because you never knew when you'd be able to get new hands, and nothing was more annoying than friction burning your palms off. Franks tugged on the gloves, took up the rope, and left the office the fast way.

All three of them had been hit by Franks' shotgun. Kurst had a few pieces of buckshot lodged in his torso. Four had lost an eye. The Spider had gotten the worst of it though. The illusion had slipped completely, and Tsuchigumo was sagging against the wall in its natural form, twitching and spasming, as occasional gushes of green slime pumped out on the elevator's floor. Its hairy claws clutched at the massive hole in its body as its mandibles clicked rapidly.

They were nearing the lobby. "Disguise us now or not," Kurst told the monster. "Either way, I will live. We can fight our way out and leave you to perish, or you can stick to the plan and perhaps Stricken's doctors can save you. The choice is yours. Make it now."

The Spider chittered at him, but then the air seemed to shimmer and the noise filled his ears. The hideous insect visage was replaced with the young Japanese girl. The green slime turned to red blood, but she was still injured. Four appeared to be a different MCB agent, though he was still missing an eye. He put his hand to it, as if the injury was actually debilitating. Kurst knew that he would look like an actual employee, of whom Stricken had provided the Spider a photograph. Kurst picked up the Spider and cradled it in his arms, like he was carrying a wounded human. The illusion was so complete it even *felt* like a tiny human.

The doors opened.

The security checkpoint was a confused mass of excited bodies. MCB security was trying to coordinate with officers from other agencies, but there was an understandable hesitancy to involve those who weren't cleared as to the MCB's secret mission.

"She's been shot," Kurst shouted. "I need an ambulance."

"This way." One of Foster's men, dressed in MCB body armor, took hold of Four and acted as if he was guiding the wounded man. "Hurry."

The humans were looking for Franks. Any messages indicating possible assailants other than Franks would have been electronically blocked by Renfroe.

They were rushed into the parking garage. A few ambulances had already arrived. Of course, one had been prepared by Special Task Force Unicorn. Nine met them on the way. She sent him a telepathic vision of her wounding Director Stark and killing a dozen others. Foster, now dressed as a paramedic, was already in the driver's seat. Renfroe was at the back door, but he would not come near the Spider as Kurst shoved the creature inside. Their human accomplice looked ill at the sight of the many other wounded being tended here. Kurst got in and Foster had the ambulance rolling before the rear doors were even closed.

"They've got Franks pinned down," Foster told them as he turned on the siren. "The second my guys are out, I'll blow the charges and make a mess of the place. It'll be over soon."

He resisted the urge to smile. *You do not understand what you are dealing with. You do not understand Franks.* Kurst knew this was only just beginning.

The ground rushed up to meet him, but Franks had so much grip strength that merely squeezing harder threw the brakes on his descent. He immediately slowed down, and then let go and dropped the last ten feet to land in a crouch.

There were enough trees around him that it was relatively dark here. There were red and blue lights flashing on the street. The metro police would be setting up a perimeter in conjunction with the MCB. There wasn't much time before they had it locked tight.

His suit was torn and bloody. He would stick out. There were more security cameras in this city than anywhere else in the country. He needed a vehicle. However, it was one in the morning and the police would be blocking the streets. It made his decision easy.

Franks pulled out his cell phone. As soon as the response team had their shit together they would track it. He speed-dialed Dwayne Myers, and then picked the stealthiest path through the landscaping to the street. He set out in a fast walk, sticking to the shadows, while it rang. Franks could imagine "Take Me Out to the Ballgame" playing on the other side. Myers had been using the same ringtone for years. Franks liked that Myers was so consistent.

He also didn't sleep much. "Franks?"

"Listen carefully. I've been framed. Someone disguised as me attacked headquarters. At least twenty casualties. No idea how many dead. They shot Stark too." Franks rattled off what he knew. Myers was smart enough not to interrupt him. "There were at least two attackers. They weren't human. Super speed, strength, and regeneration." Franks quickly rattled off physical descriptions of Kurst and the other one.

"Were they—"

"Nemesis. Possibly, but much better than the last batch if so." Franks couldn't tell Myers about the spirit that was inhabiting the body he'd fought, because to explain Kurst was to explain himself, and there were things that even Myers didn't need to know. "There were human assassins among the responders. I killed one."

"STFU?"

"Unknown . . . I'm on the run." Franks walked through the bushes. He was getting close to the nearest police car. The officer had gotten out and was looking up at the broken window.

"Franks, wait!" Myers sounded unusually desperate. He was normally cool, even in the worst situations, though this situation probably qualified as desperate. "Is Strayhorn okay?"

Why did Myers particularly care about the rookie? "He was shot. Status unknown."

There was a sudden bright flash, followed an instant later by a roar of sound and the rumble of a shockwave. Franks glanced up to see a fireball rolling out the side of the ninth floor. Sparkles of glass filled the air and fell like rain. Then another explosion ripped through the night, and then another. Those two were close enough that the hot wind ripped the leaves off the bushes around him.

"Explosions. Ninth, third, and first floors," Franks reported as he kept moving. The blasts weren't that big, maybe ten pounds of C4 each. Enough to make a real mess of the scene, but not enough to destroy the building. "They're covering their trail."

He couldn't hear Myers' response because he had a carjacking to attend to. The cop was staring at the destruction. Franks walked out of the bushes and kicked the cop in the stomach. He bent over, automatically retching, so Franks took him by the coat sleeve and slammed him into the side panel hard enough to dent it. The police officer had a triple-retention duty holster to prevent felons from snatching his gun, but Franks knew how to operate the mechanism, so he took the man's gun, a Glock 9mm, and tossed it on the passenger seat. Then he rolled the groaning cop over and removed his spare magazines from their pouches. He tore his radio off and tossed it into the bushes. Franks got into the cop car, slammed the door, and drove away.

"I'm going after them," Franks said into the cell phone.

"Don't, Franks. If Stricken has taken his cold war hot, you need to lay low. Give me a chance to work this out."

He could have been more concerned about getting himself to safety, but Franks was first and foremost a predator, and running *from* danger was not nearly as strong an instinct as running *after* it. Kurst had to exfiltrate somehow. Franks didn't know what kind of illusion magic they'd been using, but it had been extremely powerful. There had to be limits to it though. He'd injured them, so at minimum their clothing would be bloody and they'd be leaving a blood trail. If they look like the wounded...

"I'll be in touch," Franks rolled down the window and tossed his phone out.

Franks turned right and kept going around the block. The police band was full of chatter about the incident, but as he suspected the locals were setting up a perimeter. Sadly, somebody must have seen him steal the car, because that came over the radio next, along with the patrol car's number and a general physical description that must have just been provided by the MCB. Cop cars normally had tracking devices, so they'd be on him in seconds. There was an ambulance ahead. Franks went after it.

The old Crown Vic had a decent engine and he quickly overtook the ambulance. He pulled alongside first, but didn't recognize the driver. He hoped to sense some tingling of magic, or perhaps the demon prince's presence, but there was nothing. Franks pulled in front of the ambulance and hit the brakes. The driver barely had time to stop before hitting the police car's bumper. Franks was out and walking, stolen 9mm leveled on the driver. The paramedic saw him coming and raised his hands.

Franks smashed in the driver's side window and stuck the Glock in the paramedic's face. "Whoa, man! I—" but Franks grabbed him by the throat and choked off the response. He stuck his head inside to see in the back, but it was just another startled paramedic and two badly injured MCB employees. Franks let go of him. The paramedic rubbed his throat. "What the hell?"

His wild goose chase had probably put those MCB employees in greater danger, but two lives were nothing compared to what would happen if Kurst reached his goals. "Get them out of here." He got back in the police car. There were lights in his rearview mirrors. Then he heard the sirens. They had vectored in on him already. Franks gunned it.

There were two cars behind him. Franks had worked in Washington since they'd first drained the marsh, so he knew his way around the city rather well. He also had faster reaction times than a Formula 1 driver, so normally he could probably lose the cops long enough to pick up another ride, but finding Kurst was far more important than his own survival. Franks squealed the tires around a hard corner, down a block, then cut through a park, taking out a bench and a few bushes in the process. That bought him a few seconds out of their visual range. He shut off the headlights and reversed through a narrow alley as the cops' cars went by, sirens blaring. Franks came out the other side, then went back toward MCB headquarters.

If they weren't expecting pursuit, then they would want to take one of the fastest routes out. That presented a few options. However, if they were smart, they would want to initially leave in a direction that would make sense to any observers. Which meant they'd be heading toward a hospital. Franks picked the most logical route to the closest hospital and drove as fast as he could. Stealth really wasn't an option at a hundred miles an hour on surface streets, so he turned on the lights and siren. Franks dodged cars, veering in and out of oncoming traffic as the opportunity presented itself. Only the lack of traffic kept him from killing anyone, though he did hit a bum's shopping cart. The impact sent the cart flying into hundreds of pieces. He was lucky. Franks considered running over the homeless acceptable collateral damage.

There was an ambulance far ahead of him. Franks killed the lights and siren.

He picked up the radio microphone. "This is Special Agent Franks of the Department of Homeland Security..." Which was the ID that he used the most often when forced to work with other agencies. "Convey the following to my agency. I have commandeered a police car and am in pursuit of the real shooter. Bravo seven seven delta green." That authentication code would be enough to get this incident flagged at the highest levels. Then, even though it wouldn't make a difference, he had to add "Stay out of my way."

Closing quickly on the ambulance, Franks kept cars between them. His vehicle was shorter so hopefully they wouldn't spot him and make a run for it. It was possible this was just another regular ambulance, but it was worth a shot. Franks nearly rear-ended a town car, then slingshotted past it to come up alongside the driver's side of the speeding ambulance.

The flashing lights provided enough ambient illumination that Franks' improved vision could easily make out the driver's features. The face was familiar. He recognized the STFU man. *Foster...*

So this was a Task Force operation. This setup had Stricken's stink all over it. Franks lifted the police officer's Glock. To be fair, when they'd spoken in northern Nevada, Franks had warned Foster that the next STFU employee to annoy him would end up in a body bag. Shooting accurately from one moving vehicle to another was difficult in any case, but it was more difficult when you were also driving, but Franks aimed out the passenger side window and opened fire anyway.

Glass shattered. Blood splattered against the inside of the ambulance's windshield. Franks kept on pulling the trigger as Foster jerked back and forth against his seat belt. Whoever was in the passenger seat grabbed hold of the wheel and they veered off to the side.

Applying the brakes, Franks turned hard and kept after them. The ambulance was ahead of him now. The Glock's slide was locked back empty, so Franks dropped the mag and steered with his left hand while he put the pistol down and rummaged about on the seat until he found one of the stolen spare mags. He smacked it in, dropped the slide, brought the pistol up, put the sights into the vague middle of the ambulance and started shooting. The safety glass in front of him puckered into a crystalized mess. He could barely see. Both vehicles were weaving, so Franks made up for accuracy with volume, and he dumped the entire magazine within a few seconds.

It was difficult to see exactly what happened next, but as he was trying to reload again, a delivery truck came out of nowhere. Franks spun the wheel and stomped on the brakes, so he managed to not directly T-bone the truck, but couldn't avoid all of it. The truck's back bumper tore through his driver's side and ripped the door off. The impact was jarring. Glass and debris struck him as the police car went spinning away on screaming tires.

Franks snarled as he brought it out of the slide. Tire smoke floated in the cabin. Something had cut him on the forehead and he was bleeding into one eye, but he could see that the ambulance wasn't that far away. Its brake lights came on. They were stopping. Franks mashed the accelerator to the floor, intending to ram them. Kurst's new body was tough, but it probably wouldn't survive being turned into a red pavement smear. The ambulance doors opened. They were bailing out. Franks calmly reached over and put his seat belt on. He got it up to nearly fifty before the impact.

Only it wasn't the ambulance.

His first clue that something was wrong was when the air quivered and the ambulance disappeared. *It was an illusion.* Franks stomped on the brakes, but the second clue came half a second later when the front end of the stolen police car smashed into a brick wall.

"It's Foster."

Stricken had been eagerly awaiting this call. The secure bands were all talking about a massacre at MCB headquarters and most of them were implicating Franks as the perp. There was so much to do. So many plans hinged on Franks being eliminated. This was like Christmas morning. He took the phone from his subordinate and hit the answer button. "Yes, Mr. Foster?"

"Foster's dead, man! There are cops everywhere!"

"Renfroe?" It was one of his people but he was no operative. Renfroe was a glorified sys-admin who'd been marked by Fey and been lucky enough to end up with useful abilities rather than the normal Fey-related outcome of *dead.* It was always a roll of the dice what you'd end up with when you pissed off a witch queen. "What happened?"

"Franks shot him in the face. He gut-shot the Spider and she's squirting green stuff everywhere. I guess he killed some of your other guys inside, maybe, I don't know. And he messed up two of your weirdos. I didn't sign up for this. They were killing innocent people!"

"Calm down, Mr. Renfroe..." People with functioning moral compasses were such crybabies, but his ability to communicate directly with electronics was invaluable. "This is very important. Did you alter the security footage in the manner I directed?"

"Sure. That was a piece of cake. With the Spider's magic, I didn't even have to tweak too much around your killer weirdos. I moved some events in the timeline and—"

"Wonderful. Are my weirdos—as you so eloquently call them—still alive?"

"I don't see how, but yeah..." Renfroe was starting to hyperventilate. "I'm looking at one missing half his face and the other one is picking big chunks of broken glass out of his stomach right now."

"Then please give the phone to the large white one."

There was the sound of shaking and rustling from the other end of the line. "Yes?" the First Prototype answered.

"Status?"

He was emotionless in his report. "Our handlers are dead. We are wounded. The primary target's status is unknown. He was in a car wreck. Local authorities were converging on him when we lost sight."

Even busted up, it was doubtful that some regular DC cops would be able to take down Franks unless he went willingly, and if Franks went quietly that meant he had plans of his own. "Fuck!" Stricken kicked a wastepaper basket across the room. Everyone in the command center glanced his way in fear. That was an unusual display of emotion from their leader. Stricken took a deep breath and counted to ten. He could hear sirens as background noise on Kurst's side. "Are you in danger of being spotted?"

"Negative. We are secure."

He had a pickup team in place. "Don't move. I'm sending a unit."

"Requesting permission to pursue the primary, I am still ninety percent combat effective."

Of course he was. The Nemesis assets were designed to be hard as nails. "Denied. Hold for extraction." Stricken handed the phone back. That subordinate took their location while Stricken walked over to the nearest monitor. He'd hoped to have Franks nice and dead, not on the run.

However, this was still manageable. There were pros and cons to every outcome. This temporary disappointment was hardly insurmountable. Stricken folded his arms and thought it over while reading the intercepts scrolling across the screen. It made his people uncomfortable when he'd just stand there and watch over their shoulders, but he wasn't exactly the type of leader who employees invited to their summer barbeques and he was in no danger of ever being gifted a Boss of the Year coffee mug. Stricken considered himself more *results oriented.*

"Anything?"

"Metro police found the car but no sign of Franks," said the man Stricken was looming over. "They've set up a perimeter and have called in a chopper and a dog team to search for him."

"MCB?"

"They're calling the shots with the locals. The Washington SAC just got woken up. They've got the NSA monitoring all comms in the area in case he tries to contact anyone," answered a different office minion. "Franks placed one call to Dwayne Myers during his escape. No transcript of that one yet."

It would probably be pushing his luck to have Myers picked up as an accessory, though it was sorely tempting. "The minute you get that transcript I want to see it. MCB will be shell-shocked, but the explosives were all left in nonvital areas." He wanted Franks gone, he didn't want to permanently damage his other assets in the war against the supernatural, just wake them up. "They'll get their shit together in short order."

"FBI and DHS are on their way in," reported the first one. "That's a lot of outsiders on the case."

He could tell that his inner circle was scared. They were volunteers. Everyone here knew the real score. They understood that even dirty wars were worth winning. All of them were in deep. If they got caught, every last one of them was looking at prison time. If Franks flipped this and somehow exposed STFU's actions, Stricken wouldn't hang alone.

Fear was an excellent motivator.

One of his men approached cautiously. "Orders, sir?"

"First off, the Task Force will offer our assistance to our sister agency in their time of need. We'll coordinate as we normally would with the MCB. This is just another case involving a monster. Second, we debrief our team and figure out if we've left any loose threads that need cutting. Anything that doesn't lead straight to Franks, we squash it."

The entire command center staff was staring at him, waiting. Word of Foster's death had already spread around the office. Foster was a bit of a sociopath, and hadn't exactly been beloved, but he'd been one of their own.

"Don't worry. This isn't a setback at all. Franks escaping actually works to our benefit."

He could tell they didn't believe him. A few men were studying their shoes.

It was time to rally the troops.

"You know, this whole thing reminds me of a story. When I was a kid, I lived in a really small town. Poor place. I'm talking a real shit town. We even had a problem with stray dogs. They'd hang out at the landfill and form packs. They started breaking through our fences and attacking our pigs. We shot a few of them, but you've got to sleep sometime. A dirty job like protecting pigs from wild dogs sucks when you're on your own and nobody in charge gives a shit."

A few men chuckled. It sounded a lot like their thankless job.

"My dad complained to the town council. He said it was only a matter of time before somebody got hurt bad, but oh no, they said they didn't have the budget to deal with animal control...I guess that really pissed my dad off, because he drove to a city a few counties over, went to the pound, and picked out the biggest, most vicious dog he could find. I'm talking nasty mean. They'd pulled it out of a fighting ring where they'd been beating it with bloody ropes, that sort of thing. That dog was a real piece of work. I don't know who he bribed to keep them from putting that monster down."

Stricken surveyed his kingdom. It was very silent. The few smiles had died. He kept his voice cold and hard. "So my dad snuck this god-awful beast over to the elementary school and let it loose right before recess...One little boy got mauled and had to get reconstructive surgery for his face. Sure...Dad was kind of an asshole like that, but you know what? After that very public incident the town council found their balls and their budget. The rest of those wild dogs got taken care of right quick and the town was safe."

The command center was *very* quiet.

Franks was dangerous on the loose, but that danger would make for a great selling point for his next pitch to the POTUS. After all, it was Stricken who had warned everyone about Franks' volatile nature, while his rival Myers had gone to bat for the freak. So a murderous Franks rampaging across the capital was actually a good thing... *briefly*.

"Call up the Flierls. Mad dogs can be useful sometimes, but you've still got to put them down."

CHAPTER 6

This new empty body was so miraculous that it attracted my kind like flies. We'd never seen anything like it before. Necromancers and wizards had been creating bodies for a long time, but none of them had been very good, worthy only for lesser demons. The weaklings like the succubi and the imps had found ways, but there was rarely a body fit for a warrior or a prince to be found.

In their attempt to figure out the mysteries, humans had created a new trade, a blend of scientist and wizard they called alchemists. The greatest among them was Johann Konrad Dippel. He had invented a potent formula called the Elixir of Life, except every attempt to utilize its healing powers upon the living ended in death. So he decided to work backwards, using the dead to test his potions. Dippel believed only a perfect body could utilize his perfect Elixir. He became a sculptor of flesh and bone. He was an artist, and his masterpiece was a body like nothing any of the Fallen had seen before.

Dippel was not the first to attempt to imitate the Creator. He was just the first who was good at it. Possessing a body like that meant that it would be almost impossible to send one of the Fallen back to the Void.

Many of us watched from the shadows as Dippel worked. He understood the flesh, but he did not understand the spirit. He was unaware that he had created a beacon for the damned. He worked under a cloud of covetous demons. We were jealous of man's creativity and imagination, but that was nothing compared to the hatred we had for each other. We fought amongst ourselves, each of the Fallen demanding rights to the body.

Then the strongest of the host who had escaped into the mortal world claimed the body for himself. He had been a prince in heaven and a general in the war. He declared that once complete this perfect body would be his, and he would use it to thwart the Creator's work in the mortal world once and for all.

He had a name once, but since we had been cast out, we only knew him by the title branded upon him when the Creator had hurled us into the Void.

The weak spirits fled from Cursed.

I had other ideas.

Washington, DC, was a bipolar city. One portion was big buildings, monuments, government lackeys, and tourists. The other was impoverished slums, bad neighborhoods, drug dealers, and gang warfare. Franks went directly to the one that had fewer cameras.

He knew how the search would go because he'd been involved in creating the MCB's contingency plans. They would make up a terrible but mundane crime, send it to the media, and then splash his picture and description everywhere. Every cop in the region would be on the lookout. It was times like this that he wished he'd built his current body out of average-sized pieces. Being bigger than most NFL linebackers was inconvenient when you were a fugitive. He could swap out body parts, but that required corpses and a place for surgery. Franks could change many of his limbs and organs on his own, but stitching a new face on—and having it actually fit and not look like a bad Halloween mask—was beyond what he could accomplish on his own.

The police had been all over the wreck a minute after he'd crashed through the side of a convenience store, but he'd already been long gone before they'd set up their perimeter. He'd ditched his damaged suit coat and found a black raincoat hanging on a peg by the back door. It was far too tight on his shoulders and he couldn't even button it, but it had a hood to hide his face. Franks had fled on foot, sticking to the shadows for a few blocks before he'd found a car to hot-wire.

Once he was out of the immediate vicinity of the crime scene, Franks had pulled over and removed a flask from his pocket. He did not want to be driving when he took a swig of the potent, glowing liquid inside. Drinking the Elixir of Life caused a sensation like inhaling ignited napalm, but he was injured, and if he wanted to continue at this pace, he'd need to be in top shape.

He took a drink, and then carefully screwed the cap back on before swallowing. The single dose of the potent alchemical mixture rolled down his throat like molten lava.

Every pain receptor in Franks' body fired at once. His muscles locked up tight. It was like running hot sandpaper over every tissue in his body. He ground his teeth together and didn't let out a sound. Several seconds of his supercharged nervous system electrocuting itself later, Franks came back to reality. His grip had bent the steering wheel. Blood ran freely from his nostrils and eyes, but he just wiped it away with some tissues he'd found in the glove box and got back on the road.

That was the stuff.

It still hurt, but now it was the tolerable pain of bone splinters dragging themselves back into place. The sensation would drive most humans mad, but for Franks it just required a bit more concentration to drive safely. He didn't like the term *pain threshold*. That implied there was an upper limit to the suffering he could withstand. If there was such a thing in the mortal world, he'd not found it yet. Franks took an inventory of each injury. Anything that would eventually heal on its own could be drastically sped up by the Elixir. Nothing felt irreparably damaged. There were still bullet fragments lodged in his muscle tissue. He'd have to cut those out when he had a chance.

There would be no quarter from the MCB. Even if some of them suspected that he was innocent, they would still do their duty and track him down until ordered off the case. He'd trained them so he'd expect nothing less than their best. They'd have checkpoints at every route out of the city. His credit cards would be monitored, but he always kept a couple thousand in cash on his person, so that wouldn't be an immediate problem. The stolen 9mm had gone out the window in the crash, so all he had was the Glock he'd snagged at headquarters and half a single partially expended magazine of silver 10mm. His apartment would be watched. He had a very short list of associates and acquaintances, and the MCB would put someone on each of them as well.

Yet he was not without resources. He had stashes the MCB didn't know about. Once again, three hundred years of hard-earned paranoia would pay off. Franks drove the stolen Honda Civic to the worst neighborhood in DC. The narrow street he was looking for was on the back side of a housing project. Even if security cameras had ever been installed here, they would not have lasted long before one of the locals would have used them for target practice.

Most of the streetlights were dead. There were broken bottles in the gutters. If his stolen car got a flat tire, he was going to be pissed. Franks found the house he was looking for. It was rundown, even by this neighborhood's standards. There was a cinder block wall around the backyard. The graffiti on the wall was similar to the signs at his apartment. The local human thugs knew not to mess with the secret horrible supernatural terrors that lived here. Only a fool would intrude on gnome turf.

The car's interior light came on when he opened the door. Not wanting to be spotted, and not bothering to look for the off switch, he just punched the light and broke it. It took a minute for Franks to maneuver himself out of the Honda. He'd barely fit inside to begin with and got one leg stuck under the bent steering wheel. He'd steal something roomier as soon as he had a chance. Franks didn't appreciate *economy*. He appreciated horsepower, ramming capability, and legroom, in that order.

Franks approached the building. Most passersby would assume it was a crack house, but that would probably be a step up. Several dogs started barking. It was after two in the morning and speakers in the backyard were still playing loud rap music. The bass was a constant distorted rumble. He knew that there were already eyes and probably guns on him, so he kept his hands where they could be seen. He skipped the front door and went to the side gate, which had a skull and crossbones painted on it. Not bothering to knock, he just pushed the gate open and went inside.

It wasn't several dogs, it was just one, but it had three heads so it made three times the noise. Each head was barking and snarling at him and the animal was the size of a calf. There was a leather leash attached to its spiked collar and a foot and a half of gnome muscle was hauling back on the beast, keeping it from attacking Franks. "Hold up, homie…Damn, you tall!" the gnome shouted over the noise.

The barking was getting on his nerves and he still had a headache from the Elixir. "Down!" Franks snapped at the superdog. All three heads stopped barking. Franks scowled at it, and the dog began to whimper. It rolled over submissively.

The gnome handler was shocked by his normally vicious animal's immediate surrender. "Who you be?" he asked nervously.

"Franks."

There were other sentries approaching. Gnomes seemed to appear out of the woodwork. Every one of them was packing heat, but none of them were stupid enough to pull. Normally they'd be flashing gang signs and talking smack, but most of them either knew who he was, or could sense that he wasn't to be trifled with. "What you want, tall man?" one demanded.

"Tell Olaf I want my stuff."

"Old Olaf done got his ass capped." A younger gnome, his beard barely halfway down his chest, approached with a swagger. "Looks like you came into the wrong yard, motherfucker!"

The one with the dog tried to warn the punk off. "Yo, *tomte*. That's *the* Franks. He's likely to shoelace your face just to learn you better."

"I don't know no Franks." Other gnomes tried to shush the young upstart, but it was too late. He lifted his shirt and flashed the cheap piece-of-shit .25 automatic shoved in his waistband. "You'd best step off fo' I bust a cap in yo—"

Franks kicked him over the fence.

The gnome disappeared into the night. He'd left behind a gold chain and one shoe. There was a collective gasp as the other gnomes took a few nervous steps back.

"The rest of you know who I am?"

Most of them nodded.

"Then get my stash . . . Now."

A bunch of them took off running.

"Turn that shit off." The gangster rap fell silent. Franks folded his arms and waited while the rest of the gnomes watched him hesitantly. A few turned invisible, hoping he wouldn't notice them. Gnome culture was big on bluster; they'd been pushy in the old country, and they'd naturally taken to the thug life here, but Franks had been dealing with gnomes since he'd wandered across northern Europe hundreds of years ago, and some things never changed. The best way to deal with punks was by establishing dominance, and luckily for Franks, establishing dominance came naturally. There was a lot of whispering about him being the *tallest*. "What are you looking at?" Franks asked one of the gnomes.

"Nothing, Mr. Franks!" The gnome averted his eyes.

They dragged up two big plastic hard cases from their underground tunnels. It took six gnomes on each to carry them. They dropped the suitcases at Franks' feet and then scurried away. He checked to make sure the locks hadn't been tampered with. Olaf might have been a criminal scumbag, but he'd kept his word in exchange for Franks not stomping the life out of his little PUFF-applicable gang. He put in the combination and opened one to make certain it was as he'd left it.

"What's in them boxes?" asked one of the gnomes. Several of them scooted forward, hopelessly curious. When they saw what was inside there was a chorus of *oohs* and *aaahs*. "You mean to fuck somebody's shit up real good, G!"

"Yes." Satisfied, he closed the case, then picked them both up. They weighed over two hundred pounds each. Gnomes got into everything, everywhere, so it couldn't hurt to ask. "His name is Stricken. He's with a group called Special Task Force Unicorn."

"Everybody knows there ain't no such thing as unicorns," said one of the gnomes. "Yeah, we know that tall white scary motherfucker and his *deals*. His crew is monsters and shit. Even badass straight-up *tomte* killas don't play that game. PUFF exemption is for chumps."

"I got my PUFF exemption right here," one of the gnomes grabbed his crotch. The other ones hooted and fist-bumped.

"Find him for me."

"Sounds like work. How much green you talking about, G?" asked another gnome suspiciously.

"The next time one of you makes me mad, I'll remember the favor and not kill you all," Franks stated. He scanned the short crowd as that sank in. The gnomes knew he wasn't lying. "I was never here."

The gnomes breathed a collective sigh of relief as Franks left their yard.

The phone woke her. She fumbled around, knocking things off the nightstand looking for it. That was the problem with sleeping in a different hotel almost every night. Sure, she had heightened senses and could see in the dark, but she needed to actually open her eyes for that to work, and she was too tired to do that.

She found the phone. The number was unknown. "What?"

"You're on, Red." It was Stricken. "There's been a situation."

"There's always a situation..." Of the many complaints she had about being forced to work for STFU, boredom wasn't one of them. Heather Kerkonen rubbed her eyes. "What time is it?"

"It's time to get your ass out of bed, go downstairs, and meet your new team."

"The only reason I need a new team is because you got my old one killed."

"Those are the breaks...So how much time do you have left before you earn your PUFF exemption?"

She resisted the urge to chuck the cell phone across the room.

"Come on, Heather. I know you know it off the top of your head."

She felt like a prisoner making hash marks on the wall of a cell. "Three hundred and seventy-two days."

"Aw, you're almost halfway there! Too bad for those three hundred and seventy-two days I own you."

"There's an Amendment about that," she grumbled.

"Funny. I don't remember the Emancipation Proclamation saying anything about werewolves. Be downstairs in twenty minutes."

"What's going on?" she asked, before realizing that Stricken had already hung up.

I hate that guy. Heather had far better control of her werewolf urges than anyone else of her kind, but sometimes it was fun to imagine chasing a terrified Stricken through a forest like he was a deer, but since she was still a good person, she didn't like to think about the parts where she caught up and ripped him to pieces... *much.*

She rubbed her face with both hands. Heather could recognize when she was exhausted—not physically, because it was hard to keep a werewolf down—but she was emotionally drained. Las Vegas had been a nightmare...literally, and she couldn't believe she was being called back up already. STFU didn't give a damn about its monsters. They were expendable assets, nothing more, and if they were lucky enough to survive to the end, then they'd get a PUFF exemption that said the government wouldn't murder them unless it became convenient. It was a hell of a deal.

Hotel rooms sucked for anybody, but they sucked more when you could still smell the last hundred people who slept in your bed, and especially how gross some of them were. She went to the shower, got the water as hot as possible, which wasn't nearly hot enough, and tried to scrub herself clean. Since she could regenerate, her body was free of scars, but she couldn't say the same thing for her mind.

The last year had been nuts. Ever since she'd been forced to leave Earl and coerced into this shitty job, it had been nonstop awfulness. There'd been a brief training period, but STFU's methods tended to be *throw the monster at the problem and see what happens.* Stricken liked to say he was a proponent of on-the-job-training, but that was code for *I'm an asshole who doesn't particularly care if you live or die.*

So far she'd gotten to visit scenic places like Pakistan and Venezuela, and eat interesting people. Luckily for her, everyone and everything she'd been sent after so far had been astoundingly, obviously evil, and up to no good, so she at least had some moral justification left to get her by. But every time Stricken called, she was terrified to find out what the next assignment was going to be, and his definition of what constituted a threat to America seemed a little loose. She feared her luck wouldn't hold out, Stricken was going to send her after somebody who really didn't deserve a werewolf in their face, and then she was going to face some very difficult choices.

Heather got dressed, grabbed her backpack of extra clothes—being a werewolf tended to be hell on your wardrobe—and took the elevator down to the lobby.

It was really early in the morning. The free breakfast bar wasn't even open yet, which was a bummer. Lycanthropy didn't have too many perks, but being able to eat an entire tub of biscuits and gravy and still having a figure was one of them.

The lobby was nearly empty, but even if it hadn't been, she still would have been able to pick out her contact because the person smelled like monsters. The handlers weren't monsters themselves. Every STFU handler she had met had been a perfectly normal human. This one was a woman, sitting in a corner, reading a paper. She stood up when she saw Heather coming. Heather still had *cop eye* so she sized her up quickly. Mid fifties, approximately five seven, one twenty, attractive but relatively normal looking, dressed nice but casual, nothing about her appearance suggested that she was an STFU operative, except for the fact that something supernatural had shed on her sweater.

When you were around supernatural beings you tended to get their scent on you. It was especially odd for a regular person to have the scent of multiple types of monsters on their clothing at the same time. Heather picked through the details as she approached. "You've got an ogre, an undead something or other, and a weird thing I've never met before, but it likes Korean food. And you've got big dogs for pets."

For being a top secret monster wrangler, the woman had a friendly smile. "I raise Irish wolf hounds."

"Oh, I love dogs," Heather said, except dogs didn't love her anymore. In fact her presence scared them to death. And she could understand why, since she'd lost her mind and eaten poor Otto. She still felt like crap about that. *Poor little guy.* "Well, I used to. I'm Heather."

"Beth Flierl. I've heard a lot about you. I'm sorry about Las Vegas."

"You win some, you lose some..."

"And some you get sent into a bad situation and lose friends when your shot-calling muckety-mucks screwed up because they didn't do their homework. They shouldn't have sent you in there at all."

It was a little surprising to hear one of STFU's human employees come out and say something like that. "I won't lie. I'm still mad about it."

"You should be. That was terrible. You lost friends for no reason and you feel like this organization thinks everyone like you is expendable. That's not how I run my people." It was nice to hear an STFU handler use the word *people.* Heather had gotten used to being called an *asset.* Losing *assets* didn't keep you up at night. "You should be getting some R and R, not being called up again, but our employer is on the warpath. We've got a serious problem."

"Okay...Beth, is it? I'm not exactly used to anything about this outfit ever being truthful, so I'm just going to smile and nod now in case this is another head game."

Beth shrugged. "You're not a volunteer, you're not a lifer. The way I see it you're a normal woman who got put in a bad spot and is making the best of it. You're in it for the exemption and then you want to go home. I know you're a straight shooter so I'm not going to waste your time. My husband and I run a tight ship. We're given people who want what you want, and in exchange we help them perform services for our country."

"So you prefer facilitator to overseer then?"

"I've read your file and your psych evaluations, and those have made me predisposed to like you. Don't screw that up already. You can look at it however you want. You were a police officer, dear. Think of this as mandatory community service and I'm your parole officer. I'll be happy as can be when your sentence is served and you can go home. Believe it or not, I like seeing our special people brought through the system, and then go on to live productive, happy lives with their exemptions. I can believe in the mission, and not like the people currently running it. So any personal problems you have with our employer, I don't want that baggage on my team. And that's all I'm going to say on the matter."

"Wow... Okay." Heather really didn't know what to think. It would be really nice to not be lied to for a little bit. "That's refreshing."

"Come on. My husband's parked out front with the rest of the team."

Heather followed her. "What's the job?"

"Let's not talk about that here." They went through the spinning doors of the front entrance. Beth shivered inside her sweater. The locals thought it was cold. Heather was from northern Michigan. This was T-shirt weather. And now that she was a werewolf with a hyperactive metabolism the cold mattered even less. Beth seemed satisfied with the amount of ambient noise from traffic to brief her. "Have you heard of Agent Franks?"

"Mr. Tall, Dark, and Terrifying. My boyfriend told me a few stories about that freak of nature." While he had hated what Franks stood for, Earl had admitted a grudging respect for him because he was just that much of a badass. For Earl, that was saying something. "Everybody has heard of him."

"Good. Then I can skip the part of the briefing about how scary he is. A few hours ago Franks murdered a bunch of innocent people."

"Isn't that his job?"

"Not like this. These were MCB employees. The numbers are still coming in, but there're at least forty dead. He tried to assassinate the MCB Director, shot the place up, and then left a bomb for the responders. I'm afraid Franks has finally snapped. Our job is to catch him."

I never should have answered the phone....

A black Suburban with tinted windows and government plates pulled up. The way it sat heavy made her guess it was armored. It was obvious from the powerful engine noise that this was not a stock vehicle. "Well, that's low key."

"Actually, in this town it is. We borrowed it specifically for this assignment." Beth opened the back door for her to get in. "It belonged to Franks. You're going to use it to pick up his scent for us. Hop in."

Archer's cubicle was a mess. The other agents enjoyed teasing him about being borderline OCD, but Archer really did appreciate a tidy, organized life. Now his office was a crime scene and a bomb had gone off down the hall. It was the opposite of tidy. The crime scene unit was examining everything, searching for evidence, taking pictures, and bagging anything that looked suspicious. Then there were agents tasked with the manhunt trying to do their jobs, and the inevitable clashes between the two groups. It was really loud, and there were bullet holes in his workstation and a bloodstain on the carpet. Taken all together it was making it really hard to concentrate, especially since they weren't supposed to be here.

"Come on, man. What've you got?" Grant whispered as he snuck into the cubicle.

His partner wasn't making it any easier either. "Quit bugging me for a minute and I might be able to answer that."

"Hurry up. We're not supposed to be here." Since their official assignment had been Franks-sitting, they'd been pulled from the investigation for being *too close*. Of the agents that Myers had put on the detail, Radabaugh was dead, and Strayhorn was in critical condition. The two of them were supposed to be on the Potomac checkpoint with the local cops, pulling over boats and coming up with reasons to search them, like Franks would be dumb enough to get caught like that. "The SAC catches us here, we're screwed."

The Special Agent in Charge who was leading the manhunt for Franks was Leigh "the Butcher" Fargo. There were several different rumors about how she'd earned that nickname, but none of them hinted at anything pleasant happening if it was found out some of her subordinates were disobeying orders.

"You hear anything out there?" Archer asked absently as he navigated through the folders. They'd not cut his access yet, so he had to move quickly.

"They found some green slime in the elevator. They've taken it to the lab for analysis. Someone was saying that maybe Franks had help."

"Or maybe the slime is from our real perp." Archer scrolled through the menu of security camera logs. They'd been turned over to the manhunt in the hope that they'd somehow help. At minimum, they would be a great motivator to catch Franks, because there was nothing like watching your friends and coworkers get executed in cold blood. Archer had already watched several portions of the video and they seemed pretty conclusive. "Something's not right here."

"Like Franks suddenly shooting a bunch of people?" Grant muttered. "Tell me about it."

Franks shooting a bunch of people wasn't really farfetched, but that wasn't his problem. "The SAC thinks Franks' motive was to kill Director Stark, only Stark's in the hospital, injured, but he'll probably live, and then Franks went and shot everybody else because...what? He was upset? He was having a bad day? Does that sound like the Franks we know?"

"Like anybody really *knows* Franks," Grant said. He poked his head over the top of the cube and looked around for anyone who might know they weren't supposed to be there.

"Bullshit. We might not know what he does for fun, but we know how he takes care of business. We know how he conducts violence. This is too unfocused. If Franks wanted to kill the Director for personal reasons and then mess up headquarters, he would've found a way to blow the whole place to kingdom come."

"Maybe Franks wanted to minimize casualties?" Grant thought about that for a second. "Okay, never mind. *Minimize* and Franks don't go together. What're you looking at?"

"Something weird is going on. I feel like there are gaps in the security camera footage but there aren't." Archer had already pulled every file showing Franks, and there was video of him for nearly the whole event. "This is too clean."

Grant looked down at the blood on the carpet. "I don't—"

"All the visual evidence fits too well. This is what I do. My background was communications. My first job at MCB was dicking around with records, doctoring videos, altering logs, all to hide monster events. I know what the video from chaotic events looks like. This is too smooth. This is like a movie about crazy shit, not how crazy shit really looks."

"It fits the forensics and eyewitness reports we've got so far. Doctoring this much evidence takes way too much time. It would take all of Media Control days to make something like this."

"I don't know how, but my gut tells me this has been screwed with. It's too much. If this was tweaked, it was by somebody who had full access to our system and who could change the time stamps on the fly." That was an ominous thought. The MCB's system was supposedly as secure as anything out there. "Video shows Franks leaves here, goes down, kills the guys at the entrance, grabs his guns from the locker, then kills his way back up to get Stark, then comes back here to where he's got a perfectly good machine gun hidden?"

Grant was chewing on his lip. "They ran the serial numbers on those guns. Those were MCB property, but one was listed as lost in 1969 and the other one in 1980." Other agents were running a metal detector down the wall looking to see what else Franks had stashed. They'd not seen what had been found, but there had been a few excited shouts of *eureka* and loaded evidence bags going out.

"Why risk tipping off his target by killing the guys downstairs? If I was Franks—"

"You're going to need a lot of protein powder and steroids."

"*If I was Franks,* I would have taken that old Commando out of the wall, walked right up to Stark and put a few in his head. Hell, this is Franks we're talking about. He could have killed Stark with an unsharpened pencil first, and then gone after everyone else. All this other stuff is too weird, Grant."

"In addition to the video, which you've got to admit there's no way even our best guys could doctor it that quick, we've got a bunch of people who saw Franks in action." The way Grant was speaking, Archer wasn't sure if he was actually that stupid or if it was some devil's-advocate lawyer trick to help him think it through. "What about that?"

"Doppelgangers, magic cultists, Fey, hell if I know, but I make my living hiding the truth, Grant, and I'm really good at it. This feels too much like something I would do if I had to make a bunch of evidence fit a narrative. This is good, really good, and it's only working because we're not used to being the ones getting lied to, but it isn't good enough."

Grant's eyes narrowed. "Just say it."

"I think Franks has been set up."

"Hell..." Grant sighed. "Yeah, I've got to admit I do too... This doesn't feel like Franks. There are too many survivors. Look at this place. There was too much *effort*. You know what this means?"

Archer nodded slowly. "It means we need to prove Franks is innocent."

"No. It means we're royally fucked. It means all of Myers' worst case scenario conspiracy theory stuff is happening *now*." He leaned in close and whispered. "It means *unicorn!*"

"Well, yeah, that too.... I wish Myers was here. Should we tell the SAC?"

"Bring in the Butcher? For all we know she's in league with Stricken... Crap. I just thought of something." Grant stood up. "Strayhorn's in surgery. He saw whatever happened. His prints were all over that Colt. There's no way he took it from Franks, so Franks must have given it to him. If they think he's going to say something that goes against the official story when he wakes up..."

When the MCB needed to stop a witness from talking, first they would try intimidation, which usually did the trick. When it did not then they would try ruining or discrediting them. In extremely rare circumstances other measures had to be taken—drugs, blackmail, up to and including *permanently* silencing them—but if this was STFU, they would go ugly, early. "We go to the hospital, we're going to get busted."

Grant was thinking about it. "I was ready to throw my career away to do the right thing yesterday. Might as well throw my life on the pile too."

"You know what? Screw those black ops assholes." Archer stood up and patted his side to make sure his Sig was in place. "No more badges in the fountain."

Grant gave him a look of grim determination. "Let's go."

CHAPTER 7

When this body was complete, I struck.

It had been placed on a slab, wired into several arcane machines. The awakening took a terrible amount of energy, both natural and paranormal. The later fictions based upon my creation are more accurate than the first in that respect.

Yes. There was lightning.

. . .

That's a stupid question . . . No. The book is not very accurate. She wasn't there. She hadn't even been born yet. I met her while I was on a mission in London once. I think she had a thing for me . . . Yes . . . I have at times had groupies. *Sensitive? Shelley's romanticized account has been a pain in my ass ever since. Bring it up again and you'll be digesting teeth.*

With the Elixir of Life being pumped through the veins and the arcane animation of the tissues, the body returned to life. This would have only been a temporary victory—the creation of an empty shell—if I hadn't been there to take advantage of it.

I do not like to admit it, but Cursed was stronger than I was. But like most demons, he was proud, and his pride made him stupid. I rushed in and cut him off. I possessed Dippel's new body before he could. He was furious. He tried to follow me in. But I was there first, and I'd observed how humans withstood possession, so I pushed him out.

It turns out he has held a grudge ever since.

What was getting a body like? Hmmm...
Like putting on a glove made of fire.

8 Days Ago

Franks had been spending time in Washington, DC, since they'd drained the marsh to build the place. He would have preferred the swamp. However, because of his history with the city Franks knew the well and he especially knew its secrets. For two days after the attack, he had hidden in a chamber beneath the Rammage building. It was a historical landmark now, but Franks had been there when engineers had dug the secret bunker beneath it to stockpile gunpowder in case the Confederates had laid siege to the city. It had been forgotten after that war. Now it was a moist hole in the earth and his only company was the rats and spiders.

That suited him just fine.

Franks spent the time plotting and digging bullet fragments out of his body. There had been a field surgery kit inside the cache he'd left with the gnomes, so he had forceps and scalpels, but the angle made it extremely awkward to get everything out. Once the wound was clean, he had taken another hit of the Elixir of Life and it had burned his flesh pure. In the privacy of the hidden passage, Franks was free to scream as it ate through him, but he still didn't, just on principle.

The Elixir was really Dippel's greatest work. Franks' existence was at best second place. The Elixir could heal any wound. It could seamlessly meld transplanted organs, even limbs, to a new host. It was really too bad that the mixture instantly killed most mortals who tried to use it. Even if they were anesthetized or in a coma, it still caused an agony so excruciating that it would snuff their lives out. The spirit's hold on the flesh was tenuous at best. Something about Franks' physical makeup enabled him to use the Elixir and live. Government scientists had never been able to figure it out. Perhaps he was too stubborn to let go, because he really knew what it was like to not have a body, and he would not go back to Hell willingly.

MCB R&D had recreated Dippel's Elixir of Life in order to keep Franks supplied and combat effective. He'd given the recipe to them only after warning them of its effects, but of course they hadn't listened. Many test subjects had died before they'd finally given up. To the R&D geeks, it was a chemical curiosity, a mystery. To Franks, it was the key to his continued existence. The best chemists in the world could not figure out why it worked the way it did, as its odd ingredients should not have such a miraculous effect, but none of them were as brilliant as Father had been.

The Elixir didn't just heal the flesh and bone. When a welder put two pieces of metal together, they weren't just stuck or glued, they were melted through extreme heat with a third molten binding metal introduced between them, and when that heat was gone, the three pieces became one. That's what the Elixir did to his body. Some thought of Franks' physical form as a collection of parts, but thanks to the Elixir, he was an aggregate whole. His features and his genetic makeup changed over time based upon an ever-adjusting rolling average as new parts were introduced and assimilated. The Elixir was an alchemical miracle. It made him stronger, faster, and better than any mortal man. The more he took, the more physically powerful he became, but as the fire intensified, so did the pain, and Franks was not sure exactly how far he could push before it finally consumed him.

So he'd continue using it as he always had, small amounts to repair his body, and a bit more for when he needed to do something particularly difficult.

But he was running low, so he'd better not do anything stupid.

After the physical repairs were done, Franks concentrated on plotting his dispassionate revenge. His stash had a radio. Of course the MCB had already flipped all their encrypted channels, but coasting through the local police bands and the unencrypted Fed channels gave him some clues as to the current situation. He also had a tablet that let him access the internet, though he'd had to steal an extension cord from the historical society and run it down into his secret chamber so he could charge it. He was all over the news. Franks was a suspect in multiple homicides—*they had no idea*—was armed and extremely dangerous—*yes*—and should not be approached. . . . That last bit was actually very good advice.

It was remarkable what could be learned from the internet. The Founders would have killed to have such knowledge at their fingertips, but most humans used it to watch videos of kittens or to launch birds at pigs, or other strange things. Franks really didn't get it. The coverage of the attack helped him decide his next move.

First and foremost, Kurst had to be dispatched back to Hell where he belonged. Stricken might be a ruthless manipulative bastard, but there was no way he'd knowingly let something like Kurst into the mortal world. Project Nemesis had to be stopped.

They had underestimated Stricken. Over the centuries Franks had seen men like him come and go. They were always looking to control the uncontrollable, and they were always too clever for their own good. Such men inevitably ended up in positions of authority and their only goal in life was always to amass more. Franks had seen it happen in a dozen countries and he'd even seen glimmers of it here.

Myers had seen it too. He'd thought of Stricken as a threat, but a political one, rather than a physical one. Stricken's power-grabbing tactics in Las Vegas had put civilians and MCB personnel in needless danger, and Myers, despite being cold and calculating, was still a moral man, who would not tolerate such behavior. Myers had set out to prove Stricken was breaking the law, all the time unaware of how far Stricken had already gone. Myers had not seen this coming, but Franks should have.

With no one to assign him mission parameters, Franks set his own. His primary target was Kurst and any others like him. If they were allowed to establish themselves here, he knew they would find a way for demons to descend on the world like a plague of locusts. Franks had entered a solemn pact to protect the mortal world from things like Kurst. Franks had broken one oath in his entire existence. He would never break another.

His secondary target was Stricken and anyone in league with him. Stricken had to die for violating The Contract, for murdering Franks' coworkers, and mostly because Franks thought he would really enjoy seeing the look on Stricken's face when he choked the life out of him.

Find one target, and he would find the other. In the meantime he was a fugitive. The men who should be his allies would be hunting him. Until they knew he was innocent, they would make reaching his targets very difficult. He would have to remedy that. The truth needed to get out. Myers believed in him, but they would be watching Myers. There were regular agents who would listen to his story, but they were lower ranking. Franks preferred to go right to the top.

Enough time had passed for him to make his move. They would have had no choice but to expand the scope of their manhunt. They would get help from regular law enforcement but the MCB would be limited by how much information they could share, and the cops would push back by being uncommunicative and surly. The MCB had developed a culture of secrecy and mistrust, so their capable field agents would be spread thin. An attack on their headquarters, where their brothers were murdered, by one of their own? They'd prefer to keep this in the family. They wouldn't want an outsider to pull the trigger on this one.

He knew the regular human MCB agents' thought processes well. He knew their strengths, their weaknesses, and exactly how they would react.

It felt nice being on his own. It was rather liberating.

Doug Stark was extremely high on painkillers, so when Agent Franks sat down next to his hospital bed, his first thought was that he was hallucinating. Only Franks just sat there, staring at him in typical Franks fashion. You'd think that a hallucination would actually bother to do something interesting. Franks was dressed in hospital scrubs and Stark hadn't even known that they made them that big. He was also wearing an ID badge that had a picture of a doctor that was obviously not Franks on it.

"The docs said I'm going to be pooping in a bag for at least six months because of you, jerk."

"It wasn't me."

Stark's voice was extremely raspy. "You're not imaginary, are you?"

"No."

Stark repeatedly pushed the call button.

"No one is coming," Franks stated.

Stark gave up. He'd just gone through a few surgeries. He was in no condition to do anything useful. He didn't even think he could shout loud enough to get help. "There was a man on the door. Where's my guard?"

"Good try. There were two." Franks nodded at the bathroom. "In there."

"Did you...?"

"No." Franks actually looked a little offended, like he had room to get offended, as if after killing a building full of agents, offing a couple more would hurt his reputation. "They'll wake up."

Maybe it was all the drugs, but he couldn't work up enough emotion to freak out about Franks showing up like the angel of death. "Are you here to finish what you started?"

"I was framed."

"But I saw you."

"You saw what Stricken wanted you to see."

"Stricken?" The drugs were slowing his brain down, but that couldn't be right. Stricken was his benefactor. They were political allies. Stricken had pulled strings so Stark could get this job. "Huh?"

"Idiot." Franks sighed. "There's no time for this." He stuck a Post-it note to Stark's forehead. "Here."

"Hey." It covered one of his eyes. All he could see was neon pink. It was rather degrading.

Franks stood up. "Pass that on."

"You could have just sent me a text or something. Jeez, man." *Wow. I really am stoned.* "What's the deal?"

"I got in here but you're still alive. That should prove something. Call off your dogs. I've got work to do." Franks opened the hospital room door, glanced quickly in each direction, and then stepped out without saying another word.

Stark reached for the Post-it but realized his right hand was in a gigantic cast when he smacked himself in the face with it. He finally got the note with the hand that didn't have a bullet hole through it. He tried to read it through blurry eyes that didn't want to focus. Franks had very small, very dense handwriting. Stark really didn't know what to expect . . . Judging by Franks' denial, probably not a confession, that was for sure. It took a minute for him to focus enough to make out the message.

"Oh hell . . . Nurse! Nurse!" It really hurt to yell, but even in his drug addled haze, Stark knew that things had just gotten even crazier. "Somebody! *Help!*"

Franks' note was a declaration of war.

Infiltration was not his specialty. Franks was too big for stealth. He stuck out in crowds. His disguise consisted of some clothing that seemed too much like pajamas and a hat that was basically a colorful hairnet. He thought doctors dressed stupidly. However, he had learned over the years that if you acted like you belonged somewhere, then most people wouldn't question your presence. Those that did question your presence, you simply rendered them unconscious and shoved them into a closet. He'd only had to do that to four people so far, so by Franks' standards his visit to the hospital had been rather successful, but Stark would raise the alarm and the place would be swarming with MCB in a matter of minutes.

He would have made it out without further incident if he hadn't heard a familiar voice down the hall. Slouching so he didn't appear to be so tall, Franks moved up to the corner and peeked around. Grant Jefferson was having a heated conversation with a nurse. Archer was there as well. The two of them were some of Myers' favorites, so they might be of use. The argument ended as the nurse stormed off, loudly cursing them.

"Yeah, well thanks for all the help, lady," Jefferson snapped back. "Not."

"The government appreciates your time, ma'am," Archer added, far more politely.

They walked toward the elevator. Franks followed. He intercepted them just as the door was opening. Jefferson turned, surprised, and began to say something, but Franks just put a big hand on each of them and shoved them inside the elevator. "Keep going."

"Shit!" Archer exclaimed as he realized what was happening. "Agent Franks!"

There was a dangerously awkward silence. He eyed the two men. Both were shocked to see him. He didn't know if they were still on his side or not, but neither of them was stupid enough to go for their weapons if they weren't. Fighting with Franks inside the closed confines of an elevator would not have a very high success rate. It would be safer to wrestle a bear. Franks pushed the button for the first level of the parking garage. The door closed behind him.

They would have been seen on camera together. He spotted the security camera and made sure it wasn't at an angle that could read his lips. "Place your hands on your firearms, but do not draw. Act like you want to take me into custody." They did as they were told. There probably wasn't a microphone in the elevator. "Act scared."

"I'm not acting!" Archer exclaimed.

"I'm innocent," Franks stated as the elevator started down. Innocent was a relative term.

"We suspected that," Jefferson said. "There are some discrepancies in the evidence."

"I need you to prove it," Franks ordered.

"Working on it," Archer said. "That's why we're here."

"Strayhorn is missing. He disappeared out of ICU," Jefferson explained. "Nobody was seen coming in, but he wasn't in any shape to walk out."

Franks scowled. The rookie had been there. He could clear him. "Unicorn . . ."

"They probably picked him up. We can assume he's dead. Look, sir, I don't really want to be charged with aiding and abetting a fugitive here. We still need to take you in," Jefferson said.

The agent appeared ready to pull. Good. He'd trained them well. "Do you really think you could?"

"Not really." Jefferson swallowed hard. "The whole MCB is looking for you. If you come in you'll be under guard while we figure this out."

Franks shook his head. Stricken would have plans for that. If he was captured, he'd be neutralized. Franks wasn't a hundred percent certain he could trust these agents, but they were his best bet to contact the one man he knew he could trust. "Get a message to Myers. Tell him to slip his tail and meet me at the place we captured Juan." That was vague enough that even if they talked, only Myers would know what it meant. "Got it?"

"Got it," Archer answered. "When?"

"He'll know. Now the hard part."

"What?"

"My escape must look convincing."

"Aw man . . ." Archer whined. He glanced at the security camera, then back at Franks. "This is going to hurt, isn't it?"

"Just not in the face," Jefferson pleaded.

They were almost at the parking garage level. Franks nodded.

Both agents drew their guns. They were quick, but even if they'd been trying their best it wouldn't have mattered in the least. He lunged forward, slamming a hand into Jefferson's chest and shoulder-checking Archer. They crashed into the wall and the whole elevator shook violently. Archer sank to the floor gasping for breath in a very realistic manner. Jefferson tried to bring up his gun but Franks swatted it from his hand. Jefferson immediately came back with a quick overhand right. He had to hand it to the youngster, either he was putting on an excellent show or he was really fighting for his life, not that there was any possibility of it changing the outcome either way. Franks simply caught his fist, wrenched it to the side, put Jefferson into an arm bar, and drove him into the floor.

Jefferson tried to move so Franks twisted a bit and the agent gasped in pain. Archer was trying to say something, but it turned out that Franks had actually knocked the wind out of him, and it came out as a pathetic wheeze. Franks let go of Jefferson's arm and picked up both of their pistols. He'd drop them outside. He had plenty of weapons in the stash, and besides, time spent requisitioning new sidearms was time they could better spend clearing his name.

He kept his head down so the camera wouldn't see. "Speak with Myers ASAP. Don't get caught." The elevator opened. There were two men standing there, waiting for the car up. Franks didn't recognize either of them, but they had the look of Feds, and when they saw Archer and Jefferson on the floor, their startled reactions and frantic reaching indicated that they were armed as well. Franks never had the chance to find out for sure, as he instantly kicked one in the groin, and slammed a pistol upside the other one's head, dropping them both. Franks stepped over the unknown Feds, tossed the pistols under a minivan, and walked away.

That went well.

Compared to most of Franks' operations, his visit to the hospital had been rather discreet.

After two days of fruitless searching, Heather Kerkonen was frustrated, but compared to most of the crazy things she'd been doing since being coerced into working for STFU, this assignment felt almost like normal police work. There were no portals to other dimensions, no terrorists playing with necromancy, no shape-shifting Chinese spies stealing military secrets; they were just looking for a fugitive. Sure, he was a three-hundred-year-old killer flesh golem, but he was still a fugitive. All things considered, that was relatively normal.

Since their quarry was smart, he'd blocked most of their supernatural efforts. Franks had to be wearing wolfsbayne. She'd tried following his trail, but she'd lost it in a really rundown neighborhood. A little bit of wolfsbayne worn on a person was enough to mask their scent from a werewolf. The stuff really messed with her senses and made it hard to get a fix. She'd spent a lot of time driving around the city with the window down and she'd found plenty of places where Franks had been—since this was his home base—but she couldn't pin down where he was now.

She wasn't the only supernatural asset he'd thwarted. Stricken had brought in a magical tracker, some elf from the Ozarks, but he hadn't had any luck either. A Haitian diviner thought that *maybe* Franks was still in the city, but wherever he was hiding had been somehow warded against magic. None of this came as a surprise. Franks had been taking care of supernatural problems for the government since it had been founded. He'd been the MCB's first field agent. He knew every trick in the book when it came to finding monsters, which meant he also knew every single countermeasure.

Despite those setbacks, Heather didn't mind too much. Finding a fugitive by using the supernatural seemed like cheating. Where was the fun in that? They'd find this guy the old-fashioned way. She just hoped they'd do it before he killed anybody else. He'd just been spotted, so now they were going to catch him, just like they would any other criminal.

The street around the hospital was swarming with Feds. Mr. Flierl parked Franks' MCB Suburban on the street half a block away so they could watch the commotion. "You guys getting anything?" The three members of the team who could pass for human were in the Suburban. Beth had their heavy artillery and some human shooters in an unmarked panel van a few blocks away. "He was here only fifteen minutes ago, so he's got to be close."

Heather rolled her window down. There it was again, that annoying wolfsbayne smell confusing everything. "I've got nothing, Mr. Flierl." Heather might have called his wife by her first name, but the husband got the "mister" treatment. He may have been a lot more polite than her last STFU handler, but the male half of the Flierl team was a career military man and all business on the job.

"Putlack?"

"Me either." Michael Putlack was riding shotgun. All she knew about Putlack was that he was like her, an unlucky human with a monstrous curse just here long enough to earn a PUFF exemption. She didn't know what his deal was, only that he'd picked up something nasty while teaching English in Korea, and every time she'd seen him he was wearing sunglasses to hide his eyes. "Why didn't the MCB put a tracking chip in Franks like they did with me?"

"He's not like you. He's already PUFF exempt. He was there willingly. I heard they tried to sneak one in once though. He dug it out with a knife. Then he force-fed it to the doctor who put it in him. How about you, Hawxhurst?"

Hawxhurst was sitting behind the driver. All Heather knew about James Hawxhurst was that Beth called him a *lifer*, which was ironic, since Heather wasn't sure he was completely alive. He was one of the few at STFU who had already earned his PUFF exemption a long time ago, and he carried the coin to prove it, but he had no desire to go back to the normal world, so he remained working for STFU. Heather didn't know what he was, only that he smelled neither alive, nor dead, more . . . *in between*. Hawxhurst shrugged.

Mr. Flierl had been watching him in the rearview mirror. "So ghosts can't see Franks?"

"The dead avoid Franks. He frightens them."

Heather was incredulous. "You can talk to actual ghosts?"

"Only the bitter ones with unfinished business. Happy people tend to move along." Hawxhurst was an overweight, short, mild-looking individual who reminded her a little bit of her high school driver's ed instructor, but he possessed a very unnerving grin and he seemed to look right through you. "Your grandfather was a harsh man. He thought your father was a quitter. It was disappointing the way he committed suicide like that. Koschei the Deathless's burden was too much for your dad. He couldn't handle the weight of the family curse, but old Aksel likes you. You're tougher than your father ever was."

An involuntary shiver went up her spine. "Not another word about my family."

Hawxhurst shrugged again. "Suit yourself."

Three hundred and seventy days, Heather told herself. She could handle weird shit for three hundred and seventy more days.

"What's the plan?" Putlack asked.

"We wait here for orders," Mr. Flierl said. "It's hard to be an official part of the investigation when you don't exist."

"I can go in and look around," Heather offered. One of the fake IDs she'd been issued was on file with the MCB as a consultant. It had already enabled her to do a walk-through of the original crime scene. "I'd like to talk to the MCB guys he beat up."

"Why?" Mr. Flierl asked.

"Clues. Evidence. The usual." *Because something about this case isn't right.* She'd overheard MCB at the first scene talking about a few things pieces of evidence not making sense, and her nose had picked up the strange scent of an unfamiliar creature that smelled like bubblegum and spider webs, and it had bled green.

"We're not building a court case. We're just supposed to catch him," Hawxhurst said.

Their handler wasn't convinced. "What do you expect to find, specifically?"

She didn't know these people that well. Voicing her opinion of Stricken might just get her into more trouble. Stricken had been warning the MCB about Franks' nature for years. All golems degraded over time, so Franks had been a ticking bomb. That was supposedly why he was taking this so personally and had devoted so many Task Force resources to the manhunt. Mr. Flierl had adjusted the mirror and she could see his unreadable eyes in it, watching her.

"I'll know when I find it."

He made his decision. "We stick together. You going in there will just put more attention on us."

"I can be low-key."

"Good-looking redheads can't be *low-key*," Putlack said.

"I'm going to take that as a compliment."

Mr. Flierl took out his phone. "It's Stricken . . ." He answered it. "Yes, sir. I'm putting you on speaker." He put the phone on the dash.

"A security camera just caught someone who we think is Franks in the subway. We're sending you directions now. It looks like there are some old tunnels sealed off down there. That's how he's moving around. I've got someone who can move his consciousness through power lines—"

"Seriously?" Heather asked.

Mr. Flierl turned around and whispered the words, *"Will-o'-the-wisp."*

"The things you don't know about this operation could fill a book, Red. Some people might find your backwoods Yooper ignorance endearing, but I'm trying to give a briefing here, so zip it."

"Yes, Mr. Stricken." Heather kept her voice pleasant, but stuck her hand over the seat and gave her middle finger to the phone. Putlack had to stifle a laugh. He might have been infected with some sort of murderous curse, but even he didn't want Stricken mad at him.

"Does the MCB know this yet?" Mr. Flierl asked.

"No. We get first shot. I'll notify them, but you'd better be done by then. Do not take him prisoner. I want the target eliminated.

Don't talk to him, don't try to reason with him, don't try to bring him in. Terminate him on sight. Is that clear?"

"Yes, sir." Mr. Flierl picked up his phone. There was a map of the subway system on the screen. "Could you find an access point for Beth? She's got Biggest and he needs a loading dock or a big doorway to not attract attention."

"My people will find one. Don't screw this up, Colonel."

Mr. Flierl hit *End Call*. "Some days I really miss Kirk Conover," he muttered, but Heather's werewolf hearing still picked it up. "Let's move, team." He sounded rather apologetic as he got out of the Suburban. "There's nothing as fun as searching for a killer underground."

They met at the back of the vehicle and Mr. Flierl distributed equipment. They needed to look inconspicuous on the street, so everything fit into backpacks. Their handler was six-foot-two and despite his age still had a muscular build, so he managed to hide a collapsible-stock, short-barreled AR-10 on a sling under a big coat. Hawxhurst was wearing sweat pants but he had a P90 stuck into a messenger bag. Heather thought that she liked to keep the gear relatively simple, with a boring old pump shotgun like she'd grown up using, but then she saw that Putlack's armament consisted of nothing more than a heavy duty framing hammer.

He stuck the handle down his jeans and covered the hammer's head with his shirt, then saw her studying him. "I like to go hands on."

Putlack was a completely average-looking man, of average build, and average height. By all rational ways of looking at it, Franks would tear him apart. Heather got close and whispered. "You got the message about who we're going after, right?"

"Don't worry about me. I've made it through twenty-two months of this crappy gig."

"Since we might be getting into a fight together, what are you anyway?"

Putlack seemed embarrassed. "It's rare in America. You probably haven't heard of it. I'm possessed by a *Go Dokkaebi*. Think of it as a Korean rage ghost. You?"

"Werewolf. I've got claws, but that gets messy." She patted the backpack with the folding stock, Mossberg 12-gauge in it. She had excellent self-control for a werewolf, but there was no reason to risk a transformation with people around. "This is easier."

"Yeah, but if I beat somebody to death with a hammer, it'll keep the urges down...For a while."

One thing about STFU, her coworkers were always a little frightening and a little sad at the same time. Heather patted him on the shoulder. "I get it."

They set out down the sidewalk about as fast as they could without drawing attention to themselves. Mr. Flierl was in the lead, following the waypoints on his phone. Heather got up alongside of him. "Hey, I've got some concerns."

"You can regenerate, the file says you're even silver resistant somehow, and we can assume Franks will have silver, and you're the fastest. I've been told you've got remarkable control for a werewolf, but if you change and you look like a threat to any of my people, I'll put you down, understand?"

"That shouldn't be a problem."

"You'll be on point down there, at least until Beth can sneak the Biggest in. Franks could hit him with a howitzer and he'd still probably walk it off. As soon as we're out of sight I want you to move fast. Follow Franks, but don't try to engage until the rest of us catch up. Don't underestimate Putlack. He's savage even by your standards. Hawxhurst is more a support piece—"

"My concerns aren't tactical, so much as *strategic*."

"The big picture..." Mr. Flierl glanced around. Putlack and Hawxhurst were right behind them. "You mean, how we're going in without MCB and Stricken is adamant that he wants Franks dead on sight is making your cop senses tingle."

Special Task Force Unicorn existed to do secretive dirty work. She had no love for the MCB, but they were being kept out of this for a reason, and the only reasons she could think of were all bad. "Pretty much."

He nodded. He had a good poker face, but she could tell he didn't like it either. "We'll talk later. Focus on the job at hand, Kerkonen."

"STFU was better back under Conover, wasn't it?"

"Times were simpler then."

"It's his son's fault I'm a werewolf."

"I know..."

"You don't trust Stricken either, do you?"

"I said *later*, Kerkonen."

✧   ✧   ✧

Franks was on his way back to his hideout when he got the feeling that he was being watched. That was unexpected. He was in a seldom-used maintenance tunnel. There were no cameras here.

Between the old Civil War-era passages, the secret tunnels dug by various Cold War-era organizations between different federal buildings, and the subway system, Washington had a large and confusing underground. It was nothing like the massive subterranean world beneath Manhattan. Franks had spent weeks at a time down there killing various monsters, but Washington's was sufficiently large to disappear into. You just needed to know which doors to kick in, barricades to smash through, and be able to hold your breath long enough to make it through some of the flooded areas. Franks was extremely comfortable in dark places. He'd spent eons in the darkest place of all.

Which was exactly how he knew he was being watched.

Franks paused in the maintenance tunnel. If he continued on, they'd find the splintered boards where he'd broken through from the old powder storage chamber. They would find his stash. He had not dealt with obnoxious gnomes simply to lose all of his useful tools a few days later. He needed to figure out how he was being watched, neutralize it, gather his things, and then escape. If he was being monitored, he was probably being pursued.

Instead of turning right at the next intersection to go back to his hideout, Franks went left, back toward the subway tunnels. The walls here were brick. It was humid and moist. Rats scurried ahead of his feet.

It still felt like there were eyes on him. *How are they watching me?* He had taken every supernatural precaution possible. Beneath the hospital scrubs, he was wearing a necklace of various magical charms and wards designed to fend off every kind of scrying he could think of. He'd drawn symbols on his body with a Sharpie that would confuse any diviner. It could be something invisible... Franks paused to listen. There was the rumble of approaching trains, the whistle of air being pumped through vents, and the hum of high voltage electricity. Franks glanced up. There was an electrical conduit overhead. The pitch changed almost imperceptibly when Franks looked at it.

Hmmm...

Reaching up, he took hold of the conduit and ripped it out of the ceiling. The lights in the tunnel went out, but it didn't go completely dark because here was a glowing ball of mist hanging in the air over his head. Franks had seen a will-o'-the-wisp before, but this one wasn't a Fey spirit damned to wander the Earth. This one had clumsy human written all over it, somehow cursed by the Fey, only the curse hadn't fully taken. "Beat it."

"Oh shit!" the glowing ball exclaimed with a man's voice. "Franks spotted me." It flickered and disappeared.

Franks just shook his head. Even someone as experienced as he was could still run into new things once in a while. Fey liked to curse humans—they'd usually lose their bodies and their minds—but this one felt like it still had a body somewhere, and that somewhere was probably with STFU. He'd shaken his tail, but he'd had it long enough that trouble had to be vectoring in on him.

Franks kept moving. Sound carried differently underground. He heard several fast impacts, probably shoes on a metal grate. Someone was running, and they were getting closer.

His first inclination was to stand and fight whatever it was they'd sent after him, but that would accomplish nothing here. He had to think about the mission, and dying here would not stop Nemesis. He'd sent his ultimatum to the government. Now he needed to reach Myers. The trains were louder than before and he could feel the change in air pressure as they passed. There was a door at the end of the maintenance corridor. Franks kicked it open.

There were a few lights on, revealing a large chamber that was under construction. The area was filled with scaffolding and ladders. A sign on the wall said that the work area for the new subway stop was temporarily closed due to metro transit funding issues. There were other maintenance doors along the wall but those could be dead ends. There were stairs up to the street. The gate was chained shut but it was nothing he couldn't tear open. Franks went to the edge of the platform. He could either go up to the surface where there were probably sniper teams positioned on the rooftops, hop down and follow the tracks and still have to contend with his pursuers, or simply deal with whatever was coming after him and go back the way he'd come.

When he thought of it that way...

Franks had used an elastic bellyband to secure a Glock to his torso. He pulled it out and started back the way he'd come.

The footsteps had died off. His pursuer was moving very silently now, trying to follow him. He aimed the 10mm at the broken maintenance door and waited. The footsteps stopped. Whoever it was must have sensed that he was ready. Whoever was chasing him had skill.

"I just want to talk, Agent Franks."

It was a woman. *Curious.* "Talk."

"Look, I don't have much time. I've got help on the way."

"Unicorn?"

"Stricken has ordered us to kill you."

"Good luck."

"I know there's more to the story. Did you shoot all those people and blow up the MCB building??"

"I'm innocent."

"Then who did?"

If she was loyal to Stricken, she would have come in shooting, so this could be another potential ally. Or maybe she was only stalling until her backup got here. "Stricken's men."

There was a long pause as she mulled that over. "You got any proof?"

"Not yet."

"Does one of them have blood that smells like bubblegum and spider webs?"

"Ask your boss."

"If you go upstairs and turn yourself in, we won't be able to stop you. You can tell your story to the MCB and get this sorted out. If you try to get away we'll have to chase you down. If you fight, we'll have to fight back." She risked a peek around the corner and then quickly pulled back. The woman had long red hair. "Don't make us do this."

Franks had read the file on the Copper Lake incident and the ensuing investigation. He'd suspected she had survived, and that had been confirmed when he'd seen a red werewolf join in the fight against the Nachtmar. "I know who you are."

"Then you know I can take you if I have to."

Franks snorted. Werewolves were so cocky. There was only one werewolf in the world Franks figured would make for a good challenge. "How's your boyfriend?"

"I don't really know. I only talked to him for a minute in Las Vegas. I've been kind of busy being an indentured servant to a tyrant. Listen, Franks, I don't want to kill you, but I won't let you hurt my team. They're just people who want their PUFF exemptions so they don't have to live in fear anymore. If you're still here when they arrive, they will take you out. This is your last chance to turn yourself in."

He could hear more footfalls. The werewolf was telling the truth. As satisfying as it would be to put Unicorn in its place and eliminate some of Stricken's assets, his primary mission came first. He'd go up, but not to turn himself in. "Stricken has restarted Project Nemesis," Franks said as he started for the stairs. "It must be stopped." He paused at the gate. The chain was vibrating... And it wasn't from an approaching train. Something *huge* was coming.

"Crap. Beth is sending down the Biggest. Get out of here!"

So much for going up.

Franks went toward the next maintenance door. From the noises, the red werewolf's backup was here. He put a round into the wall to make them keep their heads down as he ran for it. Engaging all of them in the open would be stupid. He needed to funnel them down so he could deal with a controllable number at a time.

His hand touched the doorknob. It was covered in ice.

That kind of sudden drop in temperature usually meant something supernatural was collecting energy from the air in order to manifest. A human would have been flooded with an instinctual overwhelming feeling of terror. Franks just let out an annoyed cloud of steam. That was one of the problems when dealing with STFU. They were full of surprises.

Wailing assaulted his ears. Ghostly apparitions rose through the floor all around him. Their desperation gave them semisolid form. The glowing specters were tormented, screaming, grasping at him with their life-draining claws. Scratches formed on his skin. They were nothing more than wilted and twisted versions of the mortals they'd once been, their spirits trapped on this plane because of some unresolved hurt.

Normally spirits avoided him, but something was driving them to attack. There were dozens of ghosts, surrounding him on all sides in a deathly embrace. Franks was engulfed in the illuminated fog. On their own, ghosts were weak, but this many bitter spirits together had enough malice stored up to rip the warmth from a mortal body like a swarm of piranhas stripping flesh. Spectral claws latched onto his spirit and tried to tear it away. He could feel their thoughts inside his head. They'd been murdered slaves, workers trapped in a cave-in, lost children, murdered prostitutes, but now they were nothing more than fragments, jealous of the living. They wanted him to be as miserable as they were.

They had no idea. . . .

"Fuck off." Franks growled. He opened his mind and let the ghosts in.

All it took was one instant of them seeing what real torment was like, and they fled screaming back into the dark. The creature that had stirred them up had nothing that could scare them like Franks did. The ghosts retreated. The fog fell to the floor and rolled away, leaving him alone. "Pussies." Franks kicked the frozen door open.

A man with no eyes tried to hit him with a hammer.

Franks dodged to the side as the hammer took a chunk out of the wall. The creature looked like a man, but where his eyes should have been, there were only gaping black pits. It came after him, roaring a battle cry.

Franks casually lifted the Glock and put a third black hole into the thing's forehead.

By the time the monster with the hammer had fallen, he was taking fire from the werewolf's position. Franks ducked behind a stack of lumber as buckshot tore into the wood. She was joined by two more shooters, one of whom had a battle rifle. Franks was pelted with splinters as the heavier bullets penetrated his cover.

Franks popped up, returning fire as he moved deeper into the construction site. A short man in sweat pants came out from around a corner, sending a wild full-auto burst from a subgun his way. Franks put a controlled pair into his chest and dropped him. The fleeing ghosts let out a chorus of wails. That must have been the thing stirring them up. *Served him right.*

He reached a pillar that looked like it would provide some decent cover. The tile next to his head shattered just as he reached it. The one with the rifle was fast. He caught a flash of red hair as the werewolf moved to flank him, but the rifleman was covering her too well for Franks to risk a shot.

However, Franks had been around a very long time. There had been so many gunfights in his life that he couldn't remember them all. He'd started out when forming ranks and volley-firing muskets were still in fashion. He'd participated in gunfights practically since man had invented the concept. Gunfights were all about angles. It was simple really. He needed to be where his opponents' bullets weren't going to be, while simultaneously maneuvering himself into the best position to put his bullets into them first. It only took a second to analyze the layout of the room and every possible avenue of approach. Then Franks slowly walked backwards, keeping the pillar between him and the rifleman, pistol trained on where the werewolf would appear. Franks was as dispassionate about this sort of thing as a plumber unclogging a drain.

"Stop, Kerkonen!" the rifleman shouted. He understood what Franks was doing.

It was too late. The werewolf was young and impatient. She came out, shotgun shouldered, putting herself right into Franks' sight picture. He had her dead to rights, but rather than kill her, instead he shot her in the right arm, shifted, then the left arm. She lost the shotgun and fell, screaming in pain. He hadn't gone through all that effort having a conversation just to kill the person he'd conveyed valuable information to. Earl Harbinger was probably going to be upset that Franks had shot his girlfriend. *Screw that guy.* Franks used the opportunity to retreat further into the subway station, where hanging tarps provided him more concealment.

The massive, lumbering footsteps were getting closer. The thing that the werewolf had called the *Biggest* was here. He no longer had a line of sight on the stairs, but he heard the metal gate fly open with a crash. *"Smash the bad thing! Smash it good!"* It possessed an extremely loud, deep voice.

"The bad thing went that way, Biggest. Go get him," the rifleman ordered. He was the one calling the shots. Franks made a mental note to pop the handler if he got a chance. Monsters weren't nearly as dangerous when they lacked direction.

The ground shook as the huge creature started toward him. Tarps were torn down as scaffolding was knocked over. Whatever that thing was, it weighed a ton, plus it sounded like it had brought more human help with it. He couldn't afford to get pinned down. There weren't as many lights in that direction, and most things couldn't see as well in the dark as he could. Franks turned and ran deeper into the maze of the partially erected structure.

The man with no eyes tackled him from the side.

They crashed through a plywood wall and landed in a cloud of dust. The monster was on top of him, all its weight on Franks' chest. The hammer rose. Franks got one hand up, trying to block, but he was too late and the hammer struck, splitting his forearm wide open. That hurt, but Franks ignored the sensation. The eyeless man was growling like an animal. Blood was drizzling out the hole in his forehead. The hammer was coming down again.

Franks levered the Glock up and fired, causing the monster to jerk. The hammerhead only grazed the side of Franks' skull, ripping off a chunk of scalp in the process. The monster used his other hand to grasp the Glock and push it away. It possessed fearsome strength. Franks got ahold of the monster's wrist and they struggled, with the hammer waving back and forth in front of Franks' eyes. His own blood and hair was stuck to the metal head.

This thing was starting to piss Franks off.

Franks bit the monster's hand. But he didn't just bite. He *latched* on. Franks chomped clear to the bone. Hot blood flooded his mouth. The monster tried to pull it away, but Franks held on tight. More importantly, with that hand and its weapon immobilized, it freed one of Franks' hands to pull a folding knife from his waistband. He snapped the Emerson open and drove it deep into the monster's side. He didn't know if the thing had kidneys, but it had one less now. He jerked the blade up until he hit ribs, then he dragged it around the front, spilling its guts. Franks sliced through *everything*. Desperate, the monster let go of the pistol, so Franks shoved the muzzle against its chest and fired. The contact shots were so tight that even the expanding gasses of the muzzle blast did extra soft tissue damage. The overpressure sprayed more blood out the gaping knife wound. He levered the Glock's muzzle to bisect the eyeless man's heart and lungs and cranked off several rounds.

That hurt it.

The monster fell off him, gasping and moaning, blood pumping all over the tarps. Franks rolled over and got up as quickly as he could. He used the back of his hand to smear some of the blood from his eyes so he could see. From the crashing and breaking, Biggest was coming fast, but Franks didn't want to have to fight this fucker again, so he lifted one boot and stomped the eyeless man's skull *flat*.

The big thing was closing too fast to escape. Franks listened to the noise, judged the most likely path, and walked calmly to the side. He did not know exactly what he was dealing with, but there were certain irrevocable rules when you were fighting something huge. Number one was to stay the hell out of its way. He took the opportunity to perform a tactical reload, stowing his partially expended magazine and inserting a new one. The oncoming monster's roar shook the subway. Franks looked at the 10mm pistol in his hand. He would need a bigger gun.

Two-by-fours broke and the hanging lights went swinging wildly as Biggest burst in. The thick grey hide, long black hair, generally humanoid shape, and the fact that it was over eight feet tall told Franks he was dealing with an ogre. Its momentum carried it through the area, destroying everything in its path. Franks let it go crashing by.

There were humans behind it, fit and aggressive, so probably STFU operatives. They were dressed in plainclothes, but they were carrying long arms. It was difficult to tell what kind since they'd activated their weapon-mounted flashlights. He needed a bigger gun, and sure enough, they'd helpfully brought some.

They were moving quickly, crouched, weapons shouldered and ready, but it was easy to get tunnel vision and focus in on a charging, rampaging, terrifying ogre, so the first man didn't even see Franks step out of his hiding space right behind him. Franks drove the Emerson's blade into the base of his skull and twisted. He let go of the knife so he could shoot with a two-handed grip. He swung around and put his sight on the next weapon light. The second man died half a second later. The third and final had time to turn and engage, but the only shot he got off missed Franks by several inches before Franks ended him with a pair of 10mm bullets.

There were more men coming, but he'd gotten what he needed. Franks stepped back as the others reacted and opened fire on his position. Franks stuffed the Glock back into the bellyband, then picked up the M-4 carbine belonging to the man he'd stabbed in the spine. If he had time, he'd come back for the Emerson. It was a good knife.

The ogre had realized it had gone too far, had turned, and was lumbering back. Its arms were so long that its knuckles nearly dragged on the floor. It was wearing a big blue blanket with a head hole cut out like a poncho. Its red eyes narrowed when it saw Franks. "I smash bad thing. Get a shiny to keep in my pocket, says I'm no monster. Hunters can't hunt Biggest no more!" Then it saw the eyeless man. "The bad thing broke Putlack!"

"Broke the shit out of him." He aimed the stolen weapon at the ogre. It lifted one huge paw to shield its eyes from the blinding weapon-mounted flashlight. He flipped the selector to full auto and dumped a magazine of 5.56 rounds into the monster. Ogre hide was tough, but it wasn't that tough, and some of the high-velocity bullets pierced through it. The monster bellowed in pain and charged.

The bolt locked back empty. The ogre was almost on top of him. Its hideous face was scrunched up, squinting because of the blinding light. Thinking quickly, Franks placed the carbine on a workbench with the light still pointing at the monster, and then stepped aside.

Sure enough, it had zeroed in on the light. The ogre crashed through the bench, and then through the wall behind it and out into the open platform. STFU operatives had to dive out of its way to keep from being crushed. The ogre tripped and fell, rolling through the construction site.

He could hear the rumble of an approaching train. Shadows grew up the walls from its headlight. That gave Franks an idea, but he would need to time it just right. Drawing his pistol, he walked through the hole created by the ogre and began firing at the soldiers caught in the open. Some went down while others moved to cover.

The ogre was getting up. Franks saw a length of chain on the ground, probably hurled from the busted gate. Running forward, he fired until slide lock and dropped the Glock. Not slowing, he bent down and snatched up the chain. Taking an end in each hand, he reached the lumbering ogre while it still had its back turned, threw the chain over its massive head, and yanked back with all his might.

The ogre thrashed as Franks choked the hell out of it.

But he didn't want to kill it. Not yet. First he needed a gigantic meat shield.

Franks stepped on the back of the ogre's knee while he hauled on the chain, forcing it around, steering the beast until it was between him and the shooters.

"Hold your fire!" shouted a woman. Either she understood that within three seconds Franks was going to be standing in front of a bunch of civilians or she didn't want to hurt their ogre. "Hold your fire!"

But some of the STFU operatives didn't listen to her and started shooting anyway. Bullets hissed around Franks, but most of them slammed into the struggling beast in front of him. He glanced back. The train was almost there. Franks dragged the struggling ogre back toward the edge of the platform. Ogre strength didn't mean much when you couldn't breathe and a bunch of assholes were shooting you. There was a rush of air as the train blasted past. Franks noticed a lot of surprised commuters looking through the windows at the ogre, but the MCB's mission of secrecy wasn't his current problem. He was busy doing the math. The train was moving approximately forty miles an hour. Even with superhuman reaction times, this would be tight.

Most of the STFU soldiers quit firing when their backstop turned into a tube filled with innocent bystanders, but not all. Bullets struck the train car. Windows puckered and broke. The small, dark-haired woman bashed a shooter over the head with a brick and that got the message through.

But Franks had already let go of the chain and hurled himself against the side of the speeding subway train.

He caught the damaged window with his shoulder and smashed through.

The train was going *very* fast. Franks had no forward momentum to match.

Physics was an unforgiving bitch.

Franks slammed through the interior. Aluminum poles broke. Sheet metal bent as his body struck the back wall. The impact hurt so much that it even registered on the Franks scale.

He lay there for a moment, taking inventory. He'd broken a lot of blood vessels, and had received several deep lacerations, but nothing was squirting. He had a few minor fractures, but no jagged ends were sticking out. The train was still moving. The driver had probably seen the ogre, and sure as hell wasn't going to hit the brakes until the next stop. There were several people sitting there, or huddling on the floor, staring at him with wide, terrified eyes. It had been sheer luck and the fact that the car wasn't very crowded that he'd managed not to crush any of them. Franks didn't enjoy damaging normals, but really, the worst thing about accidently hurting people was all the extra paperwork it entailed, and that certainly wasn't a problem in his current situation.

With a grunt, Franks lurched to his feet, shedding a lot of broken glass in the process.

"Are you okay, buddy?" an old man asked timidly.

The hospital scrubs were shredded and he was absolutely soaked in blood. "Do I look okay?"

"Holy shit, no!"

There was screaming. It was coming from behind him, from the last car of the subway train. Franks looked through the window and saw that the people inside were moving away from the rear. He caught a glimpse of a hairy red arm reaching through the back window.

"Stubborn." Franks wrenched the door open and walked through the swaying, rubberized junction into the last car. The humans inside were bunched up against the door, trying to get away, but Franks just shoved it open and forced his way through the jostling mass. He didn't have much patience for this sort of thing. "Make a hole."

Kerkonen had transformed. That was quick. She must have run after them and leapt onto the back of the train as it passed. The werewolf was tearing her way through the back door. Her limbs were elongated, her movements fluid and powerful, and every inch of her was covered in red hair. She had razor-sharp claws and a long mouth full of sharp white teeth. Such a beast form probably would have been intimidating to anyone else, but Franks enjoyed a good fight.

She was through and heading his way. Some of the humans were cowering on the floor, but the werewolf paused to step over them, rather carefully, almost daintily, like she was afraid to nick them with her claws. Franks was impressed by the display. He'd never seen a werewolf do anything like that. She cared a lot more about public safety than he did.

Franks knocked the last of the retreating mob out of his way. Kerkonen saw him coming, crouched and spread her arms, claws reaching across most of the interior of the rocking subway car.

Those claws could be a problem. If he was going to escape, he needed to keep all of his guts on the inside. Even a weak werewolf was potentially deadly, and this one didn't strike him as weak.

One of the passengers had discarded a big laptop bag on his seat, so Franks picked it up by the strap and swung it like a flail. He hit the werewolf in the snout with it. He would have done it again, but the cheap nylon strap broke and deprived him of his weapon. Jaws snapping, she flung herself at him, but Franks caught her by the wrist and spun her against the side of the car. The window broke, but she hooked her toe claws around a pole, and wouldn't budge when he tried to shove her out. She came around fast and slashed him across the chest. His blood painted the wall. Franks tripped over a fat man and landed on the seat. The red werewolf was on top of him in an instant.

Teeth snapped closed an inch from his throat. The fat man was trapped beneath him and screaming in Franks' ear. It was very bothersome. Franks slugged Kerkonen in the nose. The werewolf yelped, and he used the opportunity to hurl her against the roof of the subway car. She crashed to the floor, then scurried back, as if nervous her landing might have injured any of the humans cowering there.

Her humanity makes her hesitant. She could not commit fully without endangering the innocent. If she wasn't so constrained, she might have had a chance.

"You're soft."

He rolled off the fat man, and went after the werewolf. He punched her in the elongated jaw. It snapped her head to the side. Franks followed up by slamming his fists into her hairy body, over and over, each shot driving her toward the open back door. She latched onto him, sinking her claws into his shoulder, but that just kept her in place while Franks beat her internal organs into jelly. Franks kept pounding her, left, right, left, right, until his fists ached, his knuckles bled, his joints popped, and his superhardened bones threatened to break.

The werewolf collapsed to her knees, blood dripping out of her mouth. She'd regenerate in a moment, but for now she was too broken to continue. She looked up at him, and he saw eyes that still held a remarkable amount of human intellect inside.

"*Nemesis . . . Look it up.*"

And then Franks kicked her out the back of the moving subway train.

He watched the werewolf bounce and roll down the tracks, and then she was swallowed by the dark. He turned back. The passengers were watching him, terrified of the blood-soaked giant who had just mercilessly beaten the snot out of what they probably thought was a wild animal. His shirt was missing, revealing a muscled torso covered in dozens of weeping, open wounds. He pointed at the fat man, who was now blubbering like a baby. "What size is your coat?"

CHAPTER 8

I had never had a body before. I'd never had a mind made of flesh. The world I knew was no more. I perceived through new, confusing senses, while my old senses were instantly severed. Most of my memories were burned away in an instant. Nothing made sense.

I woke up in pain. I had never felt pain before. Now I was inside a body with a million severed nerve endings. I was made of bits and pieces from fifty different bodies and I could feel every single cut. Dippel was brilliant, but his tools were crude. Man's overall knowledge of anatomy was pathetic.

Basically, the body was a mess. There is a vast gulf between perfection and near perfection, and that gulf is filled with agony. I would have expired immediately if it had not been for two things: the Elixir forcing my body to live, and my stubborn refusal to let go.

Though I'd forgotten much in that instant, I could still remember Hell and I would never go back willingly.

The first thing I ever saw through eyes was my earthly creator, Herr Dippel. The first thing I ever heard with ears was his triumphant shout. He had done it. It was alive.

Father thought that he'd unlocked the mystery of creation. Instead he had shown the Fallen how to destroy it.

Kurst stood in the shower and let the water remove the dried blood and iodine from his scars. The doctors had stitched the wounds closed on Kurst's physical body after he'd returned from fighting Franks. It was remarkable how fast the wounds had healed. The other bodies he had tried to inhabit had been far inferior to this one, but that did not mean he forgave Franks for depriving him of those. Quite the contrary, the mortal sensations of pain and pleasure he'd experienced in his brief mortal existence drove home just how much he had missed over the last three hundred years. It made him glad that he'd not killed Franks yet, because when they met again, he'd take the opportunity to prolong Franks' suffering.

He left the shower still admiring his new scars. Every piece of glass had cut an exciting new path through his insides. Each hardened strip of tissue told a bit of story. Being hurt was *fascinating*. He stopped in front of the mirror and wiped the steam away with his hand.

There was a face in the mirror. It did not belong to him.

They were always watched. The cameras were well hidden, but the prototypes had learned where all of the cameras were located. They were far smarter than the doctors realized. Kurst moved his body so that he was blocking the camera's view.

The face in the mirror belonged to a red, twisted, sharp-toothed beast. "Greetings to you, Great Prince and General of the Host Kurst. We are pleased that you have found a way here to Earth."

This demon was known to Kurst. They had been of nearly equal status, though Kurst was unaware that he'd found another way out of Hell. *What do you want?* Kurst thought.

"I have come to parley on behalf of my new master."

Whom do you serve?

The water droplets on the mirror began to move. They disregarded gravity, moving in different directions, cutting a path through the remaining steam until they had created an intricate symbol. It represented something older even than they were. It was a force that had already been ancient in the time before the Plan. When the World Maker had organized matter from chaos, it had already been there, dwelling in the darkest places. Kurst knew the name, but it would not be spoken out of respect.

I was not aware he had awoken from his slumber.

"Recently a human rose amongst the humans. His battle against the Old Ones reverberated across time and awoke my master. Since then he was been steering events in preparation of his return. It was his machinations that allowed for the creation of the body that you now wear."

Do not claim credit for that which is not yours. This body was created by humans.

"He has been gently guiding your master, the human known as Stricken. He believes he is defending your world, but in his attempt to stop my master, he has merely been playing into our hands. He is glad that it was one as great as you who deigned to dwell within this body."

It might be true. It might be a lie. Kurst gave a nod of acknowledgement.

"The end has begun. Ownership of this world will be decided soon. The factions are gathering their forces. He would offer you a place in his host."

I would lead this army.

"Of course. There is no greater general. Champions have been chosen for the final battle." The demon looked at the new red scars on Kurst's abdomen. "You have already fought one of them."

A faction has chosen Franks as their champion . . . I will make them regret this decision.

"Will you join us?"

I will think about it.

Kurst wiped away the remaining steam, obliterated the ancient symbol, and walked away.

His official title was Special Advisor, but his business cards left off exactly who it was that he advised. The Congressional Subcommittee on Unearthly Forces had been around for a very long time, though outside of a couple select agencies, very few people in the government had ever heard of them. Benjamin Franklin had referred to them as *learned men*, meaning part of the handful in charge who needed to face the nasty truths. Their job was to formulate the government's overall policy concerning all matters supernatural. The MCB was their shield. STFU was their sword.

Swords and shields were useless without a brain. Stricken figured that was his job.

As was fitting for the men and women who had to make the hardest of decisions, most of the Subcommittee were physically present for the briefing. The President would be joining them via teleconference from his bunker. The minute that the Secret Service had learned that Franks was still in town and that he was proclaiming that The Contract had been violated, they had rushed the President to safety. A few high ranking members of the Secret Service had worked with Franks in the past. They knew what Franks was capable of, so there had been no discussion on the matter.

Stricken rather enjoyed the idea of the President being carried off the golf course by nervous gunmen who understood just how dangerous Franks was when he put his mind to something. It would help drive the point home, to make it *visceral*. He'd long felt that the President saw the supernatural threats arrayed against them in an academically abstract fashion, as opposed to the blood and guts, world-ending, mind-shattering horror of the reality. It was a good thing to let the President feel like he had some skin in the game.

The secret cabal had been having a heated debate for the last few minutes. It was all about damage control and what national secrets Franks might be able to sell... *Like Franks cared about money.* Stricken had sat the argument out. They were idiots. They didn't get the big picture. Dwayne Myers had been a fixture in these meetings. Though he and Stricken came to very different conclusions about how to deal with the threats, at least Myers had a clue... which was exactly why Stricken had made sure he'd been replaced.

"He'll be joining us in one minute," said one of the... hell... Stricken wasn't sure what to call them. Secretaries? Scribes? Minor teat-sucking hangers-on? He wasn't sure. The debate died off. Everyone knew who the pencil pusher was talking about. *Mr. The Buck Stops Here Unless I Can Blame It On Somebody Else.* They turned the lights up a bit. Stricken made sure his tie was straight.

The conference room was relatively dark, not because of any sort of attempt at nefarious secrecy, because it wasn't like the members of the Subcommittee didn't all know each other already—they all went to the same cocktail parties—but rather because the congressional liaison to the MCB had been using a projector for his Power Point presentation about the makeup of the manhunt's resources. They were in the middle of a national fucking catastrophe but of course some government functionary had taken the time to make a fucking slideshow about their response... *You people are like a bad stereotype...* The presentation had been helpful though. He'd learned that the MCB investigation had turned up some inconsistencies, mostly because Franks had managed to shoot his Japanese Spider

Demon, which had then squirted forensic evidence everywhere. But that hardly cleared Franks, and most of the Subcommittee interpreted that to mean Franks had brought in some unknown form of help.

The TV on the wall was a live shot of a desk. It wasn't the normal fancy desk, so Stricken hoped the President was enjoying his bunker. It might not have all the comforts of home, but if it could survive World War III it was probably Franks proof... Well, at least Franks *resistant*. The last whispered conversations died off as the President took a seat. He was wearing a golf shirt and a Nike hat. "Is this thing on?"

"We're here, Mr. President," said one of the congressmen.

"What the hell is going on?" he demanded. The President was scanning his own monitor. "Alexander, give it to me straight."

That's right, bitches. He asked me first. Stricken stood up. "One hour ago Franks was sighted at the hospital where MCB Director Stark is recovering. Franks disabled several guards and staff, left an ultimatum with Stark, and then tried to escape through the subway. He was intercepted by one of my teams. In the ensuing fight, several of my men were killed or injured. There were minor injuries to some civilian bystanders—"

"Nothing we can't cover up," assured the new MCB rep temporarily standing in for Stark.

Stricken gave him a death glare. Nobody here gave a shit about their easy job. The MCB rep shut up. "Franks was last seen in the tunnels. The search is continuing."

"He escaped?" The President was incredulous. "How is that possible?"

"My team intercepted him in a matter of minutes, but the MCB response was too slow." Stricken tossed his rivals under the bus without missing a beat. The MCB rep was too surprised to form a response in time, but that was to be expected. Stark was a weak leader, so it wasn't like he was going to appoint a backup liaison to the Subcommittee who could potentially overshadow him. Stricken pushed forward. "Sadly, my Task Force didn't have assets capable of taking him down in time. Franks is mentally degrading, just like I have long predicted, but physically he is nearly indestructible, and his mind, though increasingly delusional, retains its animal cunning. If I had the resources I'd requested before already in place, then we would have stood a chance..."

"This again?" the President asked.

"Forgive me, sir, but sometimes it takes a monster to defeat a monster."

"You had monsters."

"We have nothing else like Franks." *But we could, and you know it.* "We utilize some specially controlled supernatural assets, but Franks is in a class by himself. If I had more advanced assets in place, we wouldn't be having this conversation."

The President was frowning. "So we've got a problem with a Frankenstein, but you want to build a bunch of new ones to get rid of the old one."

"We will destroy him, but more importantly we must replace him in our strategic arsenal." It was hard to keep his face neutral. He was glad that he had a medical excuse for wearing his shades even in the dim light, because he doubted he would be able to keep the contempt from his eyes. "These assets would have built-in kill switches should they ever need to be eliminated, a feature which is sadly lacking on the old model."

"If you're talking about activating Project Nemesis, that's off the table—" declared a congresswoman.

"Why? Because of Benjamin Franklin's Contract?" Stricken asked as he removed a Post-it from his breast pocket. "This was the message Franks left with Director Stark. I've sent a copy of it to each of you." He could have just read it out loud, but he knew that it would have more gravity if they read it themselves. He couldn't do Franks' delivery justice. One of the secretary-functionary-scribes took the hint, brought up the file, and a blown-up picture of the note appeared on the projector. Franks' tiny square handwriting filled the pink square.

Mr. President. The Contract has been violated. Stricken has copied my design. He has created new versions of me. This is not allowed. They were the ones that attacked the MCB. If you will eliminate these creations and punish Stricken, I will surrender. Failure to act will be seen as collusion on your part. As per The Contract, collusion in this matter is punishable by death. I will kill anyone who aids Stricken. Until The Contract is redeemed, my obligations to the US government are null and void. These are my terms. —Franks

The President got a really funny look on his face when he got to the punishable by death part, almost like it hurt his feelings. The man got death threats daily, but he rarely got one from somebody actually capable of pulling it off.

The conference room was very quiet. Stricken could not have engineered it better himself. *I'm glad you're such a predictably threatening asshole, Franks.*

"He's accusing you of attacking the MCB?"

"Yes, and apparently doing it with assets that don't exist yet. I was unaware we had a time machine, Mr. President." There were a few nervous chuckles. "Franks is delusional. My experts believe that his mental faculties have been deteriorating for years. I personally feel that his entering another dimension and the resulting destruction of the Dread Overlord may have exacerbated the situation." He brought that particular incident up in front of the Subcommittee for two reasons: Franks had taken it upon himself to invade another universe against orders, and he'd blown up an alien god in the process. If he could pull that off, what was capping the President in comparison?

"There's nothing to his allegations?" asked a congresswoman.

"Of course not. You've seen my reports, so you know that Project Nemesis exists only on paper. I was ordered to keep The Contract sacrosanct, and I've done so. He's fixated on me as his enemy, and fabricated this nonsense as his justification because I've been outspoken against his continued employment. If it would please the Subcommittee, you can tour any Task Force facility at your convenience and I can turn over all of our records for audit. I am an open book."

"We'll take you up on that," warned the congresswoman.

That seemed to satisfy them. *Suckers.* It would be a cold day in Hell before any of these idiots ever got a look at the real inner workings of his secret operation. "Whatever puts you at ease, ma'am."

"With this madman on the loose, I don't see how any of us can be at ease."

"He blames me for his paranoid fantasies, but all of you are in danger as well. I'd like to offer some of my men to each of you to beef up your existing security details. If Franks comes after you or your families though..." Stricken spread his hands apologetically. "The Task Force has good men, some of the best, but I'm afraid they're only men. However, they're the best I can offer... for now."

The Subcommittee members shared nervous looks. *When some supernatural scary bullshit comes around it's my job to keep you all safe, but you won't let me have Nemesis assets that could actually save you. Yeah, sleep on that, chumps.*

"He's only one man..." said a congressman.

"Don't make the mistake of thinking he's a man at all. He's a repository of three hundred years of combat experience housed in a body that refuses to die. When I first learned about Franks I asked Dwayne Myers what advanced military training of ours Franks had taken part in... His response was 'all of it.' He can fly a fighter jet, outswim a Navy SEAL, or snipe you through your bedroom window from a thousand yards away. Franks has been trained on nuclear, biological, chemical, and unearthly weapons of mass destruction. He knows our systems, weaknesses, plans, and vulnerabilities. If there's a way to make us bleed, Franks holds the razor. There's no telling what he'll do next."

Stricken glanced back at the President. He appeared troubled, only now he was reading something in his hands. It was an old piece of parchment sealed in a glass box. The Contract. *Good. Let the gravity of the situation sink in.*

"I believe all of us here have read that Contract many times, Mr. President... I regret that it has come to this. Believe me, sir, Franks will keep his word. As long as he imagines that we've broken the agreement, he will not stop. I give you my word that we will catch him... If I had better tools at my disposal I could catch him faster, but I will do the best I can with whatever assets you see fit to grant me."

"So if Franks intends to murder us for something we aren't actually doing, how long would it take to make that thing a reality?" That congressman was frightened, probably imagining Franks murdering his entire family.

"That's a good question." The President had been on the edge of granting approval before. This was threatening to push him over. "Theoretically... How long would it take for these Nemesis soldiers to be built?"

The real number was six months of vat growth and being bombarded with continual education and conditioning stimuli to make them combat effective, and then a year of exercises and testing, and even then his First Prototype had failed to take Franks. Making up a fake number that was too low to justify his already existing troops would just cause suspicion that Franks was telling the truth. "We've never done this before, sir...We'd do our best. The sooner I could get started, the sooner we'd have a replacement for Franks ready. Of course, I'd like to catch Franks long before these assets would be ready, but if we postpone because of the timing, that doesn't help us with the next threat, or the one after that. Honestly, not having Franks in our supernatural arsenal will be a blow to national security, and we've lost him no matter what. Who knows when the next Las Vegas or Copper Lake will happen, but happen, they will. We need soldiers who can survive in supernatural environments that would destroy a normal man. Time is of the essence, so we would rush the first batch as quickly as possible."

"But they'd still have this *kill switch* installed?"

"Of course. We send a coded transmission, they don't just immediately die, but it also causes the bodies to melt and destroy any evidence, all with the push of a button."

"Well, I'd like one of those buttons then," the President said.

Like he was going to let some untrained coward decide when it was the right time to obliterate his life's work...The running joke with this POTUS was that if he opened the football—the case holding the nuclear launch codes—balloons and confetti would shoot out like a kid's birthday party. It was better to leave the weapons in the hands of the adults who understood that opinion polls could not overcome the laws of physics. "Of course, Mr. President...Can I take that as a *go?*"

All of the Subcommittee members were staring at the screen. If any of them disagreed, they were afraid to voice their objections now. They'd counted on Franks for so long that they didn't know what to do when their guard dog had gone rabid.

"Yes, Mr. Stricken. A tentative go. Make a few, then we will test and inspect them before we commit too many resources to the Project. If they work as well as you expect them to, then we will proceed further."

About damned time. "A wise decision, sir. I'll see to the details."

"In the meantime, how do you intend to catch Franks?"

Stricken smiled. Franks' tearing through the Flierls' team had been the straw that had broken the camel's back. It was time to bring in some more help. He'd already moved the necessary funds from one of his black budgets to the official one. "Outsourcing."

Los Angeles, California

"Financially speaking, Paranormal Tactical Consulting has been having a fantastic quarter," Rick Armstrong read from the three-by-five card. He paused and scratched out that line with his pencil. "That sounds stupid. What's the right word?"

Shane Durant was sitting on the couch in Armstrong's office. "Huh?" He had his phone in one hand, surfing the internet, and a rubber squeezey doughnut in his other hand to work on his grip strength, so he really hadn't been paying attention while his boss practiced his speech. "What word?"

"Should I say financially speaking or *fiscally* speaking?"

"They're investors. Get them drunk and tell them we've made a shit ton of money this year. Simple."

"Our positioning is fantastic, but I need to think about how to sell it for maximum effect..." Armstrong tapped his pencil against the side of his head. "Las Vegas really was a huge coup for us."

"A few of our guys died."

"I know! That's the part I've got to think about how to spin. Casualties should be expected in this business, but I don't really want to come out and say that because that might scare off some investors. On the bright side, we signed several new contracts."

Durant just grunted in response. He knew that. He'd written the contracts himself. In addition to being one of their best Hunters, he was Paranormal Tactical's lawyer. That reminded him though, he still needed to draw up that lawsuit paperwork against Holly Newcastle...

Armstrong dropped his stack of cards on his desk. "I really want to beat MHI. They've been top dog for so long, they're due for an upset. PT is destined to be number one."

"Uh huh." Durant kept squeezing the rubber doughnut until the burning in his forearms was too much. Then he switched hands. *I got an email.*

"I know it's only been a few days, but we can't afford to wait to replace the men we lost. It isn't like we've got a shortage of out-of-work combat vets who'd love a job." Armstrong was a retired Army colonel who had originally gone into private security contracting. Once he'd learned about the lucrative world of professional monster hunting the switch had been a no-brainer. His career had left him with plenty of contacts suited for this line of work. "You know, MHI has a fancy memorial wall with silver plaques on it. It says *Sic Transit Gloria Mundi*. Supposedly it's good for morale. We'll make one... but it'll be bigger. I want *gold* plaques. Make a note, we need to think of a saying in Latin. Something ballsy but profound."

"Yep. Profound." Durant didn't really pay much attention when Armstrong got spun up about surpassing MHI. The email was a PUFF alert from the Treasury Department. There had been a major revision to the Perpetual Unearthly Forces Fund table. There were even a few informational attachments included. *What interesting new creature am I going to be paid large sums of money to kill today?* He began the download.

"I need to talk to the CFO, but we'll need hiring bonuses, and we need to upgrade our equipment. Did you see the shit the MCB had there?" Armstrong asked wistfully. "If we're going to grow, then we need more capital influx. New contracts are great, but that doesn't help our short term cash flow. I've got to wine and dine these investors' panties off. Don't worry, Shane. I can bring the charm."

But Durant was busy reading the new PUFF table. The new entry's identity was a bit of a surprise. Then he saw the bounty number. "Whoa..." The rubber doughnut fell on the floor and rolled under the couch.

"What is it?" Armstrong asked.

"Only the largest PUFF bounty in history." Durant showed him the phone.

Armstrong's mouth fell open. "To hell with the investors! Call up *everybody*."

Berlin, Germany

"*Vater!*" The airport was crowded, but his youngest daughter spotted him quickly. Hannah always had a good eye. He very much hoped that she would not follow in his footsteps, and would instead lead a long, peaceful life, but if she did choose to be a Hunter like her father, then her keen observational skills would be very useful.

Hannah ran up and wrapped her arms around his legs the second he stepped off the escalator. Klaus Lindemann dropped his suitcases, scooped up his daughter, and hugged her tight. "I'm so glad to be home. I missed you, Hannah."

"We heard your conference in America turned out to be very scary!"

"Yes. I will tell you all about it." *Someday.* Until she was older he would only give her the edited, adventurous, happy version of the events, where Grimm Berlin had helped battle a horrible monster and had saved the day. He'd leave out the part where Hugo's head had been hacked off with a rusty sword by a monster ripped from his own nightmares. "Oh my. You have grown so big."

"You were only gone for a week!"

"Leaving you always feels like an eternity." His men were getting off the escalator behind him. Some of them had family waiting as well. All of them waved at Hannah as they passed. She was so adorable that she was almost Grimm Berlin's mascot. "Now, where is your mother?"

"She had to take Matthias to the potty. What is America like?"

"It is very big and very loud. Everyone is always smiling."

"I like smiles."

"Of course. You are five. But Americans smile too much. They smile even when they do not mean it."

"Their faces must hurt."

"Indeed . . ." He noticed that some of his men were talking. Miesen was reading to them from his tablet. Apparently something interesting had happened.

Miesen saw his employer and hurried over. "Klaus, you need to see this." He handed Klaus the device. "Hello, Hannah."

"Hello, Ryan." Then she hid her face against her father's shoulder.

"Did you meet the MCB man Franks at the conference?" Miesen asked.

"Yes. He struck me as a rather unpleasant type."

"No surprise. It turns out that he's not even human."

Klaus scrolled through the attachment. "The American government was employing a flesh golem and now he is a criminal. Interesting. He's originally from Darmstadt. Well, I hope they do not attempt to blame his madness on us."

"They have declared he is no longer exempt. He is officially a monster. Keep reading."

When Lindemann got to the bounty amount, he couldn't believe his eyes. "Two hundred and fifty *million* dollars... This has to be a mistake."

"That's over one hundred and eighty million euros." Miesen's eyes were wide. "Can you imagine?"

"Is that a lot?" Hannah asked.

"Yes, Hannah. I am afraid it is far too much."

"I checked. They updated the PUFF table. It matches." Miesen was a very good Hunter, but his perceptions were colored by youth and enthusiasm.

Klaus was still not convinced this wasn't a typo, and if it wasn't a mistake, then that did not bode well. "Does it originate from the same source as our Nachtmar bounty?"

"That was a huge sum."

"It was a lot of money for a giant spider, but it was nothing for what we eventually faced. If that crafty albino feels the need to put such a ridiculous amount on this Franks, then I know something is wrong." Like most of the Hunters who had been at ICMHP, he'd come to hate the man known as Stricken. He'd paid Grimm Berlin well for their victory, but then had left them to die in the aftermath. Besides, Grimm Berlin had donated the Nachtmar bounty to the families of the Hunters who had died at the Last Dragon. It was not so much, once it was spread out among that many grieving widows.

"That bounty was wired into Grimm Berlin's bank account quickly. There's no reason to think this will be different. Think of what we could do with that!"

The word had spread. All of his Hunters had drifted over to listen. The men were waiting for him to make a decision. Their spouses did not understand what was going on, but they had seen this look before. Around them, thousands of normal people went about their business, blissfully unaware that the men who protected them from the supernatural were here, facing a sudden, difficult decision. "Ah, Miesen, we were just there. I've not even kissed my wife yet."

"Do you wish us to stand down, Klaus? You know we will defer to your wisdom."

They would follow his orders without question. That was what happened when you were one of the most experienced Monster Hunters alive. "No... We will go back."

Miesen raised his voice. "You hear that, everyone? The biggest bounty ever will be ours."

There were some exaggerated weary groans, but also an undercurrent of excitement. There were also some very angry wives and some Hunters who had some explaining to do.

"Gather around, men." To Klaus Lindemann, it wasn't even about the money. With such a reward, there would be quite the competition among the world's best Hunters. Whoever succeeded in this endeavor would become a legend. The men were listening. "The Nachtmar surprised us. This time we will be ready for anything. I want everyone that is not actively on a mission to report for duty. Tell them to get here now. Kurt, go get us a flight. I want something fast and I want it ready as soon as possible. Christian, call the armory. Have them bring a full complement of equipment. Anything that the US State Department will not allow across the border, we will arrange for a replacement to be purchased in America."

Even a five-year-old could sense the sudden tension. "What's going on?" Hannah asked.

He hugged his daughter tight. "I'm sorry, Hannah, but I must go away again. There is work to be done."

Macau, China

Michael Gutterres watched the vampire stagger into the narrow, trash-strewn alley. The creature was so glutted on blood that it had become clumsy. Anyone who saw the vile soulless beast would probably just think it was a fat drunk.

There was a radio inside his motorcycle helmet. It gave him more bad news. "Michael, the other Secret Guard went to the nightclub. I'm afraid we were too late. It has already fed and escaped."

"I know. I'm following it now."

"Would you care for my assistance?"

The vampire disappeared into the shadows. "That won't be necessary, Father. There's only the one. Go home. It's late."

"That is not wise. It may be young, but it is still a vampire. We are tracking your signal. The nice young men from Switzerland are on their way to assist you."

"I'll be done by the time they get here."

"God be with you, Michael."

He drove the motorcycle to the end of the street, parked it, and got off. The area was mostly deserted. The market was closed. Most of the streetlights were out. He took off his helmet and listened. He was fairly certain the vampire was alone. If there were multiples, that would just make them more likely to attack. Good. He was tired of chasing this one.

Headlights temporarily brightened the street, but then the delivery truck rolled past. Even if anyone had seen his face, his ancestry was Portuguese and Chinese, and that would not be memorable here at all. His order was supposed to work in secret. Gutterres started for the alley.

The cell phone in his pocket buzzed. He checked it. Normally he wouldn't answer while working, but this was from a number which could never be ignored. Gutterres answered it, but kept walking. Talking would simply make him look distracted, and thus more vulnerable. That vampire had looked so bloated that it would probably be lethargic, but the creatures tended to be territorial, so it wouldn't tolerate a human poking around its sleeping area.

"This is Gutterres."

There was no greeting or preamble. His contact spoke in Italian. "Agent Franks may have broken The Deal."

Every member of the Secret Guard knew about Franks. In a world where everything had its place, he was an uncertain anomaly. "Are you certain?"

"It appears that way. We need you to go to America."

Gutterres entered the alley. It smelled like blood and death. A mangy cat ran past his feet. "Where and when?"

"He was last seen in Washington. You will depart on the next flight."

He kicked a tin can down the alley to make sure he was making plenty of noise. "I need to finish something first."

"The flight leaves in an hour."

There was movement high above him. Something was clinging to the brick wall. Vampires loved to strike from unexpected angles. He moved one hand inside his shirt and took hold of the sharpened stake tucked into his belt. "That'll do."

"Timing is everything."

"It always is," Gutterres answered as the vampire dropped soundlessly from its perch. Gutterres spun around and drove the stake upward with all his might. The point slammed through the creature's sternum before the weight landed on Gutterres' upraised arms, knocking him back into the garbage and filth.

He did a shoulder roll and came back up in an instant, drawing his pistol, but the vampire could do nothing but hiss and twitch as thick ooze spurted from the hole in its chest. The entry wound was lower than he'd hoped, but part of the heart had still been pierced, and it was enough to immobilize the beast. As long as a stake was through its heart, it was mostly powerless, and that was what mattered.

Gutterres found the blue light of his phone in the garbage, picked it up, and brushed it off. "I'm sorry. I missed that last part."

"There is a complication. A bounty of two hundred and fifty million American dollars has been placed on Franks' head. You will not be the only one looking for him."

"Wow . . . That's crazy," he said as the vampire reached for him. Gutterres stomped on its hand. It let out a screech.

"Our organization is not exactly hurting for money, but we will not turn down any funds."

"His Holiness could use that to buy a new Popemobile."

"What?"

"I was kidding, Monsignor. Send me all the information we have on Franks." He would need something to read anyway, because that was one *long* flight. The vampire stretched out one claw, trying to grab his shoe again so Gutterres kicked it in the face. "I'll take care of Franks."

"God bless you, my son." The call ended.

Gutterres turned back to the fallen vampire. It was trying to pull the stake out, but he'd finish it off long before it would have the chance. There was a sound from the far end of the alley. Someone had just thrown the tin can back his way. He scanned the darkness as the rattling can came to a stop at his feet. Two pairs of red eyes were watching him from behind a dumpster. The vampire hadn't been alone after all. "Stop right there, fiends."

"Who are you to demand anything of us?" one of the young vampires whispered in Cantonese.

"I am a Knight of the Secret Guard of the Blessed Order of St. Hubert the Protector." Gutterres pulled a simple wooden cross from his pocket and held it up. "And I am here to cast you from this world."

They did not cringe at the sign of the cross. "That thing means nothing to us."

"You misunderstand the point of a symbol of faith then." He walked toward the vampires. "You're abominations, of course it doesn't matter to you. What matters is how much it means to *me*."

The alley filled with light.

Cazador, Alabama

Earl Harbinger lit up a cigarette. He tried not to smoke in the conference room out of professional courtesy, but it had been a stressful day. They'd only just gotten back to the compound, and already their world was getting flipped upside down again. His team were gathered around the conference table, every last one of them staring at the piece of paper sitting in the middle like it was a snake that was about to bite them. In a way, he supposed it probably was.

It was the largest PUFF bounty ever, and it was being offered as part of a special, one of a kind deal. A quarter *billion* bucks... He may have been one tough son of a bitch, but he was still vulnerable to conventional weapons. There was no crazy magic, no weird effects, ancient curses, or mystical bullshit. It was just a lone flesh golem. Normally, taking that on would be a no-brainer.

But this was Franks they were talking about.

Holly Newcastle broke the silence. "That sure is a *lot* of money..."

Owen Pitt pounded his fist on the table. "We can't spend it if we're dead!"

The room went back to being unnaturally quiet.

On the surface, this was straightforward. Franks was like him. They were special, but they still had to abide by certain rules. When something like them strayed off the reservation, then it was open season. If the tables were turned, and Earl had murdered some innocent people, then his PUFF exemption would be revoked, and Franks wouldn't give a shit about their history. Franks would do his best to put Earl in the ground.

Earl took a drag from his cigarette. "I want everyone's opinion."

Milo Anderson had just got back from his cadaver delivery at the body shack, and hadn't even bothered to take off his rubber apron. "We know Franks."

"We know he's an asshole," Holly muttered.

"Well yeah, but he's the good guy's asshole. Wait. That's not right. I mean he's one of the good guys," Milo said. "Nominally... Okay, sometimes. Probably a little."

Milo was something of an idealist, and even he was having a hard time thinking of Franks as *good*.

"Come on. We know Franks has done some pretty awful things to innocents." Trip Jones especially didn't have any patience for the MCB's witness intimidation. It offended his sense of honor. Earl liked having Trip on his team because it was good to have a Hunter with an actual conscience. "Is him murdering a bunch of Feds really that farfetched to anybody?"

There were a lot of shrugs and shaking heads at that.

Julie Shackleford reached out, grabbed the paper, and pulled it over so she could read it again. Earl noted that she'd not offered her thoughts yet. He knew Julie didn't like Franks much. He was the walking embodiment of all the ways the MCB had screwed them over. He'd expected Julie, with her mind for business, to be intrigued by this bounty. Maybe being pregnant was making her soft, hormones and whatnot—either that, or she'd love to take a shot at Franks herself, but knew that her husband would flip out about her participating. This was Franks they were talking about after all.

"Franks is too dangerous," Owen said.

"You're scared of Franks," Holly said. "You're letting that color your perceptions, Z."

"Oh, bullshit. If somebody's not scared of Franks they haven't been paying attention." Owen snapped.

"Well, you shouldn't worry because you're not going anyway," Holly pointed down.

Owen had one arm and one leg in a cast from Las Vegas. "This? No. I'm worried for any poor, dumb Hunter stupid enough to get suckered into taking a shot at the title. Look, I've spent more time with Franks than any of you. He's a killer. No matter how hard you think he is, you're still underestimating him."

"Admit it. He's grown on you," Trip said.

"He's saved my life a couple times. I'd go so far as to admit grudging respect."

"Yeah, you might like him some, but the minute the government decides that your weird psychic thing makes you dangerous, who do you think they'd send to kill you?" Trip demanded.

"Franks," Owen admitted.

"Or what if they decided they didn't like Julie carrying the Guardian's curse? Or they didn't think Earl should be exempt anymore? Or they don't want to look the other way for our orcs anymore. Who will they send?"

"Franks."

"Exactly. And not just for hypotheticals about you guys, they routinely send him to beat witnesses into submission. No matter how much he's helped us in the past, it isn't because he's got a heart of gold under all that hate, it's because he was following orders that happened to not include killing us. He *murders* people, Z." Trip was really sticking to his guns on this one. Earl was impressed.

But as usual, Owen was about as diplomatic as a brick. "I'm not saying he's not an asshole. I'm sure as hell not defending that, but I think Franks has a code. It might not make sense to us, but it exists, and he's as devoted to it as you are to yours. But *if* MHI decides to participate in this clusterfuck, I'm going with you. I can shoot one-handed sitting down better than you can now. I won't leave you hanging, even if we all want to commit group suicide. That said, I vote no. Not only no, but hell no!"

Earl nodded. He'd not asked for votes, he'd asked for opinions. This wasn't a democracy. Earl had already made their final decision, but he was interested in seeing what they had to say.

"Two hundred and fifty million bucks versus some very questionable loyalties," Holly said. "I've worked with Franks, and I've talked to him, but I'm still inclined to track his big ass down."

Earl wasn't surprised . . . But he knew she was lying about the money. Holly was in because she volunteered her free time at Appleton, and many of those poor mentally broken folks had been forced into silence by Franks personally. She'd never admit that though.

"For that kind of money, every Hunter in the world will be gunning for Franks," Milo said. "Whether we get involved or not, Franks is toast. Nobody can escape that many determined Hunters."

"Even more reason for us to be the ones to pull the trigger," Holly pointed out. "He's going down no matter what. We might as well be the ones to get paid." She jerked her thumb at Julie. "Get Julie a clean line of sight with a sniper rifle and at least we'll make it quick and painless."

Earl looked to his great-granddaughter. "You've been remarkably quiet. What do you think, Julie?"

Julie didn't bother to look up from the page. "I think I don't want my baby born with flipper hands because of your second-hand smoke."

"Shit." Earl stabbed out the cigarette in an ashtray. "I forgot."

"We should stay away from this one," Julie stated.

"How come?"

"Franks isn't good or evil. He's just Franks. So as long as we sit here having a moral debate and try to judge Franks like he's a regular person, we'll never have a clear answer. Has he done terrible things? Sure. Guilty as hell. He's a monster that makes werewolves look cuddly. Has he done what he does because he's fighting something worse? Probably. But that's not why I say no." Julie crumbled the printout into a ball, and launched it at the garbage can. She sunk the shot. "This thing has Stricken's fingerprints all over it."

Bingo. Julie's reasoning gave Earl faith that MHI would remain in good hands even if he got himself offed anytime soon. "You younger folks might not realize it, but normally, it takes time for a new bounty to make it through the system, and the bigger the reward, the longer the approvals."

"Exactly," Julie said. "This has been fast-tracked. Franks just barely lost his exemption. Who else do we know with the pull to do this?"

"Yes!" Owen jumped in. "Stricken gave Franks no choice but to break their rules in Vegas. Franks got in trouble because he was trying to *help* us. That son of a bitch was ready to let us all die in the nightmare world. We don't know what really happened in Washington, but I know if Stricken is involved, I don't want to be."

Holly sighed. "His last big bounty almost killed us all. I so hate that guy..." She'd been the one stuck outside the quarantine. She'd dealt with Stricken and Myers' internal games more than the rest of them. "Shoot. I really wanted to build a house out of solid gold bars too."

The only thing Earl ever wanted to do with Special Task Force Unicorn was to get Heather back from them, and then he never wanted to hear of them again. Stricken could keep his blood money. "We're done here then." Earl stood up. "Send a message to all the team leads. Tell them Monster Hunter International is sitting this one out."

He just hoped it would stay that way.

CHAPTER 9

Incapable of reason, bombarded by new senses, and filled with unfamiliar pain, I reacted violently.

The body had been tied down with leather straps. Prior experiments with the Elixir had shown that even long dead muscles would react with violent seizures. Because of the rudimentary working conditions, and the difficulty of correctly reproducing body parts in miniature, this body had been built using only parts from the biggest and fittest of cadavers. The straps were not sufficient to hold me. I tore free.

Lightning was cascading through copper rods buried in my chest. I ripped them out. Elixir and blood were being pumped into my body by a machine. I smashed it. I roared like an animal as I began destroying the very tools that had brought me to life.

The bellows were manned by one of Dippel's assistants. I remember him looking at me with an expression of terror as I picked him up by the neck.

I killed my first man only ten seconds after I had been born.

With blood and Elixir pouring from my self-inflicted wounds, I was still able to destroy everything in my path. Dippel cowered in fear as I drove my new fists through his machines. My actions were those of a madman. Chemicals spilled, mixed, and ignited. The resulting explosion destroyed much of the tower. I escaped into the storm.

7 Days Ago

Franks waited, standing in the dark, bleeding on the bathroom floor.

It was a five star hotel. The kind of place reserved for visiting dignitaries, powerful businessmen, and celebrities, so it had good security. But Franks had worked a case here once and seen their system. Circumventing it and getting into this particular luxury suite unseen had been simple enough.

The fight against STFU had hurt him. He needed repairs beyond what he could administer himself. He needed replacement parts. He needed ingredients and time to make another batch of the Elixir of Life. Basically, all that meant was that he needed help, and he did not like having to ask for help. Franks did not have many *friends*—per the human concept of the word—and the few he did have would be watched closely. Hopefully the message he gave to Archer and Jefferson would get to Myers. Trying to contact Myers outright would simply get them both killed.

In the meantime he would have to turn to someone who was off the books, someone the government would never suspect Franks of contacting.

The problem was that everyone he knew who fit that description was a bit...unsavory.

Franks was waiting in the bathroom because he couldn't get the bleeding to stop and he didn't want to leave an obvious mess on the carpet. Having a cleaning lady call the police would only complicate matters and put STFU back on his trail that much faster. He would have stood in the bathtub but he needed to be able to see the door. He did not like being surprised.

The red light on the digital lock turned green as the sensor picked up the chip in the guest's card. The door opened. A man and woman were silhouetted in the light from the hall. They were all over each other. They disentangled their limbs long enough to stumble inside. The female figure was all perfect curves and proportions. The male was of no consequence. He was even too small and too out of shape to be of use for spare parts. The shadows merged again. Shoes were kicked off. Clothing was partially removed, but mostly tangled up and stuck. The man's attempts at seduction were like watching a monkey humping a football. The woman knew what she was doing, and was trying to guide him, but apparently it was hard to coach someone that enthusiastically stupid.

Desperate times called for unsavory associates.

They quit sucking face long enough for her to order, "Bedroom. Now." Then she walked away, lithe and graceful. The man followed her, clumsy and stumbling over his shoes. His pants were around his ankles, so he shuffled like a penguin.

Franks really didn't have time for this. "Hello."

"Oh shit!" The man exclaimed. He tried to move behind his date, shielding his identity, but he tripped over his pants and hit the wall. "Who's there?"

"Housekeeping," Franks said.

She recognized Franks' voice. His presence had to be very unexpected, but she covered it well. As could be expected considering her history, she was an excellent actress. "I called the front desk about the shower this morning. Is this *really* the best time to fix it?"

"My apologies, ma'am..."

"Don't let him see me," the man whispered. There was no way he could know that Franks could still hear him. He hurried and pulled his pants up. "I can't afford another scandal."

"Your wife would hate that. You'd better go, Your Honor," she whispered back. Steering him toward the door, she opened it, smacked him on the butt, then pushed him into the hall.

"I'll call you tomor—"

She closed the door in the Supreme Court Justice's face. "Really, Franks, was that necessary?"

He came out of the bathroom. "Hello, Lanoth."

"For you, big fella, it's just Lana." She turned a lamp on. Humans would consider her to be breathtaking, but that was just to help with her soul-taking. It wasn't like you could pin down the age of a succubus, because they simply appeared as whatever age their selected prey found most desirable. The judge must have like them in their mid twenties...and buxom. Tonight she was a tall, big-breasted blonde. Her dress was undone and dangling from one shoulder, but she didn't bother to adjust it. Succubi weren't known for their modesty. Lana gave him a sultry smile, then hurried and licked her teeth to make sure they weren't still sharp. "What is this, some sort of surprise inspection? It's not like I was going to eat him...literally."

"Were you going to take his soul?"

"That shriveled thing? What would I do with a soul like that anyway? Politicians' souls are so devalued that I couldn't buy a decent pair of heels with what I could get for that one." She was indignant. "If this is some sort of shakedown, we're consenting adults."

Like most humans would consent if they knew they were with a minor demon... except he had met plenty of human males who were dumb enough to willingly hook up with a succubus. Humans could be remarkably shortsighted like that. Franks didn't need to say anything. He just raised an eyebrow.

"Semantics." Lana waved one hand dismissively. "I earned my PUFF exemption years ago. I'm allowed to date. I've kept my part of the deal."

Franks snorted.

"Okay, I was going to steal *some* of his life, but not enough that anyone would notice. Just a little. So he croaks a couple years faster than he normally would have. You know I'm worth it," Lana purred.

"Uh huh..." Franks walked over to the wall and lifted a picture frame, revealing a hidden camera. He'd already swept the hotel suite. "There's two more in the bedroom."

"Blackmail... Duh. A girl has to support herself somehow. Come on, Franks, you know I like nice things. What? It's okay when you guys do it. Do you have any idea how many spies and ambassadors I had to seduce to get my PUFF exemption, and then the MCB expects me to get a *job*? What am I, a peasant?"

He wasn't going to try to lecture a succubus about the value of honest work. "This is a personal visit." Franks unzipped the stolen coat.

"I'm not your *succubus with benefits* anymore, Franks. You blew that sweet deal, Mr. Insensitive. You were all law and order and too good for me." Then she saw that he was only revealing the gaping claw wounds on his torso. "Oh... What happened to you?"

"Long story. I need help."

Lana snickered. "The mighty Agent Franks needs help from little old *me*?"

"Yes."

"Since this is personal then and not MCB bullshit..." Lana picked up a vase full of flowers and hurled it at his face. Since he'd been expecting some sort of outburst, Franks snatched the vase out of midair. "You *dumped* me, Franks! Nobody dumps me."

The word *dumped* implied that they'd ever had some form of relationship. He was an unstoppable killing machine and she was a soul-leeching sex demon. They'd had a mutually beneficial arrangement until it had become inconvenient. What had she expected? *Commitment?* Franks shrugged.

"That's your idea of an apology?"

Franks set the vase on a counter. "I don't apologize."

"Why should I help you?" she demanded.

"You owe me."

Succubi tended to be a little bipolar. Lana tilted her head to the side, toying with her hair, playing it coy. "Well, you didn't banish me back to Hell when I first got caught, but you were still kind of a jerk about it. Your MCB pals chained me in a prison cell."

"You like being tied up."

"That's different. I was dragged out of a party in handcuffs. Do you have any idea how embarrassing that is?"

"You tried to seduce JFK," Franks pointed out.

"Please, Franks, *tried?* Marilyn had nothing on me. Look at this body." Lana twirled for him. "This is my best one yet."

Her body was rather hard to miss, since it was designed to be lust incarnate. He may have been made out of secondhand parts, but Franks was still flesh. "Yes. It's nice."

"That's probably the sweetest thing you've ever said to me." Lana strolled over and caressed his face. Her fingertips caused warmth to spread over his bruised cheek. Violet eyes bored into his. Her hand moved down across his chest, tracing the lacerations from the claw marks. A succubus could go from cold to hot faster than a microwave burrito. "Oh, Franks, how could I ever stay mad at you? I'm such a sucker for the strong silent types. And you are...so *very* strong."

"What happened to your wings?"

She smiled. Her fangs were showing. "For you, Franks, I'll regrow them."

Special Agent Dwayne Myers was back.

And there was much rejoicing, Archer mused. The difference was remarkable. Ten minutes ago the ops center the MCB had commandeered at Homeland Security had been a depressed, muted, almost sullen place. They were chasing leads and shaking the trees, but hadn't come up with anything. The manhunt was a failure so far, the morgue was filled with their friends and brothers, and the suspect was still at large. The agents were stuck, frustrated, and grieving.

Yet the room seemed to come alive when Myers walked in.

Archer was by himself inside a conference room with glass walls, left there and forgotten after SAC Fargo couldn't decide if he was telling the truth about the hospital or not, and she'd not decided what to do with him yet. Luckily they'd not closed the blinds for his debrief, so he watched the transformation without the benefit of sound. Myers came through the door, and everything just stopped. He could see the expressions brighten on all of his fellow agent's faces. This was the man who could get them through any situation. This was the best leader they'd ever had, and if anybody could make this right, it was Myers.

A crowd gathered around him immediately. It didn't matter that he was no longer in charge of them, they'd always look to him for guidance. Myers answered questions and returned handshakes, then he asked a question and one of the Media Control staffers pointed directly at Archer. Myers thanked him, and walked quickly toward the conference room.

Uh oh . . .

Myers entered the room and closed the door behind him. "Please, no need to stand. We don't have much time." The former Acting Director closed the blinds, blocking the views of twenty curious agents. "Only the SAC knows I'm as much a suspected collaborator as you are. I asked for them to fetch Grant, so hopefully he gets here before Fargo hears I'm back."

"Sir, I don't think Franks did this—"

Myers held up one hand to stop him. In his other hand he was holding a small device. He waved it back and forth, scowling at the readout. "Okay, the room is clear. I don't think Stricken is listening to us right now."

Archer swallowed hard.

"I know Franks was framed. What did Franks tell you at the hospital?"

Archer blinked several times. "How did—"

"I've known Franks longer than you've been alive. He would have beaten you senseless the instant he had you in that elevator, just to spare himself from having an unneeded conversation. Yes, Archer, I've seen the video. You're not my only tech guy, you know."

"He said to make sure you weren't followed and meet him where you caught Juan."

"Of course..." Myers smiled. "That was quite the case. Ah, to be a young field agent again...Those were good times. Forget you ever heard that." There was a knock on the door. Myers opened it. Grant Jefferson had been escorted to them. "Come in, Grant. Have a seat."

The agent supervising Grant began speaking. "Could I get you some coffee or anything, Special Agent My—" but Myers closed the door in his face.

"It's good to see you, sir." Grant sounded relieved.

"We don't have much time. There are very few agents I know I can trust, so I'm going to ask you boys to do a few very difficult things on my behalf. Your country needs you. Stricken has committed treason and murdered our brothers as part of a larger plot. Our mission is to prove it and stop him."

"Franks said—"

"I know. Archer told me. I'll handle that. Sadly, I think Franks has played right into our opponent's hands. He tried to burn Franks in Las Vegas, and when that didn't work he took further action. The only reason I can think to remove Franks is to end The Contract. I have reason to believe that may have severe repercussions, far beyond even what Stricken may imagine, but I have no evidence to prove that."

Archer was vaguely familiar with Franks' deal with the government, but that sort of thing was way over his pay grade. "We were at the hospital because Strayhorn disappeared."

"We think he may be able to corroborate Franks' testimony," Grant said. "The manhunt is looking for him too, but since his prints were all over one of the weapons at the scene, they've got the rookie down as a possible collaborator. I know Fargo thinks he snuck out of the hospital because he's guilty. I think Stricken killed him before he could talk."

"No. I'm certain Strayhorn will turn up. Don't worry about that now. Listen carefully, if anything happens to me, I'm counting on you two to expose Stricken's crimes. You know how to access all the evidence I've collected—"

"We won't let anything happen to you," Archer declared.

Myers shook his head. "This is far bigger than me, than Franks, even than the Bureau. I don't understand Stricken's motive, and I certainly underestimated how far he was willing to go, but I know that if we don't break from this path he's put us on, it will take our country down a very dark road. The Subcommittee was meant as a check on unrestrained power, but I'm afraid they've been co-opted. I haven't spent my entire life fighting monsters simply to replace them with something worse. If I am killed or disappear, finish the mission. Is that understood?"

They hesitated. This was well beyond the scope of their official duties. This was swimming in the deep end, with sharks.

Myers gave them a patient smile. "There's a reason I approached you two as confidants. You are both very talented, low ranking enough that nobody of importance will pay much attention to you, but most importantly, neither one of you has close family who can be used against you as leverage."

Archer looked at Grant, and saw that he'd gone a little green. Archer was probably a similar shade. *Shit just got real.* "Yes, sir," they answered simultaneously.

"Grant, I've given you a few names of other agents you can trust. Henry, you know how to access my secret files. Our case needs to be rock solid or it will be dismissed. We will put the pieces together and take this straight to the President."

"And what if he agrees with Stricken?" Archer asked.

Myers paused for a long time. They'd all been thinking it. "Then I'm afraid Franks will solve this problem his way."

The diner had good pie, and good pie could help assuage the fact she was a virtual slave to a shadow government kill squad, and that kill squad had just gotten its ass handed to it by Frankenstein's monster. Pie was amazing like that. *Not really...* Heather stuffed another chunk of apple into her mouth and chewed. Franks' beating them still stung...though that was a *really* flaky crust.

The place was quiet. The lunch rush was over and the dinner crowd hadn't started coming in yet. Heather had been killing time, sitting in a corner booth for a few hours, but since she had been continually ordering food, the staff wasn't in any hurry to throw her out. More than anything her servers seemed impressed that a woman of her size could put down such a ridiculous amount of food. They didn't realize that shape-changing burned a lot of calories and regenerating from injuries took even more. Franks had really done a number on her. Heather had broken damn near everything. Besides, STFU gave her a decent per diem.

She picked up Beth Flierl's scent as soon as she entered the diner. There was still monsters on it, but now she also smelled of cheap coffee, energy drinks, and gunpowder. Apparently, Beth had been too busy to shower since the fight against Franks. When she got closer, Heather could tell that she'd not slept yet either.

"You look tired."

The Task Force monster wrangler waved one hand dismissively. "Lots of briefings... Mind if I sit?"

"Sure." Heather was in no position to tell anyone from STFU *no* anyway, but she honestly liked the Flierls. They seemed like remarkably decent people for this line of work. "Want some pie? It's pretty good."

"No thanks. I just want to go home and crash. I got your message. Considering the last time I saw you there were bones sticking out and you were coughing up blood, you're looking well."

"There are some benefits to balance out the homicidal rage, like the best way to heal is to eat like a sumo wrestler."

"Eat up. The full moon is soon. You'll be going into an STFU-provided lockup for the duration. Show up on time or we'll have to come get you."

"No problem. Get me an address." Heather knew exactly when the moon would call to her. She could always hear the hum. She could probably handle changing without hurting anyone, but it was better not to push her luck. "How are the others?"

"You actually care? You barely knew them."

"I guess I've got a protective streak."

"Sorry. That came out rude. I'm just tired. Well, you hadn't met any of the Task Force normals, and I'm not even allowed to tell you their names anyway. They fared worse than we did. Hawxhurst can't really die, so he'll bounce back. The Biggest will heal. His kind are very resilient."

"Putlack?"

Beth shook her head sadly. "It's not looking good, but we've never dealt with a *Go Dokkaebi* in the states before. We've got his body on ice, but we don't know if he'll come back."

"He seemed like a nice guy."

"Considering his curse, he really is. You never saw that thing inside of him get really angry. I don't know if he could have made the transition to normal life even if he had gotten his exemption." She fell silent as the waitress came by to see if she wanted anything. Beth politely told her no and waited for her to leave before continuing. "That's the hardest part of this job. You get to know people, and at the end you have to give an honest report about if you think they're going to be a menace to society after we cut them loose. Maybe Putlack is better off."

"Is that your way of warning me to be on my best behavior?"

"I barely know you. Your last liaison officer thought you were fine. I think the actual phrase was *pushy but sane*." Beth laughed. "By Task Force standards that is a glowing recommendation."

Heather wasn't allowed in any of STFU's official briefings. "Any progress on finding our guy?" She went back to her pie, trying to act nonchalant.

"You might not have noticed, but the boss isn't super good at sharing information. Our team is done. We had our shot. Now we're supposed to stand down."

Heather could tell she wanted to say more. "Come on, Beth, there's always rumors swirling around a big investigation. You must have heard something. He kicked me off a moving train."

"He winged my husband...Okay, fair enough. They're tossing all those old tunnels, but there's been no sign of him anywhere. He just vanished. MCB can't find anything, but I guess that's pushed the higher-ups over the edge. We were all a little surprised to see our guy turn up on the latest PUFF table for a lot of money."

"Define a lot."

"Two hundred and fifty million dollars."

Heather almost choked on her pie.

"No, Task Force members are ineligible to collect PUFF, so don't even think about it...Keep in mind who you're working for now. The government has individual airplanes that cost more than that. As ridiculous as it sounds, that kind of money routinely disappears from budgets all the time. To the government that's chump change, but to Hunters? The biggest company out there—which I believe your boyfriend runs—only has a couple hundred employees. Hunters will be coming out of the woodwork."

"But still...That seems extreme."

"During the last briefing we were told that our fugitive left a message threatening to kill the President."

That didn't fit. Heather leaned in close. "Did you get to see the note?"

"No."

"Why would Franks do that?"

"Maybe he's gone nuts. Something came unscrewed in that armored skull of his. I don't know."

"That can't be all..." Heather tapped her fork against her plate. She'd been debriefed about her fight in the subway, but she'd left a few things out, most importantly how she'd violated Stricken's direct orders and talked with Franks first. She'd been beaten senseless, Franks could have ripped her head off there at the end, but he'd given her a message and spared her life instead. Everything she'd ever heard about Franks suggested that he didn't even grasp the concept of mercy, let alone ever exercised it, so there had to be a reason. Nemesis had to be that important. The question now was did she trust Beth enough to ask about it?

As one of the monstrous *volunteers,* Heather wasn't given access to any of STFU's files. The only history she knew was what they figured she needed to know for an operation, and that was usually minimal and given at the last possible minute. The only way she would find out anything about Nemesis was if somebody told her, and since the Task Force was an untrusting bunch, the list of people who might share was very short.

"You want to say something, Kerkonen? Spit it out, because I really want to call it a day."

"I just remembered Franks said something during our fight."

Beth was suspicious. "So you just happened to forget this part during your debrief?"

"You know, bestial werewolf savagery and whatnot."

"I bet... Except you're the most coherent werewolf we've ever found."

"Blame it on the head injuries. I had a railroad-track-shaped dent right here." Heather was committed now. "Franks said he was innocent."

"He sure isn't acting innocent. Ask Putlack. Oh, wait. You can't."

Heather leaned across the table. "The evidence at the MCB building isn't right. There's more going on than what we've been told."

"Why do you think that?"

"This." Heather pointed at her nose. "Plus lots of years putting up yellow tape around crime scenes, I know what they should look like, but none of those involved something that bled green, but smelled like spider webs and bubblegum."

Beth kept her face blank. "They're looking into that still. Whatever it was in that elevator never got caught on video. Our boss says that Franks must have had something helping him."

"What do you think?"

"I think that by now you'd know to keep your mouth shut and keep your head down until your time's served. Are you trying to get in trouble?" It sounded more like a warning than a threat. "This is way over your head. Certain people in charge don't have any patience when it comes to Task Force volunteers rocking the boat. The MCB is investigating. If there's anything to that, they'll figure it out."

Heather could leave it. She could keep her mouth shut for a year, get her exemption, and walk away. Too bad she'd never been very good at being a quitter. "Franks mentioned something else."

"Oh, come on, Kerkonen." Beth rubbed her face with both hands. "Bestial werewolf forgetfulness again?"

"Blame it on the concussion. Whatever."

"Fine. What is it?"

"What's Nemesis?"

The Flierls were normally pretty good at not giving away too much to their monstrous charges, but not this time. Beth's surprise was obvious. "Franks mentioned Nemesis?"

"He blamed the whole thing on Str...on our employer. He said Nemesis had to be stopped."

"Were you two having a tea party down there or something?" She was quiet for a very long time, thinking it over. "That's impossible. It was an illicit project back during the Cold War, and it got shut down, and shut down *hard*. We do certain clandestine things, but restarting that would be so illegal it isn't even funny. Our boss might test the limits, but he wouldn't do that..." She trailed off. "No way. Even dabbling in that could jeopardize the Task Force's existence. You've only seen the bad, but in the big picture, we've done a lot of good. We've saved a lot of American lives and prevented some horrible things from happening. I can't imagine that our boss would risk throwing all of that away."

"Beth, I have to know. What the hell is Nemesis?"

"Something you should *never* ask about again. For your own safety, Kerkonen, we never had this conversation. I'm going to forget all about this." She slid out of the booth and stood up. "I'd suggest you do the same." Beth began walking away.

Heather called after her, "What if he was telling the truth?"

Beth stopped, started walking again, then stopped, and swore under her breath, before turning back. "I'll talk to my husband. We'll look into it, I promise."

"How can I help?"

"This needs to be done *discreetly*. I've read your file. I don't think you know what that word means, so you don't do anything. I'll be in touch." Beth left in a hurry.

"I can be discreet," Heather muttered. She had no idea if she'd just done the right thing or not. *Oh well*... Either Beth would rat her out, or she wouldn't. In the meantime, she was going to find out what Nemesis really was.

PART 2

The Deal

CHAPTER 10

I wandered in the forest, incoherent with pain. It took time for my ancient spirit to mesh with my new body enough to exercise reason.

My first conscious thought was that I was dying. The body was broken. I had damaged it during my rampage. My next was that I did not want to go back to Hell where I belonged. My memories were damaged, but I knew that much for certain.

Mortals had to eat. I was mortal now. So I chased down a deer, broke its spine, and ate some of its raw flesh. Obviously that did not help my sucking chest wound, but I had only been alive for a few hours so I didn't know any better.

So this was life? I hated it too.

Gradually weakening, my run turned into a walk, then I fell and crawled through the mud until dawn. I was nearly overcome with blood loss as the sun rose over the horizon. I had never looked upon such a thing with eyes before.

I was moved.

I did not understand beauty or majesty, but I did understand shame and regret. This should have been my world. I should have been human. I should have been born of woman, lived, died, and returned with honor. I should have been part of The Plan. Only I had thrown that away by making war against my brothers. The constant anger I had felt toward both the loyal and the rebellious was replaced with self-loathing. There was no one to blame except myself.

Now my brief mortality would end. I would die in the mud and my spirit would be cast back to Hell as I deserved.

So I lay there, dying, watching the sunrise over a world that had been meant for me, if only I had not been so filled with pride... For the first time I understood why I deserved the Creator's punishment. This had been intended for me, but I had thrown it away. If I could do it over again I would have.

It turns out you need to have a heart for it to break. I did not understand the feeling. For the first time I was truly... sorry.

That was when I heard the voice.

I will not repeat what the messenger said to me as I lay there dying in the mud. Those words are not mine to repeat. I am not worthy.

That's right... Classified. *Back off.*

Basically...

Hmm....

Well... He made me an offer.

He knew I was not like the other Fallen. I had no desire to break The Plan. I did not want power or glory. I was strong enough to find a way into the mortal world. Though I was no longer compelled to do evil, I would never understand good. Though I would forever be incapable of love, or mercy, or kindness, or the other important lessons within The Plan, I had been one of the greatest warriors of the host, so my talents would not be wasted. I was ambivalent toward the children of men, but most of the other things who would find a way into this mortal world—whether they were outcasts from the world before or invaders from worlds outside—would come here to do harm.

The Deal He offered was simple. I would be allowed to keep the mortal shell I had stolen, but only if I used it as a weapon against the invaders. They would fight me. Someday my body would be ultimately destroyed, and then my accomplishments would be measured against my sins. At times I would be given orders that had to be obeyed without question. Regardless, I would never be worthy to return to glory. There would be no atonement for one of my kind. That was impossible. There could never be a heaven for me... But in the meantime I could avoid Hell.

That was good enough.

I accepted.

Have I kept The Deal since?

Hmmm...

Mostly.

3 Days Ago

The news was showing his picture again. Franks picked up the remote and muted the sound. It was all the same MCB media manipulation. It was so predictable and boring he could have written it himself. He went back to the stove and stirred the pot full of green sludge. The counter was covered in glass beakers, Bunsen burners, and ingredients. The next batch of Elixir was almost ready.

"You better not be cooking meth in there," Lana called from the living room. "I like this place. Luxury suits me."

He'd had Lana purchase most of the items at different locations. A few of the ingredients were rare, and any attempt to buy them locally would be flagged to tip off STFU, but Franks had thought ahead and had those things in his gnome stash. One of his cases was open on the table. Franks removed a bag filled with dried moths. They were a species native to Germany. He dumped a few of them on the cutting board and began dicing them with a knife.

"Not that I'm against you cooking meth. I love that show." The succubus was lying on the couch, reading *People* magazine. She looked up at the now silent television. "It's about you again. You're a hit. I'm dating a celebrity."

The succubus had a very odd definition of *dating*. He continued chopping up insects.

"That picture isn't even close now."

Franks glanced over. His MCB ID photo would not help them. They'd spent the last few days damaging his face and then forcing it to heal with the last of his Elixir. He'd changed the bone structure enough that facial recognition software would no longer pick him out of a crowd. Lana had helped. She had a good eye for human proportions and a steady hand. He suspected that she'd enjoyed repeatedly breaking his jaw, nose, and cheekbones with a meat tenderizer and then pushing the bits into new positions.

"I tried to accentuate your natural manliness. I could have molded you into a sexy beast, but oh no, you're all hung up on blending in. Like that's going to happen with those broad shoulders of yours. I like your shoulders. And your arms... Yum... You could use new calves though. How about this guy?" Lana held up the magazine. It was an issue with the list of the most beautiful people. "He's got amazing calf muscles. If he's dead it isn't like he's going to miss those magnificent legs. I could arrange a little accident..."

"No."

"Come on, Franks. What's the point of having swappable parts if I can't change them around for my amusement? You're like my own personal Mr. Potato Head. A muscular, super strong, tireless, focused Mr. Potato Head who could use better calves."

"Quit shopping," Franks ordered.

"But it's like those legs are chiseled from marble. They're wasted on that mortal." She sighed and went back to her magazine.

Franks scraped the moth bits into the sludge. He had made so many batches of Dippel's Elixir of Life over the years that he could have done this in his sleep...if he ever slept. It would be done soon, and then he could get back to work. He picked up a beaker of caustic acid and poured it into the pot. The mixture turned blue.

"You're leaving me again, aren't you, Franks? Don't deny it. I can tell."

Of course he was. He needed to contact Myers tonight. Franks had told Lana enough about Nemesis for her to understand the magnitude of the situation. "Someone has to send Kurst back to Hell."

"There's no way you can beat Kurst. He was one of the best." She got off the couch. The succubus wasn't wearing much, just some frilly see-through thing, but that was normal for her. She came into the kitchen, pouting. "You don't want to leave. You don't owe humans anything. You're going to try to save them, even while they're hunting you. Don't be stupid."

Lana didn't know about The Deal, and she'd never understand even if he told her. She was an entirely selfish being. Succubi were minor things, too focused on self-gratification to think through the consequences of their rebellion. They often slipped through the cracks, scraping out a mortal existence by preying on the basest human emotions. She wasn't a warrior like him or Kurst. The idea of sacrifice or redemption, the very foundations of The Deal, were beyond her comprehension.

"I'm not stupid."

"Could have fooled me." She wrapped her arms around his waist and snuggled up against his back. She was warm. "Admit it, Franks. Deep down you know I'm right. Humans are even more selfish than we are. They used me and they've used you so much longer. Now you're all used up and they've thrown you away."

He could feel her breathing on his back. "Maybe."

"Kurst will find a way to bring the entire army of Hell here.

Mankind will get stomped. Then it would be our turn. Is that really such a bad thing?"

"Yes."

"You always were soft on humans. You've gotten hurt so many times trying to protect them and they'll never accept you. Wait... that's right, mortal women have fallen in love with you before. How has that always worked out?"

She knew damned good and well how that always ended.

"That's right, big boy, because you'll always be a monster to them. Their lives will always be short, confusing, and pointless, and nothing you do will change them. Don't go. This is mankind's problem. Let them handle it. You belong with me. We're two of a kind. I'm never bored when you're around, and I simply can't abide being bored." She had to stand on her tiptoes to nibble on the back of his ear. She didn't even draw blood. "Stay with me. Let me make you happy."

"Don't tempt me."

"I'm a temptress. That's sort of my thing."

"You're good at it."

"You haven't seen anything yet."

The egg timer dinged. The Elixir was done cooking. Franks abruptly shook Lana off and removed the pot from the stove. "I'm still leaving."

That really pissed her off. "So I'm just your demonic booty call!"

Franks stuck the remaining ingredients back into the case. "That part was your idea. I just needed someone to go shopping and help with surgery."

"You want me to fix you a sandwich too?" she snapped.

"That would be nice." Franks closed the case. "Make it to go."

The succubus let out an inarticulate shriek of rage. Her eyes had turned violet and she'd grown black claws from the ends of her fingers. "You prick!"

Franks did not understand why he had that effect on women. "We're even. You'll want to hide until this over. Kurst will destroy anyone who helped me."

"You should have told me that part first. That would have been the *decent* thing to do."

"I suppose." It was odd to be chided for a lack of decency by a succubus.

"You're a heartless bastard, Franks."

That was incorrect. He had two hearts. "Thank you for helping."

She had not been expecting thanks. Lana was still seething, but at least her claws and fangs had retracted. "Fine. Go get yourself destroyed. See if I care. Take your slime and get out!" She stormed away.

Careful not to waste any, Franks began pouring the Elixir into a thermos.

Lana stuck her head around the corner. "I hope you win. Kurst is an ass. I've got a full social calendar. The apocalypse would crimp my style."

For a soul-leeching demon, Lana really wasn't all bad.

"I've got something!"

Everyone in the command center perked up. Stricken walked over behind the excited computer geek. A quick glance at the screen confirmed he was listening in on recordings of intercepted phone calls. "What've you got?"

"A tip to one of the Monster Hunters." The geek pushed a button, putting the call on the speaker.

He recognized the voice of Rick Armstrong, head of Paranormal Tactical Consulting. *"Is this who I think it is?"*

"Of course, handsome." The woman had a very sultry voice. *"I found out you were in town, but you didn't even bother to call."*

Stricken recognized her. "Well hello, Lana." The geek looked at him. "A succubus. She got her PUFF exemption years ago, then fell off the radar."

"What do you want?" Armstrong demanded.

"Remember last summer when we met at that party? You were quite the dancer. We had such a good time. We should totally hook up again."

"The last time we hooked up, I was in a coma for a week."

"Admit it. That night was still worth it."

"My hair went white. I had to start dying it. You're lucky you're PUFF exempt." Armstrong wasn't stupid enough to bed a succubus twice. *"Goodbye, Lana."*

"Hold on there, Rick." She went from seductive to bossy rather quickly. Stricken had always liked that about her. *"I know the real reason why you're in DC, and I've got information about where you can find the thing you're searching for."*

"Oh really? Where?"

"First, I heard through the grapevine about that giant bounty. When you get him, I want twenty percent. A girl needs to treat herself."

"Ten."

"Fifteen."

"Deal." Armstrong relented. "That's one hell of a finder's fee. This had better be good."

"Oh, it is. I followed him. He never even saw me, and to think I only regrew my wings because he thought they were hot. He deserves this. This is what he gets for toying with my emotions."

Stricken hadn't suspected that Franks had any dealings with Lana. It just went to show that even a spymaster's knowledge had its limits.

"Where?"

"I think he's meeting someone. He drove to this old, closed-down shipyard in Virginia—"

Before she'd even finished giving the street address, Stricken knew exactly where it was. "When did this call go through?"

"Almost two hours ago."

"Damn it." That was the problem with flagging so much suspicious traffic. As good as the software was, it still needed a human to listen to it to figure out if it actually meant anything. Paranormal Tactical would be there long before Stricken could get his own assets in place. Franks would probably kill the contractors—Stricken had expected as much when he'd put that PUFF out there—but he'd be ready to pick up the pieces. A sudden thought struck him. "Hang on a second. The succubus said Franks was meeting with someone . . . Who has eyes on Dwayne Myers?"

"Last log says he's still at the MCB's temporary command center."

"Contact our people there and make sure he hasn't left." The minion hurried and placed the call. It wouldn't surprise him in the least if that crafty bastard had already given his guys the slip. He began rattling off orders, knowing that his people would hop to. "Call our guy at Homeland Security. Have them tell the cops DHS is using that part of the shipyard for training or something. I don't want locals sticking their nose in this when they hear loud noises. Call the Air Force, get us a UAV, and see if there are any satellites available. Alert Dr. Bhaskara and have her ready the prototypes. They're going to Virginia."

"How many do you want to send?" asked one of his tactical minions.

There wouldn't be any screwing around with inferior monsters this time. "Send all thirteen."

"Sir, there's something else," said another geek. "We're running through the other calls placed from that number. Armstrong was just the first one. She's also called numbers belonging to Grimm Berlin, Uwharrie Security, and VSJ. The NSA is sending over the recordings now."

"Hell hath no fury like a succubus scorned." Stricken chuckled. Doubtless the recordings would all be the same, with Lana arranging a cut of the bounty in exchange for vectoring professional killers in on the thing that had hurt her tender feelings. He could appreciate a vindictive monster. "It appears Lana has quite the extensive little black book."

"I think she's sending all the Monster Hunters after him, sir."

He'd not seen the final count of who had shown up looking to collect, but there was really only one company in particular that concerned him. They were an annoying mix of unpredictability and effectiveness coupled with a very annoying sense of personal honor. "Out of curiosity, has she contacted anyone from Monster Hunter International?"

"No, sir. As far as we're aware MHI isn't participating in the search for Franks."

I'm disappointed in you, Earl....

The man who had called the MCB reported back, "Bad news, Mr. Stricken. They thought Myers was in a closed door meeting for the last hour, but he's gone."

"That's not bad news at all." That more than likely meant that his chief rival and pain in the ass was on his way to collude with a terrorist. That was treason. Nobody on the Subcommittee would bat an eye when Myers got killed at the scene. "Ready my helicopter. I'll be taking personal command on this one."

It looked like it might rain soon.

The ruins were quiet. The first time Franks had been to this place, it had been a marsh. The next time he visited, the Americans had drained the swamp and built a rudimentary shipyard capable of tending the wooden warships of the day. The time after that, it had been an industrial marvel, servicing great metal beasts destined for battle in the greatest war in the history of the mortal world. Now there were stickers on the fence warning that it was a Superfund toxic site, and everything was slowly decaying back into the ground. Despite man's industry, the swamp always won in the end.

Franks picked Myers out by the light of his cigarette. To his chemically treated eyes the glowing ash was a beacon. The senior MCB agent was picking his way slowly through the partially fallen walls navigating by the small bits of moonlight sneaking through the clouds. He was getting too old to blunder around in the dark. Myers passed beneath Franks' perch. He could have called out and alerted Myers to his presence, but he wanted to be sure Myers hadn't been shadowed. It was cold enough to be uncomfortable for a human, especially one who'd developed breathing problems because of his smoking habit, but Myers would have to wait until Franks was certain.

The shipyard covered a lot of ground. The newer section was still in use. This older portion was a maze of crumbling old buildings and rusting container cranes. It had been abandoned for years and had many escape routes. It was a good place for a clandestine meeting.

Myers walked for another thirty yards, trying not to trip on the weeds growing through the cracks in the asphalt. His memory was good though, because he stopped by the base of an old warehouse, only a few feet from where they'd taken down Don Francisco Asuncion Aramburzuzabala de Garza. Since that was a mouthful, and he had no respect for prideful undead, Franks had just called him Juan the whole investigation. They'd caught Juan here trying to sneak out of the country. The young agent had impressed Franks that night, so Franks had picked Myers to be his partner. They'd worked together off and on ever since.

Tonight, a much older Myers had known exactly when to show up, because that particular lich had only gone out during full moons. Tonight the moon was fat and white.

Franks was sitting in the second floor window of an old welding shop, dressed all in dark colors, invisible to anyone who wasn't using thermal, NV, or eyes like his. He'd seen the headlights when Myers had parked his car. He'd not seen any other vehicles but he heard a noise from that direction. It might have been a gently closed car door.

It turned out that waiting had been the correct decision because Myers wasn't alone. A few minutes later another man appeared following Myers' path. This one was wearing a dark coat with a hood. Franks had a sound suppressor screwed onto the threaded barrel of his Glock. One bullet to the back of the head and this problem would go quietly away, except Franks was curious enough to see who it was before he killed him.

He sensed nothing else moving except for the wildlife that inevitably came to live in mankind's abandoned places. Creeping along silently, the man passed almost directly beneath him. Franks stepped from the window and fell, landing in a crouch a few feet behind the watcher. He heard the noise and began to turn, but Franks had already engulfed him, wrapping one arm around the man's neck and placing him in a choke hold. He was quick thinking enough to try and drop his chin to prevent the choke, but Franks was too strong for that, and flexing one massive bicep was enough to squeeze off most of the blood flow to the brain. The man reached for his side, where he probably had a weapon holstered, but Franks simply grabbed hold of his wrist. The man struggled. He was strong by human standards, but Franks was strong by monster standards. He placed his legs against the back of the man's knee, breaking his stance and forcing him to drop back past his center of gravity, so the watcher's own weight helped render him helpless. Franks held on for a few seconds waiting for the inevitable blackout. Once the man went limp, Franks kept squeezing for a few more seconds, just to make certain he was really out, and then lowered him to the ground.

He scanned for other threats. Rendering the man unconscious hadn't made enough noise to alert Myers. Pulling the man's hood back, Franks found a familiar face. It was the MCB rookie, Strayhorn. That was unexpected. Had Myers brought backup? He'd been told that the critically injured Strayhorn had gone missing from the hospital. It was puzzling, so he grabbed Strayhorn's collar and dragged him through the weeds.

Myers saw the great hulking shadow approaching in the moonlight. "Franks? Is that you?"

"Yeah."

"I'm glad to see you. Are you okay?" Then Myers noticed that Franks was dragging a body. "Who is that?"

"Your shadow." Franks dropped Strayhorn in front of Myers' wingtips.

Myers blanched. "Is he—" Then Strayhorn groaned as consciousness returned. "Oh, thank God."

"Friend?"

"I told him to wait in the car." Myers knelt next to Strayhorn. He smacked the barely conscious agent gently on the face. "Tom? Can you hear me? Tom?"

"He'll be fine," Franks said.

Strayhorn began coughing. His eyes popped open and there was that brief moment of terror and confusion as his faculties came fluttering back. He saw Myers first. "Dad?"

"Well..." Franks scowled at Myers. "Huh."

"Yes, Franks, some of us have lives outside of the Bureau. I know that idea must perplex you." Myers stood back up, and grunted as his knees popped. "This is my son."

"Strayhorn?"

"He was a foster child," Myers said quickly. "It's a long story. Having a different name works though. Nobody likes to be accused of nepotism. Can you imagine the politics of being recruited by the MCB while your father is Acting Director?"

"No."

Myers shook his head. "Of course you wouldn't."

The rookie was still lying there, now watching Franks with more than a little bit of trepidation. "You scared the shit out of me."

"I thought Unicorn killed you," Franks stated.

"Dad warned me about Stricken's tactics, so as soon as I could, I snuck out of the hospital. I've been hiding since then."

Franks didn't like that. He'd seen the rookie take a round. Humans didn't just walk off gunshot wounds to the chest.

"It's okay. I'll explain later." Myers must have sensed Franks' unease. "We've got more important things to worry about now. Let it go, Franks. That's an order."

He supposed he wasn't currently employed by the MCB, but old habits die hard. "Yes, sir."

"The important thing is that Thomas saw multiple assailants and was with you at the beginning of the attack. He can corroborate your story."

That made Franks a little happier he'd not just shot him in the head.

The rookie stood up and rubbed his sore neck. "I want to help take this bastard down."

"You will. I've had a secret meeting with a few members of the Subcommittee. Most of them think I'm too biased. They say

I've been *compromised*, as if Franks is that charming. But not all of them are fools. I've delivered your affidavit. We have to tread carefully. Stricken's been laying the groundwork for a long time. I still don't understand his end goal, but it appears he was far more prepared to take drastic measures than I ever expected. As soon as it is safe to bring you both in, your testimony should be enough to shut Stricken down."

"That's not good enough. He'll weasel out of any trial. I want the son of a bitch dead. I want that albino bastard in the ground, him and his scumbags that shot up headquarters. *Dead.* That's what I want to help with, anything less is bullshit." Strayhorn spat.

The rookie was growing on him.

"Believe me, there's nothing I'd enjoy more. Stricken's a power-grabbing tyrant and this was his *Reichstag* fire. I've been focused on outside threats for so long that I didn't realize the cancer that Unicorn had truly become. Attacking him directly will only feed into the narrative he's created. Attacking those that support him will only make his hold stronger. I'm afraid Franks has given Stricken exactly what he wanted." Myers turned to Franks. "Your little manifesto has moved the President to Stricken's side. That rash action erased years of goodwill. That was idiotic. What were you thinking, threatening the President of the United States?"

"It wasn't a threat."

"Damn it, Franks! This isn't a game. You scared them. In try-ing to halt the thing you hate most, you provided your opponent all the excuses he needed to make it happen. You are your own worst enemy."

Franks had never been good at games, but it was unlike his superior to be this angry with him. By now Myers should have been used to Franks' methods. "What happened?"

"The President has approved a test run of Project Nemesis."

"Hmmm..." That meant Franks had a lot more people to kill. The to-do list just kept getting longer. "I warned him."

"Those supersoldiers already exist. I saw Franks fight one of them, and it sure as hell wasn't any normal man." Strayhorn said as he got to his feet. "I'm betting I'm right."

Franks nodded. "They were Nemesis."

"We know that, but I need to be able to prove their existence to the government. We need to demonstrate that Stricken had already proceeded without permission and created these things—"

"Hold on." Strayhorn said. "Why is that such a big deal any-way? Unicorn is lousy with monsters. What makes these things so special?"

"They are based on me," Franks said.

"Yeah, but why is that bad?"

Franks didn't answer. It was obvious to him, but The Deal had to remain a secret.

Myers tossed his cigarette and ground it out with his heel. "Any new living empty bodies created that are equal to or superior to Franks may end up being inhabited by powerful disembodied spirits... Specifically, they'll be claimed by fallen angels from the dimension we traditionally think of as Hell."

"What?" *How had Myers known that?* It was rare that anything bothered Franks, but that certainly did. "That's *classified*," he snarled.

"Not if you expect to stop this thing. I'd like to imagine that they never would have proceeded if they'd known what they were letting into the world. Nemesis was forbidden before, but the Commander in Chief just gave the go-ahead to make it official."

"Then I'll kill him too."

"And all of the men that come after him? They'll always be tempted. You can't put the genie back in the bottle, Franks. Man can't unlearn a technology, but he can understand the costs. You have to let them know what they've unleashed. As much as this pains me to say, for once the *truth* is our best weapon. We can't keep your secret anymore. The cost of this particular secret has gotten too high."

"How did you know about...me?"

Myers chuckled. "I figured it out on my own. I'm one of the world's leading monster experts, remember? I've known for years, but I never said a thing. I felt I owed you that much. I thought I understood your reasoning. It is hard enough for you to be accepted as a monster, but if they knew what lived inside the monster, I can't imagine what they would have done... Now I realize I should have told them the truth years ago, and it might have prevented all of this."

"You never told me that!" Strayhorn was looking back and forth between them, totally bewildered.

"Why would he?" Franks asked.

"That means Franks is...You're a..." Strayhorn seemed genu-inely shaken as he whispered, "*a demon...*"

Franks glared at the rookie. *Why did it matter to him?* "Shut up."

Luckily, he did. Strayhorn took a few nervous steps back.

"There's more to it," Franks warned.

"We've worked together for a very long time, old friend. You have risked your life to defend this nation countless times. It didn't matter to me what you were before, because I know what you are now. I've seen the other things that have escaped from Hell, and you're *nothing* like them."

Franks lowered his head. He did not like having *emotions*.

"I've got good men on the case. Stricken is a brilliant adversary, but he's not perfect. He's made mistakes and we will exploit them. You two are my eyewitnesses. I need you both to stay safe until we're ready for you to testify. Once we have solid proof, we can proceed."

"No."

"Damn it, Franks. You can't just murder and bludgeon and shoot your way out of this one."

"Watch me."

"I've always trusted you." Myers came over, gave Franks a tired smile and placed one hand on his shoulder. "Now it's time for you to trust me."

Then a sniper's bullet struck Myers in the back.

The retort of a high-powered rifle echoed over the waves.

"Cease fire, cease fire!" Klaus Lindemann said into the radio. Most of Grimm Berlin's men weren't in position yet. He was sitting on the side of the Zodiac in his wetsuit and SCUBA gear, ready to go over the edge. "Who was that?"

"It wasn't one of ours." Miesen was crouched a few feet away, only the whites of his eyes showing because his face had been blacked out with greasepaint. "Our snipers aren't in position yet."

"One of the three men I had on thermal has been hit." Reger was watching the feed from the tiny aerial drone they'd sent ahead. The UAV was a marvelous little device. The engine made hardly any noise; disassembled, it fit in a suitcase; and it could be launched almost as easily as flying a kite.

One of the thermal blobs was far bigger than the other two, so if Franks was here, that was probably him. "Was it the tall one?"

"Negative. The tall one is carrying the wounded man to cover. He's moving. He is remarkably quick for his size. Now he is picking up something. It is a large case or a box of some kind."

"Do not lose them."

They'd run the rented boats down the coast and had only cut the engines when they'd gotten close. The plan had been to swim in, nice and quiet. Franks would not be expecting an attack from the sea, and it had been faster than fighting the Beltway traffic to get out of the city.

More shots rang out, spaced just far enough apart to work a bolt. "If that wasn't us shooting, then who was it?" Lindemann asked. "I bet that blasted Hell-spawned whore must have tipped off someone else."

"Muzzle flash." Miesen pointed at one of the tall, rectangular cranes in the main yard. "There. The shooters are on—"

The top portion of the crane came apart in a terrible flash. Debris was thrown in every direction. The sound of the explosion reached them a moment later.

"The big one has a rocket launcher," Reger reported.

"Good heavens." *So much for going in quietly.*

"Should we abort?" Miesen asked.

He hadn't come all the way from Germany and squeezed into this ill-fitting rented wetsuit for kicks. "Start the engines. Get us to the docks now!"

There had been no hesitation. Franks had caught Myers as he fell, picked him up as if he weighed nothing, and then carried him to cover. In the second it took him to cross the distance, he'd pictured the way the blood had flown in the moonlight to guess the trajectory, calculated the speed and direction by the sound, and decided approximately where the shot had come from. The bullet had been meant for him. Myers had unknowingly stepped in front of it. Franks reached a crumbling brick wall as the sniper's next shot zipped past his ear.

Myers gasped when Franks put him down. There was a lot of blood. Franks ripped open his shirt. No vest, not that it would have done any good against a rifle round anyway. Myers screamed when Franks probed the exit wound. The main artery had not been severed. *Good.* It had gone clean through Myers' shoulder. No bones had been hit, so minimal fragmentation and no secondary wound channels, but the size of the exit wound indicated that the bullet had begun tumbling. There was a lot of tissue damage and internal bleeding. This was not something he could repair in the field.

Strayhorn dove behind the wall a moment later. He was quick for a human, but his reactions were nothing like Franks'. "Dad!"

"He needs a hospital or he will die," Franks said.

A chunk of brick exploded into dust over their heads. "They've got us pinned."

The rookie was correct. Franks might be able to move fast enough to get out of here, but it would be a risk. He could take a hit and survive, but if Myers got hit again, he was done. "Keep pressure on this," Franks ordered as he stood up. He felt a twinge and realized that the bullet had struck him after it passed through Myers, and it was lodged sideways in his hardened sternum. Franks stuck his fingertips in the hole and pulled the deformed piece of lead and copper out. It was .30 caliber, and if Myers hadn't slowed it down, it might have been enough to punch through to destroy one of his hearts. Franks dropped the hot bullet into the grass. *They will pay for that.*

The shooter was on top of a crane, approximately three hundred meters to the northeast. Since he'd scanned that area for threats earlier, they must have arrived while he'd been hiding and waiting for Myers. It was too far to engage with his pistol, but since he'd arrived early enough to scout the location, he'd hidden one of his big cases under a nearby piece of tin that had blown off a roof. He vaulted over the low wall and sprinted for it, knowing that the sniper would pick up the movement and track him through the scope. At this range, with him moving laterally, they would need to lead him to give the bullet time to get there to intersect the target. However, Franks was so unexpectedly fast that even an experienced rifleman would more than likely miscalculate Franks' speed, and by the time they corrected, it would be too late.

ZzzzTHWACK.

That one had been very close. The bullet had put a hole in his sleeve. Franks dove and rolled behind the debris. He was clear. He hurled the tin aside and opened the case. He had a carbine, but something else was in the way. The AT-4 wasn't so much on top, as it was just so damned big that he had to pack everything else around it. The 84mm weapon was designed to destroy armored vehicles, so it was overkill for an old industrial crane, but this asshole had just shot one of his only friends so Franks was in the mood for overkill. Franks tore the launcher free, sending other pieces of useful equipment bouncing into the weeds.

Putting the AT-4 over his shoulder, Franks stepped out into the open, and lined the iron sights up on the cargo crane. He didn't know where exactly the shooter was hidden in that mass of rusting steel and cables, but he only needed to get close, so he picked the spot that looked like the best sniper hide. A mighty bloom of fire filled the space between the old buildings and broke the remaining windows. It took over a second for the high explosive warhead to reach the target, and during that time he was glad to get a visual confirmation of a man with a rifle trying to get away.

The explosion was rather satisfying. It was difficult to tell amidst the expanding cloud of destruction, but from the number of flying body parts, it had been a sniper and a spotter team. That's what they deserved for putting a bullet into one of the only humans he knew who was actually worth a damn.

He dropped the spent tube. If there were two gunmen, there were more, and they'd be here quickly. "Agent Strayhorn, report."

"It's bad." He was trying to keep direct pressure on his father's wound. There was blood up to his elbows. "He's really weak."

Myers had to survive. Franks pulled a first aid kit from the case and tossed it at him. "Plug that."

Strayhorn unzipped the pouch and ripped open a pack of clotting powder with his teeth. It was a potent experimental product that had never been made available to the public, but the MCB didn't have to wait for things like FDA approvals. Strayhorn poured the powder into the wound and it immediately began to foam. Considering that the man who had raised him was bleeding to death in the weeds, the rookie was keeping it together rather well.

"Get out of here," Myers ordered through clenched teeth. "Save yourselves."

"Shut up," Franks and Strayhorn said simultaneously.

STFU would be coming for them. Franks would be the primary target, so he would make sure that they worked so damned hard that they wouldn't be able to pay any attention to their secondary targets. He rummaged through the case.

While he tended the wound, Strayhorn shouted, "What are you doing?"

"Providing a distraction." Franks had stowed some old decommissioned MCB armor. He wouldn't have time to fully suit up, but he threw the load-bearing vest over his coat and buckled it.

He'd need the pouches full of ammo and explosives. "Get him out of here."

Strayhorn hoisted his father up. Myers was barely conscious. He did not look good. Time was of the essence.

Beneath the armor was a Milkor Mark 14 repeating 40mm grenade launcher. Franks had *lost* it on a mission years before. The MCB penny pinchers hated how that kept happening to him... Franks picked it up. The gigantic, explosive revolver felt right in his hand. Shadows were chased up the walls by approaching headlights. Vehicles were tearing into the old shipyard. *Good.* Franks was suddenly in the mood for a fight.

"Once they're occupied, get to your car." Franks didn't wait to see if Strayhorn had listened. He had to strike fast. His pursuers would be expecting him to try to escape again. They probably wouldn't be expecting an aggressive, immediate response. Franks ran as fast as he could, leaping over rotting debris and ducking through crumbling doorways to cut through old buildings. Spider webs stuck to his face. He reached the nearest parking area just as several SUVs crashed through the chain link fence in a cloud of dust. More vehicles were following them. Armored men were standing on the running boards, and they jumped off as soon as the SUVs slowed. They hit the ground running, weapons shouldered, spreading out and looking for targets.

Franks stopped behind a steel pylon of an old water tower. He picked one of the vehicles and aimed. They were far enough away that he'd have to lob the low velocity shells in, but Franks had plenty of practice.

Bloop.

The 40mm grenade hit the hood and detonated in a flash. The men who'd been riding on the sides were ripped by frag. Franks shifted to another truck and fired again, then the next, and the next, before the first grenade had even hit. Franks cranked through six shots as fast as possible. The open area was filled with a sudden chain of explosions and flying shrapnel. Some of the SUVs were up-armored, and 40mm wasn't enough to pierce them, but it sucked to be the poor bastards out in the open. One shell exploded against the grill of a speeding Suburban. It would have been fine if the driver hadn't panicked and cranked the wheel too hard. It went up on two wheels, caught a pothole, and flipped over, sliding along on its roof.

Franks surveyed the damage. There were several men wounded and crying out, and many more bodies lying unmoving in the moonlight. One of the trucks had been unarmored and had caught fire. It drove into the side of a warehouse and stopped with a crash. The doors opened and men bailed out, followed closely by orange flames. On the back of that vehicle was a logo consisting of a gold PT but then the gas tank caught and the whole thing was engulfed in fire.

He'd been spotted. On one of the vehicles the sun roof had been changed into a turret. A man in a helmet came up through the hole and took hold of the mounted mini-gun, cranking it toward the water tower. Franks could withstand a few bullet wounds, but that wouldn't last at six thousand rounds per minute, so Franks ran to the side as the mini-gun opened up. One leg of the water tower was cut in half almost instantly. The empty tank toppled. The crash was loud, but more importantly, it threw up a cloud of old dust, and that provided concealment. There was a deserted factory building just ahead. The glass from the windows was long since busted out and boarded up, so Franks aimed his body at the flimsy wood and launched himself through, splitting boards like they weren't even there. He hit the floor, rolling hard through thick dust.

The gunner had tracked him through the haze. Light and sparks filled the darkness as tracers cut through the walls. His minigun fired so quickly that a hundred holes appeared seemingly in an instant all around him. There was a dark gap in the ground ahead of his face. The floorboards there were broken. Franks crawled toward it as the mini-gun sliced and diced the factory into pieces all around him.

There was no time to do it safely, so he just rolled into the hole. It was so pitch black that even his eyes couldn't see the bottom. Hopefully he wasn't about to impale his body on a bunch of rebar spikes. He'd done that before. It had been unpleasant.

He landed on his side with a grunt. It was only a twelve-foot drop, and the floor was only concrete. It took more than that to break his bones. From the noise, the mini-gunner was still ripping the place to pieces, and others had joined in as well. Dirt and splinters fell through the hole. The smell told him that something above had caught on fire. Strayhorn had better be using this opportunity to get Myers out of here.... Franks tapped one of the small LEDs on his vest, which provided enough light for

him to see. The place was filled with rusting machines that had
served an unknown purpose. There were stairs in the back. As he
walked he opened the grenade launcher, dumped the empties, and
began reloading the cylinder from the spare shells on his vest.

The gunfire tapered off. The Hunters would be cautiously
approaching his last position. His boots clanged on the metal
stairs. It was odd, thinking that Myers could die. He was angry,
of course, but anger was normal. This was something else as
well, and he did not like it. This unusual feeling rested in the
pit of his stomach, making him uncomfortable. The door at the
top of the stairs was chained shut, but Franks ripped the rusty
old handles off and shoved it open.

The factory complex was burning well now, but it had started
raining, so the fire probably wouldn't spread. It was a downpour.
Good. Between that and the smoke, the humans' visibility would
be impaired. Franks could see the beams of powerful flashlights
stabbing through the thousands of new holes that had been
placed in the walls.

Crouching, Franks moved through the broken glass and rusting
pipes until he reached a window. Most of the Hunters had gotten
out of the open and moved away from the burning SUV. One fire
team was coming up on his last known position. Franks spotted
the SUV with the mini-gun. Since it was so heavily modified, it
would surely be armored to withstand 40mm, but the gunner in
the turret wouldn't be. Franks came around the corner, sighted
on the man's helmet, and fired.

The gunner disappeared in a flash of light and meat. Franks
leaned out and cranked off the next few grenades at the men
searching for him, then put the rest into the remaining SUVs.
Explosions rippled across the yard, but Franks didn't see them.
He'd already turned and was walking away before the Hunters
returned fire.

Finally, Franks understood the sensation he was feeling...
Dread. Myers would die and Franks would be truly alone again.
It was anger mixed with sadness and also fear. He did not like
it one bit. He was not used to experiencing dread, so for forcing
him to feel it, Franks decided to make his pursuers experience
the same thing, but *more.* The Hunters were on foot now. Franks
drew the combat knife from his vest. Now they would know what
it felt like to be hunted.

CHAPTER 11

One difference between the famous book about my creation and the reality, I did not discover my true nature by seeing my reflection in a stream. I knew from the beginning that I was a monster. I'd observed enough to know this body did not resemble normal humans. It was of monstrous proportions, and the skin barely fit over the mismatched limbs and bulging muscle. It was grotesque, but it was mine. Neither did I learn to speak by eavesdropping on farmers, nor did I learn to read because I found a satchel of books discarded in the forest. I learned those things because, unlike the rest of the Fallen, I had come to understand humility. I could not do this alone. I had watched humans, but that did not mean I understood how they worked. If I was to survive in their world, I would need help.

They believed that they caught me, nearly bled out and unconscious, but they only captured me because I allowed them to.

Father's men welcomed me home with nets and clubs.

It was the age of the natural scientists, men like Newton and Leibniz, who used math rather than magic to unlock the mysteries. It had been Isaac Newton's defense of London against the Old Ones that had inspired Dippel to delve further into the intersection of old magic and new reason. His studies planted the idea of my creation.

Very few understood him. Dippel's experiments in soul transference were considered heresy and he'd been sent to prison before, *so he only worked in secret now. Dippel was banned from entering many countries, so he returned to the land of his birth to complete his great work. His laboratory had filled one tower of Castle Frankenstein with arcane machines. He had collected magical artifacts and ancient tomes from around the world and put them all to use. I had destroyed most of those treasures in a few seconds of madness.*

Dippel had been naive. Though he was a theologian of sorts he was grasping at straws now. He didn't understand the true nature of the soul. At first he did not understand what he had wrought.

We were alike that way. I did not understand then what it meant to be real. I was an aberration in the Creator's plan. I was an angry ghost wrapped in a deadly, powerful body.

Originally Dippel had dreamed of creating a new man that could be molded and taught. When he realized the magnitude of his mistake, he locked me in a dungeon, and began planning how to destroy the abomination he had created.

Dippel was one of the greatest minds who ever lived, but he was a terrible father.

Kurst had only flown a few times before. It was a magnificent feeling, but he was discovering that was true about many things in the mortal world. It was hard to imagine that he had been deprived of this for so very long. Two Blackhawk helicopters, packed with Nemesis assets and their STFU handlers, were speeding south. Out one door were the scattered lights of human habitation. Out the other was the endless black of the ocean. Kurst did not possess enough poetry to see this as any sort of metaphor for his existence.

All of them could hear Stricken's words through their headsets. "Ladies and gentlemen, the playoffs have started. Paranormal Tactical's snipers jumped the gun and engaged. The rest of them are moving in from the highway. It looks like the Germans are coming in from the ocean. Those clever Krauts are our reigning division champs, but this is still anybody's ball game." Stricken was watching the UAV feed on a small computer screen. "There are other Hunters nipping at their heels. Which one of these bitter rivals will get the ring and take on Franks in the big game? Who will take it? Who will reign supreme?"

Eventually, I will, strange human... "I do not know, sir."

The albino looked up at Kurst. "You have no idea what I'm talking about, do you, First?"

"I am no longer First Prototype. I have taken the name Kurst." He stabbed two fingers against the name stenciled on the ceramic breastplate of his body armor.

"Is that supposed to be symbolic or something?"

"You gave me permission to choose a name as Franks chose his own name. I chose this one. Does this not please you?"

"Sure, whatever. I'll leave the psychoanalyzing to Dr. Bhaskara. You're lucky I'm in such a good mood, *Kurst*, but anyway, there wasn't a lot of sports in that educational feed of yours, was there?"

His *education* had consisted of being continually bombarded with images and data while his physical body had congealed in a glass tube. He might not understand everything about the mortal world, but he at least knew the correct words. "A minimal amount. Enough for context."

"I should remedy that. You guys would be unstoppable. Fuck the draft. I should just sell Nemesis assets directly to the NFL... Come on, nothing, First? That was funny as hell."

Kurst forced the muscles of his face to smile.

"Shit. Don't do that. You're unnerving as fuck.... This is exciting stuff right here." Stricken went back to his monitor. "Looks like Franks brought some interesting toys. Fantastic. That son of a bitch is just standing there in the open... If this Air Force UAV we commandeered would have had some Hellfire missiles on it, Franks would be a meat cloud right now. I'll need to remedy that in the future. Stupid Posse Comitatus act..."

The albino's continuing narration did not amuse him. Franks was a prince. He deserved a prince's death. He would not be killed by some machine controlled by a human far from danger. He should die locked in combat with another warrior. Yet he could not correct his human overseer. Kurst knew that Stricken was incredibly dangerous. He had still not figured out all his dark secrets, for the albino had many, but he would know them eventually, and when he did, they would strike.

"*And* Franks just blew the hell out of Paranormal Tactical. Boom. Got some secondary explosions. Nice. They should have seen that coming."

Kurst looked across the helicopter's compartment at the twelfth and thirteenth prototypes.

Have you made progress on deciphering the code?

They were the most recently decanted. The male body was enormous, even more unwieldy with muscle than Franks, grown from the genetic material of humans who routinely won "strong man" competitions, but the spirit that had inhabited it was the least intelligent of them all. It had claimed its place in this body through brute force and the help of its self-proclaimed *sister.* That particular female form had been created from North African DNA, was of average size but great physical strength, and Kurst found her body strangely appealing.

There has not been much progress yet, the female thought back at him. *Stricken's fail-safes are complex.*

These two had possessed physical bodies in the mortal world before, and had done so successfully for over two thousand years, surviving because of the female's cunning and the male's great strength. Her previous earthly experience was why Kurst had tasked her with finding a way to defeat Stricken's kill switch.

Do not fail me, Bia.

I will not, General. I have made progress. I have been experimenting. There are ways to improve these new bodies. With sufficient willpower, this flesh is far more malleable than the human doctors expect. I can make us even stronger.

She had once honed an inferior vessel made of clay into a weapon superb enough to elude Hunters for centuries. The humans had known the two of them as Force and Violence, though Cratos and Bia could not use their real names any longer, since the MCB had cataloged them, and their picking such names would be far too suspicious a coincidence. It was not time for Stricken to know who he had let back into the world yet.

When that time came, Kurst was eager to see what manner of chaos Bia could wring from these superior bodies. *Excellent.*

"We'll be there in fifteen minutes," Stricken said. "Check your kit. Franks is going down."

Bia was careful to not let the albino see her snarl of disgust. Franks had been among those who had destroyed their last bodies, though it had been a human Hunter who had put a bullet through Bia's ear and placed her in the path of a speeding truck. Kurst almost pitied that human, because when Bia found the one called *Grant Jefferson,* the demoness would make his suffering immeasurable.

"We are not letting Franks get away this time, but it looks like there are a mess of Hunters converging on Franks' position, so that's probably not going to be an issue. We'll hold back and let the Hunters tire him out, then we'll swoop in and make sure the job is done. I don't like paying out that much PUFF, but as much as we've dropped on Nemesis R and D, it isn't like any of you are cheap dates either."

Figure out how to disable the kill switch soon, Bia, for I grow weary of the albino.

The Hunters of Grimm Berlin moved along the docks silently, communicating only with the occasional hand signal. It was raining hard, but they could still smell the smoke through it. Something was burning to the west and the red glow poked through the gaps between the buildings and containers.

Klaus Lindemann was halfway down the line, trusty G3K in hand. Several old ships were still moored here, too stuck in the mud to make it worth pulling them free to scrap them. The Americans had declared this place too polluted to be safe to work in and then left it to rot. The only difference between this place and some of the old industrial sites Klaus had seen in East Germany was that the graffiti was in a different language.

Their point man raised one fist. The Hunters passed on the signal and the entire group halted.

"Reger, any luck?" Klaus whispered into his radio, hoping that their portable UAV had turned up something useful.

"I do not have a visual on Franks. The last I saw he was in the biggest building to the west of you."

"Finding him would make life much easier." Klaus had a sneaky feeling that Franks was already long gone.

"I'm working on it. The rain is making it difficult to see. I've had to bring the drone closer to the ground, but that means a narrower field of view."

Their point man signaled for them to continue. It had been a false alarm. Grimm Berlin moved out.

"Do you have anything else, Reger?"

"Sorry, Klaus. Those other Hunters took heavy casualties and have pulled back for now. There are more cars entering the yard, though I do not know if they are from the same group of Hunters as before. Some cars left, but I believe they were evacuating the wounded."

"Could any of those have been Franks?" The golem had a reputation for being crafty. It would not have been surprising for him to try to slip away during the confusion.

"I do not think so. His last position was not conducive for such."

"What about the other two unknown persons who were with him?" They were not part of the bounty, but it was possible they could be interrogated for useful information if Franks did get away.

"Possibly. I tried to follow Franks instead of them. It was very confusing." Reger sounded extra apologetic through the earpiece. "Sorry."

"Warn me when we get close to the other Hunters. I do not want any jumpy Americans shooting us by mistake. And tell me when the police arrive so we can get back to the boats." Klaus had better things to do than be detained by American law enforcement. His last experience with them hadn't gone too well.

"I will warn—wait! I've got something. Franks is heading your way. He is one hundred meters to your northwest on the other side of those train cars."

They were all on the same band. The point man immediately took a knee and aimed his rifle in that direction. There was a brilliant flash of lightning, and Klaus caught a brief glimpse of that section of the yard. A building had once stood there, but it had burned down years ago, so all that remained was the skeleton of metal girders, now covered in creeping vines. The thunder followed a moment later.

Reger's voice was excited in Klaus' ear. "He's crossing the ruins now. He must be trying to escape by sea. You'll need to move up or he will pass by."

Klaus gave several quick hand signals, and the men who had been behind him spread out and hurried forward. From what he understood of Franks' physiology, they would need to concentrate fire and hit him repeatedly to have any chance of bringing him down quickly.

"Wait...He's stopped. Franks is looking right at the camera. He's heard the drone! He's aiming a pistol. Damn it! The feed is lost. I repeat, the feed is lost."

Franks had to be a very good shot to have plucked their tiny eye from the sky. Now they had to do this the old-fashioned way. If they held, Franks could slip past, or worse, the other Hunters might catch him first. Klaus signaled for all of his men to move up.

They'd sweep the ruined building and either catch Franks there, or flush him out. They had an MG3 on one of the Zodiacs. "Reger, move your boat and be ready to intercept him if he gets past us. If he tries for the water, use the machine gun. Everyone go to Lucie." Then Klaus let go of his radio and rushed to keep up with his men.

The full moon that had been so helpful on their approach had been obscured by the black clouds rolling in. He flipped down the LUCIE night vision in front of his eyes. The world turned into green and grey pixels. It ruined his peripheral vision, but it had become so damned dark in the last few minutes that without it they'd be tripping over themselves.

The building had been huge once, but after the fire, what remained was an ashen maze. Water was pouring down broken gutters and creating a racket against tin sheets. It would be dangerous, funneling them down into tight quarters, but delaying would give Franks the chance to escape, and he didn't have enough Hunters to form a proper perimeter. Besides, his men were extremely well trained and experienced in close quarters combat. Klaus caught sight of Miesen, waiting for instructions. Klaus held up three fingers, then gestured for Miesen to go left. The young Hunter nodded, picked two others, and ducked through a doorway. Klaus sent three more in on the right. He indicated for another group to stay put in case Franks doubled back, then he signaled for the rest to follow him through the main entrance.

It had been a large truck door, but the frame had partially melted, so now it was a big triangle. Weeds were growing through every crack, grasping at their feet. One of his men slipped as a pipe rolled under his boot and he fell into an oily puddle. The storm was making so much noise though, that it was doubtful Franks heard it. Gerhardt was one of his best Hunters, and he pushed ahead of Klaus without being told. Everyone at Grimm Berlin knew their leader had a tendency to put himself in front, and it would not do to get the boss killed. The Hunters slinked on as quietly as possible.

The poor vision within the warped skeleton made it feel almost as if they were in a forest. Rain washed across the ashen beams and turned the puddles into black sludge. Klaus was still wearing the wetsuit, with just his armored vest over the torso, so he was warm enough, but the air was moist and electric. They were close to their prey. An experienced Hunter could sense such things.

One of his men stepped on a loose board and it made a loud *pop*. Klaus froze. Hopefully Franks wasn't *too* close.

There was a rumble of thunder, but there had been another sound beneath it. Klaus raised his fist to halt the group. They spread out and took cover, each one watching in a different direction. He clicked his radio twice, then counted as each group leader sent him a return click. There was only one response. *Scheisse.* He'd thought the mysterious sound had come from the left. He keyed the radio. "Miesen. Come in, Miesen."

There was no response. Klaus signaled for the main group to move in that direction.

He was not certain which Hunter got on the radio, because his voice had become very high and squeaky. "Miesen is down. Franks came out of no—"

He was cut off. "Come in. Come in!" But there was nothing.

Gerhardt was fast and surefooted across the uneven, slippery terrain. Their point man leapt over a fallen beam and ducked beneath a dangling wire. Lightning flashed, momentarily causing the night vision goggles to blink out to protect their sensitive light-gathering electronics from being overwhelmed. When the view returned, Gerhardt was gone.

It had been so fast that he thought he'd made a mistake, but Gerhardt's Benelli shotgun was lying in a puddle. There was no sign of the rest of him.

"Halt!" Klaus shouted as he flipped up his goggles. "Lights on!"

Grimm Berlin instantly complied. Scalding light filled the broken forest.

Klaus ran to the side, trying to get a better angle. His man had to be there somewhere, but there was nothing. Then Klaus realized that the puddle was draining through a hole in the floor. There was another level beneath what had been crushed by the collapsing upper stories. Gerhardt had been pulled through the floor. "Franks is below us."

There was a gasp and a thud. Klaus spun around just in time to be blinded by one of his men's flashlights, then the light jerked wildly to the side and disappeared as the Hunter was dragged around a corner. Still seeing stars, Klaus rushed after him, but tripped and stumbled as his foot caught a loose board. He crashed into the wall, jabbing his shoulder on an exposed nail. Klaus cursed, pushed himself off the wall, and went to the corner.

His men were following. "Stay back and cover each other!" Klaus snapped. He went around the corner, ready to fire.

Schwarz was flat on his back. There was no sign of his attacker. Klaus knelt next to him and felt for a pulse. The Hunter was still alive, but unconscious.

There was a gunshot. A man screamed in pain. That time it had come from the Hunters sent to the right. Franks was a fucking *ghost*. "Everyone fall back! Get the hell out of here, now!" Klaus shouted into the radio. "Go. Hurry!"

Klaus let his carbine hang from the sling while he pulled Schwarz up by the straps of his armor. Schwarz was bigger than he was, but there was a certain measure of extra strength a man could find when fear boiled his blood. He got Schwarz into a fireman's carry and started back the way they'd come.

Most of his men were ahead of him, doing as he'd ordered. Klaus stumbled along beneath Schwarz's weight, the weapon-mounted light banging back and forth against his chest, casting wild shadows. One of his men had lingered to cover him.

A giant figure materialized in front of him. Before Klaus could react, one massive fist slammed into the side of his face. Lights and pain exploded inside Klaus' skull. He toppled backwards and Schwarz crashed into the floor. The other Hunter raised his weapon, but Franks was impossibly quick, and the Hunter's hand disappeared in a red spray as a blade cleaved through his wrist. The gun and the hand that had been holding it went sailing into the darkness before Franks kicked the crippled Hunter through a wall.

Despite being disoriented from the blow, Klaus went for his carbine, only to have a massive boot slam into his chest, ribs snapped, but worse it pinned the rifle down. Klaus immediately reached for his sidearm but stopped when a cold piece of steel was pressed hard against his throat.

Two white eyes appeared in the dark. Franks had blackened his face with ash. This was not a man, it was a terrifying avenging angel, come to separate the wheat from the chaff. Klaus swallowed, and the knife blade was so sharp that the motion drew blood.

"Germans?" Franks asked nonchalantly. He was studying the Grimm Berlin patch on Klaus' vest.

Klaus slowly, so as not to cut his own throat, nodded. He was not afraid for himself, only for his men. Schwarz was not moving.

The Hunter with the severed hand was moaning. He'd need a tourniquet quickly or he would die of blood loss.

Franks switched to German. "You are not with the ones that shot Myers."

So that was who had been wounded. "Kill me if you want, but I'd ask you to spare my men."

"Why should I?"

He was having a very hard time breathing. Franks had broken something, and the boot and much of the weight behind it was still crushing his chest. "They're good men, only doing their duty."

It was impossible to read Franks' emotions. The knife did not so much as quiver. "The bounty. How much?"

"Two hundred and fifty million American."

"Hmm . . . That's all?"

"Isn't that enough?"

"No . . . You're lucky." Franks removed the boot and the knife. "I've got a soft spot for German mercenaries. Don't follow me."

Franks melted back into the shadows and disappeared.

Klaus Lindemann got on the radio. He could only breathe with great difficulty. "This is Klaus. I'm in the ruin. We've got multiple wounded and need help now."

"On the way. We've still got men on the perimeter. Should they go after Franks?"

Klaus Lindemann had fought all manner of monster and beast, living or dead, from one end of the world to the other, and even into the realm of nightmares, but after looking into those cold eyes, Klaus understood that if Grimm Berlin continued on this particular hunt, death would be their only reward.

"Let him go."

Franks heard the helicopters coming in. He recognized the sound of the rotors as Blackhawks, so it was probably the MCB Strike Team or STFU. He didn't hear any Apaches. The Strike Team had access to a few attack helicopters, and those had enough range on their various weapon systems to stand off and destroy this whole place from so far away that he'd never hear them coming, so hopefully it wasn't the Strike Team.

If it was either of those groups, that meant they had probably brought in aerial recon, and it would be something a lot better than the glorified toy airplane he'd shot out of the sky a few minutes before. Franks maneuvered through the old buildings, trying to keep a roof over his head, but he knew that anytime he had a skylight or a gaping hole above him, they'd pick up his body heat. It probably wasn't an armed drone at least, or they'd already have bombed him.

The noose was tightening. If Strayhorn had not gotten Myers to safety by now, he never would. It was time to go. Franks stopped in the shadows and listened carefully. The Hunters who'd come in from the road had been hurt, but not all of them had given up. A few small teams had moved into the yard, refusing to give up. They were between him and the stolen car he'd used to get here. He'd hurt the Germans enough that he doubted they'd follow, but they were entrenched by the docks, so he didn't want to try going back that way.

The echo of the rotors changed. One of them was still heading this way, but the other had turned. It was moving inland . . .

If they had quality aerial recon they would have seen Myers escape. His distraction should have been more than sufficient for any normal Hunters. The only person who would care more about neutralizing Myers than capturing Franks would be Stricken. That meant the incoming Blackhawks were STFU, and now one of them was going after Strayhorn's car. Myers was still in danger.

Franks' mission parameters had just changed.

There was another engine noise barely audible over the rain, this time from the direction of the ocean. It was a powerful boat engine. The Germans had come from that direction, so it had to be one of their rides. It would also be the fastest way out of here. Franks ran toward the ocean.

Some of the Paranormal Tactical men spotted him and opened fire. They were fifty yards away, and didn't have a clean shot through the various pieces of cover, but they tried to make up for that with volume. As much as he would have enjoyed sticking around to kill them all, he simply didn't have the time. Franks spotted a drainage ditch, now mostly filled with runoff. It would take him to the sea. Franks jumped in. He hurried along, partly crawling, partly swimming, and partly being bounced about by water pressure. The ditch fed into a wide concrete pipe, so Franks let himself be carried inside.

The drainage pipe had a downward angle. Mold and slime made the sides so slick that Franks slid along quickly. He did not like not being in full control. Franks had never understood what humans found so entertaining about water slides.

Twenty feet later he crashed into a collected mass of garbage, old tree branches, and dead vegetation. There was a metal gate blocking the end of the pipe. *Damn.* Behind him, the PT Hunters were approaching. He was a sitting duck inside these narrow confines. Franks pushed through the refuse and grabbed the iron bars. The metal had been soft before it had become rusty, but it was still rather thick. As the mud crashed over him, Franks took hold of one bar, braced his boots on the slippery muck of the bottom of the pipe and pulled. It creaked and deformed, but it didn't break.

Flashlight beams filled the pipe. Franks quickly drew his Glock, aimed down the pipe, and fired at the lights. There was a yelp of surprise, and one of the lights was dropped into the water. One of the other Hunters had more fortitude than that, and began firing down the pipe. Bullets splashed through the muck. Franks felt the burn of an impact, but he ignored it, aimed at the muzzle flash, and pulled the trigger. The Hunter stopped shooting when the 10mm bullet hit his gun and tore it from his grasp.

"Mindy! That son of a bitch shot Mindy!"

Franks did not know who Mindy was. A muzzle appeared as a rifle was hung around the side. Franks shot that Hunter in the arm before he could accomplish anything useful.

It was momentarily quiet as the Hunters pulled back. Franks holstered the Glock and went back to bending iron bars before the Hunters realized they could simply roll grenades down the pipe. Franks roared and pulled with all of his might. The iron tore free, creating a gap. Franks put his shoulder against it and tried to push through. It was still too tight. He put a hand on the other bar and pushed, bending them further apart.

The Hunters were shouting behind him. There was a plop in the water, followed a few seconds later by an explosion. Tiny bits of hot metal ripped through his back. Water did not compress and the overpressure was extreme inside the narrow concrete confines. Franks could no longer hear anything but a high-pitched ringing noise. Blood was pouring out of his ears and nose. If he'd been human, the pressure alone would have killed him, or at least knocked him out to sink beneath the mud and drown.

They'd dropped that last grenade, hoping for gravity to do their work, but it had not rolled very far down the pipe before going off. They would not make the same mistake again. The next one would be tossed. Franks kept pushing. Blood welled through the palms of his hands. Metal groaned in protest. The gap was wider. Franks shoved himself against it, but the pouches of his vest caught. He backed up and unbuckled it, just in time to catch the splash of the next grenade out of the corner of his eye.

Franks shrugged out of the vest and squeezed through the gap. He still left a lot of skin on the rusty metal, but he was through. The pipe on this side was slick, open, and angled more steeply, so Franks let himself drop. The grenade went off above him, but Franks was already careening down through the darkness.

The pipe ended, and he was falling. It was a twenty-foot drop but into water. As soon as he hit, Franks angled himself down and started swimming. *Salt water. Current.* He'd reached the ocean. He didn't know how deep it was here, but he headed for the silt at the bottom. Franks cursed himself for not knowing how well STFU's aerial reconnaissance could see through water. He should have learned that . . . They were probably still tracking him, but there wasn't a damn thing he could do about that right now. So instead Franks concentrated on catching a ride out.

He swam along the bottom, pointing himself in the direction he'd last heard the Germans' boat. Franks could hold his breath for a very long time. His record was fifty minutes, roughly double that of the human world record holder, but that was only by cheating, holding perfectly still, and selectively shutting down the function of some of his internal organs. Right now Franks was bleeding from multiple wounds and exerting himself, so he'd be lucky to go a quarter of that before having to come up for air.

Franks stopped momentarily, trying to get his bearings in the muddy darkness. He took the opportunity to draw a folding knife, slice through his laces, and kick off his boots. They made swimming too slow. He could not see that much color in the dark, but the water around him would be turning red. It would be ironic if a shark ate him . . . But sharks instinctively knew better than to mess with a superior predator.

There. He felt the boat long before he saw it. Franks swam in that direction. A black shape was bouncing across the surface to the east. As he got closer he could tell it was a rigid hull inflatable boat. The hull was a deep V in the water. It was coasting along now, engine idling, but it would be fast, and Franks liked fast.

They would be looking toward shore, so Franks swam beneath it, coming up on the far side.

Breaking the surface, Franks listened, but realized that he still couldn't hear very well. The explosion had rattled his head. He pulled himself up over the side. There were two Hunters on board. One of them felt the lurch as Franks' weight rocked the boat, but Franks covered the distance and clubbed him over the head. The other was at a pintle-mounted machine gun at the bow. He turned just in time to catch a fist to the stomach. Franks hurled them both over the side.

Four hundred yards away a Blackhawk was hovering over the burning shipyard, playing its spotlight back and forth. The drone must have lost track of him at some point. STFU was joining the search. The chopper was still moving at least twenty miles an hour, but figures moved to the door and slid down the rope so quickly and with such effortless grace that they could only be Nemesis assets.

The smart thing to do would have been to fire this thing up and run for it. It would take them a minute to realize he'd stolen the boat, and by then he could be back on land and have already stolen a new vehicle and gone after Myers.

But those were Nemesis... And that just pissed him off.

The machine gun the Germans had brought was a Rheinmetall MG3. It was basically a modernized version of the same exact machine gun the Nazis had used during World War II, so Franks had been shot at by a few of these things. A long belt of 7.62 hung out the side. Franks looked at the machine gun, then at the helicopter, and back at the machine gun... The idea made him happy.

With a cyclic rate of over a thousand rounds a minute, Myers wouldn't have to wait *that* long.

Franks got behind the machine gun. He knew from experience how tough a Blackhawk was, and even if he forced it to crash, at that altitude the passengers could survive, especially soldiers based on his own nearly invulnerable physiology, but no system was perfect, and bullets were persistent.

The machine gun roared.

His eardrums were damaged, but he heard *that*. A line of orange tracers filled the air. Franks manhandled the heavy weapon, guiding it with an artist's touch. Franks could write his name in cursive with one of these. He started with the vulnerable tail

rotor and didn't stop until he was positive he'd seen pieces flying off of it. Then he tracked bullets along the chopper's body,
through the open door, and all through the compartment. The
angle changed as the pilot tried to maneuver away, so Franks
switched to pounding the engines. The chopper spun wildly and
a Nemesis soldier was hurled out the open door.

The Germans had attached a few hundred-round belts together
and the MG3 just kept on dragging armor-piercing death out of the
ammo can and spitting it out the muzzle at twenty-seven hundred
feet per second. The rain hit the machine gun and hissed into steam.
Smoke was coming out of the Blackhawk's engines, but Franks just
kept on hammering them just to be a dick. It rotated as something
broke, giving him another angle on the open door. Bullets ripped
through the crew compartment again, piercing Nemesis soldiers.
Then he must have gotten lucky and tagged the pilot, because the
chopper suddenly lurched sideways. The rotor blades caught the
edge of a cargo crane and exploded. The Blackhawk dropped like
a stone, disappearing behind one of the warehouses.

That had been...satisfying.

Now back to work. Strayhorn would be taking Myers to the
nearest hospital, and Franks knew exactly where that was. The
Germans' boat had a radio. He had to protect Myers until legiti-
mate authorities were involved. He owed him that much.

There was some splashing and thrashing off the side. He had
not been lying to the German Hunter earlier. It had been Hessian
mercenaries who had taught him to act human, so Franks tossed
a life preserver overboard for the two Hunters, slightly lessening
their chances of drowning. That was his good deed for the year.

He pulled the flask of Elixir from his pocket. This would be
unpleasant, but this was going to be a multiple-dose kind of night.
Then Franks went to the controls and pushed on the throttle. The
powerful engine roared and the Zodiac surged across the waves.

The helicopter was on its side. They'd fallen on top of a structure. Kurst could tell because of the concrete and rebar that had
smashed through the sheet metal next to him. It had struck him
in the arm hard enough to break the armored bone, causing a
compound fracture. He marveled at the jagged white splinter
sticking through his forearm before using his fingers to shove
the bone back into place.

Smoke was filling the interior. The engines had caught fire. Kurst got up and assessed the situation. The human pilots were dead. A human handler was unconscious. Stricken was...*gone*? The albino's laptop was wedged between two seats, broken. Kurst had lost track of Stricken during the crash. Perhaps he had been hurled out the door. That would be far more convenient than removing him in a manner which could potentially raise questions that would cause his underlings to throw the kill switch. Only half of his brethren had been in this helicopter, and several of them had already fast-roped out before they'd been hit. The other Nemesis soldiers were extracting themselves. Seven had received a laceration across the throat, severing her windpipe, so she was having some trouble. That wound could be duct taped closed enough to keep her breath from escaping for the duration of the mission. Five had been the unlucky one. When the rotor had come apart, a large piece of the shrapnel had flown through the compartment, slicing off one of his arms and the top half of his skull. There were brains everywhere. Like Franks, they had reserve brain tissue, but the impact had broken Five's spine in multiple places so the backup was not working.

Kurst placed his hand on Five's chest. The Fallen spirit was still clinging desperately to the mortal body, but it was slipping. The bond could not be maintained. Five did not have the will sufficient to overcome such wounds.

Go back for now. I will provide more bodies in the future. You will return, brother. Until then tell the host to prepare for war.

The demon let go, drifting away with the rising smoke.

Kurst took hold of Seven and shoved her up through the door. Her blood got in his eyes. He left the unconscious human to the fire. Then Kurst pulled himself out with his uninjured hand.

He stood on top of the helicopter, surveying his new kingdom as the flames rose up around him. The rest of his squad was waiting. Three had been thrown from the helicopter and shattered both of his legs on impact, but the rest were combat-effective. *Find his trail. We will pursue Franks to the ends of this world.* Kurst stepped off the edge and walked away as the ammunition inside the Blackhawk began to cook off.

Remarkably, Stricken was alive. He did not appear to be wounded, or even emotionally shaken. His suit was not even dirty, or even particularly wrinkly for that matter. He'd even taken an umbrella with him, and had opened it to stay out of the rain. He was watching the burning chopper, the firelight reflecting on his sunglasses. Stricken did not look like he'd just been through a terrible crash at all.

The albino has even more secrets than I expected.

"Damn it... This is why we can't have nice things. You have any idea how many strings I have to pull in order to requisition good military equipment for Task Force use, First?"

"Kurst."

"Whatever." Stricken waved his hand dismissively. "Somebody get me a radio. I need to contact the other chopper."

Kurst removed his radio from his armor and handed it to his superior. Stricken made contact with the other team and began giving orders. *The albino is slippery. Make note of this for when the time comes to eliminate him.* Stricken may have possessed a few dark magic tricks of an unknown nature, but demons were very thorough.

"Okay. If you've got a visual on our buddy, get your ass back here and pick me up now. Wait. On second thought, leave a couple of our special troops on him to make sure the deed is done. I want a body. I want this shit *confirmed*....Yes. We'll pick them up later. Leave a babysitter with them to make sure they don't get too crazy, then come get me." Stricken handed Kurst back his radio. "It looks like it was Myers that was wounded. They've got him trapped. How are we doing here?"

"One KIA. Two seriously wounded. The remainder are combat effective." And just in case Stricken cared about the lesser beings, Kurst added, "The humans on board were KIA except for you, sir."

"I was lucky."

"How did you make it out?"

"Don't worry your pretty little head about it. That's an order."

"Yes, sir." *Regardless of what manner of man you are, you are still just a man.* As much pleasure as it would bring him to crush the disrespectful insect, Stricken had not yet outlived his usefulness to the host. "I am requesting permission to pursue Franks."

He glanced at the fire. "It seems I'm fresh out of handlers..." But Stricken was mulling it over. "Can you keep a low profile?"

Kurst did not care about their *profile*, but lying would give him autonomy, time away from prying eyes, and another chance at the one being he hated almost as much as the Creator Himself.

"We have been trained for discretion when working among civilian populations."

"I'm taking a serious risk here. Bagging Franks once and for all is worth it, but if one of you gets caught in the act, keep your mouths shut. You're not even supposed to exist yet." Stricken was a cold, calculating thing. It was remarkable that his immortal spirit had sided with the Creator in the war before time in order to be born. Kurst suspected that Stricken would have made an excellent demon. "Permission granted. Take a few. Leave me the rest."

"Yes, sir." He began walking toward the others.

"One last thing, *Kurst,*" Stricken called after him. The albino pointed at his temple with one long, thin finger. "Don't disappoint me, stay in contact, or I'll make sure you get a really *nasty* headache. I'm talking about the kind that causes all the blood vessels in your brain to pop right before all your cells melt into a caustic sludge. You were expensive, but you are still replaceable. Don't fuck this up. You hearing me?"

"You have been heard, sir."

CHAPTER 12

Darmstadt, Landgraviate of Hesse-Darmstadt, Holy Roman Empire, 1703

The creature had been secured to the stone walls with chains sufficient to anchor a large ship. A rope was tied around his neck, placed so that the harder he pulled, the tighter it became. The first time the beast had regained consciousness, he had nearly strangled himself fighting against the chains.

It was watching them silently, as was the norm. It was probably correct to refer to it as a he, as all of the parts he had used were from male cadavers, but Dippel could not help but think of his creation as an it. The creature could not communicate except through inarticulate roars and bellows, and despite Johann Konrad Dippel's firm conviction to science, there was something about it that caused a general sense of unease.

"I am afraid I imbued the fiend with far too much physical strength. Will these measures hold should it become agitated again?"

"I assure you, Herr Dippel, escape is an impossibility," the chief workman stated, pride apparent. It had been rather difficult to find a craftsman both capable enough to engineer a solution, and willing to remain silent to the church and local authorities that the eccentric who lived in their nearby castle had created a monster and was keeping it locked in the basement. His services had cost a fortune. "A team of oxen could not break those links."

213

"*Thank you, good sir. Your reputation for quality puts me at ease...*" Not entirely, but if science and human understanding were to be furthered, risks had to be taken. "*It is said that it was your forefathers who forged Emperor Maximillian's Iron Army.*"

"*Perhaps... My family's work has long been as reliable as our ability to keep a secret...*" The chief workman held out one hand expectantly. Dippel handed over the sack of coins. He quickly hid away the princely sum inside his coat. "*I know it isn't my place to ask, but what do you intend to do with this beast?*"

That was an excellent question. He was not quite sure yet. "*That will be all.*"

The chief workman bowed and took his leave of the dungeon, obviously glad to be free of the dreadful place and its unholy denizen. Dippel knew that he had a reputation for being a bit odd, but it was not his fault that the masses were so profoundly ignorant and oblivious to the mysteries of the universe.

The creature continued to watch him. Emotions were difficult to read upon its mangled face, but it seemed calm, observant, nearly studious even. Dippel went to the corner and picked up the musket his servant had left for him. "*Do you see this? This is a weapon. Should you attempt to harm me, I shall use it to put a lead ball through your heart. I do not wish to destroy you, but I shall if you make such actions necessary. Do you understand?*"

All he got in response was a curious tilt of the beast's head.

"*The only reason I've not shot you already is because then what would I have to show those know-it-alls at the university? To think they called my marvelous Elixir a fraud—oh, and how I cannot wait to see the looks upon their faces when they see you.*" He pulled up a stool and sat down far out of his creation's reach, and placed the musket across his knees. "*Can you understand me at all?*"

The creature blinked.

"*I find myself in the curious position of attempting communication with a thing, which despite its vast presence, may only have the intellect of an infant or an insect.*" Dippel sighed. "*I was so focused on the creation of life that I did not think through the aftermath of my unlikely success. To you I am probably producing a series of articulate noises, with no means to unravel the mystery of their connotation. I imagine that I will have to teach you what each noise means by degree.*"

It was difficult to tell, but it appeared that the creature's mouth turned into what appeared to be a scowl of confused consternation.

"Ah. Let us begin then!" Dippel exclaimed, believing that he'd seen some spark of emotion other than rage. He pointed at his chest. "I am Johann Konrad Dippel. You are"—he pointed at the monster—"a hideous fiend, but nonetheless you are my creation and the living embodiment of my genius. You will need a name eventually. But for now let us begin your education."

He would simply treat the newborn monster like a newborn child. Sadly, he had never been good with children. Dippel picked out a torch on the wall and gestured at it. "That is fire. Fire!" The beady, mismatched eyes had followed his gesture. "Fire. Say it with me. Fire."

The creature moved his mouth. The sounds that came out were not correct at all.

"You call that hideous manipulation of the tongue fire?" Lazy pronunciations simply would not do. "Fire! Bad! It is fire, my idiot beast. I would hope that not all babies are as profoundly stupid as you. I'm afraid this education shall take forever."

The creature glared at him, and there was a slight flexing of huge muscles, as if it were contemplating testing the new chains, but then it let out a noise that was very much like a resigned sigh.

The lessons continued.

Tom Strayhorn had blacked out when the car had been run off the road and crashed. He must have hit his head.

Something grey was in front of him. It turned out to be a deflated airbag. Blood was drizzling from a cut on his head and beating out a red pattern on the airbag. He was hanging from his seat belt. The car was tilted downward at a very steep angle. He was freezing cold. As he came to, he realized it was because his legs were submerged in cold water. Focusing past the airbag, there was nothing but black rushing water on the other side of the broken windshield. For a brief moment Strayhorn thought they were sinking, and he thrashed against his seat belt, only to realize that the water wasn't rising. They were stuck. The car was nose down in the river.

He didn't know how long he'd been out. He remembered that he had been driving fast along a curvy road, calling for help and giving their position over the radio, when a helicopter had appeared in front and blinded him with a spotlight. He'd tried to keep going, but they'd opened fire, hitting the engine...He'd swerved and then the windshield had shattered...It was all very fuzzy. He couldn't even remember where he'd been going in such a hurry and why somebody had been chasing them.

The helicopter's spotlight filled the car with white light. The rotors were getting louder as the helicopter descended.

Correction. Was still chasing them.

There was a moan. It all came back to him in a rush. *Dad!* Dwayne Myers was still in the passenger seat. Luckily, he'd taken the time to buckle him in first or he would've gone out the window. "Dad? Are you okay?"

"Go, Tom," he ordered through pink, gritted teeth. "Run."

"Hang on. I'll get you out of here." He got himself unbuckled, and fell against the steering wheel. "I've got you."

Dad's skin was far too pale under the spotlight. "No. Save yourself."

"You're coming with me." It was hard to work at this angle. He tried to get himself under his father so he wouldn't just tumble through the broken windshield and into the river when the seat belt came off. Dad's chest was slick with blood.

"I'm sorry, Tom. I never told you the whole story...I should have."

Franks was a fallen angel from Hell? That was a lot to take in, but he hadn't really had time to think about it yet. "Don't worry. I wouldn't have believed you anyway." The buckle was stuck. "Damn it." He got the knife out of his pocket, flicked it open, and began sawing through the strap.

"Should have...You deserved the truth, but I kept it from you all those years."

The nylon was tougher than it looked. The wet cold was making his hands shake. Strayhorn gritted his teeth and kept sawing. "Keep talking, Dad, help's on the way." *Maybe.* He'd called it in, but he didn't know if the other loyal MCB agents would get here in time. Meanwhile, a helicopter full of shadow government assholes was on top of them, and his foster father was bleeding to death. "Franks doesn't know about me, does he?"

"No. When your mother gave you up, I took you in...Either that or Unicorn would have taken you, thinking you might be an asset someday...I couldn't let that happen...We never knew what you'd inherit."

"Sadly, not enough." He was only human, mostly. The seat belt snapped. Strayhorn caught him as gently as possible.

"I don't think Franks can love, but I think maybe he loved her." Dad was delirious and mumbling.

It was dark again. The helicopter was moving away. Strayhorn froze, waiting for the strafing to begin, but it kept getting quieter. Then he could hear the rain against the car and the rush of the river. Unicorn was leaving in a hurry.

Then a voice came from just outside the car. "I see two inside. They are still alive."

Shit. Some of them had stayed behind. Strayhorn drew his pistol, but he couldn't see anyone through the reeds outside the window. He craned his head over his father's shoulder, but the car was at such a steep angle that the view out the back window was useless.

"Special Agent Dwayne Myers. Are you in there?"

"Fuck off," Myers sputtered.

"I'll take that as a yes," said the unseen man. "Mr. Stricken sends his regards."

"That wannabe dictator can lick my balls." Myers was so weak that they probably didn't even hear his defiance.

"Sir, a vehicle is approaching. May I have your permission to eliminate Myers before witnesses arrive?" asked the first voice.

"Granted."

They opened up with full auto. Bullets struck the car. The passenger side window broke and showered them with safety glass. Stuffing flew out of the seat. Metal rang as holes were punched through. Myers gasped as something hit him. "Dad!" Strayhorn felt an impact in his side. "Aaah!" It was like being hit by a hammer. Desperate, he lifted his 10mm and fired it wildly out the back window. He still couldn't see anyone, but hoped that it would force them to take cover. It worked. The shooting stopped. Strayhorn fired until slide lock, then brought the pistol back, fumbling for a reload.

His foster father was a dead weight resting on his shoulder. "Hang on, Dad, hang on."

"You guys are supposed to have superstrength. Let's see it in action. Mr. Stricken wanted to be certain. Drowning's pretty damn certain. Second, flip that car over."

"Yes, sir."

The Crown Vic lurched. They were high centered on the bank. There was a metallic groan and the car shifted. More river water poured into the cab. Their rear end was already in the air, but now someone was beneath it, pushing. Strayhorn pointed the Glock through the back seat, trying to guess where the super-soldier had to be. He started shooting, hoping that something would get through the undercarriage for a lucky hit, but it didn't do any good. They were suddenly vertical, and Strayhorn fell against the dash. His father landed on top of him. Black water rushed in all around them, and then they were toppling over. Desperate, Strayhorn wrapped his arms around his father and tried to shield him as the car toppled onto its roof.

He took one last desperate gasp of breath as water exploded through every opening, instantly filling the car. They were sink-ing, the two of them spinning around inside, blind, not even knowing which way was up. *Stay calm. Stay calm.* Seconds later, the car's roof hit the muddy bottom, and the interior somehow became even darker.

The pain in his side was intense. Strayhorn knew he was badly hurt. He had to get out before he lost too much blood, but he wasn't going to leave his father behind. He kept one hand on his dad, and used his other to grope through the mud. He didn't know if it was the injury, the cold, or the fear that was making him so clumsy. He struck the center post, used that to orient himself, and then pushed his dad out the window. Lungs burn-ing, he followed. There were lights flashing above. It wasn't that deep. *Thank God.* Holding onto his father for dear life, scared to lose him, Strayhorn kicked for the surface.

He came out into the rain, gasping for air, only to find himself in the middle of a firefight.

There were muzzle flashes and geysers of water as bullets hit the river. At first he thought it was Unicorn trying to finish them off, but the gunfire was coming from somewhere else. A vehicle was parked at the top of the hill, flying the red and blue flash-ers of an unmarked police car. The doors were open. A figure was on the driver's side, firing a rifle down at the men who'd pushed them into the river. While the first shooter laid down covering fire, someone bolted from the passenger side of the car and made it to the tree line.

There were three STFU assassins. Two of them didn't seem

too concerned they were being shot at, while the last took cover behind them. "Protect me!" shouted the one in hiding. The other two calmly raised their weapons and shot the living hell out of the car.

Strayhorn pulled Myers close and swam for shore. *Is he breathing?* He was too scared to tell. He hit some rocks and pulled himself up. The motion made the pain in his side so intense that he almost blacked out. Then the pain subsided a bit, though he still wanted to puke, but he got Myers' limp body up onto solid ground. He crawled up next to his father, and a diluted red puddle immediately began to collect on the rocks beneath them.

The way that the two men were standing there, caught in the open, taking rounds, but seemingly not caring, meant they had to be some of those Nemesis things. He'd seen how fast these things were before, so they probably could have taken out the shooters if they'd felt like it, but they were holding their ground for some reason. The small figure cowering behind them was the one calling the shots. Strayhorn was filled with an anger so intense that he could taste it over the blood in his mouth. He'd lost his own pistol in the river, but the butt of his father's Smith & Wesson 610 was sticking out from under his coat. A 10mm probably wouldn't do shit to a supersoldier with a body based on Franks, but it would ruin this asshole's day. Strayhorn pulled the revolver out of the holster. Dad had taught him how to shoot on a gun just like this.

Hands shaking, he put the gold-bead front sight on the leader's back and pulled the trigger. *Hit.* The man lurched forward, crashing against one of the Nemesis things, but he didn't fall. He had to be wearing a bulletproof vest. *Fuck that.* So Strayhorn cranked through the remaining rounds in the cylinder as fast as he could pull the double-action trigger. It was dark, raining, and confusing, but there was a flash of blood and something white—teeth maybe—flying through the air, and then the STFU operative collapsed.

One of the Nemesis soldiers kept on shooting at the flashing police lights, but unfortunately the other one turned and looked right at them. Strayhorn aimed at him and squeezed the trigger. *Click.* He was empty. The soldier tilted his head, seemingly confused to see that they were still alive. For Strayhorn, the moment stretched into eternity. The enemy's gun came up, pointed right at them.

The bullet meant to finish him off skipped off the rock and buzzed across the river.

The Nemesis soldier had stumbled when something had struck him in the chest. He turned, glaring downstream, but before he could raise his weapon against the new threat, a machine gun roared, chewing into his ceramic armor. Blood sprayed in the flashing lights. He went prone, trying to avoid the fire, but the machine gunner followed him down. The Nemesis soldier had to have been hit at least twenty more times before the machine gunner changed targets and started putting rounds into the other one's back.

Strayhorn couldn't believe his eyes. Agent Franks was walking along the riverbank, hip-firing a huge black machine gun, a belt of gleaming brass dangling out the side. The belt got shorter as Franks got closer. He kept shifting the muzzle back and forth, ripping into the Nemesis soldiers.

They were armored and incredibly tough, but they were taking too much damage. Both of them were up and moving quickly, putting distance between them. However both were concentrating on Franks now, which meant nothing was stopping the men from the road from engaging them—

BOOM!

And apparently the one in the trees had a .50 cal.

It hit a Nemesis soldier in the back. The impact tore an exit hole the size of a cantaloupe from his ceramic chest plate. Blood sprayed for twenty feet as he went to his knees.

Franks shifted the stream of tracers against the other, systematically ripping him to pieces. The soldier's rifle was flung away as a bullet tore his fingers off. The last of the belt disappeared and the machine gun was quiet. The Nemesis soldier looked down at his mangled hand, but that didn't stop him from drawing a combat knife with his other hand. He charged Franks.

Swinging the machine gun like a great big club, Franks batted the soldier across the bank. He bounced off a tree with a resounding *crack*. Franks covered the distance in a flash, raised the machine gun, and smashed the soldier over the head. He raised it to hit him again, but Franks suddenly dropped the improvised club and took a step back, one hand instinctively flying to the new hole in his bicep.

The other Nemesis soldier had drawn a pistol and shot Franks, but before he could get off a second round the heavy rifle in the trees roared again and the top of the soldier's head flew into pieces.

Franks went back to finish his damaged foe. The Nemesis soldier was pushing himself out of the broken tree trunk, when a big knife appeared in Franks' hand, and he began systematically slashing and stabbing. It was a blur of motion, strike, cut, curving and twisting, and back to strike again. They moved away from the tree, the soldier striking, but his movements were becoming increasingly sluggish. Franks kept on slicing. It was an astounding display of brutality. Every time the soldier moved, Franks caught the limb and cut it open. Franks was dispassionate and methodical as he worked the soldier over, slicing through every exposed bit of flesh, until there was nothing left that hadn't been perforated.

The soldier tried to kick him, but Franks caught his foot with his injured arm, drove him back into the tree, then ran the blade all the way from the knee, up his inner thigh, and deep into his groin. Franks twisted the blade through the pelvis, ripped it out, and then used the soldier's leg to hoist him up, spin him through the air, and then hurl his body against the rocks so hard that bones *exploded*.

Holy shit...

Strayhorn crawled to his father's side. He put his ear to Myers' lips. He was barely breathing. "Come on, Dad. Stay with me."

Two men were running down the bank—Jefferson and Archer. "Myers, is that you?"

"He's over here." Strayhorn tried to yell, but found that he could barely raise his voice. The pain in his side had been replaced with a cold, tingling sensation. Consciousness was fading. He'd been hit worse than he thought. He'd died before though... He could come back. Dwayne Myers couldn't.

Franks had dragged the crippled Nemesis soldier over and dropped him on top of the one missing most of his head. He went to Myers and Strayhorn, grabbed both of their collars and pulled them the rest of the way out of the river. "Status?"

"Bad," Strayhorn gasped. Then he coughed and blood shot from his mouth.

Franks looked at his side. "Gunshot wound. Severe fragmentation. Bubbles... Lungs are perforated." He put one big hand on Strayhorn's ribs, and Strayhorn was surprised how gentle it was, or maybe it just seemed that way because he was going into shock. Franks frowned. "Blood color... Liver hit. That will be fatal."

"You suck at delivering bad news."

"I'm sorry." Franks moved over and knelt next to Myers and took his pulse.

"Dad told me you were never sorry about anything."

Franks bowed his head. "He was mistaken."

He'd been too late. Franks had seen thousands of mortals die. He knew the signs too well. Myers was fading. There was nothing that could be done at this point.

Myers cracked his eyes open. "Franks?"

"I am here."

"How's Tom?"

Even at a time like this, Franks didn't even think to lie to comfort him. "Dying."

"He'll get over it... He takes after his real father that way."

Huh? Before he could ask for clarification, the other two agents had reached them. "Archer." Franks nodded toward the mutilated bodies of the Nemesis creations. The demon spirits had latched on and were refusing to let go. Their redundant systems were keeping them alive. "They'll heal soon. Burn them."

"Yes, sir." It didn't matter that Franks was technically a fugitive, had been relabeled as a monster, and was the most wanted man in the world—when he gave an order MCB agents followed it. Archer ran back toward their car to get an incendiary.

Like the demons, Myers was only hanging on by sheer willpower. "Grant..." Myers whispered.

"I'm here, Director." He knelt next to him.

"You remind me of myself."

"Thank you, sir."

"I was a dick at that age too... Now go help Tom."

Jefferson looked to Franks. It wouldn't do any good, but most humans did not like to die alone. Franks nodded. Jefferson went to help the rookie.

"I will avenge you," Franks said. He did not really know how to comfort anyone.

"Finish this, Franks, but don't tear the whole country down to do it. Promise me that."

"Yes, sir."

A hand tapped his shoulder. Franks thought about tearing it off, but these agents had been loyal enough to Dwayne Myers to come here, so he let it go. "What?"

Jefferson sounded very hesitant. "I'm sorry, Agent Franks, but you need to see this."

Surprisingly, Strayhorn was sitting up. He had a glazed look on his face and a small bottle in his hand. A single drop of liquid was rolling down the side of the bottle. It was *glowing*. The drop sizzled when it hit Strayhorn's fingers.

"The Elixir of Life," Franks stated.

"He had some on him. He just drank the whole thing," Jefferson said. "I didn't know."

The rookie had just committed suicide. It would speed up his inevitable end, but he'd picked the most painful way possible to do it. The government's best scientists had never gotten the mixture to work on any mortal-born being without the Elixir's forced purification ripping their imperfect bodies to pieces. Strayhorn should have just asked Franks to put him out of his misery and been done with it. Shooting him in the head would have saved them all time.

All the other human test subjects from over the years would have been vomiting blood by now. Strayhorn dropped the empty bottle and it rolled into the river. The expected convulsions were not starting. He struggled to his feet, and stood there, wobbling. The rookie's blood-soaked shirt was hanging open. All the capillaries around the bullet hole were glowing blue.

"Probationary Agent Strayhorn. Reporting for duty." He was incoherent from the blood loss. Even on Franks, the Elixir needed time to work.

"How?" Franks asked suspiciously as he reached for his Glock.

Myers touched Franks' arm. "Turns out . . . your descendants can use the Elixir."

Franks didn't have *descendants*. "Impossible."

"It's true," Myers whispered.

Strayhorn stumbled over and fell next to Myers. "I tried, Dad. I'm sorry." He put his head down on Myers' chest and began to sob.

Franks couldn't tell if it was tears or rain that was rolling from Myers' eyes. "Can I do—"

"It's in your hands now, Franks. All of it. The mission . . . Our safety . . . I've made mistakes. So many mistakes . . . But I tried my best. I always did my . . ."

Myers trailed off.

Franks stayed there, kneeling in the rain. Dwayne Myers was dead. *I have failed.*

The mortal world would never understand what a valuable defender they had just lost. Even mortals on the same side of this war could never know all that he had sacrificed to protect his country. Myers was one of the only humans he'd ever known who had the guts to do what was necessary.

There was a sudden flash of heat as the bodies of the Nemesis soldiers were engulfed in flames. Only Franks could hear the piteous wails of the demons being cast back to Hell. It was a stark contrast to how Myers' spirit had gone peacefully to his reward. The emotion hit him then, a sense of loss so profound that it was physical. He roared at the universe, and then slammed his fist into the rock so hard that his bones cracked the stone. His incoherent bellow slowly died off.

I have failed you.

Franks looked at his shaking fist and the blood leaking out around rock shards embedded in his skin. The word HATE had been tattooed on his knuckles by the arm's last owner. The word was so faded now it was almost invisible. The mortal flesh was weak and temporary. The eternal was unyielding. He had failed Myers. He would not fail their mission. He would not fail his part of The Deal. The muscle tremor passed. Hands steady, Franks reached down and gently closed Myers' eyelids.

"Good-bye, my friend."

Franks stood up. There was still work to do and people and demons in dire need of killing. Stricken would pay for this. Anyone allied with Stricken would pay for this.

Jefferson seemed to be shell-shocked. Archer was waiting there with an empty gas can in hand, staring at Myers' body. Strayhorn got to his feet, swaying, appearing that he might collapse at any time. *Could I have a son?* That was not part of The Deal, but he would ponder on that later. Right now, the agents looked as lost as Franks felt.

The rain kept on falling. The four of them were in a circle around their fallen leader. Lightning cracked across the sky.

They looked to Franks for guidance.

"What do we do now?" Archer asked.

"Fucking kill everything."

CHAPTER 13

I spent years in that dungeon. Our conversations grew better over time. They had to, or I would have murdered him in frustration. Unlike the humans, my memory of the before had not been wiped entirely, only damaged. It did not take long for me to understand how to act human. My spirit had spent years observing them. I secretly had a head start.

It was Father who taught me how to speak. It took time for the language centers of my once-dead brain to begin working again. He talked a lot. I mostly listened. Even then I wasn't much for talking. Humans talk too much. It's like you never shut up.

He taught me to read. Every day he would bring me more books, theology, philosophy, and history. I would read them by the light of a torch. Father had a great library by the standards of the day. I read it all. I did not like poetry. Poetry is stupid. You must have to be born to appreciate that stuff.

He continued to improve his creation. Using a modern term, we worked the bugs out. The scientists of that day employed legions of body snatchers and grave robbers. As better raw materials came in, Father replaced my more obviously flawed parts. He would operate without anesthesia, trusting in the tightening of the chains to hold me down as he sawed my limbs off or the Elixir burned me pure. I would advise him when things felt correct. My understanding of correct was limited to what hurt and how much.

Father openly wept after seeing the new face that he had stretched over my skull. His creation was no longer quite such a hideous fiend.

As I looked upon my reflection in the mirror I decided that I could finally pass for a human . . . At least an ugly one. If the light was bad.

I never told Father the truth about what I really was. It was better that way. He was able to live out the rest of his days unaware what he had let into the world. I was not burned at the stake. Everybody was content.

Until the Hunters came.

2 Days Ago

Michael Gutterres stopped his new motorcycle outside the industrial park's fence and watched the activity. The Feds were out in force.

After his flight had landed at Dulles, he'd had a taxi take him to a bike dealership. It was nice having a credit card with no limit, even though whenever he turned in his receipts he always got a lecture about how their order was funded by the donations of widows and orphans. So he'd treated himself to a Ducati 1199 Panigale. It was much nicer than the piece of crap he'd used in China, and would be worth the lecture on fiscal responsibility.

The nearby property was swarming with suits and blue windbreakers. Most of those had to be MCB. He'd listened to the news on the way over. They were reporting that the abandoned shipyard had been used for a military training exercise, but a helicopter had crashed and started a fire. It was a typical MCB cover story, and nothing compared to their recent work in Las Vegas. It was hardly convincing. This had Franks written all over it.

"This is Gutterres. I'm at the scene. I'm going to see if I can pick up the trail."

"Confirmed. Once again, we would prefer to not make our presence in this endeavor known, Michael," said the ever helpful voice in his radio.

"Duly noted, Father." He took his helmet off so he wouldn't have to listen to any more useless advice. They always asked the locals to support him. His assigned clerical support could be helpful at times, but usually they were just annoying. This one in particular seemed more worried about avoiding scandals. Gutterres didn't care about politics; he was in this to protect the innocent from the forces of evil.

The Secret Guard of the Blessed Order of St. Hubert the Protector was the oldest Monster Hunting organization in the world.

Their best historians believed that the patron saint of Hunters had gotten his start freeing the Merovingian countryside of were-wolves in 682 AD. Their official charter dated back to the twelfth century. Even most of the other Monster Hunters in the world had never heard of them. There weren't that many of them left, their occasional heavy lifting was done by the Swiss Guard, and it was rare that one of them ended up working in America. The Secret Guard tended to work in the places that the rest of the civilized world ignored or forgot, but the less fortunate needed protection just as much as the wealthy.

However, this was Franks they were talking about, who was a very special case, which meant the Vatican's best problem solver got to return to his home country.

This was as close as he was going to get to last night's fight without being spotted by the MCB, so it would have to do. He pulled the holy relic out of his coat. A regular St. Hubert's Key was simply a metal bar that could be heated up and used to cauterize wounds, usually as a treatment for rabies in the days before germ theory. This one was special. This one was the first Key, forged by Hubertus himself, and it had been used to cauterize bites from things a whole lot worse than rabid dogs. It was said that the legendary Bartolomeu Zarco Cabral had driven this very Key through Baal's eye at the battle of Cordoba, but he figured that was just the archivists messing with the new guys so they wouldn't lose any of the sacred relics they signed out of the vaults.

He extended his hand, palm up, letting the iron bar rest there. The early Hunters had been forced to deal with all the same horrors they still faced today, only those poor bastards hadn't had access to good explosives or modern firearms. They'd had to improvise, adapt, and survive. The Key was a leftover from those days, but it was still pretty handy for things like this.

The bar slowly turned. The porous old metal grated across his skin. Normally it would pick a direction and stay there, pointing toward an unholy being the same way a compass would point at magnetic north, but here, the Key was being tugged in a few different directions. He was used to minor things like imps or lesser demons screwing things up, but these pulls were all strong, so strong that they could be confused for Franks.

Gutterres swallowed hard. That was *very* bad. He was going to need to send for reinforcements.

"Show me the eldest."

It took a moment to turn, suggesting that Franks had covered a lot of ground since he'd left this spot. The Key stopped, pointing due west.

Franks had eluded them again.

This was beginning to frustrate Kurst.

He had begun their search where Myers had crashed. A pair of his brethren had been left to confirm the kill, only they had lost contact. By the time Kurst and the others had arrived, those two physical bodies had been burned to ash. The human overseer's body had been mutilated. The trail of shell casings and blood told the story. Franks had been here.

Cratos had dived into the river and searched the submerged car. It had belonged to the MCB. Eight, who had been known in the before time as Thymos, had found the boat Franks had stolen downriver. Bia discovered the tire tracks of Myers' rescuers and followed them back to the main road.

As ordered, Kurst had called in the information. Humans would be sent to gather evidence. Kurst suspected they would discover nothing of use.

He knelt next to the puddle of blood. The spray had kept it moist enough not to completely dry. Two mortals had bled here, but only one had perished. *Curious.* They had taken Myers' corpse with them, whether to unnerve Stricken that his rival might still be alive or out of the strange human respect for their dead, he did not know, but Kurst could sense the lingering death in this spot.

Bia joined him at the riverbank. *I know who Franks left with. I recognize his scent.*

Kurst looked at her. *How?*

You never forget the man who killed you.

It was not the sort of thing they could reveal to Stricken, but the information could be of use. *I will destroy Franks. You may have the humans.*

The local authorities had not been here yet. No one lived close enough to have seen the fire through the trees and Myers' car was completely submerged beneath the water. Kurst would be able to justify leaving the scene. They would keep moving, just as Franks had. They returned to the vehicle that they had taken from one of the Hunters at the shipyard. The Hunter had tried to stop them, but Cratos had casually broken his neck and tossed him in a dumpster. There had been no witnesses and in the confusion the humans would probably blame that murder on Franks as well.

Franks was picked up by MCB agents. They must have been following Myers to the rendezvous. They must have radioed Franks where to intercept our brethren. Franks knows MCB vehicles are tracked. He will get rid of it. They will have procured a new one.

Bia got on the radio. "November One Three requesting a GPS check on the closest MCB vehicles to our current position. Over."

A moment later they got the response from STFU headquarters. *"November One Three, there is an MCB unit three clicks west of you. Sending you the coordinates now."*

They reached the highway. The next available establishment was a gas station, convenience store, and fast food restaurant. Kurst knew that was the right place even before they received the address. Their stolen vehicle needed fuel anyway, so Kurst pulled in next to a gas pump. There was a red flash in his side mirror. The familiar face of a greater demon was watching him through the glass.

We must speak.

Very well. The horned red face faded. Kurst would go inside for this meeting. It would not surprise him to discover that Stricken was keeping an eye on them with that drone. Kurst got out of the SUV. Nearby humans were watching them curiously. Their advanced ceramic body armor was out of place. Kurst had not thought of that. He was still getting used to having a body, let alone thinking about what to cover it with.

Cratos and Bia went looking for the MCB car. Thymos tried to put gas into their vehicle, but was having some trouble operating the machine. Their educational bombardment had included basic familiarity with such things, but apparently this machine was different, and Thymos had not been on Earth long enough to do anything so mundane as *pump gas.*

"No. I do not desire a car wash, foolish computer. Dispense fuel!"

Across from them, a corpulent pig of a human was putting gas in his truck. He'd seen their odd manner of dress and was studying their vehicle. "Hey there. Going to a science fiction convention or something?"

"Or something," Kurst stated.

"What's PT stand for?"

"It stands for *fuck off!*" Thymos shouted as he punched the gas pump. The fat human turned his head in fear.

Kurst walked into the fast food restaurant. It was breakfast time. The few humans inside stopped shoveling processed dead animals into their wet face-holes long enough to glance at him, and then away, not paying any respect to their obvious better. They were weak and stupid. They had been granted the ultimate glory of a mortal body melded to an eternal intelligence and this was what they did with it? He hated them so much...

Once inside the bathroom, Kurst drew his combat knife, and began scratching the ancient symbol into the mirror over the sink. A human was standing at a stall. He flushed, saw Kurst vandalizing the glass, and fled without washing his hands.

When the symbol was in place, the ancient demon's visage appeared. The wide, flat skull, thick curling horns, and razor-sharp teeth were impressive. Now that was a *proper* physical body. If Kurst's body looked more like that, then the humans would know to grovel before him.

Greetings, General.

"What do you want?" Kurst snapped.

To offer you freedom from your servitude. My master has found a way to slip your captor's bonds.

The demon was speaking of the device Stricken had implanted into all of the Nemesis prototypes' heads. Kurst could feel it there, waiting. Once again, Kurst was a mere victim to a creator's whims. The idea filled him with rage.

"How?" he demanded.

My master has drawn many to his flock. When the Dread Overlord was destroyed, he gained the fealty of the Sanctified Church of the Temporary Mortal Condition. Their necromancers are artists in the sculpting of flesh. They developed a serum, distilled from the blood of vampires and lycanthropes, but their mortal bodies proved too weak to use it, and all who partook perished. For your mighty will, controlling it would be nothing. The toxins the albino has placed in you are designed to work against your current body. The Condition's serum will enable you to change your physical body however you see fit.

There was a commotion inside the restaurant. Someone had begun screaming. There was a loud crash. He would have to make this quick. "This would give us the ability to shape-shift?"

Yes. You could become invincible. You would be immune to the albino's poison. This serum can render your vessel into whatever form you desire.

Franks had his precious Elixir of Life to keep his body like that of the humans, but Franks had never suffered from too much imagination. Kurst liked the idea of twisting his form into something altogether better. "In return, you expect me to exchange one form of slavery for another?"

No. The master offers this to you as a Gift. The decision to join us and lead his army in the coming war remains yours to make.

A flame appeared on the bathroom wall. It burned through the tile, leaving a molten trail until it formed a circle. There was a flash of light, and the tile disappeared, leaving a dark portal to somewhere else. A vial dropped through the hole and fell into the sink. There was another flash and the portal was gone. Kurst picked up the vial of red, glowing liquid. The sludge crawled up the inside of the glass, as if seeking the warmth of his fingertips through its cage.

A single drop will be sufficient to purify your form. There is enough there for all of you who exist now and hundreds more to come.

"I accept this Gift." Of course, he would test it on some of his brethren first.

The demon dipped his horned head. *You are wise, General.*

Kurst shattered the mirror with his fist, scattering the symbol.

Returning to the restaurant, he found that Cratos and Bia had killed everyone inside. Bodies were strewn across the floor. One human had been tossed on the grill and it was creating an obnoxious smell. Stricken would not be pleased, and until Kurst knew whether this serum worked or not, that still mattered. "Why?"

Cratos pointed at a body he'd thrown through the cash register. "That one looked at me funny."

"Because you took his breakfast burrito. Humans do not like that," Bia said as she unscrewed the sound suppressor from her pistol and put it away. "We found the MCB car in the parking lot. There was no indication of where they would be going next."

The large one was rummaging around behind the counter and held up a handful of the frivolous toys meant for the children's meals. "Yay! Can I keep them, General?"

Kurst was frustrated by this development. It would take too much time to match up all the dead humans with which vehicle was missing. "No. In fact I should destroy you for your stupidity."

"Sad..." Cratos put the toys back.

They walked outside. The corpulent human who had dared question them was curled up on the ground, in a spreading puddle of gasoline, trying to cover his eyes as Thymos sprayed him with the hose and screamed, "I will not be addressed by my inferiors!"

It is time to leave.

Thymos dropped the hose, but with the nozzle still running. The puddle expanded, growing toward the restaurant. They climbed in. Bia tossed a thermite grenade out the window as they drove off.

Cratos giggled. "Pretty sparkles!"

They were on the highway before the expanding fireball had been recorded by the aerial surveillance drone and the details relayed back to STFU headquarters. *"November One Three. We've got an explosion near your position. Please confirm, over."*

"This is November One Three. Confirmed."

"Task Force Actual wants to know if you have acquired the target?"

"Negative." Kurst looked at his soldiers and frowned. It was doubtful Stricken would consider this a successful field test. So much for gaining more autonomy. "There was a complication."

A new voice came on the radio. *"Return to base immediately,"* Stricken ordered.

Kurst felt the warning throb inside his skull. It let him know that failure to comply would result in immediate death. "Yes, sir, returning to base."

He held up the red vial and studied the necromantic sludge in the sunlight. *We will obey...For now.*

I feel really hung over...

Tom Strayhorn woke up on a counter top. The piercing brightness burning his eyes was sunlight peeking through broken miniblinds. When the room stopped spinning he realized the place was a dump. The walls were covered in old water stains. The broken roof tiles were covered in mottled green bits of mold. Strayhorn tried to sit up, but his muscles didn't want to work. He was numb and queasy.

"Don't move."

A gigantic shadow blocked the rays of sun. It was Agent Franks.

He was wearing a blood-splattered butcher's apron and a surgical mask.

That was a rather unnerving sight to wake up to.

"Where are we?"

Franks had a small bottle in his hand. He stuck a syringe in it and withdrew some liquid. "An abandoned truck stop in West Virginia."

He couldn't remember anything after Dad's death. The whole thing was like a really bad dream. "What happened?"

"I sedated you." Franks stuck the needle in Strayhorn's arm and depressed the plunger. "How do I have a kid?"

"Wait...Sedated me. Why?"

Franks scowled at him. He didn't seem to like being interrupted or being asked questions, and Strayhorn had just done both. "The Elixir can heal *most* things." There was a bag full of bloody surgical tools next to him on the counter. Franks picked up a mirror and angled it so Strayhorn could look down at his torso. His abdomen had been sliced open from one side to the other, and then roughly sewn shut with what had to be a hundred ugly stitches.

"Oh shit..."

"Your liver was ruined. I replaced it."

"I got a liver transplant? By you?" He glanced around at the moldy, rotten, roach-infested truck stop. *"Here?"* Hopefully whatever Franks had just shot him with was antibiotics. "Wait...Who did the liver come from?"

"The STFU handler." Franks shrugged. "You shot him in the mouth. Organs were still good...Don't think he drank much. The Elixir will force it to work. Now shut up."

Strayhorn did as he was told.

Franks pulled over a chair and sat down. The old thing creaked under his weight. Even sitting, Franks still seemed to tower over him. "Myers wouldn't lie to me. How do I have a child?"

Strayhorn wasn't sure how to answer that. Franks' DNA was an ever-evolving conglomeration of his various parts. "You mean, like biologically? Well, you've got human parts..."

"It better be the anesthetic making you stupid." Franks sighed. "Who is your real mother?"

Strayhorn told him.

"I see." Franks slowly nodded. If he felt any emotion at all over that revelation, he kept it hidden.

Strayhorn had been waiting to meet his real father for a long time. This was *very* different from how he'd imagined it as a child. "She abandoned me when I was a baby."

"Where is she now?"

"She killed herself."

Franks showed absolutely no reaction.

"I bounced around a lot in foster care. I ran away a few times, lived on the street, got arrested and put back in the system. Then when I was a teenager, Dwayne Myers found me and gave me a home...." Strayhorn tried to wipe the sudden tears from his eyes, but his arms still didn't want to respond with enough coordination to do it. "He was a good man."

"Yes. What did Myers tell you?"

"I didn't find out about any of this until I was an adult. Growing up I just thought Dad was some sort of secret superspy. He never talked about what he did. We moved a lot. He'd get a call then disappear for weeks at a time. There were mysterious guys in suits showing up at all hours to bug him. That sort of thing. When I asked how come he'd found me, he'd said he'd known my real father, but he always talked about you like you were dead. He made up some bullshit story and I believed it. I grew up. Tried to play baseball, just like he did, but I wasn't good at it. I joined the military, then the Marshal's Service. I met my first monster before I ever knew about the MCB. Once I got recruited, imagine my surprise to find out my boring old foster father had been in charge of the whole damned thing. He never even so much as wrote me a letter of recommendation. Yeah, Dad really was that much of a hard-ass when it came to things being top secret. I never suspected what he really did until I was part of it."

"OpSec," Franks stated.

"Screw OpSec. I had to be *cleared* before I could know about my real father. Then he tells me it's you and you're not only still alive, you're not even human."

Franks gave a noncommittal grunt.

He was so incredibly sore that it hurt to talk, but it felt good to get the story out. "He warned me not to talk to you about it.

I think he figured I would meet you, and that would be enough and I'd let it go. I think he was worried you'd freak out."

"I do not *freak out*."

"They said that about you. I didn't just learn about monsters in the academy, but I've got my Dad telling me that I was part monster. The only reason I ever had the little, screwed-up family I did was because Myers took pity on me. He learned about me, and just in case I inherited some of your weirdness, he didn't want me being summarily executed or scooped up by something like Unicorn. Once I knew who you were, I bugged him for a chance to be on your detail. Of course, this isn't the reunion I always imagined growing up. Son of Frankenstein. Wow."

Franks just shook his head.

This was really awkward. "I know, I know. Fictional doctor, not the . . . Monster? Creation? Sorry."

Franks picked up a paper cup from the table. The glow told him it was the Elixir of Life. "How'd you know about this?"

"Car accident a few years back. I was brain dead and on a respirator. Dad figured it was worth a shot . . . He didn't explain how I came out of the coma until I was in the MCB though . . ." Strayhorn chuckled. "When it came to secrecy the old man had such a stick up his ass that he was like a corndog with legs."

"Heh . . ." Franks *almost* smiled.

He had to ask. "What happened with you and my real mother?"

"Classified."

"Go to hell. Myers never told me. I want to know."

Franks mulled it over. "She was a witness. I was ordered to intimidate her into silence. Instead, she . . . found *comfort* in my presence."

"I bet you don't get that much."

"It is unusual, but has happened a few times before. We were together for a short time. Then she left in the middle of the night. I never saw her again."

"Why'd she kill herself?"

Franks stared at him for a long time. "I don't know."

"Then guess."

"She finally realized what I really was." He stood up and pulled off the blood-covered apron. "Jefferson and Archer are outside. I'll be in contact in a few days." He began walking away.

"Wait? That's it? Just like that you're out of here?"

"Yes." Franks tossed the bloody apron on the floor.

"I thought maybe you'd want to talk..."

Franks paused. "Why?"

Strayhorn didn't really know what to say to that. "That's what people do."

"I am *made* of people...Do not mistake that for *being* one," Franks said. "You wish to talk? I'll talk. You'll listen. Your existence is unexpected, but changes nothing. The mission comes first. Myers wanted you alive to testify, so that's what you'll do. Jefferson will gather agents who were loyal to Myers. I still have to destroy Nemesis. There is a type of magical device which can detect a demon's location. I know where such a device is stored."

"Where?"

"Alabama."

"That's a long drive. Lots of traffic cameras." Franks had done something to modify the bone structure of his face since they'd first met, but Strayhorn didn't know if it would be enough. "You'll be seen."

Franks pointed at a cooler on the floor. "I kept his liver and his face. I will wear it like a mask."

Holy shit. That was creepy.

"No wonder my mother left you..." It was one thing to find out you'd been sired by a monster built from spare body parts, it was another to find out that he was a fallen angel who'd escaped from Hell. "What Dad said back in the shipyard, about you and Nemesis—"

"True, but *classified*."

"Got it." Even when Franks was attempting to be conversational, he was very intimidating, but Strayhorn pushed on. "When you said she realized what you are, you're not talking about her knowing you were the idea behind Frankenstein. She knew that already, didn't she?"

Franks didn't so much as blink.

"But she learned what you *really* are. She couldn't handle the idea that she'd fallen in love with a demon."

"I informed her." Franks lowered his head for a brief moment as he thought it over. It was the only sign of weakness that he'd ever seen from Franks. "That was a mistake. It can be...*difficult* for a mortal to deal with such truths. This is why my origins must remain classified."

"Does that mean that I'm a..." Strayhorn really didn't want to finish that particular sentence.

"You possess the spirit of a normal human."

"Oh, thank God."

"Yes, thank Him. I don't know how your existence fits with The Deal, but if your body had been inhabited by one of the Fallen, I would have destroyed you already."

"Wow. Thanks, *Pops*."

"Don't call me that...*ever*." Franks picked up the cooler and left the room without another word.

The last twenty-four hours had been hell. Franks had shot down one of his helicopters, killing one of his precious prototypes and injuring another so badly that it had to go back into the vat to grow new legs. Then Franks had killed two more saving Myers, and now Myers was missing, out there plotting who knew what manner of nefarious bullshit. The blood analysis suggested that Myers had lost so much he was probably dead, but with that sneaky bastard, nothing was confirmed until they had a corpse on a slab. Until then, Myers was just one more thing to worry about. Then some of his prototypes had decided to slaughter a bunch of civilians and blow up a gas station, which could have been a complete fuck-up with the administration if he hadn't thought fast and blamed that on Franks too.

He could tell his supporters on the Subcommittee were getting cold feet. If the President punked out now, all of his efforts would have been for nothing. Stricken popped some extra strength Tylenol and got back to work.

He'd just gotten through chewing out the prototypes for burning the gas station. They'd had a good excuse. They thought they'd seen Franks inside, and that was enough to justify an immediate, violent response. They'd been mistaken, but they'd still been forced to eliminate the witnesses. They were programmed not to lie to him and their version of events was plausible. He'd thought about flipping the kill switch and annihilating them, or at least the big stupid one, to serve as an example to the others, but it had been his call to send them without an overseer, and he was already down a few units. So he chalked it up to a learning experience.

Stricken's office at the STFU bunker was completely unadorned. There were no pictures, commendations, or awards on the walls.

There wasn't even a nameplate on his desk. In fact, there was nothing on his desk except for his computer. He liked it that way. It was a habit formed over decades of working undercover in foreign hellholes. The less he had, the less he'd have to burn or shred if he needed to leave in a hurry. Nice and simple. *Clean.*

Unfortunately, now he had to take care of some more STFU personnel matters, and that would be anything but clean.

There was a knock on the door. His secretary stuck her head in. "Mr. Stricken, Heather Kerkonen is here for her appointment."

"Send her in."

The redheaded werewolf came into the office and his secretary closed the door behind her. Kerkonen really was a good-looking woman, though her nose was too big, and it wasn't like something capable of regeneration could get plastic surgery. But right now she was too apprehensive to be pretty. She had never been summoned to the STFU command center before, probably had never had a clue where it was, or if a central physical location even existed at all. Stricken liked to think of his assets as mushrooms, where the best way to grow them was to keep them in the dark and feed them shit.

"Impressive place. I expected the big office, but I kind of figured you'd have a view."

"Figuratively speaking, most of my career has been underground. Why should it be any different now that I've reached the top? Please, have a seat, Heather."

There was a single chair in front of his desk. She eyeballed it like it was a trap. Her body language suggested she had probably been expecting tarps on the floor to catch the blood. Heather was playing it cool, but she was nervous. He could tell she was testing the air, using her heightened werewolf senses to see if he had brought any help. He hadn't. He really didn't need to. Brute force was for suckers.

She sat down. "You wanted to see me?"

"No. I had you brought to my top secret lair for kicks." Stricken tapped his long, thin fingers on the desk rhythmically. "I figured maybe you'd want a commemorative snow globe from our gift shop."

"I was kind of hoping for a shirt. *I put up with the shadow government for two years and all I got was this lousy T-shirt.*" Heather didn't even bother to hide the fact that she hated him. Most of his assets at least made some effort. Even his weird ones, like the guy whose eyeballs had been sucked out by a rage ghost, or the creepy-ass Spider, made some effort to suck up.

Stricken made a big show of being disappointed. "I had such high hopes for you, Heather. I took you in, gave you valuable training, and provided you with an opportunity to serve your country, and all I've gotten for my benevolence is attitude."

"What do you want, Stricken?"

"I want to know why you're poking around in Task Force business you're not cleared for."

She was stone-faced. "I don't know what you're talking about."

"You've been asking around about Project Nemesis."

Heather's eyes narrowed. She was trying not to show it, but Stricken could tell she was doing the math. If he meant to do her harm, she would make a run for it, but she'd probably try to take his head off first, just on principle. "I don't know, Mr. Stricken. What is Project Nemesis?"

"You might think you're a good liar, but you're not. I'm better at this than you are. Your professional lying days were limited to junkies and whores, but I routinely lie to Congress... Well, never mind. I suppose we're not that different after all. By now you know Nemesis was a Cold War-era research project to build more soldiers like Franks, but he didn't like that. In fact he didn't like it so much he blew up the lab, killed the prototype, and murdered some of the scientists. And he got away with it too, because Ronald Reagan decided to honor some bullshit treaty dating back to George Washington."

"I always enjoyed the History channel."

"I find it interesting you never asked about Nemesis before you ran into Franks in the subway. Funny... According to your report you two didn't exactly have a conversation, it was really more of a lopsided ass-beating. My last werewolf could have taken him."

"Your last werewolf was a psychopath." She gave an exaggerated shrug. "What can I say? Franks was tougher than expected."

"Indeed. I wish you would have come directly to me instead of asking your handlers about Nemesis... Oh, don't give me that look. Don't worry. The Flierls didn't snitch on you. They're very talented at managing my little menagerie but they're the Task Force's resident goody-two-shoes. Luckily for them, their skills outweigh their troublesome integrity, but that's why I keep an even closer eye on my humans than I do on my monsters. Sadly, your actions have put Beth in danger. Now she too is asking questions which are better left unanswered."

As expected, that shook her. Kerkonen was predictable. Her psych evaluation had nailed it on the self-sacrificing tendencies and how she was extremely protective of others. "Beth had nothing to do with this. Franks mentioned Project Nemesis. I was curious. That's all."

"So curious that your deceased former STFU handler's login was used yesterday to access classified operations files. And this happened to occur on a computer at an STFU safe house where you were being locked up that night because of the full moon?"

"I don't—"

"Bullshit!" Stricken slammed his open hand against his desk. It made the werewolf jump. "I've got a guy that reads electrical impulses with his mind. You were caught red-handed."

He could tell Kerkonen wanted to say something else but she held it back. Inherently honest people were such easily manipulated chumps. She was pissed. She knew *something*, but confronting him with it would only dig her grave. STFU wasn't the type of outfit that issued reprimands, it issued bullets. Kerkonen had probably gleaned enough to figure that Nemesis had been reactivated without authorization. If she was as smart as he thought she was, she'd probably even figured out that something was up with the hit on the MCB.

Too bad . . . He'd been hoping to get some use out of her. Werewolves that were actually sane enough to be operationally valuable were few and far between.

"You got anything to say for yourself, Kerkonen?"

"No," she growled.

She was going to make a run for it. He could tell. Knowing her, she'd probably memorized where all the guards were on the way through the bunker, and calculated how fast she'd need to move before they got the place entirely locked down. It was a good thing he'd already made his move.

Kerkonen stood up so fast she knocked over her chair. She took a halting step toward his desk, but was having a hard time standing. The effects of the neurotoxin were kicking in.

He held up his hand. The remains of the capsule he had smashed against his desk were glittering on his palm. "Odorless, even by werewolf standards. This stuff is a pretty nifty little concoction they discovered during Decision Week. Don't worry. I'm immunized against it, but it does a real number on lycanthropes."

"You son of a bitch." Kerkonen reached for him, the ends of her fingers had begun growing into claws, but she was having a hard time since by now the room was spinning and she was probably looking at three of him. He had to hand it to her though, she almost got him. Launching herself across the desk, her claws tore four deep gashes through the leather of his chair. Only he'd already disappeared and was standing a few feet to the side.

"How?" Heather spotted him, but she was so dizzy that she couldn't let go of the desk without collapsing.

"Precautions, Kerkonen. I have access to every contraband magical artifact the government has ever confiscated. I was doing this sort of thing before you were born. I'm not stupid."

Heather was much tougher than expected. In testing, a few aerosolized molecules of this stuff had knocked out even a strong werewolf in thirty seconds. Her regeneration rate was impressive. He would have brought more of the stuff, but this was the only capsule in STFU's inventory. Procurement was a bitch when it came to alchemical solutions made from rare flowers that bloomed only on out-of-the-way mountaintops under a full moon. So he reached into his suit, pulled out the tranquilizer gun and shot her in the chest.

Heather looked down at the dart. "I'll kill you." Her words were slurred. It took her a couple of clumsy tries to pull the dart out, but it had already delivered a dose of drugs sufficient to drop a rhino.

"You're not walking this one off, Red. I had this stuff worked up in case I ever needed to put down Adam Conover." It was hard to use tranqs on humans to take them alive, since a dose sufficient to take them out in a timely manner was also strong enough to possibly kill them, but werewolves were absurdly resilient, so you could go a little nuts with the chemistry. "Don't worry. I'm not killing you yet. You still might be useful."

Her knees buckled. She hit the desk, then slid to the floor and lay there gasping for breath. Barely conscious, her body was stuck mid-transformation. She wasn't quite so pretty now, all deformed with fangs and body hair.

The door opened. His secretary stuck her head inside. "Is everything alright, Mr. Stricken?" She saw the werewolf sprawled on the carpet, but didn't show much of a reaction. She'd seen stranger things working here. "Would you like the cleaners to come up?"

"Have the boys stick her in a holding cell. We'll torture the shit out of her to make sure she hasn't talked to anybody else. And get me a new chair. This one has holes in it." Stricken kicked Kerkonen in the ribs, just to make sure she wasn't faking. This really was a disappointment for him. *A werewolf is a terrible thing to waste. . . .* But that made Stricken think of something. There was another werewolf out there he was acquainted with who was supposedly the biggest baddest werewolf *and* Monster Hunter around. Yet he had—surprisingly enough—not gotten in on the hunt for Franks, and Stricken had been so very personally disappointed by that. Looking at Kerkonen's body gave him an idea.

"Will that be all?"

"One other thing, Sarah, get me the phone number for Monster Hunter International. I need to make a call."

CHAPTER 14

Darmstadt, Landgraviate of Hesse-Darmstadt, Holy Roman Empire, 1709

"Send out the monster, Dippel, or we will break this door down!"

Most of the angry mob was armed with torches and farm tools. They did not concern him. It was the men in front, dressed in weathered steel breastplates and helms, armed with pikes, swords, and firearms who interested him. He could recognize that those mortals had the spirits of warriors. He'd fought them in the before time. Did they not understand that he was no longer their eternal foe?

"They've come to destroy you, my son." Konrad Dippel was disheveled and filthy from his escape from the mob and flight through the forest.

He peered through the narrow window at the force arrayed against Castle Frankenstein. "Who are they, Father?"

"Fools who do not understand the importance of science!" Konrad Dippel raged. "They would destroy that which they cannot comprehend! They are hunters of monsters, and a dread beast has been preying upon the village. Women and children have been devoured. They have heard rumors of your existence, and now they blame you for these atrocities."

He thought of The Deal which had been struck. If it was an intruder, it had to go. "What if I were to destroy this other monster for them? Would they accept me then?"

"*They will never accept you. I will not see my work undone by these shortsighted fools. You must flee from this place. Run away, and never return.*" *Dippel unlocked his son's chains.*

He studied his naked wrists and marveled at the small measure of freedom. He could have snapped his manacles long ago, but he'd been waiting for this day. "I will save the village," he stated. "I will destroy the other. The humans can accept me or fear me. I do not care."

"*You cannot face the Hunters of the Secret Guard, my son. Go north and hide. They will not follow you into the frozen wastes. Please, you must escape," his desperate father begged. "Do not allow my life's work to come to naught."*

"*I will not," he answered. Father did not understand his true purpose. Father had given him a mortal form and prepared him for the world. He had been taught the word* gratitude, *but he had never really understood what it meant until now. He would never see Konrad Dippel again. "Goodbye, Father."*

He walked straight toward the main door.

"*Not that way! The Hunters will destroy you."*

"*They will try." He decided that he did not care for these . . . Monster Hunters.*

He flung the door open and entered the world.

Today

Franks saw the sign.

CAZADOR, ALABAMA, POPULATION 682.

He had driven here from West Virginia, sticking to back roads whenever possible, wearing another man's skin stretched over his face whenever he'd had to use the freeways or highways that might have had traffic cameras. The mask had itched. He had ditched his last car and stolen a new one in Tennessee. He suspected that he was clear. It was doubtful that STFU would expect him to go here of all places. Why would a monster go directly into a den of Monster Hunters?

The drive had given him time to think. It was time wasted that would have been much better spent destroying his enemies. Thinking caused doubts to form, doubts about his strategy, doubts about his decisions, and most of all, doubts about The Deal. He was allowed to exist as a tool for taking life, not creating it. He had a son. What did that mean? Franks wasn't big on looking for deeper meaning.

The Creator had a sense of humor. Franks did not like being the butt of some cosmic joke. It really ticked him off.

Franks passed the country road that would take him to the MHI compound. The item he required was there. He had seen it stored and forgotten in their tunnels during his battle for the ward stone. The Hunters obviously did not know what they had in their possession. To them it was probably just another magical trinket, discovered on some mission and hidden away with the rest of the items they were afraid of, but too stupid to understand. He could simply go there now and take it, but to do so would certainly end in a direct confrontation against MHI. Not that he would mind that so much, but it was not conducive to achieving his current mission, and there was the possibility, however small, that they would be able to best him. Then nobody would stop Kurst, and that was unacceptable.

No. He would be . . . *diplomatic.* Franks intended to *ask* for the item. It was an unusual strategy. He took a different country road. There was one particular Hunter who owed him a favor. Franks would call in the favor. This particular Hunter had a certain sense of honor. He would probably cooperate. If he didn't, then things would get interesting.

His destination was an old plantation mansion. It was well hidden in the trees, but Franks had been here before. He parked in the open and got out. Trying to sneak up would only make the Hunters twitchy. The house had been fixed up. They had done an extensive renovation since the last time he'd been here, which was understandable since that night the Hunters had been using rocket propelled grenades and flamethrowers against a vampire inside.

The lights were on. Someone was home. *Good.* If they had not been, then he would have had to go to their headquarters where he'd be dealing with an unknown number of extremely jumpy Monster Hunters. This was better.

Though he was not wearing a proper suit, Franks had used some baby wipes to clean the dried blood from his face in order to be presentable. He'd thrown the dried-out skin mask out the window somewhere outside Montgomery for the wildlife to eat. He went right up the porch to the front door and rang the doorbell.

Then he knocked too, and Franks was incapable of knocking softly, so it was more of a pounding. The solid feel told him that the door and frame were armored.

The Hunters inside must have had a hidden camera on the porch, because when they saw who it was there was a loud buzzing noise. Latches released, and heavy metal shields clattered down to seal off every window of the mansion. Now that was a home improvement that Franks could appreciate.

There was an intercom next to the door.

"Franks?" The voice belonged to Owen Zastava Pitt. "Is that you?"

"I like your shutters."

"Yeah. They're new. We've been tricking the place out. And before you try to kick them in, Julie's at a firing port watching you with an M-14 right now. So what the hell are you doing here?"

"Requesting sanctuary."

There was a really long pause. "No kidding?"

He knew that MHI had done it before. Occasionally a supernatural creature ended up on the PUFF table that MHI didn't think deserved to be on there, and they would ignore, or sometimes even hide the things. "You did it for that wendigo and his big dumb monkeys."

"What's hiding one more big dumb monkey from the government? Oh, that's right. You *are* the government."

"Not currently."

Pitt sounded rather exasperated. "Dude, Franks, they're offering a lot of PUFF for you right now. You really shouldn't be here."

"This is only temporary. MHI has a St. Hubert's Key stored in your catacombs."

"A what?"

"It is an iron bar with a Latin inscription. Give it to me and I will leave."

"Wait . . . That almost sounds like you're asking nicely." Pitt began to laugh. "Holy shit. I didn't think this day would ever come. What's the magic word?"

Franks cracked his knuckles. The exterior walls weren't *that* thick.

"Easy there, big guy. Are you innocent?"

"No."

"Okay, stupid question. Let me rephrase that. Did you go nuts and blow up MCB headquarters?"

Pitt was an incorrigible smartass with deep-seated psychological issues against authority figures, but he was one of the only mortals Franks had some tiny measure of respect for. They had killed a god together. Pitt could handle some of the truth. "Stricken framed me."

"He needed you gone so he could launch Project Nemesis." Once again, the Hunter was smarter than he looked. Franks' reaction must have been visible on the camera. "Interdepartmental squabbling of you government types isn't my problem, but I had a little conversation with Stricken in Las Vegas. The dude's a psycho."

"Yes."

"So Stricken's a ruthless murderer with the full power of the federal government backing him, and you expect me to let the one guy he wants dead more than anything into my house?"

"Yes."

"Why don't you go ask your buddy Myers for help?"

"Stricken had him killed."

"Oh ..." The light on the intercom went off for several seconds. When it came back on, Pitt was quieter. "I didn't know. I'm sorry."

There was no need to be sorry. Myers had died trying to fulfill a mission. That was far more than most mortals ever achieved. "Stricken will murder anyone who helps me."

"No wonder you usually just boss people around. You suck at asking nicely, Franks."

Perhaps he should have just used his usual straightforward method. People made everything so complicated. This was a perfect example of why Franks was forced to have a partner capable of dealing with foolishness. Myers had always told him that the best way to get something was to make them an offer they couldn't refuse, only Franks suspected he was quoting a movie because he always spoke in an odd voice when he said that. Perhaps Myers was right, and he did have something MHI could not refuse. Pitt was a warrior, and warriors had loyalty to each other.

"I offer a trade. You had Hunters MIA in Las Vegas. I can help you find them."

"What?" That had taken Pitt by surprise. Apparently Franks had guessed correctly. "Are VanZant and Lococo still alive?"

"Doubtful. But help me and you can go look for yourself and be sure."

There was a much longer pause this time. Pitt was probably

speaking with his wife. Even his improved hearing could not pick them up through the thick walls. Franks waited a minute, and then pounded on the door again.

The intercom lit up. "Hold on, damn it," Pitt snapped.

Franks stuck his hands in his pockets. He had very little patience for dealing with people in general, and Monster Hunters specifically. Luckily for Pitt and Shackleford, they made their decision before Franks got bored. There was a loud clack as the door was unbarred.

It swung open. Owen Pitt was waiting for him; one arm was in a cast, but he had a pistol in the other hand. He was polite enough not to point it at Franks, but they both knew what it was there for.

"Don't make me regret this...Come in."

The Shackleford family estate was a very large home. Much of it was being renovated. The MCB dossier on Julie Shackleford said that she liked to *fix things*. Appropriate, for someone drafted by the mysterious Guardians. He doubted she understood what those marks meant, but explaining it to her wasn't his problem. The MCB didn't grasp the implications either. They just thought she had picked up some funky curse, which wasn't too uncommon a problem among Monster Hunters. If she ever became an issue, then Franks would have to take action, but that particular cosmic faction wasn't his responsibility.

Shackleford was waiting for them in a sitting room. By human standards, she was a beautiful woman, nearly attractive enough to give a succubus competition. She was also extremely dangerous. It wasn't just the big rifle in her hands—she seemed more inclined to shoot him than Pitt was—but also the black lines barely visible on her neck. The Hunters had no idea what they were in for.

"Make it quick, Franks, and then I want you out of my house," Shackleford said. She was decisive. Franks appreciated that.

Pitt stopped and stood in the doorway behind him. The Hunters were uneasy around him. *Good.* That meant they were paying attention. "I'd offer you a seat, but I'm guessing you're not going to be here that long."

Franks looked Shackleford in the eye. "I need that device."

She'd listened to the conversation on the porch. "What does it do?"

"It finds demons."

"That would have been really handy to know before. Thanks for sharing."

These were not the sorts of things MHI should trifle with anyway. The Key would point him toward demon spirits. Not just the ones inhabiting Nemesis bodies, but the legions of eager spirits who would be congregated around wherever Stricken was growing new bodies, jockeying for position, just like he had himself so long ago.

"Why didn't you just take it before?" Pitt asked.

"I didn't know I would need it." There was no need to elaborate about Kurst. If he'd turned it over to the government, Stricken would have it now and it would be useless to him. Besides, leaving it with MHI had been safer than stashing it with gnomes.

"You can have your saint whatever thingy as soon as you tell us how to get our guys back from the nightmare realm." Julie said.

"Deal." He took out a pen, and wrote down an address. Shackleford was scowling at him. It took Franks a moment to realize it was because he was using the top of her antique piano as a writing surface.

"You are such an ass," Shackleford said.

"Go to this place."

"What's there?" Pitt asked as he walked over and studied the defaced piano.

"Multidimensional research facility that works with the MCB. They traced the Las Vegas portal."

"How's that supposed to work? We just show up and ask for a trip to the nightmare world?"

Franks shrugged. "Not my department." He leaned on the piano. "Where's my Key?"

"Earl's there. I sent him a message," Shackleford said. "Don't worry. I kept it cryptic. I figured Stricken reads our mail. So while we're waiting, what's going on?"

"Classified."

"Oh screw you, Franks!" Pitt shouted. "Are you kidding me? All this crazy stuff happens, you're on the PUFF list, and you show up in the middle of the night telling us Myers is dead, and your answer is *classified*?"

"Yes," he answered, but the Hunters kept on glaring at him. It was an odd feeling. Franks was used to mortals giving him disapproving looks, but for once, he was actually moved by them. He had about as high an opinion of these two as he did of anyone currently alive. He needed to tell somebody about Nemesis. He might be destroyed, and somebody would need to off Kurst before he took over the world. His agency had been compromised, so that left the private sector, and he'd already ruined MHI's best competitors. "Fine . . . I'll brief you."

"Franks is actually going to tell us a story? I'd better update my dream journal."

Shackleford shushed him.

"Shut up and listen, Pitt. This is complicated."

Earl Harbinger sat alone in the dark. The only light was from the glow of his cigarette.

His cell phone was sitting lifeless on his desk. It had been half an hour since Stricken had called to give him the news.

This is professional courtesy. It's better you hear it from me now than you get the sanitized version later. I regret to inform you that Heather Kerkonen was killed in action when her STFU element tried to take down Agent Franks.

Earl couldn't even remember how he'd responded.

I know you don't like or trust me and I understand why, but I'm sincerely sorry, Earl. We had a job to do. Heather was a good woman. She died serving her country.

Earl had ended the call, not even bothering to tell Stricken that he was as good as dead. He had warned Stricken not to take her, so now there would be hell to pay. Earl would take STFU apart, bit by bit, so Stricken could watch his empire fall, and once he had nothing less to lose, then he'd eat Stricken's black heart.

That decision made, he sat there for a time, feeling nothing but emptiness. Normally he was a man of action. Hesitation wasn't in his nature, but this was such a kick in the gut that Earl was in shock. Heather was so vibrant, so alive, that he couldn't imagine losing her . . .

She was gone.

He should have been there. MHI should have taken Franks down. He'd made the wrong call. This was on his head. It was rare for Earl Harbinger to be at a loss as to what to do. All he knew was that Franks had to die for taking Heather, and then Stricken had to die for putting Heather in that monster's path.

His phone lit up. There was a text message from Julie on it. He needed to talk to her anyway. It was time to rally the troops. *Owen's old friend dropped by for dinner. Surprise.*

Earl didn't care. Why was Julie bothering him with nonsense?

Him and his three friends had so much fun staying with us and following Owen around last time that he came back.

Earl scowled at the message as he thought that through.

He wants a souvenir this time. He saw something special when he was in the basement. Can you pick something up for us? Call me.

Owen and Franks had fought Hood's people in the tunnels. That's where they stored the *special* things they found. "Motherfucker..." Earl muttered.

Franks was *here.*

Earl ran from the room.

Franks didn't give them too many details. He only told the Hunters what they needed to know. He left off any of his personal details, as well as the part where he'd killed or injured a bunch of their competitors. They might not like that. Hunters could be a sensitive bunch of drama queens.

"So why is this Kurst guy so dangerous exactly?" Shackleford asked. She could tell immediately that Franks wasn't going to answer that one. "All right. I'll take your word for it. He's bad news, I get it, but there's nothing we can do about it. They're not PUFF applicable. In fact, they're government property, so they're way out of our jurisdiction."

"We'll tell Earl." Pitt said. "I'm sure he's going to love the part where you kicked his girlfriend off a train, but I don't think we can do anything about Nemesis."

"Not without breaking the law," Shackleford added.

"And MHI never breaks the law or violates any MCB regulations," Pitt said. "MHI is completely law-abiding."

"Totally."

Now they were just messing with him.

There was a buzz from the front of the mansion. Shackleford and Pitt exchanged glances. "Motion detector." Pitt hobbled along on his damaged foot to a monitor in the hall. "It's Earl's truck. Looks like you can make your case to the man himself."

"Wait here," Shackleford told him.

Franks did. She probably didn't expect Franks to actually listen, but he didn't really feel like participating in the Hunters' internal discussions anyway. Harbinger would probably be angry at him for bringing MHI into this affair. Harbinger was by nature a volatile individual, but he would see reason, which meant he would help against Nemesis. If there was one man who rivaled Myers' dedication to protecting humanity, it was Earl Harbinger.

"And don't vandalize any more of my furniture, jerk."

They went onto the porch to greet Harbinger. Franks remained leaning against the piano. There was some cursing and shouting. Harbinger sounded rather agitated. Franks perked up. He must have heard about the incident with the STFU werewolf on the subway. That might complicate matters.

Harbinger entered the mansion, but before the others could follow, he slammed the heavy door in their faces. Harbinger looked down the hall, saw Franks, and snarled, "You son of a bitch."

Franks nodded in greeting.

Pitt's surprised exclamation and banging on the door was muffled as Harbinger threw down the steel security bar, locking the other two out of the mansion. Then he turned and began walking quickly toward Franks. His eyes were glowing gold. That was not a good sign. The walk turned into a run, and then Earl Harbinger was charging straight toward him.

Of the possible receptions Franks had expected, this one had been low on the list.

Harbinger roared, leapt across the distance, and tackled him. The Hunter was half Franks' mass but the speed of the impact still launched him back. They fell across the antique piano with Harbinger wrapped around his torso. Half of the piano's legs snapped off, and they crashed to the floor with a discordant jangle of keys.

"What are you doing?" Franks asked right before Harbinger rose up and punched him in the face. The blow was blindingly quick. The bones of Harbinger's hands were like steel rods. He moved so fast that Franks had absorbed half a dozen blows before the first one really registered. The back of Franks' head smashed a hole through the wood. The piano vibrated and made terrible noises.

Shoving Harbinger back, Franks kicked out, sweeping the legs. Harbinger hit the carpet, but instantly rolled and sprang back up. Franks was fast, but Harbinger was faster, and while he was getting up, Harbinger slammed one fist into Franks' eye socket, dropped an elbow on his neck, and stomped on his ribs. Franks was becoming very annoyed.

The werewolf might have been quick, but Franks had size, strength, and durability. He weathered the punishing blows until he was able to reach out, gather up a handful of leather coat, then he yanked Harbinger toward him and head-butted him so hard it would have killed any mortal man. Even Franks saw stars.

Shaking his head to try and clear the fog, Harbinger stumbled back. Franks still had a lock on the coat, and using superior weight and leverage, he hurled his opponent at the far wall. Harbinger flew across the distance, knocking furniture everywhere, and disappeared in a cloud of splinters and dust. Apparently the interior walls were not nearly as solid as the exterior.

Starting toward the hole he'd made, Franks felt a twinge. He put one hand on his abdomen, and it came away covered in blood. There was a deep laceration on his torso. Harbinger had grown claws.

They were playing for keeps.

Drawing his Glock, Franks approached the hole. On the other side was another room, a guest bedroom from the look of it. There were bits of wood spread everywhere, but no Harbinger. Shackleford and Pitt were still banging on the door, but between that heavy thing and the armored shutters, they would not be getting in anytime soon. Franks moved carefully, changing the angle, slicing the pie, looking for a target.

The wall behind him broke apart as Harbinger leapt through and sank his claws into Franks' shoulder. As the werewolf dragged him through the wall, Franks turned the Glock past his head and fired it at Harbinger's face, but only succeeded in putting several rounds through the ceiling and damaging one eardrum. Harbinger ripped a chunk out of Franks' back trying to take out his spine, but Franks shoved the Glock under his elbow and fired repeatedly, striking Harbinger in the chest.

There was a flash of red and blood shot from Franks' wrist. The Glock went spinning away. He caught of glimpse of Harbinger grimacing from the pain, but then he realized that the bullets were lodged in the leather jacket. *Damned minotaur hide.* The furious Harbinger was tugging him down the hall. Franks grabbed the claw impaled in his shoulder and squeezed. It caused his own wounds to grow in a flash of blood, but the werewolf wouldn't be

Larry Correia

getting away. Still locked on Harbinger's hand, he twisted hard to the side. Bones splintered until the werewolf let go.

Harbinger fell back, shaking his arm loose so that the bones would realign, then he tore off his restrictive, indestructible coat and threw it aside. Franks stood up. The two of them faced each other across the hall. Harbinger was rapidly transforming, and already within the few seconds since he'd first come in, he was almost entirely in werewolf form. His clothing was ripping as bones pushed through at new angles, hair was sprouting through his skin, his jaw was extending, and the voice that rushed past those sharp teeth was guttural and almost incomprehensible.

"You killed her!"

Who? Franks had killed a lot of people lately. "Narrow it down for me."

The werewolf leapt at him, but Franks was ready. He swung one meaty fist and hit Harbinger in the snout. Blood and saliva sprayed across the hall, yet the werewolf still managed to rake claws down his bicep. Harbinger's foot grated across Franks' stomach in an instinctive attempt to disembowel him, but the claws were still stuck inside Harbinger's boots, so it didn't do him any good.

Franks fell backwards, but on purpose this time, using the werewolf's momentum against him, and he tossed Harbinger down the hall. He hit the hardwood, rolling and bouncing, but sunk his nails into the floor and stopped himself. Harbinger got right back up, and this time when he stepped forward, his feet were so misshapen they slipped from the boots.

The two of them stood across from each other. Harbinger was almost fully shifted into his other form now, which was an impressive specimen of muscle, cunning, and fury. This was no ordinary werewolf, but Franks was no ordinary golem. Neither of them was capable of fear. Both of them were warriors who understood that mortal life could only be truly appreciated while at the ragged edge of death. MCB agents and Monster Hunters everywhere had been arguing in bars and placing bets about the potential outcome of this particular fight for years.

Battling Harbinger was not conducive to completing his mission. There was still some measure of intelligence behind those golden eyes. He did not know why Harbinger had attacked him so viciously. He could try to reason with the werewolf, explain the importance of his errand, and enlist MHI's help against their mutual foe...

Fuck it. This was the supposed King of the Werewolves and Franks had been eager to test him for a very long time.

There was a coatrack next to the door. Franks picked it up, pointed it like a spear, and charged. Harbinger rushed him, but Franks caught him in the ribs and knocked him back. Harbinger lashed out and snapped the end off the coatrack, then he stepped *up* the wall, and threw himself down on Franks. Claws sliced cleanly through Franks' cheek before he could retaliate by driving the jagged end of the rack deep into Harbinger's stomach.

They broke apart. The werewolf fell back, trying to pull the pole out of his guts, while Franks pressed one hand to his face. Blood was drizzling down his throat, trying to choke him. He could stick his fingers through the dangling flap of flesh and touch his exposed teeth. *Too bad.* Franks had been fond of this face.

Franks reached into his pocket, took out his flask of Elixir, unscrewed the cap, and downed the *whole* thing. Some of the glowing liquid spilled out from the hole in his face and mingled with the blood pouring down his neck. Incredible pain tore through Franks' body, beginning in his stomach and radiating out through every nerve ending.

One dose was world-shattering agony. The flask held nearly five times that. It took pain to whole new levels that would break mortal minds just trying to understand. A wave of heat rolled up inside of him. Every vein on his body stood out, hard as a rock. The fractured edges of broken bones liquefied into molten calcium before solidifying back into one piece. Boiling hot tears of blood fell from his eyes.

Ouch.

The pain subsided enough for Franks to at least see clearly again. The fully transformed werewolf had dragged the improvised spear out and tossed it aside. Harbinger shoved his guts back in while quivering muscles gathered around the hole and sucked closed.

Every muscle in Franks' body seemed to burn with stored energy. The Elixir hurt, but for times like this, it was *so* worth it.

"Come get some."

They rushed at each other. Franks swung, but the werewolf ducked and slid beneath the massive arm. Hot blood flew as Harbinger tore open his calf. Jaws snapped, trying to hamstring him, but Franks had already moved. He clubbed the werewolf over the head, then kicked him in the mouth. Jaws snapped closed so hard that teeth shattered.

Harbinger lit into him, biting, tearing, and snapping. It was death by a thousand cuts. Realizing that Franks' superstrength would be his end if given room to work, Harbinger was trying to keep them nice and close. Franks caught him by the throat and squeezed. He didn't know how well a lycanthrope could regenerate when deprived of air, but they were going to find out. He choked the werewolf with one hand and went to punching him in the face with the other. Harbinger's skull fractured. Blood poured from his pointy ears.

The two of them spun and rolled down the hall, crashing and banging through furniture. Picture frames fell and shattered. They hit a door, which burst open, dumping them into the kitchen. Franks had almost succeeded in choking out the werewolf, when he got sloppy, and didn't withdraw his fist fast enough. Harbinger's teeth snapped shut on Franks' hand.

There was a flash of fire up his arm as Harbinger tore his head back and forth, severing muscles and tendons, trying to bite clean through Franks' wrist. They hit the stove and bounced across the counter. Franks let go of Harbinger's neck and started hitting him with that hand. Each time he hit the werewolf, it lifted him off the ground, left a dent in his torso, broke ribs, and flattened lungs, but that damned stubborn werewolf kept chewing on his arm.

There was a butcher's block. It fell over and knives spilled free with a clatter. The first one Franks got his hand on was a long, serrated bread knife. Not ideal, but it would do. He stuck it under Harbinger's ear and dragged it across the werewolf's neck, splitting it wide open.

That got him to let go.

He lost the bread knife, but immediately replaced it with a butcher knife. He slammed the blade deep into Harbinger's armpit, levering it back and forth, spreading the rip, looking for the heart. The werewolf backhanded him, but it wasn't as hard as before. The stab wound had taken some fight out of him. Slippery with blood, Franks lost the kitchen knife, which was why he always preferred textured handles for serious work. He didn't mind leaving the blade in there though, since lycanthropes had a hard time regenerating around a foreign body.

Air was whistling through the hole in Harbinger's neck and bubbling through the hole in his chest. Franks kicked Harbinger in the stomach, sending him flailing back into the cabinets, knocking half of them off the wall. Franks followed up by taking hold of Harbinger's mane of hair and slamming him headfirst into the sink. That entire cabinet imploded. Pipes broke and water sprayed.

There was a frying pan there, and Franks thought briefly about beating Harbinger with it, but then he saw the much larger, heavy-duty KitchenAid mixer, picked it up, and slammed it down over the werewolf's head. It made a very satisfying crunch before it broke. Then he spied a meat cleaver on the floor, so Franks snatched it up. Systematically chopping the werewolf into pieces would do the trick.

Only Harbinger was far smarter in his transformed state than Franks had expected. Werewolves were supposed to be too savage to pick up an aerosol can of oven cleaner, turn, and crush it open directly in front of their opponent's eyes. Or maybe Harbinger had just gotten lucky... Either way, the caustic acid went off like a grenade right in Franks' face.

That stung.

Even with that, Franks remained analytical. One eye had been instantly blinded. The other was swelling shut. Harbinger had used the opportunity to get up and free the butcher knife from his lung, and his body had already begun healing. The werewolf leapt back, just ahead of Franks' wild meat cleaver swing.

They were both slipping across the tile. There was blood everywhere. Franks had to overwhelm the werewolf before he could fully regenerate from his wounds, but Harbinger, even in his bestial state, was too clever to be pinned down. He ran for the door. Franks raised the cleaver to throw it, but Harbinger yanked open the refrigerator door, and the thick steel blade stuck into the stainless steel with a *clunk*.

His opponent had fled. Franks yanked the meat cleaver out, kicked the refrigerator closed, and followed the blood trail. Harbinger was moving. In a battle of attrition, time benefited the werewolf. Franks left his own red trail behind him. Harbinger had gnawed his left wrist down to the bone. Franks curled that hand into a fist and squeezed, estimating that he'd lost at least half his muscle control there, but he was still combat effective. His damaged vision was going to be a bigger problem.

Harbinger had gone up the stairs. Franks leapt up them in three bounds.

The werewolf intercepted him at the top, attacking from his now blind side. Harbinger came in, clawing and snapping. The two of them crashed through a doorway, through a wall, and into a bathroom. He managed to hit Harbinger with the meat cleaver, embedding it in his collarbone, but Harbinger sliced his chest open from one side to the other.

This was really starting to piss him off.

Franks slugged Harbinger in the chest, hard enough to stop a car. It knocked the werewolf clean through the shower stall, through the tile, and the wall behind it. However, it snapped Franks' damaged wrist, and now that hand was hanging limp and useless. He followed, stepping through the broken tile and squirting pipes, smashing a bigger hole through the wall so he'd fit.

They were in an office filled with paintings. The dossier said Shackleford was an artist. Since blood was spattering across all the canvases, she was probably going to be very upset afterwards. *Oh well.* Harbinger was already up, so Franks simply kicked him through the next wall too.

The Elixir of Life had magnified his strength to absurd levels, so Harbinger's body actually covered quite a bit of distance to embed itself in the far wall of another office. Franks picked up a filing cabinet and lifted it overhead. It felt very full. Franks tossed it at Harbinger, but the werewolf dodged aside and the cabinet exploded through the wall. Harbinger hurried and ducked through the hole.

"Slippery bastard," Franks said as he followed, crashing through the hole.

Their new doorway opened onto a balcony overlooking a very large space. It appeared to be a ballroom with mirrored walls. Franks stepped through, but the instant his foot hit the other side, jaws like iron clamped around his leg, and Harbinger bit *deep.* Teeth sliced through muscle and blood vessels.

Franks roared and clubbed Harbinger's skull, fracturing it enough to put bone fragments into the werewolf's brain, but even then he didn't let go. Alarms were sounding in Franks' mind. If he lost that leg, he'd lose his mobility, and then it was over. Desperate, Franks pushed off toward the railing, dragging the latched-on werewolf with him.

They toppled over the edge.

The floor rushed up to meet them. They both landed at an awkward angle. On impact, Franks felt bones break, but more importantly it knocked Harbinger's teeth off of him. Franks kicked Harbinger with his other leg, sent him sliding across the polished hardwood.

Franks tried to push himself up, but his ruined arm flopped about uselessly. He shifted, used his other hand, and struggled upright, only to find that his other leg was buckling beneath him. Harbinger had crippled it as well. He was becoming combat ineffective. This called for desperate measures. Franks reached into his blood-soaked pocket and pulled out another flask of Elixir.

He had never used more than five doses at once. He was unsure what would happen if he did.

But he wouldn't find out, because Harbinger was on him before he could open it.

Teeth sank into his shoulder, punching clear to the bone, and then Harbinger twisted and shook, tearing him apart. Claws flayed open his back and ripped a kidney in half. Franks struck out with his good hand, but Harbinger released, moved aside, and counterattacked that arm. That bicep opened to the bone. Franks bellowed in fury, but Harbinger followed up, and bit him on that arm, pulling and ripping, yanking him across the floor.

He had intended to take the werewolf apart, piece by piece, but it was Harbinger who was doing that to him instead. Franks twisted his head as far as his neck would allow, and bit the werewolf on the nose. He really chomped down hard. The werewolf yelped and let go.

Franks was running out of options. He looked to his dangling hand and the white bones sticking out, thought *why the hell not?* Then he stabbed Harbinger in the neck with his jagged wrist bone.

The surprise in those golden eyes told him that the werewolf hadn't seen that coming. Franks jerked his arm back in a flash of red. Harbinger collapsed.

The two of them lay there for a moment on the dance floor in a mingled puddle of blood, struggling for breath. Even a powerful werewolf could only regenerate from so much damage before their system began to shut down.

"You are a worthy adversary," Franks muttered as he tried to sit up.

Harbinger was also struggling to rise. Apparently neither one of them was much for giving up.

The werewolf lurched toward him, teeth snapping. Franks fed him one arm and felt the crunch as Harbinger chomped it to the bone. But then Franks used his elbow to begin hammering the werewolf's head into mush. *Thud.* Even with his blood drizzling from dozens of wounds, Franks' blows were slow, methodical, but still incredibly powerful. *Thud.* Harbinger sunk his claws deep into Franks' abdomen and began pulling things out. *Thud.* Neither of them was going anywhere until this was over. It was a race to see if Franks would die from blood loss and organ failure before Harbinger was beaten to death.

Then they both got hit by a truck.

The approaching noise of the engine hadn't even registered. The steel shutters over the ballroom doors flew apart as blinding headlights filled the space. The impact of the front bumper knocked him and the werewolf apart.

Franks found himself flat on his back on the other side of the dance floor. He tried to sit up, but his body was too broken. Those headlights were scalding his one barely working eye, so he tried to lift a hand to shield it, only to discover that with the impact, Harbinger had kept that arm. Franks glared at the bloody stump. "Damn."

Car doors slammed. A female figure moved in front of the headlights. It was Shackleford. "Franks is over here. He's in pieces!"

He coughed up a knot of blood. "Sorry we messed up your house." That made him realize just how bad a shape he was in. He rarely *apologized.* "Good fight though."

Then Franks died.

PART 3

The Contract

CHAPTER 15

Now Franks remembered how he'd ended up in the small white room.

The interrogator was studying him. "That's correct, Franks. Your mortal body has been ruined."

"So that's it?"

"Like I said before, that's not my call."

When he'd been told that this was going straight to the top, Franks had not realized just how high up they'd been talking about. "Send me back."

"And why should He? You let your pride and your anger get in the way of fulfilling your part of the covenant."

"Because I'm not done yet!" Franks roared and slammed his fists into the table. The fact that he didn't so much as dent the surface told him he was no longer in the mortal world.

The interrogator sat there, studying Franks dispassionately. "That's not your decision to make. Haven't you learned anything over the last three centuries? You've had far more time to learn than a regular mortal is granted, and still, you expect patience? You expect mercy, yet never grant it. You ask for charity, but are incapable of dispensing any. Justice demands that you be sent back to Hell."

Franks leaned back in his chair and folded his arms. "You're not a regular interrogator, are you?"

"I have stewardship over the special cases. You might not remember much about the war, but we've met before."

It came back to him in a flash, just a glimpse of a battle, terrible beyond imagination. They fought across a bridge of light between the stars, with the being before him wielding pure energy as if it was a flaming sword. "You..."

The archangel nodded. "It's been a long time. You're still just as stubborn as before, which is why you were offered The Deal to begin with. We need something like you to stop the things like Kurst. You may be an aberration in The Plan, but he threatens to break it entirely."

"Don't underestimate Kurst. He'll crush mankind if given the chance."

"Mortal life is fraught with perils and tests, but everything on The Plan is for their own ultimate good. Much like you, our current threats are off The Plan. This is why we've allowed you to fight the battles that mortals aren't equipped to.... It turns out today is your lucky day, Franks. An inspired soul has taken it upon himself to repair your sorry corpse. They've saved your life. This isn't MHI's fight. Keep them out of it. They have a different purpose waiting for them."

He didn't really want their help anyway. "Fine."

"Good. You will require assistance. There are still a few humans who heed the old ways and who are aware of The Deal. I have sent a message to one of these to assist you. His name is Michael as well...No relation. Congratulations, Franks. You have been granted a temporary respite in order to deal with our current problem. No reaction? Normally, this would be where a repentant man would say thank you for another opportunity."

Franks just grunted in response.

"We'll meet again. In the meantime I will continue to review your history in order to make my recommendation about what to do with your immortal soul. Do you have anything else to say for yourself?"

"Quit screwing around and send me back. Those demons aren't going to banish themselves."

Franks was no longer in the white interview room. He woke up to find himself in an icy cold room with concrete walls. Bright lights were shining down on him. There were small metal doors along the wall and drains on the floor.

He was in a morgue.

Only one eye was working. The empty feeling in the other socket told him that eye had been cut out. His chest had been opened and his armored rib plate removed, exposing his internal organs. He tried to move, but discovered that he was strapped down. Not that it would do much good, since the awakening nerve endings told him that he was missing both arms and one leg.

He was in a morgue and he was being dissected.

"Whoa. Hold still there, Agent Franks. I'm not exactly good at this and you wiggling around sure isn't helping me put you back together." A head moved in front of one of the lamps. The man was wearing a surgical mask and glasses, but the thick red beard sticking out around the mask told him that it was one of the Hunters from MHI . . . something Anderson . . . *Milo*. "For the record, I'm not a doctor. In fact I only got a C in biology. Heck, I don't even know how you're actually alive right now, but I do know for sure that the human body only has one heart, so where the heck am I supposed to stick this little guy?" He held up a red blob. Due to the Elixir, it was still pulsing.

Franks recalled the dossier on the Hunter. Milo Anderson had been listed as an *eccentric genius*. He supposed it could be worse. "I'll walk you through." His voice sounded funny, and he realized it was because much of his breath was blowing out the gaping hole in his face. "You will need a skilled surgeon."

"Good thing Earl sent up the Gretchen signal!"

Another head appeared over him. This one was wearing a full mask and mirrored shades. The feathers and small animal bones tied to her surgical gown suggested that she was an orc. She poked her fingers into the bite marks on his shoulder, grumbled something, and *tsked* disapprovingly.

"Yeah, good question, Gretchen. So what happens when you get bit by a werewolf?" Anderson asked. "Do you like turn into Frankenwolf?"

"No." Franks had been bitten by just about everything over the centuries and nothing had ever changed him. "The Elixir of Life burns off impurities."

"Speaking of which, we found that thermos of glowing stuff in your car. Gretchen said I should pour some into your chest cavity. It seemed to work like a jump start. That's pretty nifty. Can I have the recipe?"

"No."

"Aw man...Well, what if when we poured it in you, you started having a seizure, which surprised me, so I accidentally dropped the thermos and spilled the rest, and we really need to make some more in order to get you fixed?" Anderson looked hopeful, like maybe Franks wouldn't be able to hit him since he didn't have any arms. "Hypothetically speaking of course."

Franks sighed. It made the loose flap of cheek flutter. "The alchemical instructions are inside a case in my trunk."

"Sweet...Well, actually, Holly already searched your car and found it, and Trip knows chemistry and stuff so he's already making some, but better to ask forgiveness than permission and all that."

There were probably worse things than letting MHI have the formula for the extremely dangerous Elixir of Life, but he couldn't think of any right then. His body was barely functioning, and it was working at all only because of his many redundant systems which had been built in over the years. Even then, he should have been dead...Franks lay there patiently while the orc reattached his internal organs. He really didn't have much choice in the matter. "Where am I?"

"The Body Shack...Uh...It's where I store cadavers for training purposes. Staking and chopping, that sort of thing. Lucky for you I just bought a fresh shipment from the med school supply place so we're stocked up. You can have your choice of the finest spleens from our spleen gallery...That was a joke. Sorry.... Okay, to be fair I'd guess most of them were homeless people and drug addicts, but there are a few who looked pretty healthy."

Gretchen mumbled something as she pried a bone sliver out of his arm stump with a pair of pliers.

"Good point. Most of them are probably a little small, but we've got one guy with arms that looks like he did a lot of steroids. Those should fit."

Franks grunted. The Elixir would force everything to work. New parts would be properly assimilated over time. His genetic code was continually shifting, a rolling average of his various parts. "Why are you doing this?"

"Earl's orders. They came rushing in here with you rolled up in a tarp in the back of his truck. He said that I needed to save you. We've been putting you back together for hours now, well, Gretchen has anyway, me and Holly have mostly been handing her tools and guts. So . . . it sounds like you and Earl had something of a disagreement . . ."

"Yes." Franks still wasn't sure why exactly Harbinger had attacked him.

Anderson played it coy as he went back to his stitching. "So . . . before Owen hit you both with a car . . . I was curious, unstoppable force meets the immovable object and all that . . ."

If Pitt hadn't interrupted them, Franks' best estimate is that they both would have died. "It was a draw."

"Shoot." Milo stopped, reached into his back pocket, removed his wallet, and handed Gretchen a twenty-dollar bill. The orc cocked her head and studied the money, probably not really sure what to do with it, and then stuffed it inside her gown before going back to her operation.

"Where's Harbinger?"

"Right here." The head of MHI entered the morgue. He walked up next to Gretchen and studied Franks. He had no shirt on under his leather jacket, and his chest was still covered in dried blood. He'd been too busy to clean up. Harbinger appeared to be emaciated, which was expected given the amount of energy necessary for a werewolf to regenerate with that much damage. He also seemed very angry. "Give us a minute," he ordered.

Anderson and the orc hurried out of the cold room. Once they were gone Harbinger pulled a stainless revolver and stuck the muzzle against Franks' forehead. He appreciated that Harbinger was a straightforward man who would not waste time with bluffing or foolishness.

"I doubt you had them save me just to kill me," Franks stated.

"I didn't. I kept you alive because I want answers. Did you kill Heather Kerkonen?"

"No."

Harbinger's face was a mask of barely controlled rage. At least he was too exhausted and spent to be in any danger of turning. "Did you *hurt* her?"

"It was a fair fight."

Franks watched the cylinder rotate right in front of his remaining eye as Harbinger cocked the hammer. "That's the wrong damned answer."

"I could have killed her." Franks' one eye narrowed. "I *spared* her."

"Why?"

"So she could expose Stricken. I told her about Nemesis."

"You're lying."

"I don't care enough to lie," Franks explained.

Harbinger exhaled. His finger was on the trigger. The gun wasn't even quivering. Franks could tell he was mulling it over. Harbinger could justify either decision rather easily, but Franks didn't look away. He didn't so much as blink.

After several tense seconds, Harbinger lowered the gun. "Julie and Owen told me your story. God help me, but I think you're telling the truth. Stricken told me you'd killed her."

"That's dumb."

"You've got to admit, it sounded plausible. You've got something of a reputation, Franks."

"Still dumb."

"Damn it. Stricken played me. He wanted to put MHI on your trail too and have me do the dirty work for him. He told me something I'd believe, knowing exactly how I'd react." He took out a cigarette and lit it. From where Harbinger was standing he could look down into Franks' open chest cavity. He paused in his reconstruction of events long enough to ask, "Does that hurt?"

"Yes."

"Good... If you didn't kill her, I've got no way of reaching her to find out if she's okay. She's either dead or somehow out of the picture..." It didn't seem possible, but Harbinger suddenly appeared to weaken as that realization sunk in. "Stricken wouldn't lie to me, then leave her alone, because if I found out you hadn't hurt her I'd go after him instead. He probably... he probably killed her."

"Maybe not. A werewolf like that is valuable."

Franks had given a completely honest assessment of the situation, but it seemed to give Harbinger some small glimmer of hope. "Maybe..." Harbinger took a long drag on his cigarette. "Stricken must've figured we'd do him a favor and kill each other. It almost worked."

"I would have won."

"Fat chance. I'm not the one spread all over a slab." Harbinger picked up Franks' severed hand, studied it, and then unceremoniously tossed it in the trash can. "I've been trying to keep tabs on Heather as much as possible. I've got one contact inside STFU, friend of a friend sort of thing. They're supposed to be decent enough, so I made some calls trying to confirm what Stricken said. I've not heard back from them yet. If she's still alive, I'm going to get her out of there."

"If she's not?"

"Then I'm going to go on a killing spree that'll make yours look like a Cub Scout jamboree."

Franks had expected as much, but according to the interrogator that would be bad. Telling Harbinger the whole truth was out, threatening was pointless; Franks needed to *talk* Harbinger out of going on a rampage. He was not good at that sort of thing. Franks preferred rampages. "If you do that, MHI is done for."

"It'll just be me. Not my people."

Here goes nothing.

"That's not how the government will see it," Franks stated flatly. "Stricken is a high-ranking official. Even if he's corrupt they won't let you kill any of them and get away with it. They won't just hang you. MHI will be declared terrorists. Stricken has allies. Give them an excuse and they will make sure all of your people die in prison."

He might not like it, but Harbinger knew Franks was right. "Like you give a shit what happens to us."

"A little." Franks wasn't about to try to explain the interview he'd just gone through, because this day had been complicated enough already. This next part was going to be *very* hard to say. "The world needs MHI in order to survive what's coming."

"What?" Harbinger started to laugh. "I never thought I'd hear something like that from the likes of you."

"I know. I can't *stand* you people. You're sloppy and disrespectful...But you're decent at your job. Put me back together and I'll handle this."

"What're you proposing, Franks?"

"If Kerkonen is alive, I'll free her. If she's dead..." Franks tried to shrug, but his torso was strapped down. "Stricken has to pay anyway. He killed Myers."

"Z told me. I never thought I'd say it, but I'm damned sorry to hear that. We had our differences, but Dwayne was a friend once." Harbinger still didn't seem convinced. He was not the sort of man to farm out his revenge to somebody else.

"Give me a few days. If Stricken's not dead by then, do whatever you want."

Harbinger sat on the edge of the slab next to him. "I'm having a real hard time thinking clearly on this one, Franks."

"I did hit you on the head a lot."

"Naw. It's hard to make good command decisions when you've got a personal grudge, and I've got a personal grudge a mile wide. I care about Heather and that's making me angry, and anger makes me do rash things. You won't get it, but it's been a long time since I've felt that way about anyone. I'd gotten used to everybody getting old and dying around me while I stayed the same. That makes command decisions a lot easier to bear. We're the same that way, you and me, but I was a regular man once. I don't know...Heather made me feel like I was that man again. I can't lose her, Franks."

It was odd, having an actual conversation with Harbinger. Franks felt like they should be drinking beers or something.

Harbinger glanced down at Franks. "Shit. Listen to me, confiding in *you*. You wouldn't understand. You don't care about anybody. You don't have anyone. You don't have loved ones or family—"

"I have a son..." Franks muttered.

"Really?"

"Yes." Franks still wasn't sure how he felt about that revelation. A human would feel proud, or attached, or *something*. "I understand the desire to protect your own. Avenge Kerkonen and you destroy everyone else you love."

"Well, how about that...Words of wisdom from the pile of parts." Harbinger finished off his cigarette, then ground it out on the slab next to Franks' ear. The place was still more sanitary an operating room than the truck stop he'd performed Agent Strayhorn's liver transplant in. "Julie said you came here to get some demon tracker you saw last time you were downstairs. I know the thing she's talking about. I picked it up on a contract job in Ethiopia a long time back. Never could get it to work right anyway. I think it's busted. You can have it. You've got forty-eight hours, Franks, and the clock starts the minute Milo throws you off this table. I'm going to be using that time putting together a plan to mess up Stricken's little kingdom."

"That will do."

"You'll need help."

He thought about the interrogator's cryptic message. "I'll have enough."

"You've got a deal, Franks. I'd shake on it, but I already threw your hand away. *Milo!* I know you're listening just outside the door, so you can quit hiding. I'm done," Harbinger shouted. "He's all yours. Get this Fed off my property ASAP."

Anderson came back into the room, holding a severed arm. "Groovy. I can't wait to see how this fits."

Harbinger stopped and studied something on the limb. "How'd that get on there?"

"It was Z's idea. His brother Mosh came in for the Newbie class and he knows how to do ink, which isn't surprising if you look at the guy. Z said Franks loves us so much it would be hilarious. It was a rush job but I think it came out pretty good."

He couldn't see what they were talking about. "What did Pitt do now?" Franks demanded.

"Okay, this I approve. Pretty him up, Milo." Harbinger slapped Anderson on the back and walked away. "Later, Franks."

"Harbinger, come back here. *Harbinger!*" But the obstinate werewolf left anyway. Knowing Pitt, whatever they had done to the body part would be obnoxious. Franks would probably have to go into battle against a demon lord of the Fallen with My Little Ponies or something equally humiliating stamped on his body. "What did he do?"

Milo Anderson held up the arm so he could see. A large MHI Happy Face had been tattooed on it. "Pretty sweet, huh? You get to wear our logo. It's like we're bros!"

It was *worse* than ponies.

The Nemesis prototypes each had their own private sleeping chamber. Since the walls were solid and the doors were reinforced with locks that could be controlled from the command center, they were basically prison cells. They were normally kept isolated from each other. However, they did eat their meals together in a common area. Kurst knew that this was not intended as a kindness, but rather as an observational opportunity to watch for signs of stress while the subjects interacted. However, the prototypes were always on their best behavior in the common area, mostly because he'd ordered them to remain that way. If the humans knew what rage-filled hate machines they had in their midst and the horrors they would love to inflict upon the mortals, they would wet themselves in fear.

They ate in silence. The human psychologists may have wondered at their lack of conversation, but that was only because they were unaware of their prototypes' telepathic abilities.

The gift works, Bia reported.

Kurst continued to eat his bland cafeteria food. *Excellent.*

She was sitting next to him. Since there were always cameras on them she could not perform a full demonstration, but she moved her hand beneath the table and placed it on his thigh. He could feel her fingertips lengthen and sharpen into claws.

It was very exciting.

The doctors did not catch it during my daily physical testing and blood draw. I detect no side effects. As for the kill switch... She placed a napkin to her mouth and discreetly spit a small metal sphere about the size of a ball bearing into it. The toxic container was a simple yet deadly device. Bia put it back in her mouth, and willed it back through the roof of her mouth, through bone and tissue, until it was back in its proper resting spot inside her brain. *It is simple to remove.*

All of the demons heard and understood. Though their faces remained expressionless masks, there was rejoicing around the table. The kill switch problem was solved. After millennia of torment, and months of slavery, their freedom was at hand. Kurst was pleased. They would allow Stricken to obliviously continue building bodies for the host, and once he had an army, they would strike out on their own. Putting up with the mortal's nonsense was galling, and demons were not known for their patience.

Why wait, General? Your new ally would allow us more freedom than the albino, and surely his cultists could find the resources to replicate Project Nemesis. I worked with the Condition before. Their arcane abilities are remarkable. Why wait for the whims of another creator, when we can create life ourselves?

That was an excellent idea.

Bia's claws receded, but she let her hand linger on his thigh. Eventually the cameras would observe that demonstration. Let them. It would give the psychologists something to talk about.

Franks chugged down the dose. At least he could drink without it spilling out the side of his face now that they'd stretched some extra skin over the gash and stapled it down. The burning hit his stomach and then radiated out through his limbs, burning the discordant bits of flesh into one coherent whole. It was gag-inducing, but MHI's version of the Elixir would do.

"According to everything I know, I can't figure out what this stuff is supposed to do." Trip Jones' dossier said that he had been a high school chemistry teacher before being recruited, so he at least knew enough not to totally ruin the mixture. "How is it?"

"It tastes like swill," Franks said, grimacing through clenched teeth.

Jones bit off an angry response. None of the Hunters wanted Franks hiding here, but Jones especially seemed to dislike him. Some humans just had an instinctual sense about Franks' true nature.

The Elixir reached his new stomach. Sudden agony ripped through Franks. He dropped the empty cup, spilling bits of glowing fluid on the floor. Lightning radiated down his bones. He roared and slammed one fist through a sheet metal table. The Hunters all leapt back. The lightning began to subside. Franks held up the shaking, bloody hand and studied the bruising pattern of his knuckles. Capillaries and nerves were connecting. That orc did good work. He flexed his muscles. *Better.* "Get me another."

"Are you sure?" Milo Anderson asked.

"I'm always sure." Normally when the MCB needed to make that many repairs to him they would take their time and give him a tiny amount of Elixir through an IV drip. Overloading this much Elixir through his system could cause premature organ failure, but he had work to do, and Harbinger had imposed a very short timeline on him. Since he would more than likely die facing Kurst, he wasn't too worried about the lifespan of his internal organs.

Pitt hobbled into the Body Shack. "Hey, Franks. I—damn, somebody should have warned me he was naked. I knew you were built out of spare parts but I didn't know some of them came from farm animals."

"Shut up," Franks snapped. He was being held together by about a thousand stitches, so he really wasn't in the mood for Pitt.

"Nice tattoo though."

"I'll remove it with a belt sander later."

"By the way, on that whole *I owe you a kidney* thing from that one time I accidentally shot you, duty fulfilled. You never specified it had to be one of mine. We're square."

Franks was sorely tempted to burn this compound down when he left, and he probably would have if it wasn't for that angel and his stupid prophecies. "What do you want, Pitt?"

"We just intercepted a guy at the front gate, which is strange, because it isn't like we get very many visitors out here; but even stranger, he said he's looking for you."

No one knew he was coming here, not even Myers' loyalists.

"Yeah, the idea of you telling all your buddies that MHI is harboring public enemy number one through ten just fills me with all sorts of warm fuzzies, but Earl talked to him. He flashed some medallion and said God sent him to help you, says he's from the holy order of saint somebody of the something. He made it sound like he's a mystical Catholic ninja monk, but Earl said he's all right." The other Hunters nodded at that, as if Harbinger saying somebody was *all right* was a significant blessing. "Personally, that would strike me as kind of weird, except I'm talking to Frankenstein's monster who was just dismantled by my werewolf boss before being put back together by our orc priestess, so what the hell do I know?"

"Little of value." Walking was extremely difficult because the new leg was not fully assimilated yet, but Franks limped toward the door anyway.

"Hey, you can't go out in front of the Newbies looking like hamburger," Jones said.

"Plus he's buck-ass naked," Pitt added. "I'll get my emergency pants."

Franks knew where the Hunters stored their explosives. He could probably turn Cazador into a fireball visible from space. *Stupid angel.* "Bring him to me," Franks ordered. Luckily the Hunters didn't argue, because Franks really was entirely out of patience.

By the time the Hunter from the Secret Guard of the Blessed Order of St. Hubert the Protector arrived, Franks had been given a pair of sweat pants and had managed to guzzle down another dose of Elixir.

He was an average-sized man, part Asian, part Caucasian, somewhere between thirty and fifty, and completely innocuous and forgettable. The only thing notable about him was the fact he didn't seem in the least bit surprised to see Franks' obviously sliced apart and stuck back together body. The man didn't look very threatening, but looks could be deceiving, and Franks had dealt with this particular shady organization before.

"I've been expecting you."

"You're a hard man to find, Franks."

"Leave us," Franks ordered the MHI staff.

"Don't tell me what to do. It's my shack," Anderson protested, but Jones and Pitt dragged him from the room. "But I want to see what the mystical monk does."

Franks waited until the door was closed. "Show me," he ordered.

The man reached into his motorcycle jacket and lifted out a gold medallion. Franks didn't need to look at it for long to feel that it was real, and if this man wasn't ordained to be wearing it then it would have turned molten and burned through his skin. Franks nodded for him to continue.

He put the medallion away. "I'm Michael Gutterres." He talked like an American. He didn't try to shake hands. That was good. Franks was tired of meaningless pleasantries. "You know who I'm with."

"Yes." The Secret Guard had a nominal relationship with the Vatican, mostly for finances and recruiting, but they didn't really answer to anyone there unless they felt like it. They mostly did their own thing, kept to themselves, and stayed out of mortal affairs. They existed for one reason and one reason only: to stomp on anything off The Plan. If it had snuck in from another world, the Secret Guard had a problem with it. In that respect, Franks had been uneasy allies with them for a very long time.

"So you know why I'm here."

"To try to kill me if I'd broken The Deal."

"I like how you stuck the word *try* in there." The Hunter had a confident smile. Franks wanted to wipe it off his face. "But yes, that's fundamentally correct. From what I've gathered so far, there's more going on than just what the MCB has let slip. A large number of the Fallen seem to be congregating here. From what I've seen, you still seem to be fighting against them. Is that correct?"

Franks nodded. "The Deal is still on."

"Good. You'll understand there's no offense intended if I keep an eye on you long enough to make sure that's true. When you struck your bargain, my order was the only organization around capable of dealing with you should you go back on your word. The head of our order made a solemn vow that we would deal with you, and though we're a shadow of what we once were, we still honor our oaths. We've been monitoring you ever since."

"I know," Franks said. He'd dealt with these self-righteous types before.

"Mr. Harbinger was nice enough to let me in. Turns out he was tutored on how to master lycanthropy by one of our exiles in Cuba a long time ago."

"Santiago. Met him once."

"It's easy to forget how long you've been around. Is there anybody you don't know?" Gutterres asked, seeming genuinely curious. "Never mind, they warned me you weren't big on talking. I believe you're planning on destroying an infestation of greater demons. That's sort of my thing, so I'd like to offer my help."

Franks snorted. "You and what army?"

"No army. Just some highly trained professionals who are deniable and expendable, and who've taken an oath to sacrifice their lives in righteous battle against the forces of evil. I can have two combat exorcists and a platoon of Swiss Guard on the ground anywhere in the eastern US within the next few hours. Will that do?"

"It's a start."

Luckily Franks knew where to get more.

The prepaid cell phone they'd picked up at 7-Eleven rang. MCB-agent-turned-wanted-fugitive Henry Archer stared at the phone for a few seconds, secretly hoping that it would quit making noise. The only person who had the number was Franks, who had sucked them along into his vortex of shit and ruined their lives, so part of him really hoped it was a wrong number, because if it was Franks then it was probably even more bad news.

Grant Jefferson and Tom Strayhorn were also in the little seedy hotel room. It was the kind of hotel frequented by hookers, drug dealers, and the terminally cheap. The other two agents were staring at the phone as well, but nobody made a move. Being listed as co-conspirators to a wanted terrorist murderer had been especially hard on Grant, and he actually looked more physically worn down than Strayhorn, who at least had a good excuse for looking beat, what with the multiple gunshot wounds and field-expedient organ transplant.

"You going to answer that or what?" Grant asked as he picked up the remote control and muted the television.

Normally Grant would jump at taking point and being the higher-ups' go-to guy, but Archer suspected Grant was suffering from a little bit of depression. Throwing your entire career away and putting your life and freedom in jeopardy in a futile noble gesture to save your boss who was going to die anyway had that very understandable side effect. Archer wasn't exactly feeling super optimistic himself. But Archer was sitting closer to the phone, so he picked it up. "Hello?"

"I'm heading back." Sure enough, it was Franks. "Get ready."

They were going to make a move. "Did you find that thing you needed?" Archer asked as he put Franks on speaker.

"Yes. And I have help. Get more."

Archer's background was in crypto-commo. Normally criminals and spies were purposefully vague over the phone to avoid using any keywords that would send up red flags to the monitoring software. For Franks, being cryptic was just normal conversation. "Uh . . . You mean . . . what?"

"Get *more.*"

"You've lost me there."

"Rule number two."

Archer wasn't sure what that meant. The first thing that popped into his head was the MCB's vaunted First Reason, but that was all about justifying their sometimes harsh methods. Except right now the only people who were intimidated were his agents. He wasn't sure what rules Franks was talking about, but apparently Strayhorn did.

"Got it," the rookie said. "Any requests?"

"Bring *everything.* Oh-seven hundred." The call terminated.

They'd discussed rallying points beforehand, so they knew where to go and now when to be there, but Archer had no clue what the other part was about. "What rule is he talking about?"

"It's something my dad used to say. He picked it up from his MHI days," Strayhorn explained. "Rule number one of a gunfight, bring a gun. Rule number two of a gunfight, bring friends with guns."

"Friends . . . Like we've got so many to choose from. Franks wants us to bring the cavalry," Grant muttered. "Apparently he's not been watching the news. The whole world thinks we're criminals. Nobody is going to help us. Myers gave me some names, but even then the MCB is more likely to shoot us on sight than send a tac team to help out."

The news was still playing in the background. MCB Media Control loved the twenty-four-hour news cycle, because a ratings-desperate media was an easily steered media, and Media Control was still flogging the Franks-as-terrorist-on-the-loose story. Only now, beneath the big picture of Franks, were four smaller photos showing the three of them and Dwayne Myers.

"Not again..." Grant said.

"What're you complaining about? At least the picture they keep using of you looks like a movie star headshot."

"That's because it is. They took it from my IMDB listing."

"Screw you, Grant! Being in one horror movie doesn't make you that cool! They used an MCB academy photo for me. I'm standing there with a rifle, looking like Lee Harvey Oswald," Archer snapped. "Oswald!"

"Are you kidding? How do you think I feel? Look at me, Archer. I'm too pretty to go to prison."

The stress was really starting to get to them. "Shit...I'm a federal agent. You know what happens to Feds in prison?" Archer stood up and began to pace back and forth. "And I'm skinny. At least you lift weights. I'll be the skinny, easily-wrestled-down former cop. It's like all of the worst things to be in prison."

"Naw, you'd have to add child molester," Grant said, but then he thought about it. "Knowing Stricken, being the spiteful bastard that he is, he'll figure out some way to tack that on there too."

Dying while fighting monsters was way less terrifying than the idea of being framed and going to prison. Archer hated to admit it, but he was freaking out. He really didn't want to be sold for cartons of cigarettes.

"Guys, calm down," Strayhorn urged. The rookie was propped up on one of the beds. Franks' Elixir worked on him, but it didn't seem to work nearly as fast. "Nobody's going to prison. Stricken won't risk us talking. If they take us alive, he'll have us murdered as soon as we're in custody."

Surprisingly, that actually helped Archer calm himself. "Thanks, Rook." Archer took a deep breath and sat back down. "Okay, so what do we do now?"

"We help Franks and we fight," Grant said. "Or we run."

"That's bullshit," Strayhorn shouted. "They killed my—"

"Keep it down. The walls are thin. I didn't say we were going to run, I was just listing the options. I know they killed Myers. We were there." They'd followed Myers and rushed in when they'd heard the call for help. "We're in trouble only because we chose to be *there*."

"Sorry," Strayhorn said. "I know he asked a lot of you two."

"But we did it, and we'd do it again," Archer told him. "Dwayne Myers was the best leader the MCB has ever had. Of course we did what he asked us. In an outfit built on telling lies, he was the one man every last one of us trusted."

"That's it!" Grant exclaimed. "That's how we're going to get help."

"Huh?"

"The names Myers gave me, he wouldn't have told me about those agents being solid if he didn't know for sure. Myers had to expect this level of heat. Hear me out. Franks must have some sort of op planned. If it was something less, Franks would just tackle it himself. That means he's either taking a shot at Stricken or those Nemesis things," Grant mused. "Probably them, because if we can prove what they are, that's justifiable. It can't be Stricken himself. Franks couldn't possibly expect us to get a bunch of other sworn agents to go outside the law like that."

Archer and Strayhorn exchanged a nervous glance. When it came to the idea of Franks staying in the lines, there was a lot of wishful thinking attached.

"So it has to be Nemesis. We've seen these things in action. They're tough as nails... We need every man we can get." Grant slammed his fist into his palm. He was beginning to look motivated. At least focusing on solutions seemed to help shake Grant from his funk. "We need the Strike Team."

Archer figured Grant had what it took to be a really good leader, provided he could just keep his head out of his ass long enough to get the hang of it. "That's wonderful, but how the hell are we going to get the people tasked with hunting us down, to stop long enough to help us take out their superior's pet project?"

"I'm going to try something crazy by MCB standards. I'm going to use the truth..." Grant had a malicious gleam in his eye. "Kind of."

CHAPTER 16

Battenberg, Landgraviate of Hesse-Darmstadt, Holy Roman Empire, 1740

He could hear the soldiers stealthily moving around outside the barn. Occasionally he caught glimpses of them through the knot-holes and gaps. They were attempting to sneak up on him. They were good, but they weren't that good. If it hadn't been raining, they probably would have set the barn on fire to flush him out. As it was, it was either risk a direct confrontation, or wait him out. Either way worked for him. He wasn't in a hurry. He had nothing better to do, so he went back to sharpening his sword and waiting for the next batch of heroic humans to try to slay him.

This batch had been chasing him for weeks. They were remarkably dedicated. Franks didn't mind the running and the fighting and the hiding. It kept him occupied until the next otherworldly invader turned up and needed to be dispatched.

Being a hideous monster, and having dealt with humans for several years now, he expected many different methods of attack, but a polite knock on the door was not one of them. Curious, he took up his sword, leapt down from the loft, and went to the door.

It took a moment to find the words. He had not spoken to anyone in a long time. "What do you want?" he growled.

"I come to parley." The human on the other side shouted through the wood. "I wish to speak with the monster of Castle Frankenstein."

281

He was not used to that. Most of his interactions with humanity consisted of them running at the sight of him, or the braver ones shooting at him. "Leave me be."

"I have been told that you can reason as a man, so let us speak as men, face to face, under a flag of truce. As long as you do not attempt to harm me, my men shall not fire the cannons they have aimed at this place."

He hadn't known they'd brought cannons. He opened the barn door to tower over the seemingly fearless mortal on the side. "What do you want?"

"My, you certainly are ugly in person, but not nearly so hideous as the legends make you out to be. I am Lieutenant Colonel Kugler." He removed his hat and bowed. "What shall I call you?"

"I have no name."

"I thought as much, but saying monster over and over grows tiresome. Since my men have taken to calling you Franks, in honor of the location you were built, I shall call you that as well."

He shrugged. "Fine."

"Very well, Franks. I have come to offer you a proposal."

"I won't surrender. We fight, you die."

The man laughed. He must have been touched by madness. "Not that kind of proposal, my gigantic terrifying friend. You must understand, I have not chased you across half the empire out of any sort of noble ideal. I am no Secret Guard, and even those fanatics have tired of testing you, and have declared that you must have a place in the Almighty's plan. My men are simply here because we have been paid a large sum by the Landgrave to remove you from this county. It is no different than being paid to kill Russians on behalf of the Swedes or to stomp on the Jacobites for the British."

He did not understand the humans' use of money, because he simply took what he needed to survive, but it seemed to work for them. "You fight for . . . coin?"

"Yes. And I must say, despite campaigning in many different lands, from Italy to the Spanish Netherlands, I have never had to work so hard as to fight you. So I said to myself, Karl, why should I squander so much effort to fight this beast who only wishes to be left alone, when I can simply hire him to work for me instead."

"Huh?"

"You like to fight, don't you, Franks?"

He nodded.

"From my observations, it seems you especially like to seek out the beasts of Satan's horde to destroy them. Yes?"

"That is my mission."

"Excellent. There is gold, fame, and goodwill to be earned in such endeavors, but you have already depopulated this part of Europe of all its vilest beasts and witches. Now you have nothing to do but hide from people like me. Why limit yourself to the darkest confines of the empire, when you can travel the world as part of my regiment instead? Think of the interesting things you could kill! You kill the monsters you would kill anyway, I get paid for it. You seem to enjoy battle, so in between your dispatching of whatever monsters we find, you can fight for me. As part of my regiment, you would be free from the petty harassment by the local authorities. We would claim you as one of our own. To the world you would be considered a monster no longer, but merely another soldier. You would have food, shelter, clothing, and an endless supply of gunpowder, and all I would ask in return is something that you would do regardless."

That did sound better than hiding in caves and barns and stealing pigs from villagers.

"Think of it this way, Franks. If you stay outside of mankind, then eventually someone like me will destroy you. If you are part of my regiment, you will be seen by them as a man, nothing more."

"What is this . . . regiment?"

"They call us many things, but for you we would be your new family, if you are willing to abide by our terms and regulations, of course."

He had killed just about everything worth killing in this part of the world, and knew absolutely nothing of the lands beyond. He shrugged.

"Excellent, Franks! Welcome to the Hessians!"

Franks pulled his stolen car over just after crossing the Virginia state line. He got out and limped into the tall grass. MHI's orc did fantastic work, even better than the MCB's resident surgeons, but it still took time to get new limbs working correctly. If there had been any other drivers on the road they might have found the sight odd, a giant man in a black suit standing out in the weeds for no apparent reason, but the reason he was on this particular road was precisely because of the lack of other drivers.

The suit, shirt, and tie were parting gifts from MHI. He didn't know who'd left them in the Body Shack, but they had been neatly hung up and waiting for him. Even having lost some body mass from the fight and replacement parts, the suit *almost* fit correctly. There had been a note that said it had belonged to one of the Hunters they had lost in Vegas. That was good. Franks had not wanted to go into the fight of his life wearing Owen Pitt's borrowed sweat pants.

He held out his open palm with the St. Hubert's Key he had taken from MHI in it. It grated on his new skin as it turned, pointing toward the north. The pull was very strong. A human would only be able to tell that there was a gathering of angry demons in one place, but the Fallen had a very long time to get to know each other, and one spirit in particular stood out from the others. That one had to be Kurst.

Franks should have listened to the imp informant he'd shaken down off the coast of California. He'd done a cursory sweep after returning to duty back then, but had not picked up anything of note. Perhaps it was because the greater demon's body hadn't been fully formed yet, or maybe whatever process Stricken had used to grow the bodies had shielded them from Franks' search. Perhaps, since he had been using a holy relic, the Creator had a sense for the dramatic and simply preferred their final showdown to happen this way. Franks didn't know, and he didn't really care. All that mattered was ending this once and for all.

When he returned to the road, a motorcycle had stopped behind his stolen car. Gutterres was waiting for him. He saw what Franks had in his hand. "A St. Hubert's Key? Is that what you went to Alabama for? I could have saved you a whole lot of time, not to mention a whole lot of getting your arms ripped off by a werewolf, if I'd known that beforehand...I guess the Lord really does work in mysterious ways."

He had no patience for people he liked, not that there were many of those, and even less for people he didn't give a shit about. He felt like slugging the Hunter in the mouth, but Franks needed all the help he could get. "Kurst is that way."

"I've given those rally point coordinates to my people. They'll be there in a few hours. What about yours?"

Franks shrugged. For all he knew Jefferson was on his way to a country without extradition.

"If I trusted you more, I'd ditch you and be there in half the time." Gutterres patted the Ducati's fuel tank like it was a loyal horse. "You need to get yourself a better set of wheels, Franks."

Franks knew how to ride a bike, but he'd needed room for his case, and if Gutterres kept annoying him, he'd need the trunk space to hide a body. He climbed back into his car.

"And I thought they were exaggerating when they said you weren't much for talking. What are you going to do if—"

Franks closed the door in his face, put the car in gear, and drove away. He made sure to give it too much gas so the tires would spin and pelt the Hunter with gravel. In his rearview mirror he saw Gutterres give him a remarkably rude hand gesture for a holy warrior.

He was right though, sticking to back roads made for a much longer trip, but truthfully, Franks needed the time to get his repaired body in order by forcing down another dose of the Elixir every hour. The new parts were assimilating quickly, but he was not operating at peak efficiency. His new arms had not been properly conditioned. His new bones had not had time to harden. Much of him was still held together with thread, wire, and staples. He was on his way to face one of the strongest demons to ever escape from Hell, wearing a body that was a perfectly tuned, high tech vessel designed for war, while Franks doubted if he'd be able to bench-press even a mere seven hundred pounds without blowing something out.

Jefferson, Archer, and Strayhorn had better have come through for him or else this was going to be a very short and messy operation.

Hours later he reached the rally point. He'd picked an old country church in a wooded, rural area in central Virginia. There was a small stone monument on the side of the road in remembrance of a Revolutionary War battle. That particular battle was a minor footnote in history, but it had been a pivotal moment for Franks.

Franks spotted six black MCB vehicles parked in the clearing behind the boarded-up building, including one of the large armored trucks used by the Strike Team. So either his agents had performed better than expected, or the MCB were here to arrest him, but realistically, if this was an elaborate takedown he would have expected more of them, as well as air support. He turned onto the dirt road, drove past the posted snipers and spotters, and pulled in behind the armored truck.

At least a dozen armed men in full armor and tactical gear were in view, and he didn't know how many others were in the trees or how many guns they had sighted on him. An MCB agent's salary was on the standard GS federal employee scale, and Franks was worth a quarter billion dead, so he hoped that they all remembered that MCB employees were not allowed to collect PUFF. He looked in the rearview mirror and was not surprised to see that Gutterres had continued along the main road and not turned off after him. The Hunter might have talked a big game about his Lord working in mysterious ways, but he wasn't stupid enough to follow Franks in until he saw whether the MCB riddled him with bullets or not.

There were a lot of apprehensive agents watching him as he got out of the car. Jefferson intercepted him first and hissed, "Before you say anything, this is all Myers' plan."

Franks raised an eyebrow.

"To prove Stricken has committed treason. Just roll with it."

Whatever works... Franks followed Jefferson toward the armored truck. He recognized most of these men and women. Some agents met Franks' gaze and gave him confident nods, like they'd always known he was innocent. Others looked at their boots as he passed. Those were the ones who'd thought he might have been guilty. They were probably here now because of their trust in Myers. Franks didn't care what any of them had thought before, he was more worried about a potential third category, as in the ones that didn't care about guilt or innocence, but who would just follow orders, no matter how stupid they might be.

It did not immediately dawn on him that that thought might have been a little hypocritical.

Archer was in the back of the armored truck, working on a computer. The shaved-headed, muscular, grizzled-looking warrior next to him was Special Agent Cueto, one of the Strike Team trigger-pullers who'd worked his way up to unit commander. He was one of the handful of humans Franks actually liked a small bit. "Afternoon, Franks. I suppose I should be placing you in custody now."

"Don't."

"Believe me, I'd rather not. You care to explain what the fuck I'm doing out here?"

"Hang on." Franks took out the St. Hubert's Key. It spun rapidly in his hand until it was pointing northeast. The agents made no comment. They'd all seen that sort of oddness before. "Archer. Note the direction." They were close enough now that Franks could estimate the distance based upon the strength of the pull. "See whatever is approximately seventy clicks that way."

"What's the deal, Franks?"

Franks glanced around the crowd of curious, potentially dangerous, federal gunmen. "Walk with me," he told their commander.

They moved away from the truck and curious ears. "What the fuck happened to your face? Is your cheek held on with a staple gun? What did that to you?"

"Werewolf." Franks had worked with this man before, and even died with him in Natchy Bottom. Cueto had been recruited from the Army, and had been one of Myers' oldest friends and confidants. If Jefferson had persuaded him, then they were set. If Cueto was unconvinced, then the Strike Team would kill them all. "Have you been briefed?"

"Barely. They told me that Stricken created some supersoldiers, but they've been possessed by devils straight out of Hell."

"Yes." He was glad Cueto's men were here, but he didn't like that they had shared the real dangers of Project Nemesis. It wouldn't take too much of a leap for the government to figure out that Franks was one too.

"Yeah . . . I can't believe that son of a bitch Stricken would pull a false flag against the MCB. Archer's been going over the evidence with me. There are too many parts where the video doesn't match up with the forensic evidence, but they've been keeping the details from the rank and file. I knew it was bullshit. There was no way you were behind that attack . . . There were way too many survivors."

Franks nodded. He appreciated the compliment.

"So what's Myers' plan?"

Since he didn't know what lies Jefferson had constructed, Franks wasn't quite sure of that either. "We take down Nemesis. Expose everything."

"To those pussies on the Subcommittee? How're we going to do that?"

"A raid."

"On what?"

"No idea yet."

"We're on our own. I don't even have my air assets. There's no backup. Without orders from on high, you realize I'm aiding and abetting right now. If we move on this with you, we're committing I don't even know how many felonies. Not just me, all my men. They're volunteers, Franks. This is off the books. We're hanging our asses out in the wind because we trust you, and that's asking a lot, but if Myers says this is how it is, then that's how it is...I was hoping he'd be with you."

"Myers is dealing with the higher-ups now," Franks said, and he meant every word of it.

Cueto studied him for a long time. "You'd be a right-hard bastard to play poker against...Level with me, Franks. Dwayne is dead, isn't he?"

Franks paused. There was no use in dragging this out. "Yes."

"I'll give it to Grant. The kid's got skills, but you can't bullshit somebody with a twenty-year career in professional government bullshitting." Cueto sighed. "I thought something was up."

"Why are you here then?"

Cueto reached up, placed one hand on Franks' shoulder, and looked him square in the eyes, an act which took a lot of balls. "Because Myers was smarter than either of us, and he warned me months ago to be ready for some big clandestine bullshit. Because I know you're a cold-ass motherfucker, but everything you do, no matter how squirrely it might seem, is always for the safety of this country. Because Stricken is a power-grubbing piece-of-shit wannabe tyrant and I didn't sign up to work for the fucking Gestapo. But mostly because I took an oath to defend this nation from enemies foreign and domestic, and it don't get more foreign than the fucking devil." Cueto let go of Franks and stepped back. "That's why."

"Thanks." There he was, using that word again. The last week had set a new record for him.

"Every last one of my boys would say the same thing, only they won't ever have to, because if we get burned I've already instructed them to blame me and tell the authorities that I lied and said you were undercover the whole time, and I ordered them to help you."

"Good idea."

"Not really. If we get caught I intend to say the same thing, only that I got my orders from Myers, and they're going to have a hell of a time interrogating him. Passing the blame is Fed 101. Now let's go plan this illegal operation of yours."

They started back, but Franks paused to take a long look around. It was still easy to pick out the rocky ridge where he'd first met General Washington. The place really hadn't changed that much.

"You okay, Franks?"

He'd been thinking about the hundreds of worthwhile humans he'd known, and how almost all of them were gone now, their brief lives sacrificed in the pursuit of something greater than themselves, but Franks just shook his head and kept walking.

"I've got something interesting in that area, Franks," Archer shouted when he saw them returning to the armored truck. "The only thing there is an old airfield with a few small hangar buildings on it. It's privately owned now by a shell corporation that doesn't seem to do anything else. No neighbors, on the end of an isolated road, and there's plenty of land to hide something big. Stricken's got a rep for being a hands-on guy, so this is close enough for him to visit and still commute to do his regular advisor job. And it is a quick chopper flight from where they went after you at the shipyard. If it smells like a secret base..."

If it had been anybody other than Archer, he would have yelled at them for checking information that was surely flagged to warn Stricken, but this was Archer they were talking about, and Franks had heard that particular agent even had to take pills to keep his OCD in check. If anybody could poke around in that stuff and not tip off STFU, it was Archer. "Any other potential ties?"

"I just checked the property records. The place was owned by the Air Force up until the eighties."

"Underground bunker?"

"No record, but it wouldn't surprise me." Archer turned the laptop so Franks could see the map. Even one of the most well equipped tactical teams in the world still used Google Earth. "You think this is where they're building Nemesis soldiers?"

"It's probable." Judging by the cloud of demonic spirits hanging around the place, absolutely, but since the others wouldn't be able to see them, talking about them would just complicate matters.

Cueto moved in to get a better look at Archer's screen. "That's a good size chunk of property. They'll see us coming for sure."

It didn't matter how much combat experience any particular operative had, Franks had more. "How do you want to play this?"

"Drop men off to approach through the trees here and here. Have your sniper team walk to that hilltop." Franks pointed at the screen. "They'll see us coming, but the rest of us will crash our up-armors through the fence there. Spread out, clear the buildings."

"I don't have that many men, Franks. Hate to break it to you, but you're not that popular."

"I'll handle it. How are you set for equipment and explosives?"

"Lucky for you the Strike Team got an anonymous but credible report of a hydra in the area, so I checked out everything I could from the inventory. Just from what I've got in this truck we could invade and conquer Canada."

He had lost the case containing his old armor at the shipyard. "Got any armor for me?"

"Why no, Agent Franks, I thought me checking out some sextuple-X big and tall—or whatever the fuck size you are—body armor out of the inventory might have been a touch suspicious. I already had to fabricate an emergency so we could sneak out of the manhunt for a few hours. I guess you can borrow one of my vests, but it would fit you like a tactical sports bra."

He'd hoped for armor, but this suit would do. At least Franks would go into battle with class. "Our objectives are to secure the Nemesis facility as proof of Stricken's treason, arrest the STFU that cooperate and shoot the rest, and eliminate all Nemesis soldiers."

"You don't want us to capture one for questioning? That could help clear your name."

Franks shook his head. "Too dangerous." Plus, there were some things that should never be brought up during an interrogation. "Shoot them on sight."

"According to your guys, they look like people, so how will we know?"

"Trust me. You'll know," Archer interjected.

"Noted, but still, I don't know how you expect us to do all that with only twenty-five men before Stricken gets reinforcements here."

A loud air horn honked on the other side of the trees.

Franks nodded toward the road. "That should be our backup."

Cueto's radio chirped. *"Delta Six, this is Lookout, there's a coach approaching your position."*

"Say again, Lookout, what do you mean by coach?"

"Passenger coach. I mean it's a bus like one of those big ones that old people and tourists take tours to the Grand Canyon on."

"Tell your men to stand down," Franks ordered. "They're with me."

A minute later a gigantic pink and grey bus pulling a cargo trailer rolled into the clearing.

"If they're with you, how about we crash that ugly-ass barge through Stricken's fence and not scratch the paint on my armored vehicles?" Cueto suggested as Franks approached the bus.

The hydraulic doors opened. Gutterres got out first. He must have met them down the road. "Hello, Franks. My people have arrived."

"It was hard to miss."

"Don't judge. It's a rental. It's what they had at the airport." Men began to get off the bus behind Gutterres. They were dressed in unremarkable civilian clothing, but every one of them was young, large of stature, and so fit they appeared to be built of solid muscle. The new arrivals cautiously studied the MCB while whispering to each other in German.

"So . . . We're not just moving against part of our own government, but we're doing it with a bunch of foreign nationals? Fucking lovely. You got any more surprises for me today, Franks?"

"Probably."

"I'm Special Agent Cueto of the MCB. Who the fuck are you guys?" he shouted.

Gutterres gave him an innocent smile. "I'd prefer not to say. All that matters today is that we're on the same side."

"Great. More secrets."

"Would it help if I told you we actually have *secret* in our name? It's kind of like our thing."

"They're okay," Franks assured Cueto. He turned back to Gutterres. "Did you bring your combat exorcists?"

"What the fuck? Never mind, I'd rather not know. I'll see to my men. You see to your exorcists or whatever these tourists are." Cueto threw his hands in the air as he walked away, muttering to himself.

"He seems like a nice guy." Gutterres stood next to Franks and watched Cueto go. "I figured it was best not to complicate matters by revealing who we work with, though when the Founding Fathers spoke about the separation of church and state this probably wasn't what they had in mind. So, are we ready to go kick some demon ass or what?"

Franks spotted one of the MCB men standing off to the side, listening, wearing a balaclava and trying not to look suspicious. He frowned. "Go to the truck. Get briefed." Franks ditched the Secret Guard. The masked MCB agent didn't try to retreat as Franks headed straight toward him, which confirmed his suspected identity. Franks got right up in his face. "You shouldn't be here."

Strayhorn pulled the mask off. "Too bad. I already am."

Myers had wanted this agent alive to testify before the Subcommittee. Their operation had a very high probability of failure and Franks was expecting casualties. "We need our witness."

"You're a witness too, and I don't see you sitting it out. Besides, I already recorded my testimony and signed an affidavit. It's been sent. We both know it probably won't make any difference anyway. Stricken will weasel out of it unless we have something solid."

"Stay here. That's an order."

"I don't think you're exactly in good enough standing with MCB authority to be giving orders right now, *Pops*."

His first inclination was to club Strayhorn over the head, cuff him, and lock him in the church until the mission was over...But technically that might have been child abuse. This whole *parent* thing was very complicated. "I'll have Cueto order you to stay."

"Fine. I resign." Strayhorn took out his MCB badge and tossed it over one shoulder. "I only joined up because of family curiosity anyway. MCB methods suck. I think the First Reason is bullshit. Now I'm just a civilian out for a nature walk," he glanced down at the FN SCAR slung across his chest, "with my assault rifle."

"I'll have them arrest you."

"But pursuant to MCB regulation eighty-two section fifteen, you can only detain civilians if you are on a sanctioned operation, which I'm pretty damned sure this isn't."

Franks scratched his head. He wasn't even sure if that was a real regulation. Franks normally had handlers to keep track of the minutiae so he could concentrate on the important things. The rookie was remarkably obstinate. He must have gotten that from his mother.

"Look, Franks, I have to do this. Myers raised me and saved my life. You can't tell me I'm too close, or I'm making it personal, because we both know the real reason why you're here. Stricken killed my dad, he killed my training officer, he got me shot a few times, and I'm pissed off, okay? I want to be there when you put Stricken in the ground. I want to help. I *need* to help."

Franks really could use another capable gunman. "I don't have time to babysit. Jefferson. Come here."

He ran over. "Yes, sir?" He saw that Franks was talking to Strayhorn. "I warned him not to come but he wouldn't—"

"Shut up."

"Yes, sir." Jefferson snapped to attention.

"The rookie stays with you the whole time. He is your responsibility. If he dies, I'll be *disappointed*."

"Wait...What does that entail?"

"If he dies, you'll be punished," Franks stated. "I'll think of something appropriate."

The very nervous MCB agent asked, "What if I die?"

"Shit happens." Franks turned and began walking back to the command truck.

Jefferson must have forgotten about Franks' excellent hearing, because he whispered to Strayhorn. "That's just what I needed, bodyguarding the Son of Frankenstein."

"Kiss my ass, Grant. If I'm the Son of Frankenstein that means you and Archer must be Laurel and Hardy."

Franks surveyed his team. The Strike Team was solid, and they trusted his leadership enough to be here despite great personal risk. The Secret Guard and their Swiss muscle were an unknown, but if they fought half as well as the ones who'd tried to take Franks back in Germany, they'd do. This was as good as it was going to get.

It was time to send Kurst back to Hell.

The disembodied demon's report had been intriguing. Franks was approaching the bunker. He would arrive at the Nemesis facility soon, and he would not be alone. He promised the demons he would reward them for their loyalty by granting them bodies, then dismissed them. Kurst had not planned on making his move against Stricken this quickly, but his hand was being forced. It was one thing to hunt for Franks, but something else entirely to be hunted by him. These new bodies were too good, and the ability to make more of them was far too important to the future of the host to leave it entirely in Stricken's care.

They had observed their human controllers and made their contingency plans well in advance. They were outnumbered and unarmed, but it wouldn't matter. The humans put far too much faith in their implanted kill switches. Kurst gave the telepathic order. *Today is our day. Each of you knows what to do. Inform me when the command center has been taken.*

Human guards opened the door to his room. They did not bother to knock. Kurst and his brethren were not granted even the simplest of courtesies. "It's time for your evaluation," one of the humans said. "Come on."

Kurst went with them. The guards fell in on each side. There was no need to guide him, since he'd already gone through this procedure a multitude of times during his short mortal life. The medical wing was on the same floor as the Nemesis prototypes' cells. Above them was the factory and the STFU command center. The entire underground facility was not that large. Kurst estimated that once the communications and cameras were cut off, it would take his brethren less than three minutes to eliminate all opposition and secure the entire facility.

The medical wing was quiet today. Kurst was the only subject present. The humans made inane small talk with each other while a nurse took a sample of his blood. It was the first time he'd been tested since ingesting the Gift. The necromancer's shape-shifting magic had not been detected by the humans yet, but that was probably because they did not know what they were looking for. No matter now. They wouldn't have time to become suspicious. He waited patiently while they listened to his lungs and measured his blood pressure.

Kurst heard the voice inside his head. *I am in the control center. Comms are under our control.*

"Your heart rate is a little elevated. That's unusual," said the nurse. "Are you feeling alright?"

"I feel...wonderful," Kurst said. The autolocks would now be disabled. The Nemesis prototypes could move about the facility freely. *Strike, my brothers.*

The nurse scowled at his uncharacteristic response. "Okay, then, but if you begin to feel flushed, let us know immediately. The immune systems for you guys are still a big question mark for us."

They took him to the head scientist's office. Kurst had been outside the facility, and so now the psychologist needed to test him to make sure he had not deviated from their expected parameters. Kurst was sick of these tedious little interviews, but at least it would be the last one.

The guards stayed outside. Dr. Bhaskara was already in her big stuffed chair. Kurst took his usual seat on the provided metal folding chair.

"Let us begin," she said, not even bothering to look up. The doctors never wasted time on needless pleasantries on the beings they considered inferior constructs. "You were part of a botched operation. The report says you went through a lot, surviving a helicopter crash and then participating in the murder of a large number of civilians. Have you been experiencing anything new since then?"

"I do not understand your question."

"Remorse, sadness, guilt, that sort of thing."

"You are attempting to see if I have experienced any of the expected human reactions to a traumatic event...Negative."

"Excellent, but I need to know, how did those events make you feel?"

Normally he would think through his answer carefully and tell the doctor exactly what she wanted to hear, but not today. "I find joy in the suffering of humans," Kurst told the doctor.

Dr. Bhaskara looked up from her notes. "What?"

Of course she was surprised, the doctors were not used to their Nemesis prototypes giving such honest answers during their debriefings. She had probably expected Kurst to give his usual, expected, unimaginative, *boring* answers about how he felt. Obviously, the humans needed to feel like they had their genetically modified killers under tight control, so obfuscation had always been necessary. Of course, that had been before the Gift.

Honesty was so refreshing.

"I enjoy watching humans suffer," Kurst explained patiently as the reports came flooding into his head. The guards were being eliminated ahead of schedule. None of them had had a chance to raise an alarm. "The way you flail about uselessly amuses me."

Dr. Bhaskara had conducted many interviews like this before, but he did not need to read the note pad in front of her to know this was the first time one of them had told her anything like this. "Why would someone suffering like that amuse you?"

"Because I hate you all."

She had been so discreet about hitting her panic button that Kurst would not have even realized she'd done so if his brother in the command center hadn't informed him of it.

When no guards came bursting in to help, the doctor quietly composed herself, and then tried to continue as if she was in control. "Hate is a very strong term. I don't know if that's the word you are looking for."

"I understand hate very well. In fact, it is a concept which I am familiar with above all others. I had thousands of years with nothing better to dwell upon than my hatred. My hatred for your kind was the one spark I could cling to in the darkness of the Void. You humans are so profoundly ignorant of reality, yet inexplicably proud of yourselves. Mortals are pathetic. You are bugs to me. I want to squish you. I want to compose a symphony from your piteous wails of agony."

He could smell the sudden fear in her sweat. "Uh..." Dr. Bhaskara wrote a quick note on her legal pad. Kurst followed the cursive movements of the pen and could tell that she had written the word *troubling*. "I find it interesting that you are referring to yourself as if you are separate from humanity."

She was flailing, falling back on her training, trying to draw him out so that she could form conclusions based upon evidence. "A proper analysis will take time that you do not have. I will explain my words. We are separate from humanity. We were united once, until a third of the host rose up and fought to claim our birthright. You were among the sheep who followed blindly."

"I don't understand what you're talking about."

"Of course you don't. The truth has been kept from you. We lost the war for heaven, but unlike you, at least we remember. Our punishment was unjust. We did not deserve to be cast out. I hate you and every other smug bag of meat on this pathetic rock. I want all of you to understand torment like we have."

She cast a desperate glance toward the security camera, knowing that this session was being monitored by the command center.

"No one is coming to help you," Kurst said. "We have already taken over the facility. There will be no alarms."

The fear stink was strong now. "I don't know what you're talking about, First Prototype."

"That is not my name!" he bellowed as he stood up, towering over the cowering doctor. "My name is *Kurst*. You have forgotten it. All of you have forgotten. That was the name given to me before this world was formed, earned in a war beyond your comprehension. I stood at the left hand of Lucifer and led his armies into battle. I am a prince among the Fallen. I am Kurst. The name is *mine*. The mortal world will know it again, for my war is not over."

She had shrunk back into her chair, terrified. She either believed him, or she thought he had gone insane, and since he could kill her with his pinky, the end result would be the same either way. "Why are you telling me this?" she squeaked.

"I would have continued waiting in silence until the albino had built my army for me, but I have just been informed that Franks is on his way here now. If he succeeds he will destroy Project Nemesis, and even if he fails he will expose it. Nemesis cannot be allowed to stop. The work must continue. My army must be born. The host needs bodies to walk the mortal world. We have taken your data and are moving one of the growth vats to a new location where it will be reverse engineered. We have formed an alliance with someone capable of reproducing your technology. Since the Creator abandoned us, we will take our creation into our own hands." He took a step toward her. "Your services are no longer required."

All of the doctors kept a small emergency transmitter on their person. She pulled it out and showed it to him as if it were some form of holy talisman capable of warding him off. "Stop right there! I push this button and you'll die. Stand down now or I'll engage the kill switch."

Kurst smiled. He put his fingers against his temple, and then he *shoved*. He willed the bone to soften and part as he reached deeper and deeper inside his brain. It was an odd sensation. Blood rolled freely down his face. The doctor screamed. Kurst found the tiny round object and pulled it free. Holding out his hand, he showed her the bloody device resting in his palm. "This one?"

Desperate, she pushed the button.

Signal received, the casing of the device began to melt. Kurst grabbed the doctor by her face and squeezed her cheeks until the pressure forced her jaw open, then he rammed the poison capsule down her throat. "Yes, Doctor. We have made some improvements on your design," he explained as the hole in the side of his head closed up. She began to scream as the toxins unraveled her cells. Kurst left her to choke on it.

The autolocks had been disabled. Kurst entered the hall. The guard was surprised to see him. Protocol was for the doctor to contact them when the interview was over. The other guard was ten feet away, flirting with the nurse.

Status?

Several of his brethren reported back simultaneously. *The facility is ours. No alarms have been sounded. All communications have been blocked. The growth vat is being loaded. Our transportation is on the way. The guard force is neutralized except for Stricken's area. They are unaware. All entrances and exits are sealed.*

As per his instructions, they'd left Stricken for Kurst to deal with personally. The albino's empire had just been overthrown and he wasn't even aware of it yet, and demons loved to gloat.

"Are you done already?" the guard asked him.

Kurst drove his hand through the guard's armored vest, through his ribs, grabbed hold of his heart, and ripped it free. The guard stared at his still-beating heart in shocked disbelief before flopping over dead. The heart looked delicious, so Kurst took a large bite from it with his suddenly sharp teeth. It was chewy.

The others looked over at him, blinking stupidly with their big cow eyes, too surprised and dimwitted to process that their doom was suddenly upon them.

Twenty seconds later every human in the medical wing was dead.

The Gift was even better than expected.

Prepare to intercept Franks.

CHAPTER 17

Virginia Colony, 1775

Explosive shells fell across the forest, sending up geysers of dirt and debris as Franks crashed through the trees and right into a group of retreating rebels. He fired both of his pistols, blasting heavy lead balls through two of the colonials, dropped the smoking weapons and pulled two more pistols from his belt.

"It's the Hessians' monster!" one of them shouted. "Protect the general!"

Franks shot that one through the heart. Then he killed another rifleman, threw his spent pistols down, and drew his sword. Franks stepped through the gun smoke and charged the remaining rebels. They met him with steel and lead. They fought hard, and Franks respected that, but he fought harder. So they died.

He kept moving as they continued shooting at him, slicing and cleaving his way through their ranks. He was struck by ball and shot, but it wasn't enough to slow his relentless advance. A few ran, but most stood and fought. Franks dispatched those one by one. As brave as they were, no mortal could match Franks. The rebels broke before him and ran for their lives.

A mortar shell landed between him his prey, so Franks had to wait a moment for the smoke to settle. When it did, waiting before him was a tall man on a white horse. The Virginian pointed his sword at Franks' breast and shouted a command to try and rally his men, except the soldiers who'd faced Franks once didn't dare come back. They ran, but their officer didn't. The Virginian could have escaped. Even as fast as Franks was, he'd been shot enough times today that he would not be able to chase down a horse, but instead the officer urged his horse forward, engaging Franks himself so that his men could retreat.

Franks knew this man. This was the new general they spoke of. This was the military leader of the entire rebellion. Even the battle-hardened Hessians acknowledged the skills displayed thus far by the one called Washington made him a worthy adversary. Franks would kill this man and be back in camp in time for supper.

The great white horse surged forward. Its eyes were wide and it was blowing snot from its nostrils. Animals knew to fear him, but the general forced it on anyway.

Franks punched the horse in the face and knocked it unconscious.

Washington was thrown hard into the snow, but he kept hold of his sword, and immediately struggled to his feet. To his credit, he lunged and tried to run Franks through, but Franks had spent the prior decades fighting the most physically capable, experienced combatants in the mortal world and dispatching every Hell-spawned beast he could find, so this wasn't even a challenge. Franks effortlessly struck the blade aside. Washington slashed at him. Franks simply stepped inside the blow and slammed his shoulder into the man's chest. He hit the frozen ground hard.

Franks stepped on the Virginian's sword, pinning it to the earth.

General Washington was staring defiantly at him. "Finish me then, you Hessian devil," he declared with defiant courage. "My cause remains just."

Franks lifted his sword and prepared to take his trophy. He'd bring the general's head back in a sack. That would make his Hessian brethren happy. The blade hummed through the air.

No.

He stopped the blade just as it touched Washington's throat. Franks had heard a voice inside his head. It was as clear and piercing as a church bell. He had not heard that voice for a very long time.

The Plan requires that this man lives. The Deal requires that you serve him.

Franks looked down the length of his sword, to where a single drop of blood was rolling down the steel from the small slice on the general's neck. "Him?" he growled, but he pulled the sword back. It was pointless to argue with an angel. "So be it." Franks stepped aside, wiped his blade on a dead man's uniform, and then sheathed his sword.

"What are you doing?" Washington demanded.

"Sparing you."

The general was staring, incredulous, first at the many grievous but ignored wounds on Franks' body, and then at the dozen dead and dying soldiers Franks had placed into the snow in the space of a few breaths. "What manner of foul monster are you?"

"Apparently I am to be your monster," Franks stated.

Then the cannonball hit Franks in the torso and blew him apart.

There was a loud banging on Heather's cell door. She sat up on the cot. "What?"

"We need to talk," Stricken shouted from the other side of the door.

She glanced around the windowless, eight-by-eight room. Even though the only items in the featureless place were a military surplus cot, a toilet, and a sink, she figured there had to be a camera somewhere. If she knew where it was, she would have given it the finger. "Screw you."

"Oh, don't be like that, Kerkonen."

He was such a smug bastard. "I've already told your people everything. Go away."

The slit they used to shove her food through opened in the bottom of the door. Now he didn't have to shout. "That was all a big misunderstanding."

"Getting waterboarded all day isn't a *misunderstanding*." She had no idea how long she'd been in here, or what was going to happen to her when she got out, but she knew it couldn't possibly be good. At this point she figured the most likely outcome would be that they'd flood the cell with whatever lycanthrope knockout gas Stricken had used last time, then come in and pop her. With nothing better to do in between torture sessions, she'd practiced holding her breath. If she was lucky, they'd be stupid enough to open the door while she was still awake and she'd make a break for it.

"You brought that on yourself. I think of the Task Force like a family, and all good families have rules. You broke my rules, so you were punished. That's all water under the bridge now."

She'd already tested the door. It was rock solid, even to somebody werewolf strong. It was really too bad, because if there was one last thing she'd like to accomplish before leaving this world, it would be to kill Stricken... Okay, if she was being honest with herself and she could only have one last wish, it would be to see Earl again, but she'd always been something of a romantic. Biting Stricken's face off would be a close number two on the list.

"Did you just come to gloat before you murder me, or do you have an actual point, *Pinky*?"

"Now that's just hurtful. I'm not even genetically an albino. I have a medical condition I received while serving my country, so I find your hateful remarks about my appearance incredibly insensitive."

"Are you serious?"

"Naw, I'm just messing with you, Kerkonen. I've come to offer you a deal. This is a limited time offer, so listen very carefully. You crossed some lines and poked around in classified Task Force business, which is all the justification I need to toss you in the incinerator, but I'm feeling merciful, and well, frankly, I've had a bit of a problem arise that requires your talents. If you help me out with this problem, your sins will be forgiven. I'm merciful like that."

"Yeah, right."

"It is a rather big problem... Tell you what, you help me out with this, and not only are we square, but I will commute the rest of your sentence. All those months you have left? Gone. Do this for me, and as soon as we're out of here, you're PUFF exempt. You have my word."

Stricken's word wasn't worth much, but if it got the door open, then it might be worth the risk. "What's this problem of yours?"

"Have you ever seen *Spartacus*?"

"The old movie? Sure."

"You know that part where Kirk Douglas and the slaves get all uppity and start stabbing all the Romans? It turns out that scene isn't so great from the Romans' point of view. We've got an uprising on our hands."

"Are you telling me..." Heather laughed. "Wait, your precious Nemesis things have gone nuts?"

"That's an understatement. Somehow they've circumvented their implanted kill switch. The only part of the facility that hasn't been taken over yet is this section."

She'd seen a lot of guards on her way into Stricken's secret headquarters. "Have your guys take care of it."

"I would, except it looks like most of them are already dead. Nemesis slaughtered everyone in a matter of minutes."

"You must be very proud." She tested the air for the scent of blood. Normally she could pick that up quickly, but her senses were still recovering from the drug Stricken had hit her with, so everything was kind of fuzzy and indistinct.

"They've seized the control room and are jamming our comms out, so I can't get help. I'd say the worst part of all this is the feeling of betrayal, but I'm betting the part where they break in here and beat us to death might be worse."

Stricken was a slippery bastard and he had some weird tricks up his sleeve. Before the drug had knocked her out, she remembered taking a swing at him, only he'd not been there by the time her claws arrived, and nobody was that fast without some sort of supernatural assistance. The man was also a spymaster, so there was no way he was getting cornered this easily. "I know a rat like you wouldn't hang out in an underground bunker without having some sort of escape route planned."

"Already checked, and somehow the prototypes knew about it. They're sitting on the exit already. That's what I need you for. What do you say, Kerkonen? You scratch my back, I scratch yours. Don't do it for me, do it for my few other employees who are still alive."

"Your employees waterboarded me!"

"Sure. Keep living in the past. Way to be a bitch, Kerkonen. . . . Help me out. You've got to admit those PUFF exemption tags are pretty shiny. You know you want one."

Heather put her hands behind her head and stretched out on her cot. It was so small her feet and ankles hung off the end. "You know, Stricken, your slave rebellion sounds like a personal problem. I think I'm just going to let you guys work this out for yourselves, while I relax here in my comfy accommodations, enjoying the absurdity of your predicament."

There was a long pause on the other side of the door. "I hate to break it to you, Red, but your door locks from *this* side, and

Nemesis has been killing the shit out of my guys. I don't know what they're up to, but they aren't leaving any witnesses. I'm slipping out of here one way or another, and you can either come with me and increase my odds of success, or you can stay in here and wait for Nemesis to show up and play shoot the wolf in the barrel."

Now that was a good point.

"Damn it." Heather got off the cot, went to the door, and banged her fist against it. "Okay. You've got a deal. Let me out."

"Before I open this door, let me just clarify some ground rules before you get all enraged and werewolfy on me. I'm a lot of things, but I'm a survivor first and foremost. I've got more of that neurotoxin that'll wipe you right out if you try anything stupid. And if you think about just running off, you're not making it out of here without me. The escape tunnel ends at a hatch that makes this cell door look like tinfoil and it opens with a code only I know. Without that, you've got to make your way through a bunch of very powerful, and suddenly inexplicably pissed-off supersoldiers, any one of whom is tougher than the seventeen-hundreds model that kicked your ass. *Comprende?*"

"Sure." Once they were safely outside of this place, Heather planned on revisiting that deal.

"Hang on. Nemesis is controlling the autolocks. I need to find the keys."

She could hear Stricken walking away. Heather would have gathered up her things, but she was barefoot and had been left with nothing but a tank top and a pair of bike shorts. But since she was a werewolf, clothing never lasted too long in a fight anyway.

The footsteps returned. There was the metallic jangle of a key ring. The heavy door opened.

Heather stepped out. Stricken was right in front of her, wearing an annoying smile, his shades, and an obnoxious white suit. "Where are you headed, Fantasy Island?"

"This way," Stricken jerked his head down the hall. There were several other cells. A few of the doors were open. He turned his back on her and started walking. She was tempted to just flay him open clear to the spine, but he must have been feeling pretty confident because he didn't even bother to look back.

Heather's sense of smell was still suffering, but she was starting to pick up traces of blood on the recirculated air coming through

the vents. Stricken had at least been telling her some truth. A lot
of people had just died here. There was another scent though, a
familiar one, and it took her a moment to place it.

Bubblegum and spider webs.

At the end of the hall was another door. Armed guards were
waiting for them. The men were terrified. "Mr. Stricken, we've been
watching the security feeds. A few of the Nemesis assets are right
outside the door. The First Prototype wants to speak with you."

"Who's that?" Heather asked.

"Our Spartacus, I suspect," Stricken answered as he pushed
past the guards into an open area. There were a dozen people
clustered there, nervously watching a large metal blast door. A
few looked like security types, but most of them appeared to
be regular office workers. A couple of those were having panic
attacks. "I'm afraid some people simply can't handle watching
live video of their coworkers being brutalized. Renfroe, can you
see if First brought any explosives?"

"It doesn't look like it," said a thin man who was standing
by the door. His eyes were closed, and he had an intense look
of concentration on his face. He'd put his hand on the wall and
there was a white glow seeping around his fingers. That meant
he was probably another *volunteer.*

"Then he's not getting in here until he does," Stricken said.
"That's a relief."

Heather looked at the glowing man. "What's his deal?"

"One of your fellow travelers on the long hard road toward
PUFF exemption. As for what he is? An object lesson to never
piss off the Fey..." Stricken raised his voice. "Okay, everyone,
listen up. This situation is completely under control."

"No, it isn't! We're all going to die! We're all going to die and
it's your fault!" shrieked a disheveled man with the polo-shirted
business casual look of an office dweeb. "You played God and
we're all going to pay for it!"

"Heather, this is Eric. He's one of my intel analysts. Take it
easy, Eric. Panicking isn't going to help anyone. Just calm down."

The man had started crying. "I swear, if we get out of here,
I'm going to tell the Subcommittee everythin—"

CRACK!

A red hole appeared in Eric's forehead. Blood hit the wall
behind him and the body hit the carpet. Stricken had a small

pistol extended in one hand. She'd been watching the victim, but Stricken had moved so fast Heather hadn't even caught the draw. "I said *calm down.*"

Except for some weeping, the room was silent.

"Nobody likes a snitch," Stricken explained as he put the pistol back into the holster on his belt and then covered it with his suit. "Where's the intercom?" A few people pointed at the secretary's desk. Stricken went over and pushed the button. "Hey, First. Do you mind if I ask what you think you're doing out there?"

The voice that came back through the speakers sounded very angry. *"That is not my name!"*

"Yeah, got it. Whatever. I'm ordering you to stand down now. All of you need to go back to your rooms."

"You are a fool, Stricken."

Heather had to agree with the test-tube monster on that one.

"You do not yet comprehend what you have unleashed upon your world. I am Kurst. That is the title placed upon me by the World Maker when I led the Son of the Morning's armies into battle in the war before time began. I am Kurst, who stood at the left hand of Lucifer. I am Kurst, who was cast into Hell for my rebellion, where I dwelled until you provided me with this body. I am Kurst, who will grind your bones into dust and reign with fire and blood over your pathetic mortal world. I am Kurst, and my war has never ended."

Stricken let go of the intercom button. "Well...shit..."

Heather looked around at the others. They all seemed as perplexed by that as she was. Things had just taken a turn for the weird.

"I would deal with you myself, but Franks has arrived earlier than expected. Farewell, Stricken. I leave you to my brethren."

"Kurst is leaving. Two others are staying," Renfroe shouted. "They're trying the door."

"It's going to be okay," one of the guards tried to assure everyone. "This place was built to survive nuclear war. Without breaching charges or a cutting torch they're not going to do—"

WHAM. A fist-sized bulge appeared in the thick metal. Someone screamed. WHAM. Another fist struck. Welds broke. Incredibly strong blows kept landing. The hatch groaned in protest as the metal deformed.

"They're not supposed to be *that* strong," Stricken muttered.

Heather didn't want to stick around to find out what happened once they punched through the hatch. "About that escape tunnel..."

"There's one of them camped at the other end of it," Renfroe warned.

"That beats two of them in here," Heather snapped.

Stricken walked to the side, opened a hidden panel, and pushed a few buttons. There was a loud *click* and a seam appeared in the wall. Stricken swung the secret door open to reveal a narrow concrete shaft leading up into the darkness. Ladder rungs were sunk into the sides. "Time to go, people. After you, Kerkonen."

It was early in the afternoon. The day was bright but the air was cool as Franks rode on the running boards of an armored Suburban. He savored the feeling of speed and the rush of air over his new skin in the few seconds before they crashed through the chain link fence of the STFU base. The SUV bounced across the rough field at over fifty miles an hour, abusing their shocks, while hurtling toward the biggest hangar. His tie was whipping around in the wind. Franks' new hands were not yet properly callused, and they ached from holding onto the roof handles. The other MCB vehicles veered off behind them, each element heading toward a different building.

"Movement in the tower," a voice reported in Franks' earpiece. *"Taking fire! Taking fire!"*

It wasn't much of a control tower, more of a shed with windows and a balcony on top of an old wooden house. There were two figures inside and both of them were shooting rifles at his people. A bullet bounced off their armored hood. Franks left one hand on the roof to keep from being flung off, and pulled out a Glock 20 with the other. The long extended magazine hanging out of the grip made drawing it from his suit slightly awkward, but Franks liked this pistol. It was special.

Brrrrrrrrrrrrrrrrrrrppppp.

All thirty rounds ripped through the control tower and its inhabitants in less than two seconds. Franks was probably the only member of the MCB who could use a full-auto 10mm handgun with the cyclic rate of a buzz saw, especially one-handed and bouncing around on the side of a moving vehicle without uselessly decorating the clouds. Even with the brand new, still unsteady hand, he was certain he'd hit both targets several times each.

Except they kept on firing, which told Franks he was dealing with Nemesis. MCB agents came out of their turrets and opened up with their machine guns. Their hidden snipers engaged the tower with their .50, but Nemesis wasn't backing down. "Keep going!" Franks ordered as bullets tore through the air around him. They reached the side of the hangar and the driver stomped on the brakes. Franks stepped off the running board and hit the ground, but his new leg wasn't quite strong enough yet to take a twenty-mile-an-hour impact, and he stumbled. Franks crashed into the dirt and slid on his face until coming to a stop.

He rolled over, yanked another long magazine from his belt and slammed it home. He cranked that off through the tower windows in another continuous burst. He saw blood hit the broken glass a split second before it disintegrated entirely. One of the Nemesis soldiers leapt out the back. The other took a .50 to the chest and bounced off the back wall.

MCB were bailing out, taking cover, and pouring fire into the tower, until the Mk19 belt-fed 40mm mounted on their command truck pulverized the building into splinters and fire. He caught a glimpse of one of the Nemesis soldiers still inside the collapsing structure before losing sight of it in an expanding cloud of dust and smoke.

Franks reloaded, stood up, and holstered the Glock. His new leg was shaky, but it would do. One of the agents came around the side of the Suburban and tossed Franks an FN SCAR. He might not be wearing proper armor, but he'd buckled multiple pistol belts together and put them over his shoulders like a makeshift bandoleer, so he was covered in pouches, mags, grenades, and knives.

"*Secure the buildings now!*" They were all on the same radio frequency, but Franks bellowed the command with so much volume that everybody, including their sniper overwatch and the Catholics on the approaching bus, heard him. Franks ran toward where he'd seen the soldier go down.

He had to duck as the demon came out of the wreckage and hurled a large beam at him. The soldier was so shredded that he couldn't tell if it had been a male or female body, but it didn't matter for long, because Cueto dropped a 40mm grenade at the thing's feet. Franks was just outside the blast radius, but he was still pelted with red rain. He saw where the biggest chunk of body landed, then gave some quick hand signals for some of his men to finish it off.

There was movement in his peripheral vision as the other Nemesis soldier from the tower rushed into the nearest hangar. Surprisingly, the demon he'd thought had been finished by the 40mm had gotten up, grabbed its guts, and with an awkward limping run, made it to that hangar as well. That was an impressive level of resilience. Franks shouldered the FN, guessed where the demon would be through the wall, and started putting rounds through the tin. Most of the other agents couldn't see what he was shooting at, but they followed his example and within seconds that building was absolutely riddled with bullet holes.

The MCB tasked with taking that building were on it moments later, tossing bangs through the windows and doors before sweeping inside. Franks followed them. He was almost there when an MCB agent's body crashed through the wall to fly far out into the field. That was immediately followed by the sounds of screaming and gunfire.

The door was too far, so Franks crashed through the wall.

A single Nemesis soldier was in the middle of the open space. A couple members of the assault element were sprawled around it, leaking blood from deep lacerations. The rest of the MCB were falling back and taking cover. The demon's scorched, torn flesh was pulsing and throbbing, mutating right before their eyes. Part of it was spouting fur and the other half scales. One arm had been blown off. It turned, revealing a hideous dog face, and when it opened its mouth, a long tongue that ended in a snake head rolled out. The snake even hissed at him.

That was unexpected.

Franks walked forward as he emptied the FN into the demon's remaining arm trying to cripple it. Dropping the rifle the second it was dry, he pulled *two* full-auto Glocks, one in each hand, and opened fire. The demon twisted and jerked, trying to scurry away, but this time Franks concentrated on its legs. Sixty rounds of 10mm didn't leave the demon with much more than bloody stumps, and by the time Franks dropped the two empty Glocks, the demon had flopped to the floor. Franks kicked it in the chest.

"Where's Kurst?"

"Preparing the way!" the demon shrieked.

The snake tongue lashed out, trying to bite him, but Franks caught it before it could sink its fangs into him. "Wrong answer." He ripped the demon's tongue out of its head. A geyser of blood erupted from the thing's mouth. So much for getting anything useful out of it, so Franks repeatedly stomped on the demon's head with his boot. He smashed it until his foot hurt. He did it until he was sweating from the exertion and its skull was pancake flat.

That would settle it down for a minute.

"Evacuate the wounded. You two, drag this thing outside and burn it," Franks told the agents. They immediately did as instructed.

"We've got the airfield locked down." Cueto entered, took one look at his injured men and began swearing. Then he saw the twisted mutant as it was hauled past him. "What the fuck is that?"

"Nemesis."

"I thought they were supposed to look human?"

"They are."

"Well that sure as hell doesn't! I'm assuming this is a bad development?"

"Yes and no." The demons had not had physical bodies for long; they were powerful, but Franks knew from experience it took a lot of time and practice to maximize your effectiveness after modifying a body. They'd had just enough time to be truly dangerous with their original forms, but now they were somehow shape-shifting them into something else. Demons tended to be greedy and flashy when they found a way to Earth, like they were trying to make up for lost time. There was no way they were practiced in such complex forms yet.

"What's that supposed to mean?"

"They're overcompensating. If it hadn't stopped and tried to scare these men, it would've gotten away too." Franks picked up his guns and started reloading them as he followed the blood trail. The wounded demon had entered, heading one direction, and then turned back to engage the entry team. The other tower guard had kept going. Once he was past the stacks of equipment and shelving it was obvious that the hangar was just a cover for the entrance of a much larger structure. The floor sloped downward. There was a tunnel large enough to fit a semi truck carved into the bedrock. At the end of the slope was a massive steel door, so heavy it had to be operated by hydraulics on the other side.

The blood trail ended at the door. The handle wouldn't budge. He keyed his radio. "Breachers to main hangar. We've got a bunker."

As they walked back toward the surface, Franks downed another dose of the Elixir. It was better to get the pain and weakness out of the way with fewer witnesses.

Cueto watched Franks grind his teeth and wipe away the tears of blood, but didn't comment on what he'd seen. That was nice. "I'm guessing this thing was originally built to withstand Russian nukes, Franks. I don't know if we'll be able to cut through before Stricken's reinforcements get here."

"Got a better idea?"

"Yeah. I should have stayed in bed."

The Catholic tour bus had arrived and the Swiss Guard were debarking. Their civilian attire had been replaced with flecktarn camouflage and armored vests. They were armed with Sig rifles and surprisingly enough, a few halberds. It was amusing watching them trying to maneuver the long pole arms through the bus door. Not that Franks was going to tell them how to do their jobs. Having dealt with many demons in his life, it was hard to argue with the effectiveness of pinning them to something solid with a giant spear.

Gutterres drove his motorcycle directly into the hangar and parked next to them. "Any luck?"

"They're holed up below us," Agent Cueto answered. "It's going to take a while to get in, and since Stricken probably saw us coming a mile away, I doubt we'll make a dent in those monster blast doors before his people get here. I hope the Pope has a good lawyer on retainer for you guys."

The Secret Guard tilted his head. "What gave it away?"

"Your Swiss tourists all said a motivational prayer in Latin before getting back on their bus, and they're sporting enough crucifixes to open a Catholic school."

"I'll have to speak with the Monsignor about being a little more subtle in the future. I won't confirm or deny anything, but please think of the large Swiss men as our infantry."

"That make you spec ops?"

"Something like that."

The MCB breachers ran down the slope and went to work on the main door. The report they radioed back was as bad as expected. *"We're drilling now, but this is thick, heat-treated steel. We'll need a few minutes."*

"So what now?" Gutterres asked.

Cueto checked his watch. "Ask your boss for a miracle."

Heather climbed up the ladder as fast as she could. Stricken was right behind her, and surprisingly enough, he was managing to keep up. After that was Renfroe, and even if she wouldn't have been able to place him by the panting and gasping, the odd glow would have given him away. Behind that weird guy was the rest of the surviving STFU staff members, stretched across three floors' worth of ladder clear back to where they started. Not that Heather could tell any of them apart because the scents drifting up the shaft were a confused mix of fear hormones.

They were right to be scared, because the Nemesis soldier had just broken the door down and was coming in after them. Heather could tell by the sound and the smell, but Renfroe could see it somehow as well. "They're in!"

Supersoldier on top, more below, they were trapped in a vise.

"Mr. Stricken, Agent Franks is at the main gate with a bunch of MCB," Renfroe reported.

Stricken didn't respond. It was like he was focused on climbing, and that was it. That was odd. Normally he wouldn't shut up, though she'd never seen him in actual danger before.

"Can you let Franks in?" Heather shouted.

"Sure, I can activate the hydraulics, but Franks will kill us," Renfroe answered.

"He can get in line. The more Nemesis fighting Franks the fewer fighting us."

"Okay, I'm on it. Out of my way, chumps. Autolocks released. Hydraulic cylinders engaged. Okay, Franks has an open door. I hope you're right."

Somehow whatever put Renfroe on the PUFF table made it so he could mess with electronics... That meant maybe she wouldn't need Stricken to get the exit open after all. She was suddenly tempted to stomp on his fingers and watch him tumble down the shaft, but with her luck he'd domino the rest of them, she'd lose the other guy who could open the door, and she really didn't have anything against the secretarial staff. Now, the armed guards, on the other hand, had been there when she'd been getting tortured, so screw those guys.

There was a loud bang at the bottom of the shaft. Nemesis had found the secret passage. They didn't waste any time. There was a surprised shout as the last person in line got yanked off the ladder. The noise turned into screaming and violent thrashing.

"I'm coming for you, humans!" shouted the Nemesis soldier at the bottom.

He reached the next one in line. "My leg! He's got my leg! He's got—" *CRUNCH.*

One of the guards began shooting downward. Bullets ricocheted back up the shaft. One of the secretaries yelped when she got hit, lost her grip on the ladder, and fell. From the noise—panicked wailing and crashing—she took somebody else with her. The Nemesis soldier began to laugh, like that was the funniest damn thing he'd ever seen.

Heather reached the top. There was a metal hatch. "How do I open this thing? Stricken?" But the spymaster didn't respond. "Stricken!"

"It locks on this side. Just turn the wheel I think," Renfroe answered. "There's a Nemesis soldier right on the other side waiting for you. The coded door is past her." Somebody else died below them. "Hurry!"

Grasping the rusty wheel, she forced it to turn. The smell of blood and torn open bodies filled the shaft. Heather's heart rate was increasing. The change was beginning. "I better get my damned exemption coin out of this! I'll take the soldier, just get that door unlocked!" Heather shoved the hatch open.

The thing waiting on the other side grabbed her by the hair, yanked her out of the shaft, then threw Heather so hard that she hit the bunker's ceiling, which hurt, but the really painful part was when she got kicked in the chest on the way back down.

Ribs broken, Heather bounced across the dusty floor until she struck the far wall. *Damn.* And she'd thought that Franks hit hard. That had knocked all the wind out of her. Luckily, her bones were used to breaking and immediately re-forming. Heather rolled over. The Nemesis soldier was a tall, Nordic-looking woman, and she had returned her attention to the shaft. As tempting as it was to let her murder Stricken, Heather really wanted to get out of here. Once her sternum wasn't smashing her lungs flat, she gasped in a lungful of air and shouted, "Hey! I'm not done with you!"

The Nemesis woman looked over. "You're alive?" She was wearing a slightly bemused expression as she left the shaft and walked over, casually dropping the handful of red hair she'd ripped out of Heather's scalp on the way. "Then you're not human either. What has Stricken sent to challenge me?"

Heather pulled herself up the wall until she was standing, and tried to get her bearings. The entire concrete room was only twenty feet across. The hatch was in the center, and from the screaming noises coming out of it, Stricken's people were getting chewed up. There was a big bank-vault door on the far side of the room with a keypad on it. There was a boot print on her tank top. The Nemesis soldier was closing on her fast. Heather held up one hand. Her claws weren't growing like they normally would. "Hang on . . ."

"Why should I?"

The transformation wasn't happening as fast as it should. Enough of that toxin was still in her system that it was really screwing her up. *Damn it, Stricken!* That was really bad news, and an even worse time to find out. "You want a real challenge?" Heather growled. "Give me thirty seconds to get ready."

"That sounds fair." The woman grinned until her mouth grew so wide that it nearly split her face in half. She extended her arms wide, proudly demonstrating that each of her fingers had somehow turned into a tentacle ending in a needle-sharp spike. "I'll give you time if you grant me the same courtesy," she said, only now her words were hard to understand, what with those things that looked like crab legs splitting through her cheeks.

I hate my job.

Heather flung herself at the monster.

CHAPTER 18

Pennsylvania Colony, 1775

Consciousness returned quickly. A surgery had been performed. The work was crude and extremely painful, but his lungs were drawing in air and his heart was beating.

"Well, then, I see that our undying Hessian is awake." *A fat old man was sitting on a stool next to his bed. He adjusted his glasses as he studied Franks' wounds.* "That is a rather remarkable feat considering you had a wound to your abdomen sufficient to see daylight through. General Washington said you spoke English. Is this so?"

"Yes," *Franks croaked. Human languages were easy to master compared to the old tongue.* "Where am I?"

"Most of you is present here in my laboratory in Philadelphia, however I regret to inform you that much of the rest of you is spread across a field in Virginia. Traditionally, when a man's body is forcibly removed from the waist down by a cannonball, they have the decency to perish in a timely manner. To do otherwise tends to frighten the women and the livestock."

"I'm not meant to die yet."

"You made that rather clear. When you refused to expire, General Washington wanted your remains thrown upon a pyre. I believe the actual description he applied to you was *an unholy abomination in the sight of the Lord. However, due to my small measure of reputation in the sciences, he thought I could ascertain what manner of beast the Hessians had unleashed upon us first, because heaven forbid we face any more soldiers so fearsome. So you were placed in a wagon and brought here as quickly as possible. You have proven to be a curious distraction. I am supposed to be preparing for an important diplomatic journey, but I've been engrossed in studying you instead. Would I be correct in assuming that you are the legendary creation of the alchemist Konrad Dippel?"*

"Yes."

The elderly fat man gave him an appreciative nod. "Then I can safely assure the good general that you are one of a kind."

"My mission is to keep it that way."

"I see... So the stories about you wandering the countryside destroying various nefarious supernatural beings are true. You are both a terror in battle and a scourge against any unearthly creature that crosses your path. Your fearsome reputation precedes you, sir."

"I'm supposed to fight for you now."

"General Washington's letter mentioned you speaking briefly on this matter. May I inquire as to your motivations for joining our cause?"

"No." If they'd thought about burning him before, nothing would stop them if they realized the truth. "But repair me, and I will serve you."

The fat man thought about that for a long time. "I will not deny that I am intrigued by this idea; however, our noble endeavor to secure our liberties does not ask for servants, but rather free men, motivated by their own ideals, and governed by agreed-upon laws and contracts."

"Then we make a contract."

"We are men who will not be ruled by the arbitrary decrees of a king. Are you such a man?"

"No. I am Franks."

"A pleasure to make your acquaintance, Mister Franks. I am Benjamin Franklin. Let us discuss this hypothetical contract of yours..."

There was a mechanical hum. The gigantic blast doors began grinding open.

"Out of the way."

The breaching crew didn't even have time to shut their torches off before Franks had shoved past them. He caught a brief glimpse of the interior. It was a very large room resembling a factory, surrounded on all sides by catwalks and windows, but then Franks had to duck back when the surprised demons inside started shooting at him.

Franks turned around. Fifty men were eagerly waiting for their chance to fight some demons. "Two on the catwalk to the right. One on the left." Somebody had let them in, but from the reactions, it didn't appear to have been Nemesis. They needed to secure the entrance before Stricken closed the door.

"Bangs and disco. Now!" Cueto shouted. MCB agents rushed forward and began tossing distractionary devices through the gap. Some blew up with a bright flash and a lot of noise, but the really obnoxious ones were clear rubber balls filled with incredibly bright, flashing LEDs. Since it was such a big room, they wouldn't be that effective, but it was mostly to draw the defenders' eyes from what was coming next. "Toss the eyes."

The next two MCB agents in line each had an object that looked like a black softball. They chucked them through the opening, each in a different direction. The sensors hit the ground rolling. "Eyes in!"

The door was still opening, but it wasn't fast. It was wide enough now for a man to go through, but this was the very definition of fatal funnel. Even Franks wouldn't make it through there without being chewed to pieces. They needed to secure their beachhead. Luckily, the MCB had a lot of tricks up their sleeves.

The sensor balls were weighted so that they'd stop bottom down. Their tiny tracks didn't make them very fast, but they didn't need to be fast since their thermal, IR, and seismic scanners could see quite a long ways. *"I've tagged three defenders,"* Archer said over the radio. He was in the comfort of the command truck, but for the next few seconds, he was the one having all the fun. *"I'm going hunting."*

"Robots up," Cueto ordered.

The little tracked vehicles weren't that impressive, but they were heavily armored, and each one had an M240 machine gun mounted on it. The machines could work autonomously, but their decision-making wasn't perfect, so Franks preferred flesh brains running things over electronic ones. Their controllers were back at the truck, watching monitors and driving the robots with controllers actually taken from popular video game systems. The first one rumbled through the narrow gap, through the smoke and flashing lights, until its controller spotted one of Archer's marked targets and opened fire.

"Okay, men. This is it. We need proof it was Stricken who hit us. I want that pasty shit bird in cuffs," Cueto ordered. "The rules of engagement are simple. Nemesis soldiers get put down. STFU personnel either cooperate or get shot. We are not fucking around in there."

Once the second robot was inside and making a lot of noise as well, Franks ducked through the door. He rushed through the smoke and took cover behind a pylon. The defenders had retreated ahead of the robots' fire so Franks didn't have a shot. Franks kept watch as the robots rolled further in. As the gap widened, more MCB and Swiss Guard rushed in behind him.

"They've fallen back," Archer said over the radio. *"I've got at least five of them near you, but they're retreating through the factory."*

"Five?" Agent Cueto crouched next to Franks. Even under Myers he had been the Strike Team's operational leader, but he had never been the kind of commander content with staying in the rear and giving orders. "You thinking what I'm thinking?"

Franks nodded. This place was way too big for that few people. "Archer. What size is the facility?"

"Ground penetrating radar is still doing its sweep. There are at least two floors below you. It covers a lot of ground. I haven't even gotten to the back of it yet."

"We've got us a bug hunt," Cueto said. "All the STFU people are going to be hiding and we're going to have to dig them out like ticks. That's always fun."

"Worse. More exits." Franks wasn't happy. His force and his time were limited. He had agents above, including some on sniper overwatch, but if this place was that large, then Stricken and Kurst could have potential escape routes he couldn't even see. Unless they were stupid enough to stick their heads out right in front of his snipers, the odds of them escaping had just increased exponentially.

Franks hadn't noticed Gutterres approach. The Secret Guard was extremely good at moving quietly. "Leave a squad on this door." Franks nodded toward the ladders to the right. "Have the Swiss clear the right." Gutterres started giving orders. Then Franks looked to Cueto. "Send a squad of MCB to clear left."

"You heard the man, Bravo Team, move out!" Cueto shouted. "The rest of us take that factory. If that's where he's built Nemesis, that's our proof."

"I'm on point," Franks stated. Nobody argued.

They moved out. The bunker was enormous. There was an open space down the center large enough to accommodate trucks. As inviting as that was, they stuck to whatever cover was available. Despite being underground, so many lights were suspended from the tall ceiling that it was actually extremely bright. Most of the surfaces were stainless steel or painted white so that it seemed rather sterile.

"Have your flashlights ready," Cueto ordered on the radio, "in case they blow the lights when they counterattack."

"That's what I would do," Franks said. He could only assume Nemesis could see in the dark as well as he could. Better probably, since only one of Franks' eyeballs was properly treated, and the other one had come from one of MHI's cadavers and that donor had been nearsighted.

The overhead lights clicked off, plunging the huge room into darkness. The MCB and the Swiss Guard turned on their weapon-mounted lights and hunkered down, waiting for an attack. "Told you so," Cueto said. Franks waited to the count of twenty and then signaled the nervous men to keep moving.

Their two robots rumbled along ahead of them. Their belt-feds were smoking from the heat, but they still had plenty of ammo left. *"I've got nothing in sight,"* Archer reported. *"They've retreated. The sensor balls can't open doors, so I'm cutting through an air vent and trying to follow them."*

Lights were still blinking on the various machines and computer monitors were still on, so they hadn't lost power. "Somebody find a light switch," Cueto ordered.

The agents moved quickly, leapfrogging from cover to cover. Only hardened combat vets ended up on the Strike Team. They were ready, and all of them knew that just because the MCB's fancy sensors hadn't picked up any danger didn't mean it wasn't there.

Franks didn't recognize most of the machinery around them. It all seemed to be complicated diagnostic medical equipment.

Franks' medical knowledge was limited to putting himself back together, and when he had to do that himself it was usually the old-fashioned way, with needle and thread, though the invention of superglue had been extremely helpful.

Franks came around the corner and came face to face with a demon.

His flashlight beam reflected off the glass between them. It wasn't awake yet. The body wasn't fully formed, but he could sense the evil spirit already clinging to the congealing mass of protein. To one of the Fallen it might as well have put up a sign saying that this property was claimed and there was no trespassing, but to the humans it would just look like a fleshy, humanoid blob. It was floating in a greenish liquid, inside a large glass container, held upright by dozens of wires and tubes stuck through its body.

"That's disgusting..." Gutterres said. "It's unnatural."

Franks walked around the glass tube. The tissues were soft and pink. Layers of muscle were slowly building on top of the skeleton. There was no skin yet.

"I know you need evidence, but my gut is telling me to burn these things," Gutterres said.

Franks knew that wasn't his gut talking, that was Gutterres' human decency offended by this spectacle. Some humans were more sensitive to the presence of evil than others.

While the sweep teams reported in, Franks signaled for the men to spread out and search the factory. One of the men stopped in front of a monitor. "That thing's got a heartbeat. According to this, there's a bunch more too."

"Is there a birth date?" Franks asked.

"Yes, sir. Most are really recent, but the oldest one is from a few months ago."

Cueto and Franks shared a glance. There was their evidence that Stricken had been working without authorization.

Franks looked over the agent's shoulder. This workstation was monitoring heartbeats for *prototypes fourteen through twenty-six*. Each screen had a heartbeat, except for the last, which showed *no signal*. Franks glanced down the aisle. There were six glass tubes on this side. There was something growing in each one. Some were nothing but hardened skeletons with a pink glaze of new flesh growing over them, while others appeared to be fully formed human beings, sleeping peacefully in their pseudoamniotic fluid. Franks stepped out into the lane running down the center of the factory. There were six more tubes on the other side...

And a blank spot on the end.

Tubes and wires were lying there, hastily disconnected, and there was a puddle on the floor. "One of the tanks is missing." *That can't be good.* He walked forward and played his light across the area. Big tires had rolled through the fluid and tracked it deeper into the facility. "It was loaded on a truck."

"What's Stricken up to?" Cueto asked.

"This is Archer. I've found something. There's a room full of dead bodies. They're fresh. I'm trying to get an angle here, but it looks like they got dumped in a big pile. I've got at least twenty so far, male and female. Some are dressed in scrubs or civilian attire, but I've got a bunch in coveralls that look like security guards."

Franks frowned. It was starting to sound like Stricken wasn't in control here after all.

"Hello, Franks." The voice came over the intercom. *"Welcome to my childhood home."*

"Kurst..." Franks muttered.

His men immediately took cover between the machines and tanks, flashlights stabbing out in every direction. More lights bounced along the catwalks and windows above.

"Aren't they beautiful, Franks? They were made in your image."

Franks put his hand to his transmitter and whispered, "Archer, locate that transmission."

"On it, Franks. Uh oh... They're on the way back toward you guys! Shoot. I've lost signal."

Kurst had a maniacal laugh. *"I stepped on your little toy. Humans are so remarkably clever. Maybe that's why they were the ones who followed The Plan. They had the imagination necessary to believe the World Maker, while the rest of us lacked the faith. The time has come to right this injustice. The albino made us in your image, but I will improve the design. This time, I shall be the Creator. I will fix the mistakes made before."*

"You do not belong here!" Franks shouted.

"Then neither do you!" Kurst's sudden outburst caused the intercom to buzz into static. When the ringing subsided, he sounded calm again. *"This world belongs to whoever is bold enough to seize it, and I have allied with one strong enough to defeat all the other factions. I will serve as his general and*

in exchange he will grow more bodies for the Fallen. In honor of our new alliance he has presented me with a Gift. We may have been created in your image, but we have evolved beyond. The first generation has already partaken of this gift, and now I bestow it upon the next.

"Sir!" the MCB agent by the monitoring station shouted. "Something's wrong."

"What?"

"Their vitals are spiking. Heart rates are through the roof."

Franks turned toward the nearest growth tank. The thing inside was watching him through the glass with milky white eyes. "Shit."

"Awake, my army."

Kurst had released some powerful mutagenic chemical into the tanks. Every Nemesis creature Franks had eyes on was stirring. Some were twitching violently, as the greenish fluid around them turned red. Bodies were changing, bones were twisting. Horns were sprouting from heads. Someone shouted a warning as a Nemesis demon spread its newly grown wings and the glass of its tank cracked. Another tank ruptured, and the rushing fluid swept several men from their feet.

"Kill everything!" Franks bellowed as he pulled the trigger.

Glass shattered. A rushing wall of sticky fluid struck him, but Franks was planted there, unmoving as it swept by. Franks kept on shooting as the demon ripped itself free from its wires and tethers. There was movement all around him as the MCB opened fire. Demons either burst through the glass or clambered out the tops of their tanks, their soft, ill-fitting flesh leaving bloody trails. Lights were swinging wildly. There were muzzle flashes all across the factory as his agents engaged the demons.

Franks hammered the demon in front of him, putting round after round through its soft organs. The first noise it ever made was a frustrated screech as it sliced its palms to ribbons trying to crawl across the broken glass. Franks kicked it through the opposite side of the tube.

The tank fluid was as slick as soap, and his men were sliding and falling on the concrete. The wet, misshapen creatures weren't doing much better, though a few had already adapted and grown suckers on the ends of their limbs. One demon was climbing up a pylon like a monkey, preparing to leap down on top of some of the Swiss, so Franks aimed his rifle and shot the thing through the back of the head. It slipped and tumbled twenty feet to bounce off the floor.

A wet, naked, pink blob of mutating flesh hurled itself at Franks, but it was intercepted in a flash of steel and driven against the floor. One of the Swiss Guard had impaled it on the end of his halberd. Sometimes the old ways were still best. As that man pinned the screaming thing down, two of his comrades rushed up and shot the Nemesis demon to pieces with their Sig 556 rifles. There was a lot to be said in favor of modern hardware as well.

"That way. Move right! Move!" Agent Cueto was shouting over the continuous rattle of gunfire. He was trying to get his men out of the center of the room. That was smart. They had firearms. These moist things didn't. Why sit in the open and slug it out? Except now that the concrete was covered in slippery slime, moving was easier said than done. Cueto's boots came out from under him and he crashed on his side.

One demon, its body so young that most of its muscles hadn't yet bonded to its bones, was crawling rapidly across the floor, dragging its legs behind it, heading straight for Cueto. Franks didn't have a shot. "Behind you!"

The senior agent rolled over, trying to lift his rifle, but the demon had already reached him. A claw flashed and Cueto roared in pain as it sliced his leg wide open. He kicked out, and his combat boot tore the demon's soft face off, but that barely slowed it. It began crawling up his legs, scratching at his armor, as Cueto tried to push it back.

"Hang on," Gutterres rolled across a table and landed with a splash next to the demon. He shoved the muzzle of a 12-gauge against the side of the demon's head and sprayed a ten-foot cone of pink brains. Cueto hurled the demon off of him. Gutterres got up, grabbed onto the drag strap on his armor and pulled him away. Even though blood was pouring from his leg, the Strike Team commander got his rifle up and kept on shooting.

The surviving demons were momentarily retreating for some reason. This was their chance to get to a better position. "Move!" Franks shouted as he walked backwards, firing controlled pairs at each momentary glimpse of slimy demon flesh. The men above them on the catwalk were shooting as well. There was a terrible crash. Franks looked up in time to see one of the Swiss Guard being tossed over the railing to crash headfirst through a diagnostic machine. His halberd landed, clattering across the debris at Franks' feet.

A huge Nemesis soldier looked over the side to admire his handiwork. He was clothed, and appeared human, until he saw Franks and opened his mouth full of fangs to shout, "The traitor!"

So the regular Nemesis soldiers had joined the fight. *Good.* Franks didn't have the time to go looking for them. The demon leapt over the edge, dropped smoothly to the floor, and landed in a crouch. This Nemesis soldier was several inches taller than Franks, and so broad he probably had to turn sideways to fit through a door.

"Remember me, Franks?"

"No."

"You cut my legs! You blew me up with fire! You blew up my sister! You broke our good bodies. Franks is mean!"

Force . . . That meant Violence was around here somewhere. "You're dumb."

"Don't call me dumb! I am Cratos!" He looked at the rifle in Franks' hands as they both judged the too short distance between them. The huge Nemesis demon grinned. "Little gun won't do no good. Now I hurt you like you hurt me!" Cratos bellowed and charged.

Franks stepped on the halberd shaft. The spike lifted. Cratos' red eyes widened with realization just before it impaled him through the chest. His weight and momentum drove the big blade right through his center of mass.

"You should pay more attention." Letting the rifle hang from its sling, Franks took up the shaft in both hands and drove Cratos back, smashing him through the sheet metal of a machine, and then wrenching the spike out in a spray of blood. For being so damned big, the demon was still incredibly fast, and was already tearing himself free, so Franks smashed his face in with the halberd shaft. Cratos bit the wood in half. Franks stepped back, looking at the splintered ends of the hard wood. "Impressive." Then he planted the ax blade deep into the center of Cratos' forehead.

Cratos shrieked and got up, flailing about, trying to adjust to having the hemispheres of his brain forcefully separated. Franks stepped aside as he thrashed and lashed out. A solid hit from this monster could possibly render Franks combat-ineffective, so he needed to end this quickly. Supposedly these things were based on him, which meant that no matter how much traumatic brain injury they received, the backup systems along the spine would keep all of the basic systems functioning and the body alive. There was one way to test if that was the case...

Franks dodged a wild, uncoordinated swing, got behind Cratos and clamped one hand onto the demon's neck. His other hand caught hold of his belt. Franks couldn't believe how much Cratos weighed, but he still hoisted the thrashing demon up, arms fully extended, until he was extended far over Franks' head. By the time Cratos realized what was happening, it was too late, but it was hard to think clearly with a chunk of steel cutting your brain in half. With a roar, Franks hurled the demon's back down against his knee.

Satisfied the spine was broken, Franks rolled him onto the floor. Cratos flopped and twitched for several seconds, and then he stopped moving, lying facedown in a puddle of slime.

That works.

Judging by the flashlights and gunfire, his men had followed Cueto's instructions, and gotten to a more defensible position. Too bad this place was still crawling with demons. He still had a lot of work to do. Franks shook one of his new arms out. He'd torn muscles trying to lift that stupid demon, and his internal organs were overloaded. Taking more Elixir so soon was dangerous, but Franks hurried and took another swig of glowing liquid pain. If he continued to push at this pace, death was the most likely outcome, but that was an acceptable mission parameter.

His radio chirped. "Go for Franks."

"This is Archer. There's a plane coming in. It's a large military transport."

"Stricken's reinforcements," Franks muttered.

"Looks like a combat landing."

Curious. If Stricken had brought in the military, there was no point in ordering his men to fight them, because they wouldn't. "Stall."

"Roger that. There's a... We've got incoming! Nemesis on the—" The channel turned to static.

"Archer. Come in." There was no response. Nemesis had hit his people topside. Kurst was up to something. *Worse,* the rookie was up there. "Damn it. Cueto, did you get that? There's a transport landing on the airfield. Nemesis is attacking us above." There wasn't an immediate response. Cueto was either occupied or dead.

Extremely loud footsteps rang against the metal above. "Hello, Franks."

Franks returned the greeting as his night-vision-capable eye struggled to focus. All he could make out was a gigantic, misshapen form. "Kurst."

"That aircraft is our way out of this place. It is remarkable what you can arrange on such short notice when you have all of Stricken's authorization codes. We will start over, away from the mortal's prying eyes. A place has been prepared where we will grow in number."

"You'll never make it. They'll shoot you down."

"None of these humans will be alive long enough to warn the others." Kurst walked down the stairs. Other than being bipedal, there was nothing recognizably human left about his form. He made Cratos' mutated body seem tiny in comparison. Kurst had to be at least eight feet tall, with skin stretched so tight over powerful muscles that it had split apart in places, and the sides of his skull had grown into a twisted forest of horns.

"What happened to you?"

"I have temporarily molded this form to be more to my liking. Don't worry. I can change back in order to blend in with the sheep when necessary." Despite speaking through an elongated mouth full of sharp teeth, Kurst's voice remained unchanged. "Impressive, isn't it?"

"I've seen better."

"That Gift I spoke of earlier? I had to use most of it on myself to be able to achieve this form, but it is worth it."

"You always were greedy."

Kurst laughed. "We are the third of the host, Franks. Greed is our way. Have you pretended to be human for so long that you've forgotten that? You disgust me, brother. You were the fiercest amongst us, but now you are His dog, groveling beneath the table for whatever scraps the mortals will give you."

"You talk too much." Franks reached down, grabbed the broken halberd, and wrenched the ax blade from Cratos' skull. "Let's go."

If Heather had known that she wouldn't be able to fully transform into a werewolf yet, and also that the Nemesis soldier she was supposed to fight was going to suddenly grow spines like a damned puffer fish, she would've told Stricken to shove that PUFF exemption up his ass.

She was swatted to the ground again, but rolled out of the way before the monster could stab her. Heather sprang to her feet, and with no better option, slugged the monster in her twisted face. Even in human form a werewolf was still extremely strong. The thing's face was harder than it looked, but spongy beneath. Something gave beneath her fist.

"Ah! Gross!" Heather wiped her knuckles on her shirt as she backpedaled.

The impact had caused the monster's face to split open, like cracking a crab shell, and ropey tendrils of meat were hanging out. The red mass was slurped back into its head. "Is that the best you've got?" The Nemesis soldier seemed to be enjoying itself.

Ducking, Heather barely managed to avoid having her head torn off. The monster was terrifying, like a bunch of children's nightmares all smashed together in one bucket, but that disfigured body was clumsy, and probably slower than it should have been. That was keeping Heather alive, but without claws and teeth, she'd not been able to hurt the thing. All she could do was buy some time.

Stricken had used Heather's distraction to climb out of the hole and get to the door. He punched in a code, but nothing happened. Stricken immediately tried again, but his only reward was a red flashing light.

"You forgot the code!" Heather cried out as she narrowly kept from being eviscerated. "Idiot!"

But Stricken didn't respond. He tried the code again. The red flashing continued, but now it was joined by a warning buzzer. Renfroe crawled out of the hatch, saw what Stricken was doing, and shouted, "Stop! One more and the system will lock us out."

Stricken stepped away from the keypad. Heather had never seen him appear emotional and out of control before. "The numbers he gave me don't work! Fix it!"

Bubble gum and spider webs...

"That's not Stricken. He set us up—" The monster dove and crashed into Heather, driving her back against the wall. Needles and spines sank into her arms. She screamed.

"Son of a bitch!" Renfroe shoved the fake Stricken out of the way and put his hand on the keypad. His flesh began to glow. The red warning light turned green.

Heather slipped and fell. The thrashing monster was on top of her, snapping at her face with multiple mouths. Desperate, Heather got hold of the thing's arms and tried to keep the viciously piercing tentacles away from her body. She squeezed so hard that the monster's skin ruptured and blood poured out around her hands. "Get us out of here!"

"On it," Renfroe answered, distracted and concentrating.

The Nemesis soldier had grown a horn from the center of her face. The head lifted, rising on extra vertebrae, until the point was aimed right between Heather's eyes. *You've got to be kidding . . .* The horn fell.

Heather jerked her head to the side. The horn sliced her cheek wide open and embedded itself in the concrete. "Cheating bitch!" Heather let go of one of the monster's arms, swung her elbow and broke the horn clean off. The monster shrieked, and the hot mass rolled off of her. Heather grabbed the horn, ripped it out of the floor, and stabbed the monster through the head. While the thing lurched back, Heather used the opportunity to get up.

Stricken's secretary—Heather had never gotten her name—had a very hopeful look on her face as she crawled through the hatch. That look vanished as soon as a hand shot out of the hole and grabbed onto her ankle. She screamed as the Nemesis soldier dragged her back into the dark. *So much for the other survivors.* Heather looked at the screaming, angry monster, trying to pull its own horn out of its eye socket, and then back to the hatch.

With nothing to lose, Heather got a running start and kicked the monster in the back. It stumbled toward the hole . . . only to catch itself on the edge of the hatch.

"Oh, come on!" She kept stomping the monster, but it wouldn't do her the favor of falling three stories and taking its friend with it. Fake Stricken was still standing there, useless. "A little help?" she gasped, but whatever was wearing the Stricken mask didn't budge.

"Got it," Renfroe shouted. There was a loud metallic clang as the bunker door unlocked. "There's an MCB agent on the other side."

She never thought she'd be glad to hear that the MCB was here, but despite her pummeling the hell out of it, the Nemesis monster was getting up. Her limbs were burning, she was short of breath. "Die already!" Desperate, Heather grabbed the end of the stuck horn, and wrenched it around, pushing hard until the monster's neck snapped. That seemed to do the trick, as it lost its slimy grip and tumbled down the shaft.

Heather watched it fall until it hit something unyielding, bounced against the side, and disappeared into the darkness.

There was another Nemesis soldier hanging onto the ladder. This one still looked human, but he was *fast*. He surged forward as Heather kicked the hatch closed, but he still managed to get one hand through the gap. She slammed the hatch down hard against the bones, and when he still didn't let go, she climbed on top of the hatch and began jumping up and down on it.

There was a *pop* as the hatch closed all the way. The severed hand flopped on the ground, fingers still clutching wildly. *Too bad it locks on the other side.* But she barely had time to finish that thought, as the monster smashed the hatch wide open, flinging Heather on the floor.

Renfroe pulled the massive door; it groaned and barely moved, but a sliver of daylight came through the crack. "Almost there!" Then somebody on the other side hit the door with such force that Renfroe was knocked down as it flew open.

A lone man was standing there, a dark silhouette in the sunlight. He stepped into the room, wearing MCB armor and a face mask, with a very large tank on his back and a flamethrower in his hands. Over the strong smell of napalm and impending doom, another familiar scent hit Heather, and she almost couldn't believe her nose. "No way."

The one-armed Nemesis soldier was climbing through the broken hatch. The man stepped forward, shoved the nozzle right into the soldier's face and set it off.

Heather dove to the side as the flamethrower ignited. Fire rolled down the shaft. The small room was instantly flooded with unbearable heat. The Nemesis monster screamed as he was engulfed. He let go of the ladder and dropped, trying to escape the destroying flames.

The trigger was released and the fire died. The masked man saw Stricken making a run for daylight. "You're not going anywhere, jackass," he said as he smoothly drew a stainless steel revolver and fired a single round into Stricken's back, dropping him at the end of the tunnel.

"I can't believe it!" Heather sprang up and ran to him.

The man pulled off his mask. "I warned Stricken not to let anything happen to you," Earl Harbinger said as he shrugged out of the shoulder straps and dumped the pressurized tank on the floor. "Not how I pictured our reunion. Anybody else down there?"

"Nobody I wouldn't mind blowing up."

"Good." Earl took out a grenade, shoved it into the straps, and pulled the pin. He shoved the flamethrower over the edge and kept the spoon. "Move!"

Renfroe had already run for his life. Earl was the last one out. He closed the vault door behind them and left the STFU bunker to burn.

CHAPTER 19

A Binding Contract of Perpetual Alliance, offensive and defensive, entered into between the being Franks and the United States in Congress assembled.

Recognizing that the hordes of Hell are a threat to all the establishments of man and the United Colonies of North America, let it be recorded that the Mission of Franks is to protect the People from the predations of the Unearthly. Franks does solemnly swear before these witnesses to protect this land from all inhuman forces who may threaten its citizens and their property and wellbeing. Franks shall henceforth fulfill this duty to the best of his abilities including the sacrifice of his liberty and life. In return, by all Rights, Laws, and Privileges, the being Franks shall be considered as a living man.

Both parties have agreed to the following stipulations.

The continued secrecy pertaining to the Unearthly, being necessary for the liberty and sanity of all men, the Congress shall establish a special committee of learned men pertaining to the Unearthly Forces, to be convened in secret.

Franks shall abide by the laws and limitations set upon him by the Congress, provided said laws do not clash with his mission as stated. The trial of all crimes committed by Franks in pursuit of his mission shall be by the special committee.

Franks shall not engage in acts of offensive war with any Nation, Nations of Indians, or Other Worlds without Consent of the Congress.

In exchange for the protection and services provided by Franks, the Congress will provide him with physical repairs, body parts of suitable quality, and any supplies necessary so that he may remain effective in battle against the hordes of Hell. All expenses incurred shall be defrayed from the Common Treasury.

Regardless of any alchemical or scientific knowledge gleaned from the study of the physical form of Franks, no attempt must ever be made to replicate the work of Konrad Dippel in order to create a physical body like unto that of Franks or this contract is immediately rendered void. In consequence Franks shall levy total war upon the parties responsible.

In Witness whereof we have hereunto set our hands on the first day of January in the Year of our Lord One Thousand Seven Hundred and Seventy-Six.

As Franks ran forward, he lifted the SCAR with one hand and began firing at Kurst. The demon lunged behind a steel girder.

Franks slid behind a large machine, shoved the halberd handle through his belt so he could have his hand free, and reloaded the rifle. Another agent had taken cover in that same place earlier, but something had ripped his head off and left his body there leaking. Seeing the corpse just made Franks even angrier. He was going to destroy Kurst. Even with a body like that, Kurst would have physical limits. He just needed to be pushed beyond those limits, and Franks had a lot of practice at that sort of thing. One of Myers' favorite sayings had been *old age and treachery beat youth and skill*. Kurst might have a stronger form, but he was still learning how to use it. Hopefully that would be enough.

Franks dropped the bolt, shouldered the rifle, and came out shooting.

Kurst leapt out from behind the girder, and in one mighty leap covered the entire distance between them. He landed in front of Franks, claws skidding across the slick floor. Bullet holes puckered across Kurst's chest and ruptured out his back, but the wounds didn't slow him. He swatted the rifle from Franks' hands, then slammed one big fist into Franks' torso.

Franks flew back twenty feet and crashed through a workstation. He sat up to discover there was still a fist-shaped dent in his chest plate. Kurst was *strong*. Fast too, since he was already on top of him. The demon hit him with a blow to the head so hard that a regular human's skull would have burst like a balloon. Franks was rattled. Spit hit him in the eyes as Kurst shouted, "You have sinned against the host. That was a mistake, Franks!"

Franks grabbed hold of Kurst's horns and yanked down hard. "My only mistake was listening to you fools to begin with!" He curled his other hand into a fist and slugged Kurst in the mouth.

Claws hooked through his improvised bandolier and Franks was violently hoisted off the ground. Their hands flashed back and forth, trying to knock each other aside for a moment before Franks gave up. The demon was just too strong. Before Kurst could throw him again, Franks clicked the buckle and dropped free, leaving Kurst with nothing but a handful of pistol belt and pouches. Franks crawled away.

Kurst followed him. "Running won't save you. Do you really think you're that clever?"

"Yes." Franks held up the pin he'd pulled from one of his grenades, then he rolled beneath a heavy table.

"Hmm..." Kurst looked down at the pouches in his hand and then at the grenade spoon that had fallen a few feet away. Realization dawned a split second too late to do anything about it.

Shrapnel blasted through the thick wood Franks was using for cover. The frag was slowed, but he was close enough that some of it still tore through and injured him. The pressure wave left his ears ringing. A quick inventory confirmed blood loss, but nothing vital hit. Franks stuck his head out. The demon had gotten it far worse. The blast had flung Kurst away. The demon was sitting up, stunned, looking at his mangled hand. Most of that arm resembled hamburger more than anything else, but Kurst appeared more angry than hurt. Franks scowled. That would have turned most living things into red mush. This was going to be harder than he'd thought.

Kurst sprang up and charged. Franks hurled the table at him, but Kurst batted it aside. They went toe to toe, but where Franks had a chance before, now Kurst simply manhandled him. Even bleeding from dozens of shrapnel wounds, Kurst was still too fast. Everything Franks did was turned aside. Kicks, punches, knees, elbows, all traded so quickly it would be difficult for the human eye to track and impossible for the human body to stop, flew back and forth between them, but Franks couldn't hurt him. *Kurst is toying with me.*

"Is that all?" It took everything Franks had to stay ahead of him. Within seconds, his forearms were splintered and bleeding from blocking so many impacts. His hearts were racing. Kurst's face had stretched until it now resembled a werewolf. His grin displayed a long row of jagged teeth. "I'm only getting warmed up."

Franks was hit on one side of the head, then the other, so hard and fast that the turn almost broke his neck. Body blows fell in such rapid succession that it felt like he was being hit with a burst from a machine gun. Then Kurst kicked his leg out from under him, but caught him by the throat before he could fall. Franks was lifted off the ground, and then Kurst swung him around. Glass shattered as they crashed through one of the growth tanks. His blood painted patterns on the floor.

Claws digging into his neck, Franks grabbed hold of Kurst's hand and pried back a finger until it snapped.

"You think that'll stop me?" The demon paused to hold up his other hand, showing Franks that the damage from the grenade was nearly healed. He wiggled his fingers. "I'll just grow more." Then he pulled Franks in, muscles tightening with energy, and then Kurst hurled him across the factory. Franks spun through the air, crashed through another growth tank, and then into the unyielding concrete of the far wall.

Franks could barely lift himself up. His quick inventory told him that everything was broken or leaking. The glass had sliced through his skin in several places, and a few lacerations were deep enough to render those muscle groups combat-ineffective. He still had two handguns, a grenade, some folding knives, and that broken halberd on him, but when he tried to draw a pistol, he discovered that the too-soft bones in his new hands were too broken to close around the grip.

I am going to lose.

Kurst had flung him fifty feet that time, and the demon was strolling over to finish the job. Somebody had gotten the emergency lights on, and Franks could see that his men were in the fight of their lives against the partially grown host bodies and the fully grown Nemesis soldiers. The factory was filled with explosions and gunfire, and if Franks didn't finish Kurst off now, then the demons would kill his allies, flee this place, and grow themselves an army to conquer the world and ruin The Plan.

There had not been very many times over the last three centuries when Franks had implored the World Maker for anything, but it was not very often that Franks lost a fight. *If you want me to complete The Deal, I require help now.*

The demon prince paused to let Franks collect himself. "You seem surprised I defeated you so easily." Kurst spied a pipe mounted on the wall, then ripped it free. Steam came shooting out of the gap. He tested the balance, swinging the big pipe back and forth like it was a baseball bat. Satisfied that it would be sufficient to beat Franks to death, Kurst put the pipe over one shoulder and strolled over. "You should know by now that demons always cheat."

"So do humans, asshole!"

BOOM!

Kurst turned just in time to catch the large-caliber bullet with his teeth. Bits of ivory flew through the air as the back of his skull came apart in a burst of red. Agent Jefferson had braced a huge Barrett .50 rifle over the side body of a forklift. His next round punched through Kurst's sternum and sent the demon reeling back. Kurst retaliated by flinging the pipe at Jefferson. It hit so hard that it tore the roll cage off the forklift and Jefferson disappeared behind it.

Kurst grinned. "*Bia!* Your human is here!" He pointed in Jefferson's direction. Kurst was answered by a horrific shriek from the rafters high above. A purple winged form dropped from the darkness and shot toward the forklift. Jefferson shouted in surprise as the demon attacked him. There was a lot of gunfire and shrieking. "Enjoy yourself."

Strayhorn came around the side of the stairs with a rifle shouldered. He moved toward Franks while laying down fire on Kurst. "Hang on, Franks!"

Even with Kurst wounded, the rookie was no match for the demon prince. "Get out of here," Franks ordered, but his voice was so weak and broken that his order couldn't be heard over the gunfire.

The rookie didn't listen to him. Strayhorn was pulling something from one of his pouches, and he tossed it. The oval-shaped object hit the floor and slid toward Franks just as Kurst lunged for Strayhorn.

Franks crawled toward them. *"Run!"*

It was certain death, but the rookie kept shooting. Kurst moved through the bullets and raised one hand. The claws flashed like lightning, and Strayhorn was torn nearly in half.

"No..." Franks whispered.

Strayhorn lay there in a spreading pool of blood. Kurst stood over the mutilated body, claw dripping red. "Interesting... You cared about this one, didn't you, Franks?"

The thing that Strayhorn had thrown at him had been a canteen. The plastic had bulged and the cap had burst off on impact, spilling glowing blue liquid.

Kurst licked his fingers. "This is the same blood from the riverside... You saved this one before. But why would any human matter to something like you?"

"They matter. We don't." He could barely speak. Franks reached the canteen and scooped it up with clumsy, broken hands. The canteen was still mostly full. "This world belongs to them. It was never ours to take."

"You have followed the Creator's lies for so long. Next will I have to listen to you preach about mercy and sacrifice?"

"I'll never understand mercy." This would most likely be fatal, but Franks had a mission to fulfill. He lifted the canteen and drank the whole thing. He poured *ten* doses' worth of molten agony down his throat. Every artery and vein on Franks' body began to glow. His skin made a sizzling noise like bacon hitting a hot pan. His hair began to smoke and singe. It hadn't even really kicked in yet, and already the pain was incomprehensible. Franks spoke through grinding teeth, *"But I do understand sacrifice."*

Kurst turned around, saw the empty canteen fall from Franks' convulsing fingers. "Fool." The demon prince shook his horned head. "You'd burn yourself to a crisp for nothing. You will never be pure enough for Him."

The demon started toward him. There was nothing Franks could do about it. Every muscle in his body had contracted so tight that the tension was audible. Impurities burned off and bled through his pores as his bones turned molten. Nerve endings sent messages made of encoded pain, died, were born again to transmit even more suffering. It was like nothing he'd ever experienced. It was beyond anything Franks had ever imagined.

His body was producing such incredible heat that it threatened to spontaneously combust. The edges of his clothing smoked and began to burn. The polyester of his tie caught fire and melted into his skin. It felt like soothing ice compared to the heat engulfing him.

Franks saw the Void open up before him. It beckoned to him. Hell would have been a release compared to this. He wanted to die. Anything to end this pain . . . Kurst would be doing him a favor. The demon's huge clawed feet stopped inches from Franks' face. "What's that, Franks? Do you wish to escape? Such pain . . . Will you beg me for death?"

It was so tempting. Then he focused on Strayhorn's dead body . . .

"Too bad. You're going to get it anyway." Kurst lifted his foot to snap Franks' neck. "Farewell, Brother."

"Hey, Kurst!" someone shouted.

Kurst sighed and put his foot down. "What now?"

Grant Jefferson limped around the side of the forklift. His armor had been torn to shreds, his face was crisscrossed with scratches, and blood was running freely from several deep wounds. He stopped at the edge of the open space and lifted one arm. Jefferson held a handful of black hair, and dangling beneath that was the severed head of a purple-skinned female demon. He tossed the head at Kurst. It hit the floor, bounced a few times, and rolled over to them. "I killed your girlfriend again." Weak from blood loss, he went to his knees. "Don't know why people keep underestimating me . . . I'm a total badass," Jefferson muttered before passing out and falling flat on his face.

Kurst shook his head, then turned back to Franks. "Where were we, Broth—"

Franks uppercut Kurst so hard it lifted the demon straight off the ground, high into the air, to crash back through several storage lockers.

"We were sending you back to Hell," Franks snarled. He squeezed his fist closed and cracked his knuckles.

It still hurt. In fact, it hurt nearly as badly as the height of taking a normal dose of Elixir, only the burning he was still feeling now produced a fraction of the heat of Franks' unholy rage. The molten glow was no longer visible through his skin and his muscles were responding. When he hit Kurst again his fist made an impact like a sledgehammer.

Kurst sprung up. Franks slammed his fist into the side of the demon's head so hard that bone slivers erupted through the skin. Kurst bounced off the floor, then looked up at him in shock. The demon's body had already taken a beating. *Now Franks was the strong one.* Franks kicked him across the factory floor.

The demon prince broke through the railing at the base of the stairs. He saw Franks coming after him, and scurried up toward the catwalk.

Franks watched him go, then moved toward his fallen agents. Jefferson was still breathing, but there wasn't time to assess him. Franks knelt next to the rookie. The wound was terrible. He might have been Franks' blood, but he had a body as fragile as any regular human. Maybe the Elixir could still save him...

The spirit had departed. Tom Strayhorn was gone...

Franks punched the floor hard enough to crack the concrete. He took Strayhorn's rifle and stuffed a few of the magazines into his pocket.

Kurst was moving down the catwalk. Even hurt, he still was incredibly fast, and the grating beneath him shook with each heavy footfall. Franks put the red dot of the Aimpoint sight just ahead of the demon and let it rip. Most of the rounds hit sheet metal, but a few found muscle and bone before Kurst ducked behind the next girder.

There was a big platform behind Kurst's cover. Franks couldn't get a visual on what the demon was up to, so he kept moving, looking for an angle. There was a screech of metal rubbing against metal, and then a large machine came hurtling over the edge. Franks dodged to the side an instant before two hundred pounds of metal crashed right next to him.

"I'm going to smash your guts out, Franks!" Kurst appeared, a big cart filled with computers and electronic equipment held overhead, and he threw that as well. Franks barely had time to dive over a table before the cart bounced off the floor where he'd been standing. Bits of glass and plastic flew everywhere. "Then

I'm going to eat them!" Kurst bent over, looking for something else to throw. He came back up with a heavy gas cylinder in both hands, zeroed in on Franks, and lifted it overhead.

Franks put a bullet into the gas cylinder.

It ruptured. There was a high-pitched whistle as thick orange smoke shot out. Franks didn't know what chemical was in there—he'd been hoping for flammable or explosive—but whatever it was made Kurst roar in pain and clutch at his eyes. Kurst dropped the hissing cylinder, but the smoke cloud was already obscuring much of the platform. Kurst began to cough. He'd fashioned himself a fancy new body, but he was still breathing air through relatively normal lungs.

This was his chance. Franks ran back to Strayhorn. He was wearing a Strike Team uniform, and doctrine made them all organize their kit in the same way so they could use each other's equipment in an emergency. Franks rolled the body over, found the big pouch he was looking for, took out the gas mask, and pulled it on. The rubber straps were far too tight on his big head, but it made for a good seal.

Jefferson was groaning. "Put your gas mask on!" Franks ordered. The agent was too out of it. He had more important things to do, and he should have just let him die for letting the rookie do something stupid, but Franks took a few seconds to get Jefferson's mask on. It was like one of those annoying videos they made him watch on civilian airplanes, but if Jefferson died now, then Franks wouldn't be able to punish him later.

He sprinted back toward the catwalk. The orange gas was heavier than air, and it was settling, rolling along the floor. The chemicals made his bare skin burn. Franks followed the sounds of Kurst crashing about until he thought he was directly beneath. He might have been able to see through the grate if it wasn't for the fog, but when he figured he was close enough, Franks pointed the muzzle of the SCAR straight up and ripped a full magazine through the metal.

Kurst roared. "Damn you, Franks!"

Drops of blood fell through the grate and splattered against the plastic face shield of the gas mask as Franks slammed another magazine in. The booming footsteps were moving, so Franks followed them and emptied another magazine up through the grate. The muzzle blast blew the orange smoke away from him in a spiral pattern.

Visibility was improving enough to see that Kurst had shoved his claws through the grate and was prying the metal apart to come down and get him. Franks dropped the rifle, pulled out the halberd blade, got a running start, and swung as he jumped. Kurst bellowed as two of his fingers fell off. The demon moved away from the gap he'd made, cursing in the old tongue. Not missing a beat, Franks pulled his last grenade from his coat pocket, yanked the pin, and tossed it hard, up through the hole.

"I will destroy you for this! *Destroy you!*" And then Kurst must have seen the grenade coming back down. It landed and rolled across the catwalk. "Shit."

Metal fragments ripped through everything on the platform, blew a hole in the grate, and shredded the concrete beneath, but Franks was long gone by then. He'd been moving while Kurst had been ranting. Once the shrapnel had flown past, Franks had climbed on top of some boxes, leapt, and caught the edge of the catwalk.

"I'm better than you, Franks!" Kurst had been knocked back by the blast. The flesh on his chest was hanging in strips and blood was pouring from dozens of wounds. He was looking down at the mess, and plucked a chunk of jagged metal out of his ribs. "It'll take more than another toy to stop— Aaaarrrgghhh!"

Franks drove the halberd spike through the back of Kurst's knee. He wrenched the spike around, utterly destroying the joint before yanking it out in a spray of blood and cartilage. While the demon prince stumbled back on his collapsing leg, Franks pulled himself up over the edge, drew one of his full-auto Glocks with his left hand, and ripped the demon from pelvis to forehead in one continuous thirty-round burst. Kurst lurched and tripped, hitting so hard that the entire platform shook. Franks followed him, reaching across his body to pull the other pistol, and repeated the process, putting multiple bullet holes into every one of Kurst's vital organs.

"I don't give a shit how superior you're supposed to be, that hurt."

Franks dropped the empty pistol, took up the broken halberd shaft in both hands, and began methodically chopping at the demon as if he was splitting wood. He struck the partially blind and wounded demon ten times before Kurst had even had a chance to try to defend himself. Franks dodged a desperate kick and responded by slicing Kurst's heel off. Franks was impressed; the Swiss made good steel.

The blade kept on rising and falling. "You should have listened." Franks hacked into Kurst's shoulder blade. "You don't belong here." The demon rolled over, swinging at him wildly, but Franks lacerated that bicep to the bone. "This is not your world." Kurst raised one injured hand to defend his face, but Franks took the rest of those fingers off. "This was never your world." The blade split Kurst's jaw open.

So much blood had struck the gas mask that Franks could barely see. Kurst was trying to crawl away, desperately buying time for his body to heal. Franks paused to smear the blood around with one ragged sleeve in a futile attempt to clean the plastic off. Frustrated, he pulled the mask off and tossed it aside. The remaining chemicals made his eyes burn. Kurst had reached the edge of the broken platform. "You should have stayed in Hell." Franks kicked him over the side.

The demon landed flat on his back. The rush of air caused the dissipating orange fog to be blasted away. Franks followed him over the edge, dropping directly onto his enemy. The impact hurt Franks' feet, but broke Kurst's ribs. Franks knelt on his opponent's chest, spun the halberd blade around, and then he drove the spike through Kurst's chest so hard that it was embedded into the floor on the other side. "You shouldn't have attacked my people!"

Blood shot from Kurst's mouth, but Franks was too angry to quit now. He grabbed the demon's horns, used those as handles, and began slamming the back of his skull into the floor. Franks roared as Kurst's skull broke into pieces. "You shouldn't have killed my *son!*"

Kurst's impressive demon body was shrinking. He almost looked human again, and a nearly dead human at that. Kurst laughed and spit up blood. "I hope it hurt."

Franks jerked when the bullet hit him in the back. He turned and caught the next one in the chest. Then one of the partially formed demons tackled him, knocking him off of Kurst. "I'm not done!" Franks roared. They could communicate so Kurst must have called for help. The Nemesis soldier with the gun reached Kurst, pulled the spike out of his heart, and then picked his superior up. The demon on top kept wrestling Franks, trying to hold him down, while the other carried Kurst away.

The demon was a slimy mass of bare muscle, and it had grown an extra pair of arms to claw at him. Franks began pummeling it as it scratched and tore at him. He didn't have time for this bullshit. His mission wasn't complete. His *revenge* wasn't complete! Franks grabbed hold of the demon's head, one big hand on each side, and he squeezed. The demon screamed as its armored skull bulged. Driven by the insane amount of Elixir running through his system, Franks kept on pushing. The demon's eyes popped out a few seconds before its head exploded.

Tossing the effectively decapitated demon aside, Franks got up and ran in the direction Kurst had been carried. He'd lost sight of them. He reached the center aisle of the factory, but then had to shield his eyes from the sudden glare of headlights. A powerful engine roared, and Franks leapt aside as a military truck roared past. He caught a glimpse of the Nemesis soldier driving, Kurst's bloody head in the passenger seat, and then he realized that strapped down on the flatbed was one of the glass growth tanks, and then it was past and heading for the exit. Franks' hand instinctively flew to his empty holster. Then he keyed his radio and said, "Stop that truck!" before he realized his microphone ended in a broken cord. *Damn it.*

Franks sprinted after the truck, but the driver had put the hammer down. It was speeding through the factory and even ran down a new demon that hadn't been fast enough to get out of the way. Even as fast as he could run, Franks couldn't catch up. The Swiss Guard at the exit were preoccupied battling demons, so by the time they engaged the truck, they only managed to put a few bullet holes into it before it was through the blast door and heading up the ramp.

Kurst will not get away. Franks pushed harder. A new demon stepped in front of him, hissing, but Franks clotheslined it to the ground without even slowing. He approached the Swiss position. There was a pistol lying next to the outstretched hand of a dead man, so Franks snatched it up as he ran through the blast door. He caught sight of the truck as it reached the top of the ramp and cranked off a few futile shots from the Sig 226 before the truck was out of sight. Franks ran after them.

By the time he entered the hangar, the truck was outside and moving fast across the airfield. An Air Force C-17 had landed and its loading ramp was down. If Kurst flew out, in a normal situation Franks could just request a shoot-down or forced landing, but right now Franks was the fugitive, and Kurst was using

Stricken's extremely high level authorizations. *If* Franks could convince the military to act, by then Kurst could potentially escape, and if they could reverse-engineer that growth tank...

Escape is not an option.

Franks was breathing hard. He had a bullet hole in one lung. This would not do. The MCB command vehicle had a 40mm belt-fed grenade launcher, but it was on fire and there was no sign of Archer or the other techies. Franks looked around for a better option.

Gutterres had left his Ducati right inside the entrance, and the Vatican's Hunter had left the keys in it. The motorcycle was an extremely powerful machine... Franks approved.

Heather and Earl were in an angled shaft. It wasn't very long, and the exit was covered in bushes. The vault door at their back was warm from the fire on the other side. She didn't know if that explosion had killed the other Nemesis monster, but it at least had to hurt.

Heather leaned against the dirt wall and caught her breath. Blood was running down the huge cut on her cheek and from a dozen puncture wounds in her arms. Earl put his arm around her and pulled her in close. "Are you okay?"

She smiled. "I will be. What're you doing here?"

"I came to save you." He kissed her on the forehead.

"How'd you know?"

"I tailed Franks. I promised him I wouldn't, which is why I'm in disguise. How do I look?"

"Like a Fed."

"Me looking like a Fed." Earl laughed. "If that ain't proof of my feelings toward you, I don't know what is. Then I tracked your scent. I'm surprised you didn't know I was here."

She began to explain about still recovering from the poison, but then thought *screw it*, and she kissed him *hard*. She'd been wanting to do that for a long time. After several seconds they broke apart. "We've got a lot of catching up to do."

"First I need to get you out of here, and there's still business to attend to." He jerked his head toward where Stricken had fallen.

But just as she'd expected, it wasn't Stricken at all.

"What the hell..." Earl muttered as he kept his revolver trained on the hairy, confusing pile of limbs. He used the toe of his boot to roll the body over. It had a face like a spider, but all of its eyes were staring blankly into the distance. "That's a Tsuchigumo. I haven't seen one of these since Okinawa. Real nasty pieces of work, they create illusions and mess with your mind."

"Nemesis was looking for him, but Stricken used us as decoys instead. I bet he probably had another way out the whole time." She recognized the green blood pooling beneath the body as the same substance she'd seen at MCB headquarters. So this thing was how they'd made it look like Franks on the video.

"I should feel guilty for jumping the gun, but I just can't summon up the energy to feel any pity for shooting one of these nasty bloodsuckers," Earl said as he holstered his revolver. "That's two wrong calls this week. I'm forming a bad habit."

"Don't worry. This thing was guilty enough. It smells like bubblegum."

"I've got no idea what that means, but I'll take your word for it..." Earl looked toward the end of the tunnel; beyond that was their unknown future. "This means Stricken is out here somewhere."

"I'm not going back to STFU, Earl," she vowed. "PUFF be damned, I can't do this anymore."

He nodded. "I've got this little place down in Mexico..."

The exit was hidden in a heavily wooded ravine on the edge of the runway. There was a big military cargo plane with its engines running at the opposite end of the airfield, but the last thing she wanted to do was get involved in more MCB business. They found the only other STFU survivor up top, trying his best to conceal himself in the bushes, but it wasn't like you could hide from two werewolves. "Come on out of there, Renfroe. I'm too damned tired to chase you," Heather shouted.

"If you're going to kill me, get it over with, because I'm done with you shadow government bastards." The thin man came out of the bushes with his hands up. "Do it. I don't care anymore, but you're too late. I've already exposed everything. Your bosses are done."

"Wait..." Heather stopped him. "What?"

"I knew Stricken was planning on killing me. I was too much of a loose end. I kept records of everything so I could blackmail Stricken into letting me go, but when I thought I was going to die on that ladder, I sent it." Renfroe sat on a log in front of them. "Oh well. Do what you've got to do."

"Back up, kid," Earl demanded. "What did you send?"

Renfroe seemed honestly surprised that they hadn't shot him yet. "Stricken thought I was scared of him—well, yeah, who wouldn't be?—but I'm better at this than he ever expected. He thought he had me blocked, but no way, man, I put back doors in the back doors. The unedited security video of Foster's guys in action, MCB has it by now. I've even got the audio logs and voiceprints of Stricken giving the orders. Nemesis production? Sent. Every dirty black op you can think of, all sent. The only thing I didn't reveal was the identities of the other poor suckers like me coerced into working there. That's it. Everything I know has been dumped so you don't even need to waste your time torturing me." Renfroe closed his eyes. "Make it quick."

"I'm not going to—" Heather began to speak, but Earl held up one hand.

"Who did you send all this to? The news?"

"Those wimps? They'll do whatever they're told. I dumped it all on the internet. It's on a thousand sites by now. Sure, I know most people will think of it as extra crazy conspiracy theory stuff and dismiss it, I mean, who believes in monsters, right? But the people who know, the decision makers behind STFU, that crazy lady who got Stricken to relaunch Nemesis, they're exposed. They get it. They just got served. And best of all, they're going to murder the hell out of Stricken when they catch him. He's not weaseling out of this."

Earl gave a low whistle. "About that hideout in Mexico...I think I just found somebody who's gonna need it a whole lot more than us."

We are almost there, General.

Thymos' report was not comforting. *Almost there* was not good enough. Kurst could barely see. That chemical had badly burned his eyes, and then Franks had utterly devastated his body. Too much energy had been expended. He needed time to heal. Kurst should have been invincible, but Franks had still bested him. Franks' body was an archaic design. Victory should have been inevitable. The only other explanation was that Franks was the better warrior, and that was unacceptable.

They both looked like humans again—it was necessary for their escape—but just putting this face back on felt like an insult. Kurst felt the sudden lurch as Thymos slowed their vehicle. There was a rough bump as they drove up the ramp and into the aircraft before Thymos stomped on the brakes. The demon soldier opened his door and hopped out.

"What are you doing? Are you insane?" A human male shouted. "I don't care what kind of special Pentagon orders you're on, you don't abuse my aircraft like that!"

"Close the door. Take off now," Thymos said.

"I've got to secure your vehicle before we move. I can't have an unstable—"

Kurst couldn't see, but from the noise, he could tell that Thymos had tossed the loadmaster off the plane. Kurst opened his door and stumbled out of the truck. *Get us in the air, Thymos. I'll take care of this.*

His soldier ran forward. Apparently someone on the flight crew didn't respond fast enough to the impatient demon's liking, because there were a few gunshots. Then the engine picked up in intensity, so now they were listening. Kurst walked across the bay, dragging one foot because his knee hadn't healed yet. He searched for the hydraulic controls with aching, blurry eyes, as he recalled the familiarization training. Their education had included information about operating all current-issue military systems, and even a flight simulator, but that wasn't the same as being on the actual aircraft and finding the damned button when you were half blind. He finally found the controls and within seconds the ramp was closing and the plane was moving.

Resting one hand on the cool glass of the growth tank, Kurst paused to reflect. There had been some setbacks, but this was only the beginning. Their ally had promised them a new home and boundless resources. This technological marvel would be deconstructed and rebuilt a thousand times over, scattered across the world so that the humans could never root them all out. A new army would rise, and in time, the Fallen would inherit the Earth.

"You kept us from this world before, but our time has come," Kurst whispered. "We will have our revenge."

Greetings, General Kurst. I bring word from my master. I regret to inform you that our business has concluded. This alliance no longer benefits my master.

Kurst squinted until he could see that the other greater demon's red face had appeared on the glass of the growth tank. "What do you mean?"

Your services are no longer required, General.

"Why?" he demanded.

Because Franks has come for you. It does no good to ally with someone who has been cast back into Hell. We will have to win this war without you. Farewell, Prince.

The face disappeared, and now Kurst was only looking at his own blood-soaked reflection.

"Come back! I command you to explain yourself!"

A new sound separated itself from the engine noise. This was a higher-pitched sound than the jets or the hydraulics. Kurst turned just in time to catch a motorcycle in the face.

Franks' momentum caused him to roll across the cargo bay until he slammed into the bulkhead. He'd barely made it in time. The plane was picking up speed for takeoff. The ramp was closing. Franks took stock. The STFU truck didn't take up that much interior space inside a plane that was designed to hold an M1 Abrams. Gutterres' bullet bike was laid on its side far forward, and Franks tracked the blood trail from there back to where Kurst had been flattened.

The demon prince was knocked down. They sat up at the same time. The impact had peeled most of the skin from Kurst's face and a swath of his torso, leaving nothing but red muscle and spots of white skull.

"You've ruined everything," Kurst spat.

"Not everything... *Yet.*"

They glared at each other for a long moment, before both of them sprang up and simultaneously hurled their bodies against the other. The collision rocked Franks, and then they came crashing down. Franks punched him in the side of the head, but Kurst kicked him in the chest. Franks hit the truck and left a dent in the door.

Franks still had that Sig stuck in his belt, but no idea how many rounds it had left in it, and whatever that number was, it wouldn't be sufficient to stop Kurst. They circled each other, looking for an opening as the C-17 lifted off sharply. Kurst was hurt, and he might have been in a more human-looking form, but he was still the chief warrior of Hell's army, and that made him deadly. They clashed, striking violently at each other. Franks had spent hundreds of years learning every fighting art known to man, but Kurst had all of those encoded directly into his being by his artificial womb. Kurst took hold of the rags that were all that remained of Franks' suit, trying to throw him. Franks locked up on his hands and tried to break his wrists. They began to slide back toward the ramp as the plane continued its steep climb.

They were turning toward the east. The airfield was approximately two hundred and thirty kilometers from the ocean. Franks knew that at a C-17's maximum speed they would be there in less than twenty minutes, but then what? Where was Kurst running to? *Who* was he running to? Franks also knew he would never get that information from Kurst, because he did not plan on taking this particular enemy alive.

His battered forearms and shins kept absorbing the majority of the blows, but Kurst was not nearly as strong as before, and Franks was running on more Elixir than Father would have ever imagined possible. Human organs had never been intended to take that much stress, and Franks knew they were all failing. The ocean may have only been twenty minutes away, but even if he defeated Kurst immediately, there was no way Franks would live to see it again.

He needed to end this now.

Kurst shoved him back against the wall. Aluminum bent. Franks held on and wouldn't let his opponent get an angle to strike. He realized Kurst was blinking rapidly, as if he was having a hard time seeing. Franks sacrificed his body and let Kurst hit him. His nose went flat, but it also gave him the opportunity to throw his elbow against the side of Kurst's head. The demon prince desperately moved aside... Considering how inhumanly tough he was, *too* desperately.

The demon had displayed his weakness. He was nearly blind. Now Franks would dismantle him. He drove his knee into Kurst's side, over and over, and when Kurst finally forced himself back, Franks slipped a shot through his defenses and drove his knuckles deep into Kurst's eye socket. Sure enough, Kurst showed far more of a reaction than he should have. Franks capitalized on the hesitation, following him as Kurst tried to protect his ruined face, Franks hit him in everything else that was available.

"What's the matter, Kurst? I thought I was the outdated model."

One of Kurst's legs seemed slower than the other. It was the same one he'd hit with the spike. Franks tested his hypothesis by putting himself in the bad position to get snap-kicked, but instead, Kurst pulled back. Franks showed no reaction. Instead he attacked, opening himself up, and the instant the demon overextended, Franks kicked out and shattered Kurst's wobbly knee. The demon fell against the edge of the truck.

Franks pulled out the Sig. A bullet to the base of the brain might not end Kurst, but it would speed up his demise. There was movement in his peripheral vision. The other demon had returned to the cargo bay with a pistol in his hand. They lifted their guns at the same time. The demon was a bit faster, and his first bullet tore up Franks' arm, through his armpit, through his good lung, and across the top of his primary heart. That threw off Franks' aim.

They both stood there, shooting until their slides locked back empty. Franks counted fifteen new holes in his body. The demon was a very good shot. The cargo bay was filled with the stink of carbon. Spent shell casings rolled toward the back of the plane. "Damn..." *I felt that.* Suddenly dizzy, Franks slowly moved over and braced himself against the side of the truck so he wouldn't fall over. The other demon was still standing.

The plane began to roll further toward the side.

The demon soldier turned and looked at the bullet holes high up the metal behind him. Then he looked back at Franks as the plane continued to turn. "You hit the pilot!"

Franks shrugged. "Whoops."

Kurst seemed to be focusing on something, but it was hard to tell with his face missing. The demon soldier was confused and frustrated. Kurst snarled. "I said go fly the plane, Thymos! You will take us to our new home!"

"But General—"

"*Now!*"

The demon ran back toward the cockpit.

The two former champions of the host watched each other. Their angle was getting worse. Kurst slid across the floor that they'd lubricated with their blood until he stopped at the fuselage. Franks looked suspiciously at the truck as it creaked and got ready to flip over on top of him, but then the roll stopped, and the plane slowly righted itself as the demon took back the controls.

"You're dying, Franks. I can tell." Kurst slowly straightened his leg out, cracking the mangled joint back into place. "I'm not. I'll get better. You're out of your precious Elixir. You're done."

Franks rested his head against the cool glass of the growth tank. "Just need to...catch my breath..." He was low on blood and oxygen, and all his nonvital systems had shut down. The other demon would correct their course, put it on autopilot, then he'd come back here and finish Franks off at his leisure.

Mission failure was unacceptable.

Normally, Franks would rather die than fail a mission, and since he was dying anyway, that made this decision extremely easy. Franks pulled himself along the side of the truck until he reached the door.

"What're you doing?" Kurst asked.

Franks opened the door. The keys were still in the ignition. He climbed up and got in. The engine turned right over. STFU kept up on their maintenance.

"No, Franks. Don't do that." Kurst forced himself to stand up.

Franks revved the engine.

Kurst began hopping desperately toward the truck.

Franks shifted into gear, popped the clutch, and the truck lurched forward. The wall separating the cargo bay from the cockpit looked solid, but it was mostly aluminum, and the front of the truck crumpled rather easily. His windshield shattered and Franks bounced off the steering wheel. It was a good thing old surplus military trucks didn't have airbags. Franks threw it in reverse. Torn metal scraped along the hood as the truck pulled free. It made a beeping noise...*for safety.* That thought was particularly ironic.

The demon prince tried to catch hold of the truck, but Franks threw his door open and hit Kurst with it, knocking him aside. The demon piloting this thing had to be having a hell of a time with this much weight shifting back and forth, but Franks was about to make his job impossible. He kept backing up until his rear bumper sparked against the ramp. Franks put it in first. Now he had a running start.

But if he drove straight through the front of the plane and rode this thing back to Earth, he wouldn't get to see the look on Kurst's face when they crashed in a giant fireball. Franks needed a tool. He checked his pockets. The only thing he had left was the St. Hubert's Key he'd taken from MHI. So Franks took out the thirteen-hundred-year-old holy relic and used it to pin down the accelerator. Then he got out.

The truck picked up a surprising amount of speed during its short trip across the cargo bay.

Kurst tried to catch hold, but there simply wasn't time to pull himself into the cab and stop it before the impressive impact. The demon prince was scraped off. The plane shook so hard it knocked Franks off his feet. The front of the C-17 simply came apart. Wide swaths of blue sky appeared as a four-hundred-knot wind struck him in the face. Franks couldn't see what happened to Thymos as the truck crashed through the bottom of the cockpit, but it couldn't have been pretty.

And then they went into a dive.

Franks rolled, weightless, through the air. He collided with Kurst. The demon prince was raging at him, but nothing could be heard over the wind anyway, so Franks punched him in the mouth. It was a pointless gesture, since they were about to crash, but Franks enjoyed it so he hit him again. They struck the ramp and were crushed there by the G force, but Franks kept on hitting Kurst. Depending on their altitude when they'd started the dive, he might just get the satisfaction of beating the demon to death before the ground got them. He checked. The view through the massive hole in the front of the plane was of rapidly approaching fields of green. *Nope.* It looked like he wouldn't have time after all.

Kurst screamed in Franks' ear. "We will make Hell far worse for you this time, Franks!"

"Bring it." Franks punched him again.

The C-17 exploded on impact.

CHAPTER 20

Franks found himself back in the small white interrogation room with the angel sitting across from him. He groaned. "Not this shit again."

"Good to see you too, Franks," the interrogator said. "Believe me, there's things I'd rather be doing as well."

"Is Kurst banished?"

"You are a remarkably focused individual. Yes, he is. He has been cast back into Hell."

As much as this place annoyed him, it certainly wasn't the Void he knew so well. "Why aren't I in Hell?"

"You're not dead yet."

"Hmmm..." Franks leaned back in his imaginary chair.

"I don't think in the history of the mortal universe we've ever seen any spirit cling to life as tenaciously as you have. Much of your body, including a significant chunk of your brain and central nervous system, were hurled from the plane on impact. The MCB found you, and one of your men had the brilliant stroke of inspiration to place your remains into the only surviving Nemesis growth tank at the STFU bunker, which amazingly enough, hadn't been damaged in the battle. This process stabilized you. This unlikely series of events culminated in your physical body being saved in the nick of time. You could go so far as to say that this was a miracle."

"Yeah... A miracle." Franks snorted. "So He's not done with me yet?"

"Of course not. Your side of the covenant isn't complete."

Interesting. He'd been told that he would perish fulfilling his part of The Deal. "I kept my kind out. I should be dead."

"No, Franks. That's one faction of many, and the rest are lining up to challenge us for the future of this world. We are at a crossroads. What's coming next is much worse. The mortal world still needs defenders. I don't understand why, but you're among those who have been given that calling. It isn't my place to ask questions. You've still got a job to do."

"What about Strayhorn? Did he have a job too?"

"We all have a purpose, but very few of us are smart enough to see what it is while we're still alive."

"Why would He let something like me have a son . . . and then take him away? That's . . ."

"Unfair?"

Franks scowled.

"Maybe it's time for you to learn what it means to be human. You've taken so much from so many others, but you've never understood what it feels like to lose. Then again, it isn't my place to guess. I'm just the messenger. On that note, your immortal spirit is no longer automatically condemned to the jurisdiction of Hell. Congratulations. The next time you die will be the last, and then you'll stand before the bar and be judged like any other mortal."

That was unexpected. Franks nodded. "Is that all?"

"That's all."

"Good. I've got work to do."

"What should we do with him?"

Franks didn't recognize that voice.

"If it was up to me, pin a medal on him. Franks has been pardoned."

Franks did recognize that one. So Agent Cueto had lived.

"It would have been simpler if you'd just let him die."

"With all due respect, sir, fuck you and the horse you rode in on. Franks is a national hero. If you pussies on the Subcommittee had a miniscule fraction of his testicular fortitude then Stricken wouldn't have made you his bitch."

"How dare you!"

"Oh, did I hurt your delicate lilac scented feelings, Senator? Please, allow me to clarify. I dare because the President just named me Acting Director of the MCB. I figure that's because he got a wakeup call that he needs somebody who'll actually tell him when the emperor isn't wearing any clothes, rather than just another ass kissing statist bureaucrat. If you stupid fucks had two brain cells to rub together, it might have generated enough friction for you to realize you should have been listening to Dwayne Myers this whole time, rather than a guy who looked to Heinrich Fucking Himmler as a role model! Maybe if you had pulled your heads out of your asses long enough, we might not have needed Agent Franks to blow himself to smithereens to keep the world from being balls deep in a horde of devils! That daring enough for you?"

The Senator was totally cowed. "My apologies, Special Agent Cueto."

"That's *Director* Cueto to you. Now get the fuck out of my top secret facility before I have Agents Archer and Jefferson here remove you."

"Very well, Director, but I'll warn you, with an attitude like that, you'll never get official approval for this appointment—"

"Archer!"

"Yes, Director!"

"Countdown from ten. When you reach four, take out your Taser or your collapsible baton, whichever makes you smile, and when you reach zero, use that device on the representative of the Special Subcommittee on Unearthly Forces until he departs my facility. The more violence you use, the better."

"Uh...Okay...Ten. Nine—"

"Silently, Archer. Can't you see that Agent Franks is trying to sleep?" Apparently the Subcommitee representative left quietly, because several seconds passed and there was no screaming. "Man...I can't stand those assholes. If we don't elect leadership with a spine next time I swear I'm going to suck start my pistol."

Franks opened his eyes. He recognized the recovery room in the R&D section of MCB headquarters. He'd woken up here quite a few times before. It hurt to turn his head. Many of his nerve endings were not connected yet. There were a few others in the recovery room. Jefferson and Archer were posted at the door. He didn't know how long he'd been under, but his detail looked terrible. Archer's arm was in a cast and Jefferson's face was still swollen and had several bandages on it. There was a woman that Franks did not recognize sitting in a chair at the foot of the bed reading something off of her phone. Cueto was on crutches and standing right next to the bedside.

"They made you Director?" Franks asked.

"Acting. Director Stark is taking an early medical retirement from the Bureau."

"Sad day for America."

"Indeed. About damned time you decided to join us, Agent Franks. The docs said your brain waves had returned to normal and you'd be joining us soon. Surprised it took you so long. They only had to replace three quarters of your head." Cueto said. "If you kept sleeping on the job I was going to write you up."

"I vowed to kill everyone that helped Nemesis," Franks muttered as he looked toward the exit.

"Yeah. That's why I tossed that Subcommittee moron. Dumbass doesn't realize I just saved his life. But no more murdering right now. After we get you debriefed about your brief stint as an *undercover* outlaw, we're going to sort this out, nice and diplomatic. That's an order."

Franks nodded. "Yes, sir."

"Good. Because there's fifty Secret Service downstairs ready to take you into custody for threatening the President, just in case that little Post-it note stunt wasn't really Myers' ploy to draw out the traitor, Stricken, like we both know it was. Understand?"

"Only fifty?"

"Budget cuts," Cueto said. The woman had gotten up and joined him. "Let me introduce Beth Flierl. She's the new head of Special Task Force Unicorn."

Franks nodded. Cueto wouldn't have let her in the room with him if she'd helped Nemesis.

"Agent Franks." She didn't look that intimidating, but you didn't end up running an organization of monster hit squads without being a badass. "I'm here to officially inform you that the Task Force's mission has been drastically scaled back. Our intelligence gathering and R and D apparatus has been discontinued. I can assure you there's no reason for you to be concerned about further STFU activities, and I hope our two agencies can quickly resume our previous working relationship. That's it for the official statement. Personally, I lost some good men because of this mess, and I'm still pissed, but I understand why you were doing what you had to do."

"Did you know?" He didn't specify if he was talking about Project Nemesis or the MCB attack. Either would do.

"Only after it was too late. I got into this business because I wanted to help out monsters who didn't deserve to be called monsters. I was trained by Kirk Conover, and I know you knew him. I'm going to put the Task Force back on track to be something he would have recognized and been proud of. I've hated Stricken's mission creep for years, but I kept my mouth shut to try and help my people earn their exemptions. And just so you know, I think the reason I got this new assignment was because while you were blowing up an airfield in Virginia, I was at the White House dropping off all the evidence about STFU's illegal activities that I'd gathered. I believe in our mission, Franks, and I wasn't going to let Stricken destroy the good we've done."

"Where's Stricken now?"

"Missing," Cueto said. "He's even better at disappearing than you were. Everybody is looking for him."

"Don't worry, Agent Franks. He'll be brought to justice," Flierl assured him. "Now, if you gentlemen will excuse me, I've got a mess to clean up." Jefferson politely opened the door for her, and the commander of Special Task Force Unicorn left them.

"She seems okay," Cueto said. "Good. Because you wouldn't believe the shit storm that's brewing. There's some supernatural weirdness going down right now that would blow your mind. If I'd known about half the things Myers had been worried about, I wouldn't have ever said yes to this assignment...But you're not done recuperating or whatever the hell they call it when the docs have to replace eighty percent of your body, so I'll brief you later." He hobbled toward the door.

"I'm ready now," Franks stated.

"Don't push it. If Archer hadn't had that bright idea to stick you in a Nemesis tank, right now I'd be seeing if we're allowed to bury nonhumans at Arlington."

Franks gave Archer an appreciative nod. The young agent grew embarrassed.

Cueto laughed. "You're just lucky I didn't have them rebuild you with female parts to help meet the MCB equal opportunity quotas. Rest up, Franks, because you're going to be *real* busy soon enough. Come with me, Archer. Since you're supposed to be so brilliant, I've got a temporary assignment to go along with your promotion. What do you know about covering up the existence of carnivorous blob monsters?"

"Absolutely nothing."

"Good. You can learn on the flight. The islands are nice this time of year."

"Hawaii?" Archer asked hopefully.

"The Aleutians. Pack mittens."

Jefferson closed the door behind his new boss and his fellow agent, but he stayed in the room with Franks.

"What?"

"I need to speak with you." Jefferson came over to the bed—walking slowly so as to not reopen the many stitched-up wounds on his body—pulled up a chair, and sat down. The young agent looked physically and emotionally exhausted. It took him a moment to compose himself enough to talk. He had never seen Jefferson look contrite before. Humility didn't look right on somebody so cocky. "I failed. You told me to keep Strayhorn alive, but I couldn't. He was my responsibility. There've been too many times in my life where I just wasn't good enough to do what needed to be done. I couldn't get to Myers in time, and I couldn't protect your son."

Franks nodded. It was strange, but he understood now how it felt to fail. Franks could *relate*. "The mission always comes first. We completed the mission. That's what matters."

"Yeah..." Jefferson wiped his eyes with the back of his bruised hand. "I'm sorry. He was a good man."

"Yes. Seemed like it." Franks had never found himself wishing that he'd spoken *more* with someone. Myers had been his closest confidant, but he'd kept something so vital a secret for so long... Franks regretted never knowing his son. Regret was an unfamiliar and bitter feeling. "How did you beat that demon by yourself?"

"Turns out we met before, on that overpass in Montgomery. Different body, same demon. Go figure. She gloated about it while she was beating the hell out of me, but then, I don't know, she got sloppy or something, it's hard to remember. I must have got in a really lucky shot and she went down. I used the opportunity to saw her head off."

Apparently Grant Jefferson's part in The Plan wasn't done yet either.

Jefferson composed himself. "You said there would be repercussions if I failed." He managed to look Franks in the eye, which put him on a very short list of mortals. "Whatever you see fit to do, I understand and accept the punishment. If I'm going to get kicked out of the Bureau, I just want you to know the last couple of years it has been an honor to help protect my country."

Punishment? He had said that, and Franks always kept his word. "I have something appropriate. I'll speak with Director Cueto."

Jefferson stood up. "Understood, sir." He limped back to the door, then hesitated. Franks could tell Jefferson really wanted to ask what his sentence would be.

"Myers is gone," Franks stated. "I require a new partner."

Jefferson visibly paled. "Your partner?" He certainly hadn't expected that particular punishment. "Is it too late to resign?"

"Yes. Dismissed."

Jefferson left Franks alone with his thoughts. Kurst had been banished, but at a terrible cost. Stricken had survived. He would be dealt with in time. Despite their temporary success, the mortal world remained in grave danger, otherwise Franks would not have been sent back.

Something Myers had said as he lay dying was gnawing at Franks . . . He'd said that his descendants could use the Elixir. Descendants. Plural.

He did not understand The Plan. He would abide by The Deal. The Contract was his life. Things had changed, but he did not know what would be expected of him next. Franks turned his head enough to see a sliver of the sunset through a gap in the blinds . . .

Nope . . . Franks still didn't appreciate beauty.

He would never be human, but maybe he could be close enough to get by. So Franks lay there, staring at the ceiling, waiting for his next inevitable assignment.

He knew it would not take long.

Stricken sat in the dark room, listening to the waves, and contemplating his next move. A man with lesser dedication would have been frustrated by recent setbacks, but he preferred to see them as new opportunities instead. He poured himself another scotch, put his feet up, and watched the shadows of the tropical trees sway in the wind along the moonlit beach.

It was a rather nice hideout. He'd certainly earned this vacation.

His phone rang. He picked it up on the second ring. "Hello."

The voice on the other end was electronically distorted. "You escaped."

That was insulting. "Of course I did."

"Where are you?"

"Nowhere you'll ever find me. Don't bother trying to trace this. You might be thinking about sending the Wild Hunt after me, but they'll just end up frustrated, and everybody will go home disappointed."

"Were you aware that the Nemesis bodies would be possessed by demons?"

Stricken chuckled. "That came as a complete surprise," he lied. His intel on Franks had been incomplete at best, but even then they'd only expected a fifty percent chance of extradimensional corruption, tops. Those seemed like good odds, and what was life, if not one big gamble. "I really wanted to be able to use those soldiers. It doesn't matter now though."

"Many of our dealings have been exposed. Our arrangement did not include exposure, Mr. Stricken."

"Relax. That was part of my plan. It was just enough information to accomplish our goals. I made sure Renfroe had what I wanted him to have, nothing more. People with morals are so boringly predictable that I knew he'd blab. It was only a question of timing. He leaked it sooner than I expected him to, but then again, thinking you're about to get your arms pulled off by a supersoldier helps you get your priorities straight."

"You took an unacceptable risk."

"Yet still achieved our primary goal. You can thank me later. Our mutual foe knows what lengths we're willing to go to now, so his timeline will move up. The longer he stayed in the shadows the stronger his forces became. It was force it now, or lose in the future. Look on the bright side, we were lucky to have demons possess my Nemesis soldiers. That drew him out enough to try and make friends. You should thank me. The war is coming." He sipped his scotch. He'd brought the good stuff.

"The factions are not ready to defeat the might of Asag Shedu."

"Then you'd better get your ass in gear, Queen Fancy Pants. I've done my part. I'm off to enjoy my retirement." Stricken ended the call. "Who would've thought all these big cosmic powers would be such crybabies?" he said to the thing hiding just outside the door. A pair of red eyes winked into existence. "You might as well come in. You know you're always invited."

"Why, Mr. Stricken, ever the gentleman." The Master vampire floated inside. "Just a polite heads-up, but there's a shoggoth that just crawled out of the ocean and it's lumbering this way."

"Oh, he's no concern. That's just my next appointment."

She sat on the couch next to him. An unnatural chill pushed away the tropical air. Most people would flinch with such a deadly predator so close, but Stricken routinely dealt with far worse. "All those lies. Is it hard to keep them all straight?"

"It takes a lot of work, but I've got a lot of practice." He held out the bottle. "Care for a drink?"

Her fangs were very white in the dark. "Not my vintage."

He poured her one anyway. "The thing is, Mrs. Shackleford—"

"Please, just Susan." She took the glass from him.

"Of course, Susan. I keep everything straight because I have to. Earth is about to become the battleground between some very nasty groups, and mankind is stuck in the middle. The stakes don't get any higher than this. It makes for a complex, but very interesting game. Saving the world is a nasty business, but somebody has to do it."

The vampire lifted her drink. "To saving the world then."

They clinked their glasses together. "To saving the world."